INDECENT WOMAN

DR. MOHSEN EL-GUINDY

2ND EDITION

WORKBOOK PRESS LLC
187 E Warm Springs Rd,
Suite B285, Las Vegas, NV 89119, USA

Website:	https://workbookpress.com/
Hotline:	1-888-818-4856
Email:	admin@workbookpress.com

Ordering Information:
Quantity sales. Special discounts are available on quantity purchases by corporations, associations, and others.
For details, contact the publisher at the address above.

ISBN-13:   978-1-954753-01-3 (Paperback Version)
             978-1-954753-02-0 (Digital Version)

REV. DATE: 09/02/2021

Chapter 1

The famous lawyer Tom Wilson owns a large law firm in New York. The revenue of the firm amounts to 750 million dollars per year. The firm employs 50 lawyers on a full-time basis in 25 offices across the United States. Quite recently, Tom Wilson expanded the company to have offices in Canada, France, England and Germany. The expansion grew to include the Arab countries with offices in Kuwait, Bahrain, and the Arab Emirates. Tom Wilson was always busy moving from one country to another to ensure that his lawyers were carrying out their duties and looking after the interests of his clients.

Tom Wilson was married to Claire Moore the daughter of one of his clients. Claire was the only child of Richard Moore the owner of gambling casinos and nightclubs along the west coast of the United States. Because she was his only child, Richard over pampered Claire beyond any limits. Her mother coddled her as well. Her heart bled if Claire had to do some work. She would not allow Clair to even fetch a glass of water.

Because Claire was pampered in her growing up days, she grew being attentions seeking and difficult to adjust with situation types. To feel happy and alive she needed from her husband attention, compliments, physical affection and emotional attachment.

Claire tried to mould Tom as per her emotional needs, but Tom was dedicated to his work and had important jobs to do than pampering her or spending more time with her. Her attempts ended up into misunderstandings, conflicts, and long arguments.

Tom Wilson lived his day according to a routine schedule. He gets up early and would go jogging while it was still dark before starting his breakfast. Claire however wakes up at noon. Tom reads the morning paper while having breakfast, and by 8 am, he is at his office reading reports. Tom travels quite often on business trips for two to three weeks each month. He often informs Claire about the sudden trip from the aeroplane.

Their marriage had resulted in a baby girl they called Daisy. Claire pampered her daughter exactly as she was pampered. She did not let Daisy do things she was capable of without extending undue help. She jumped in to help Daisy at the slightest hint of a struggle. She did not let her learn and grow. Daisy was thus deprived of numerous opportunities that were crucial for her development, and she became always dependent on her mother.

At the age of 12, Daisy grew up into a beautiful girl that was joy to watch. She took the long stature of her father, and the beautiful blond hair and the wide blue eyes of her mother.

Tom worked so hard that Clair and Daisy seldom saw him. Clair rarely had a conversation with Tom without it being interrupted by a work-related call, and she often felt as if he valued the caller more than her. This was the case pretty much all the time that Tom was at home. Clair could survive almost anything except lack of communication.

Clair lived with Tom for 12 years without passion, true love, and a normal complete sexual life. Tom seemed clueless about their sex life. His continuous work decreased his libido. Clair had to initiate sex 90% of the time and she had felt frustrated.

Clair felt alienated from Tom, gripped by an overwhelming feeling of desolation. She realized that she had little in common with him. Bitterness worked its way in her very soul. She sank into her own isolated world until she met a man who filled her and finally ended her misery.

She met this man at the mall. After shopping she went out to her car and discovered that she had a flat. She got the jack out of the trunk and began to change the flat. A nice man dressed in sexy casual outfits walked up to her and said, "I noticed you're changing a flat tire. Would you like me to take care of it for you?" Clair was grateful for his offer and accepted his help. They chatted amiably while he changed the flat. The man put the flat tire and the jack in the trunk, shut it and dusted his hands off. Clair thanked him profusely and as she was about to get in her car, he said with a broad smile on his face "how about having coffee with me?" She was astonished at his daring and sudden invitation; however, she just couldn't resist the strength and masculinity radiating from him. She accepted his invitation, and both went to a coffee shop to chat and get to know each other. After chatting, he took another step toward her:

"You are going to have sex with me."

A look of shyness crossed her face. Although his request was provocative and unexpected, she looked into his eyes with love and acceptance. The chat ended up sleeping together in a motel room. Naked in his arms she was wet and ready for him. She felt as though she had been waiting forever for this very moment…this very man. She begged him to fill her and finally end her misery, and he gave her what she needed.

Having great sex with her lover happened frequently during the next months. She fell in love with him and wanted to spend every minute with him. With him, she felt truly loved. With him, she laughed, danced, and felt alive. She experienced outbursts of frantic ferocity and desire. In fact, she lusted after him.

When Tom came home one night after a long trip to the Gulf Estates, she confronted him.

Clair: "Tom, I want a divorce!"

Tom: "What! Are you crazy? What happened?"

Clair:" I was always here for you, but you lost me with your continuous absence. I am not your property. I do not ow you my soul. You earn it."

Tom: "What does that mean? I do not understand!"

Clair: "I wanted to talk to you about what matters to me,

but you were never here for me."

Tom: "It's business darling. I work hard to support our family and make sure that you and Daisy are happy. Please try to understand."

Clair: "I am your business too Tom, but you neglected me for years. You don't make me feel like a woman. You dried me up. I was a green meadow, but you turned me into a barren desert."

Tom: "I spend good moments with you when I have time."

Clair: "Our sexual life has no passion or romance. I do not want quick sex. I want to feel your passion, but you have no time for this. You are not present with the woman you share your life with."

Tom: "I thought our marriage was perfect. You are nothing like the woman I married. It is your role to hold marriage and home together while I am busy building our future. Many couples have the same situation and managed to stay married."

Clair: "I want to feel, to give, to take, to laugh, to lust, to be so human. I deserve passion. I deserve to be loved. I deserve a man, who will give his whole heart to me."

Tom: "you're going to burn the house down and destroy everything. Is there someone in your life?"

Clair: "I have found a terrific person who swept me off my

feet. We have been together six months now. He asked me to marry him and I said: 'Of course.'" Her words were meant to torture and hurt.

Tom: "What did you find in him?"

Claire: "He made me feel wonderful, sexy, desirable, and for the first time in years, alive."

Tom: "Do you still see him?"

Clair: "Yes. Every time he comes back to town, we meet, he buys me lunch, and we go have sex. I enjoy the thrill of having sex with him. It is better than lingering idle at home."

Tom frustrated: "I am in favour of staying married Clair."

Clair: "Sorry Tom. I do not belong to you anymore. There is no use talking Tom I want a divorce."

Tom: "And how about Daisy? "

Clair:" I will leave her to you. I don't want to disturb my new life with obligations I cannot afford."

Chapter 2

Clair got the divorce and Tom lived with a wounded pride and bruised ego. Although four years had passed, it seemed as if Tom were still recovering from the sting of divorce. Being busy at work did not make him forget. He will take a long vacation to a remote place.

Now Daisy was 16 years old. She had grown from a girl into a young woman. She was spoiled like her mother. Daisy became a bit of a wild child. She skips school and goes to wild parties without telling her father. She even hosts wild parties in the house during his long absence.

Her head is filled now with boy stuff. He knew the day would come when she would tell him about her boyfriend. And that she did. She came one day and told him that she had a boyfriend she truly loved. When she said that he blurted out without thinking: "Please don't have sex".

"Don't fear anything father. I will not get pregnant." She said as if having sex was okay and being pregnant was not.

Tom feared that Daisy might inherit the bad traits of her mother and elope with a lover who might take advantage of her. He needs her to be sensible. She had to be safe. He was not going to leave her behind. He will take her with him in his trip. The trip could bring her close to him, and distract her from love, lust and infatuation.

They will go to the ancient civilization of the Pharaohs. They will spend good time in Luxor, the city of the huge Karnack Temple, which was the centre of the ancient faith of the Pharaohs.

Tom made reservations in the legendary Victorian old Cataract hotel. The hotel was comfortable and relaxing. Tom and Daisy spent several days in the hotel before visiting the most amazing places in the city of Luxor. They had their lunches and dinners in the hotel restaurant overlooking panoramic views of the Nile. The father and his daughter enjoyed the hotel's spa and relaxed in the sauna. They also used the fitness centre and enjoyed massage treatments.

Now came the time to visit the most historical and amazing places in Luxor. In Karnack Temple, they visited the precinct of Amun, the precinct of Mut, and the precinct of Montu. They enjoyed watching the sound and light show. They walked through the most impressive places in all of Egypt - the Hypostyle Hall with its 134 massive columns. They admired the many impressive sights within it.

Tom and Daisy crossed the Nile to the West Bank on a ferryboat. While crossing the Nile, Daisy beheld feluccas sailing in the Nile near the ferryboat. Their stark white sails at sunset and simple construction was eye catching and brought to her remembrance the primitive boats of the ancients. Tom noticed Daisy's amazement while watching the feluccas cruising the Nile.

"They're called "feluccas". Feluccas are an integral part of Egypt's past. These long wooden sailing boats once carried everything from pharaohs and military troops to food and supplies. Many say Don't leave Egypt without taking at least one ride on a felucca. A trip to Luxor is not complete without taking a ride on one I think." Tom said while standing on board near Daisy.

"Yes, we will take a ride on one. Why would we spend long hours on the deck of a massive boat when we could sail down the Nile on a Felucca? This is by far an awesome way to cruise the Nile River, without a cruise ship. It will be fun I am sure." She said with a happy smile on her face.

The next day, Tom and Daisy went to the prier. Tom chose a felucca of an honest looking captain to take him and Daisy around for two days. The captain pointed to a young lad in the felucca and said: "This is Mostafa my son. He is a good sailor. I taught him English to be a tourist guide in the future. He will take you around for two days. You will both enjoy the trip I am sure."

Tom seemed worried. He said hesitatingly: "But your son is so young and might not be able to..."

The captain interrupted: "He knows everything. He is well trained. I have eight boys and three girls. This boy is the mightiest and the wisest among them all."

Tom and his daughter stepped cautiously into the boat. Mostafa took Daisy by the hand and relaxed her on the seating area at the rear of the boat, outfitted with colourful fabrics and soft cushions.
She smiled at him thankfully, a smile that took up residence

inside his heart, making it glow.

At the centre of the felucca was a table offering meals and cold drinks. Tom sat beside Daisy and Mostafa was busy preparing the boat for sale. The felucca was now ready for sale and off it went.

The boat peacefully glided through the Nile River with mist lightly dampening their faces. The felucca sailed against wind, having to zig zag its way back and forth to make progress while slicing through the current.

Daisy stared plainly at Mostafa. He wore a white jellabiya and a turban, the basic traditional Egyptian garment for men. His olive skin was darkened by the sun. She saw him primitive, simple and exotic.

Tom and Daisy enjoyed breath-taking views, clear sky, and fresh air, and clear and clean River. The sparkling water at sunset was so attractive that Daisy wanted to swim.

"Mostafa is it safe to swim in the Nile?" Daisy asked Mostafa.

"Not quite, but I will take you to an ideal place for swimming."

Mostafa stopped the felucca at a suitable place for swimming and dropped the anchor. "Here you can swim but do not go far from the shore." He said pointing to the wide river.

Daisy examined the water and found it still and flat inviting her to swim. She rose to her feet with her handbag hanged around her shoulder. "Where can I change my clothes? She inquired.

"Over there." Mostafa pointed at a small locker covered by a curtain.

Daisy disappeared for a short moment then appeared wearing a skimpy bikini. She looked stunning with her white skin, blue eyes and blonde hair. The bikini emphasized the curves of her feminine body. Mostafa looked at her aghast.

He looked at her curves dancing with her hesitating steps as she approached the Felucca's edge. He wanted to touch her white flesh, but he glanced at his feet unable to face the glow radiating from her.

"Don't stray too far from shore." He warned still glancing at his feet.

She dived into the Nile and swam her way easily across its surface for 50 yards, but on her way, back a strong underneath current pushed her back to the middle of the river. She swam with a hard crawl against the current, willing to use the last of her energy to reach the shore, but she could not. Her arms cramped, the last of her breath spent. She was completely exhausted and gulped for air as the current pulled her away from the felucca. Frantically, she didn't think. She focused on getting to the shore, but the exhaustion overtook her energy. She swallowed water and suffered difficult breathing and suffocating.

She called Mostafa to come quickly to her rescue: "Mostafa I can't reach the shore."

Quickly Mostafa pulled off his jellabiya and threw his turban away. Wearing only his boxer shorts dove into the river.

He swam toward her, with sure strong strokes, his strong brown arms slicing the water with remarkable skill. He reached her. Fear and fatigue were obvious in her face. "People drown because they panic. Don't panic, just relax. Let the water carry you." He said calming her fears.

His reassuring words helped calm her rising anxiety. He turned her onto her back and put his left arm around her waist. She felt his strong arm around her waist clamping on her like a vice. With his free arm, he swam toward the shore. He helped her back to the boat, wrapped her in a blanket and seated her on a cushion.

He stood with his boxer shorts towering over her and filling the small boat. "Do you feel better now?" He asked.

"I am fine, thank you." She said smiling appreciatively.

She found herself unable to keep her eyes off him. He was eye catching especially with those boxer shorts that fitted him like a glove. She took a good look at him. He had a wealth in his hair. His jet-black hair fell down his shoulders. He was slim and quite tall, a little over six feet. His arms and shoulders were huge and smooth. His muscular pecs tapered down to a tiny waist. His legs looked strong. His thighs looked massive. His calves were very prominent. The rest of his legs long and lean. His nipples looked hard and pointed. She could see every detail of his cock and balls bulging through the thin fabric of the thin boxer shorts. His body was flawless and beautiful.

Mostafa put on the jellabiya and the turban, and then prepared green tea and offered it to his clients. Mostafa sailed again against the northwest wind. Tom was impressed with his boat handling skills, and his courage and adroitness and cool, easy-going nature.

The anchor was dropped again, and they spent the night on the bank of the river. Mostafa prepared a delicious meal for dinner then offered the passengers cold soft drinks. He brought from the boat sleeping bags, to spend the night. The experience of sleeping outside under a blanket of stars was alone worth the trip.

In the morning, Mostafa prepared breakfast in the small kitchen of the boat. The breakfast included Egyptian bread, cooked fava beans, boiled eggs, white cheese and black olive. The best way to start the day is with a warm cup of coffee. Two cups of Nescafe were then served.

So far, most of the sailing was downwind. All Mostafa had to do was to hold the sail perpendicular to the wind and let the boat be pushed from behind. Now the wind was blowing backward, and Mostafa had to sail upwind. Mostafa climbed the tall mast and released the sail. He positioned the sail as to cope with the new situation and while sailing upwind he was Patient to zigzag back and forth. The felucca sailed close to the Nile bank for an hour. The warmth of the Nubian Desert pressed against Tom and Daisy's skin as they beheld the majestic Nile.

The Felucca anchored again on the bank of an oasis where

Tom and Daisy watched the art of "Tahtib". Tahtib is an Egyptian martial art, which makes use of long sticks for battling one's opponent. It originated in pharaonic times. In a Tahtib competition, two men will battle each other with their sticks, each seeking to strike the opponent with his stick while parrying blows from the other. The Nubians battled with each other and Mostafa participated in the duels demonstrating high skill.

The Nubians then sang their melodious songs and danced their folkloric dances. Tom and Daisy could not help but to smile and enjoy dancing with the Nubians.

It was lunchtime. Tom and Daisy returned to the boat to find Mostafa has prepared for them "fatta". It consisted of layers of rice and fried bread, covered in a garlic and vinegar meat soup. Large chunks of stewed beef and deep-fried poached eggs were served along with the rice and bread base. The dessert was rice pudding with a hint of vanilla.

The meal was delicious. Tea was served to help digest the heavy meal.

The trip ended, and the boat reached the bank near Cataract hotel. The captain of the boat, Mostafa's father, was waiting for them to see if Tom and Daisy enjoyed the trip. "I wouldn't have traded this experience for anything." Tom said to the captain while shaking hands with him. Tom insisted to invite the captain to a cup of tea in the lobby of the hotel. Mostafa stayed with the boat, and Daisy went to her room to freshen up. Tom and the captain sat in the lobby talking.

Tom: "I am fond of Mostafa. He is dependable, smart and experienced. He proved to be a good sailor."

Captain: "I raised him to be a tough guy."

Tom: "He was strong and managed to sail against a strong wind. We were in good hands."

Captain: "I am happy that you liked the trip."

Tom.: "My daughter was about to drown. The strong current drifted her away from the shore. Mostafa easily rescued her and brought her back safe to the shore. I am indebted to you and to Mostafa."

Captain: "Thank you for your kindness."

Tom: "I have only one daughter – Daisy. Her mother pampered her, in other words spoiled her. I have always wished to have a son like Mostafa. A son I can rely on when my strength was failing."

Captain: "May Allah give you the son you wish for."

Tom: "I divorced Daisy's mother. We do not live together anymore. I do not intend to marry again. That son you are talking about may never come."

Captain: "Nothing is far from God. Just pray and ask for a son and Allah will arrange things for you and make your wish comes true."

Tom: "That wish had come true already when I met your son."

Captain: "I do not understand."

Tom: "I want to borrow your son for money."

Captain frowned: "What do you mean?"

Tom: "I want to take him to America to live with me and Daisy."

Captain: "What?"

Tom: "I want Mostafa to keep an eye on Daisy and protect her from every form of evil."

Captain: "What a strange proposal!"

Tom: "It's a bargain captain, a bargain."

Captain: "How much exactly is the bargain?"

Tom: "100,000 American dollars."

Captain: "Oh! I can use that money. Are you that rich?"

Tom: "Yes I am. The money is all yours if you accept that Mostafa comes with us. Try to convince him to live in a different world."

Captain: "You got yourself a deal Mr. Tom. However, you

must understand few things about Mostafa. I raised Mostafa and his brothers as god-fearing men. They enjoin good and forbid evil. Mostafa's deeds are goodness, righteousness and faithfulness."

The captain stopped talking for a long moment, and then said with signs of concern on his face: "Mostafa is a young boy with extraordinary strength. He can withstand great force or pressure. No one has the strength to subdue him. He had not attained this strength by training or exercise, it is rather a God-given strength intrusted to his care to be used in ways of goodness. I have seen him lifting a rock weighing 250 kg. He alone pulled out of the river the boat you have seen without toil or pain. I saw him ripping out a big tree of the ground from its roots. He does not know his own strength, and he thinks that his mighty actions are quite normal. This natural power could be beneficial or dangerous. It is your task to control his strength by not submitting him to stress or anger."

Tom: "Of course - I will treat him like a son. I have a sentimental weakness for Daisy. He will take care of her and protect her against all evil."

Later in the evening, the father talked to his son about Tom's proposal.

Father: "It's about time that you live in a different world. You will see a new world and new people. You love challenges, and discovering a different world is a big challenge, especially when you have to fight temptation in a liberal world. Mr. Tom gave me good money to accept sending you to America. If you accept going there I will divide the money into equal halves, one for you and one for me. I'll open a bank account for you to deposit your share."

Mostafa: "Yes father I long to see America the land of hope and liberty."

Father: "Since you have accepted going there then listen to me carefully. Always remember that Allah is watching whatever you do. He sees what you do in the middle of the day and He sees what you do in the deepest part of the night. He sees all. He hears all. There is nothing that escapes Him. If you are alone, He is the second and if you are two, He is the third. Never forget that nothing happens except by His Command and Permission. Everything lies in the Hands of Allah. No harm can befall you and no benefit can reach you except by His Will. Everything that happens in this life is ordained for a purpose. You have no recourse other than taking refuge in Him, trusting in Him, and submitting to Him. There is no place or moment in the universe that is independent of Allah. Nothing can remain out of His Sovereignty."

Mostafa: "Pray for me father."

Father: "May Allah guide you in each decision you make and be with you at every step you take. May He protect you when you fall and hear you when you call. May you always be in Allah's hand. Ameen."

Mostafa repeated after him: "Ameen."

Chapter 3

It was quite a spectacle to see Tom and Daisy walking through Cairo airport and Mostafa walking hot on their heels with his jellabiya and turban and carrying a lace straw basket as his bag. Tom tried to convince him to change his native clothes into jeans and T-shirt, but he refused. He considered wearing his native Egyptian clothing a matter of pride and dignity. Tom was a bit embarrassed, but Daisy was hilarious. She had brought home an exotic naïve creature her friends will laugh at. With such stupid clothing, he was going to make a spectacle of himself.

It was his first plane ride. Mostafa sat beside Daisy shaking with fear. When the plane took off, he closed his eyes reciting in silence some Koranic verses. After the plane straightened in the sky, he opened his eyes to see Daisy glancing at him laughing. Embarrassed shyness washed over him.

"you haven't flown before?" she asked in amusement.

"Never before."

"You travel only through sailing boats and donkeys, eh?"

"Mostly yes. I hope the trip will be safe until we reach our destination."

"It will be safe do not worry."

The breakfast was served. Mostafa ate with great appetite. He did not use fork or spoon but ate with his fingers and wiped his mouth with the back of his hand.

The plane hit turbulence and started to shake violently. Mostafa panicked and caught Daisy's hand and pressed it hard.

"Are we in danger? It seems like we dropped 100 feet!" He said shaking with fear.

"It's just turbulence. Turbulence is uncomfortable but not dangerous."

"What is turbulence?"

"Turbulence is caused by weather conditions. It is particularly obvious when flying over mountains."

"Are we going to crash? "He said trembling all over.

"Airplanes pass through turbulence every day, and no plane crashes because of it. Just fasten your seatbelt and you will be okay."

"It is already fastened." He said annoyed.

She looked into his innocent eyes and felt a strong urge to appease his fear. She laughed lightly when she remembered how he courageously saved her from drowning in the Nile, and now he was catching her hand in fear. She patted his hand and smiled at him. Her smile however was wry on her lips and her eyes mocking him. A slow Appreciative smile worked its way across his face and into his eyes.

Tom, Daisy and Mostafa arrived at Tom's mansion. Mostafa was overwhelmed to see such a gorgeous mansion with its spacious hall and rooms, and pleasant garden with vegetables and fruit in the front. Round rugs fitted beautifully in the double stair entryway. Round domes floated overtop the double staircase. The hallway was elegant with dark hardwood floors.

Tom and Daisy went to their rooms to bath and freshen up. A butler led Mostafa to his room. The room had beige walls and cheerful wood floors. The room was rich and cosy at the same time.

They all had lunch in the dining room. Mostafa was hungry. He ate with great appetite. Nothing, indeed, could be more primitive than his mode of eating. His fingers made rapid and frequent voyages from his plate to his mouth.

Tom remarked: "Daisy, this young man has a lot to learn. Teach him how to eat with fork and knife."

Daisy: "I guess I can do that. I hope he will learn fast."

Tom: "Mostafa, do you need more food?"

Mostafa: "Yes please. I am not used to small amounts of food."

Tom ushered the butler to bring more food. Mostafa devoured the food in just few seconds. He drank a glass of water, wiped his mouth with the back of his hand and burped loudly that startled everyone within earshot.

"This primitive naive creature is going to be a big show in her coming party." Daisy whispered to herself. Now she has something spectacular to show to her friends.

With signs of disapproval on his face, Tom left the table and addressed Mostafa saying: "I want to have some words with you. I'll wait for you in the drawing room."

Tom and Mostafa sat in the drawing room chatting:

Tom: "I brought you here in order to take care of Daisy."

"Mostafa: "I thought you were going to find me a job to start a new life in America!"

Tom: "Daisy is your job Mostafa. Now listen to me carefully. Daisy is a spoiled girl. Her mother pampered her, and she inherited all her bad qualities from her mother. Her mother cheated on me and eloped with a man she had sex with him while I was away in my several business trips. She didn't even care about Daisy and left her behind. I am a very busy sort of person and I do not have time to spend with Daisy. During my absence, she goes to wild parties and comes drunk accompanied by debauched boys. Daisy is reckless and irresponsible, and I tried to straighten her out but I failed."

Mostafa: "This is a strange job. I am not familiar with such kind of work."

Tom: "You will succeed in your job because what you will see from Daisy goes against your principles. Her thinking is purely carnal and animalistic. Her irresponsible behaviour will make you stand against her way of thinking in life. Your job is to protect my daughter from her evil soul. She needs protective arms, and my arms are busy working somewhere else. I will give you a good salary if you keep an eye on her.

Mostafa: "How can I protect her from her evil soul?"

Tom: "Daisy cannot prevent herself from sexual temptation. She can have sex so easily with anyone she likes. By this, she puts herself in a position where she can be hurt. Protect her from men taking advantage of her. Teach her that it's brave and strong of her to stand against the temptations of life. Make her aware of her flaws so nobody can use them against her."

Mostafa amazed: "I do not believe for a second that Daisy is that kind of girl. Is she so thoughtless, so heedless?"

Tom: "Yes she is. Protecting her is a mission. I chose you for the mission. You are pure, and uncontaminated. You are strong and courageous. You have rescued Daisy once, you can rescue her again."

Mostafa: "God has bestowed on her His divine blessings; beauty, wealth and honour. How could she trample all this into the mud?"

Tom: "It's your job to snatch her out of the mud."

Chapter 4

Tom travelled to visit some of his offices abroad. The house was now ready for Daisy. She will have a party and invite all her friends. Mostafa with his jellabiya and turban will be the laughing stock of the party.

Daisy prepared the house for the party. She bought beer and whisky to provide alcoholic drinks to her guests. She ordered the servants to clean the rooms upstairs for lovers willing to have privacy.

It was Thursday night when the party began. A great open buffet was set up where the diners will serve themselves. The guests, boys and girls, arrived one after another. The girls were dressing seductively.

Daisy received them at the entrance stunned in a plunging, thigh-high-slit black dress that highlighted her fabulous white figure. Mostafa stared at Daisy bewildered. His heart throbbed in his chest. The sight of her had all but undone him. He wanted to touch her, to feel her softness.

In the living room overlooking the hall, Mostafa sat in the alcove watching the party. Everyone lined up and began to fill their plates. After finishing eating, they moved to the drinking table and filled their glasses to the brim. After an hour drinking and chatting at the drinking table, wine drove them crazy. They ran around the house yelling and shouting like nuts.

The romantic music played. They all moved to the hall, and the boys danced with the girls. Daisy danced with a big boy and their bodies were so close that Mostafa was irritated. The boy began to kiss Daisy in the lips while holding her buttocks. Daisy was strongly responding. She kissed him back and rested her head on his shoulder as they swayed to the music. The music then stopped, and Daisy seemed to have an announcement to make.

"Boys and girls listen carefully. I have a surprise for you. I have invited you tonight to see something exotic and extraordinary. I brought you from Egypt someone from the Stone Age."

Daisy shouted aloud: "Mostafa where ae you. I know that you are around here somewhere."

Mostafa heard her mocking words about him and was terribly offended. He pulled himself together and entered the hall wearing the jellabiya and the turban. Upon seeing him, Daisy's guests laughed, and she laughed along with them.

The big boy said: "So this is the man from the Stone Age. He is supposed to walk like apes, but he is standing upright and erect. He surely combines apelike and humanlike ways of moving around."

Another boy said: "He developed from an apelike creature to human specimen. His brain must be smaller than ours."

A third boy said: "He depends for his subsistence on hunting wild animals."

Everyone was staring at him. The boys and girls looked at his clothes in disgust.

A girl said: "You wear this thing, so you do not get hot after strenuous activity, right?"

A girl by the name of Alice said: "He looks stylish to me. The jellabiya is most elegant and exotic. I see him tall, strong and attractive. In my spare time, I work in fashion modelling and we require good appearance and the right look. We need tall and well-proportioned men, with strong beautiful features and healthy skin, teeth and hair, and he has all that."

Alice kept contemplating Mostafa. She said after a long moment: "I wonder how he would look in T-shirt and jeans. I am sure he would be stunning - a sight to behold."

"Now stand still for the pictures." Alice said. With her cell phone, she began snapping pictures. The other girls followed suit.

Alice walked up to Mostafa and circled around him. She stood before him and exhaled loudly as she touched his luxurious hair and ran a finger lightly down his cheek.

"How about having sex with me?" She asked in a husky tone.

When she received no answer, she continued: "I know ways that would please you."
Daisy's eyes widened, a wave of jealousy washed over her. But how could she be jealous, and she hardly knew Mostafa – this primitive villager, and besides, she had an affair with Arnold, the big boy.

Daisy admonished her: "Leave Mostafa alone Alice. He is not the man you think he is."

As if she had not heard Daisy, Alice continued talking about her sex skills: "I am more sexually appealing in bed. I know how to sex well. I am well-schooled in sexual techniques." Alice then looked at Daisy and said: "As I understood, this is a sex party and we are supposed to engage in sexual activity with each other. I will choose this beautiful creature here." She said pointing to Mostafa.

Daisy: "You have to be kidding Alice. Are you going to make sex with that naïve, crude and unworthy peasant?"

Mostafa glanced at Daisy annoyed and offended. Her insults were as though she had just ejected a rotted fish from her mouth.

Mostafa remained calm however and did not respond to any of their sarcasm. His main concern was Daisy. He must focus only on Daisy. He did not like the way she danced with the big boy. They danced in an impudent way and she encouraged him by laughing and kissing him back.

Arnold the big boy suddenly yanked the turban right off Mostafa's head. The girls sighed upon seeing Mostafa's jet-black abundant hair falling back against his shoulders. In Egyptian rural areas, the turban is regarded as dignity and strength for the believer. Muslims wear it in emulation of the Prophet Muhammad, who is believed to have worn either a white or a black turban. Emulation of the Prophet is generally encouraged among Muslims even in seemingly superficial matters such as clothing.

Mostafa attempted to take the turban from Arnold, but he threw it to a boy, and the boy threw it to a girl. The turban turned around the hall until it reached Daisy. Daisy gave it to Mostafa laughing with a hint of apology in her eyes. Mostafa glanced at the boys and girls. Everyone was laughing at him.

"Now let's get this sex party started." Arnold said grabbing Daisy's hand and leading her upstairs to her bedroom. Alone in the bedroom they began kissing and hugging in bed, Arnold started to have an erection.

"Can you feel what I am feeling?" He said to Daisy in a husky voice.

She said: "Yes."

He began to undress her when the door was opened, and Mostafa stormed into the room, grabbed Arnold from his shoulder, and slapped his face right left, right left in quick succession. He then pushed him out of the room and closed the room with the key inserted in the keyhole and pocketed the key. Daisy found herself imprisoned in her own room.

Mostafa grabbed Arnold by his nape and pushed him downstairs to where the party was still going on.
Mostafa shouted at the boys and girls: "The party is over. Get out of here."

Seeing the sparkle of anger in Mostafa's eyes, and his hand squeezing Arnold's nape, with blood spurting from Arnold's nose, they left the house in haste.

Mostafa returned to Daisy's room and opened the door to see her standing in the middle of the room fuming. She looked at his flashing eyes and saw a face contorted in rage. The muscles of his neck bulged out as he breathed. His rage suppressed her anger a little. He dragged her by the arm to the bed. He sat her on the edge of the bed and sat on the floor before her.

"We have to talk." He said angrily.

She hit his massive shoulders so fiercely she thought the bones of her hands might crack.

"Who do you think you are? Father brought you here to work as a servant." She snapped at him.

"Your father brought me here not to work as a servant but to do something he thinks is Important. I will explain that later. Listen, and listen carefully. You made that party to ridicule me and make fun of me. Your intention was to humiliate me in front of your friends. You made me a laughing-stock."

"It's your funny dress that made you a laughing stock. Unless you change that weird dress, you will be subject of ridicule."

"You insulted me when you described me as being naïve, crude and unworthy peasant. I am sad that you are stupid and lack the creativity to call me anything else."

"What do you expect me to do? To apologize to you - never."

"I forgave you. You know why. Because there is nothing more powerful than showing forgiveness to someone who does not deserve it."

"Oh - you illiterate scoundrel. You know how to play with words." She shot at him.

"I came from people proud of their heritage. Touching their tradition with evil or mockery could bring anger and vengeance. Don't you ever make fun of me again, do you understand?"

"I don't give a shit about your tradition." She yelled at him.

She hit his shoulders with her fists again. "How dare you treat my friends like that you savage brute. How could I face them again? How dare you lock me in my room as if you owned the house? "

"I don't give a shit about your friends. They are evil and corrupted. You are bad as they are. You are all on the road to perdition."

"Who are you to interfere in my private life? It is a free country. I can do whatever I like."

"This takes us to the point why your father brought me here. He brought me here to take care of you."

"Take care of me? What do you mean by take care of you? I do not understand."

"Your father told me about your mother and how she deserted him and eloped with her lover. He said that she was a spoiled woman and had spoiled you as well. He gave me a brief about your misconduct and asked me to protect you from all evil, to protect you from your own personal hell, to protect you from you."

"You are singing his praises. So, you are here to control my life. I have no intention whatever of letting you determines my future course of action."

"I did not like the way you danced with Arnold. You showed impudence when you allowed him to take you to your room. You were laughing when he was on top of you, undressing you. Adultery is forbidden in all religions. Your Bible considers this shameful act as idolatry. Aren't you ashamed of yourself?"

"You came from an underdeveloped world and you do not know what civilization is. We are different. We think differently. We live differently."

"How different - Does that mean you have to open your legs

in every relation you have with a man?"

"So what - I and Arnold are spending a good time together. We are having fun."

"You call this indecency fun?"

"We are close to each other, we are having an affair."

"What do you mean by having an affair?"

"Kissing, hugging, you know the rest."

"I hate your lose ways."

What are you going to do? Smack my bottom if I don't do as you say?"

"Do you know other men beside Arnold?"

"It feels amazing to sleep with a new man. When we share our real selves with others, we forge the deepest connections. I am easy going and pretty much what most men want." She said willing to hurt him and humiliate him further.

"I am not happy with this at all. You are losing your honour and tarnishing the reputation of your father. These men are taking advantage of you, because you are so vulnerable and so weak to their desires. You know that?"

"I want to share and explore my desires with men. If I am interested in a man, I attempt to escalate it into sex. This creates a powerful bond between us."

"Don't you feel guilty?"
"You shouldn't feel guilty about wanting something that is natural and healthy in a romantic relationship."

"This is not love Daisy. You can have friendly connections without sex."

"But those do not entitle or guarantee you to romance. I want to love and be loved."

"You move from one man to another Daisy. You are ruining your life."

"Do not impose your outdated ideas on me. I am not your girlfriend."

"Now I understand why your father wants to protect you against your evil self. You are the devil on earth. The devil lives in you." He said feeling the awful burden her father laid upon his shoulder.

"You think I am naïve, crude and unworthy peasant. You think you are civilized and I am not. You must understand that civilization is the civilization of ethics and not wealth or power. I am not illiterate. I write and read Arabic and English. I memorize the Koran. It is all here embedded in my heart. I abide by its principles. I live my life according to its injunctions. The most honourable of people in the sight of God is not the wealthiest or the mightiest, but the god-fearing. I fear Allah and I hope to meet him clean and sinless. You have lost your direction and sinned terribly against God. You have to repent and start a new life."

"Charming Mr. know it all. You have a way with words. Spare me your preaching. Your righteousness cannot save me. Stop your boring sermon and leave me alone."

"I regret for making unworthy girl like you a priority in my life, but I promised your father to keep an eye on you. An ugly task needs to be carried out. I will be like your shadow from now on when you are out in public. I will escort you every day to college and makes sure you get back safely."

"So you will work as a watchdog guarding its master. I could have bought a German shepherd to do the job." She said willing to humiliate him further.

His pride was bitterly wounded, but he managed to suppress his anger. He rose to his feet and walked to the door. She stopped him saying: "Change into T-shirt and Jeans. I don't want to walk beside a watchdog with a jellabiya and a turban, enough embarrassment please."

Chapter 5

Daisy woke up in the morning, had a quick breakfast, and rushed to the front entrance to get into her car. The time of the lecture was due, and she was already late. A young man of striking good looks dressed in T-Shirt and jeans was standing beside her car. His stunning appearance made her heart almost stop. His beauty astounded her. She looked at him in wonder. His dark hair was pulled back at the nape of his neck. The inky blackness of his densely thick hair, the heavy lids of his glowing eyes were all oriental and gave a touch of mystery to his face. Her eyes drank in his tall frame as she approached the car. She was certain a sexier man had never walked the earth.

The good-looking man opened the car door for her. She smiled at him saying: "Do I know you?"

"It's me, Mostafa, in T-shirt and jeans." He said laughing.

Hiding her astounded features behind a cool mask, she ignored how her heartbeat hammered in her chest. She got into the car and he jumped into the passenger seat beside her. She drove the car distracted by his nearness. His achingly masculine scent drifted up and filled her nose. She took a deep breath to steady herself.

She parked the car in the campus lot. "I will attend two

lectures and be back in two hours." She said heading to one of the buildings.

"I will wait in the park." He said getting out of the car.

He sat on a wooden bench at the campus park. He contemplated the flowering trees. There was a tree with glossy dark green leaves and low spreading branches. It bore sprays of red and yellow pea-shaped flowers partly hidden by the dense foliage. Another tree bore clusters of yellow flowers at the end of the branches, together with dark green leaves. The ground under the tree was strewn with a carpet of the yellow petals and was sight to behold.

Mostafa's tongue muttered: "God is beautiful, and He loves beauty. It is for this that the whole of God's creation has been designed and created according to the highest heavenly standard of splendour. The beautiful creation proves the existence of a beautiful Creator. It shows that the Maker of perfection is truly deserving of praise."

He praised God: 'Unto Him all praise is due, at the beginning and at the end of time; and with Him rests all judgment; and unto Him shall we all be brought back.'

After the lectures, Daisy walked to the front door of the building with Layla her colleague. They went to the park to fetch Mostafa. Layla suddenly stopped and drew in a deep breath.

"I have no desire to be anywhere else on earth other than in the arms of this beautiful man." She said pointing to a group of girls surrounding a man sitting on a wooden bench in the park. Daisy looked in the direction where Layla pointed and saw Mostafa smiling to girls fighting to catch a glimpse of his superb face and figure.

"Look at this beautiful lad. The girls faint in a circle around him. He is so beautiful. It is impossible not to be fascinated by his beauty." Layla said bewildered.

"Do not say beautiful he is so masculine, so manly." Daisy said annoyed to see all these girls gathering around him.

"There is nothing derogatory to dignity or to manhood is being called beautiful, for he is that."

"Mostafa let's go." Daisy called out in a nervous tone.

"Well girls I have to go. Thank you for your kindness." He said rising to his feet.

Layla said bewildered: "Where did you find this amazing creature?"

"We were on a trip to Egypt, we brought him with us." Daisy said abruptly.

"Please introduce me to him." Layla said pleading.

"Later Layla, later." Daisy said walking in quick steps to the car with Mostafa hot on her heel.

Daisy got behind the wheel and Mostafa sat in the passenger

seat beside her. "It seems that women drop like flies around you. They find your charm irresistible." Waiting to hear his response, she could hear the loud pumping of her heart in her ears.

"That is the bounty from God. Praise and Glory be to God." He said raising his hands to the sky.

"As it seems, you can subdue women with your devastated charm. You can easily have affairs with women and..."

He knew exactly what her words might lead to - a physical fling. He was pure and chaste and was not going to add himself to her lovers list. He is not interested in just an affair. He is interested in sharing his life with a wife he could love and cherish – a good mother for his children. His religion taught him that there is no sex outside marriage, and he will not succumb to sexual temptation.

"Subject closed." He said with a serious expression on his face.

Daisy drove the car in the direction of the house, but she suddenly changed her mind. "Father is investing in Rodeo industry. He owns a Rodeo farm for breeding horses specifically to buck. Are you interested to see it? It's 100 miles from here."

"Why not."

"Okay. Off we go."

Taking him to the farm will give her more than enough time to know him better and explore his beauty. She drove in silence with thoughts whirling in her head. This crude peasant when changed into T-shirt and jeans looked like an angel bringing good tidings from heaven. His calm deep voice was ringing in her ears like the sweetest melody. He seemed confident enough to conquer obstacles and easing things up. He talked as if he owned her. She wished him to conquer her, to own her, to subdue her. She wished to nestle in his strong arms forever. At that moment, she liked nothing more than making love to him. She feared however that he might sense a turnaround in her mood, so she kept driving in silence.

"You raise horses to buck! How do you make them buck?" He said interrupting her thoughts.

"In rodeo, we don't make horses buck; we utilize horses that already have an inclination to buck. These horses are considered too dangerous for other equine activities, yet they are perfect for the events of bareback riding and saddle bronc riding."

"You people are crazy. I have never heard such a strange sport before!"

"I haven't seen horses during the trip to Luxor. Have you ever ridden a horse before?"

"No. I have been only on the back of donkeys."

She laughed until tears came to her eyes. "I will show you

what Rodeo sport really is". She said while speeding toward the farm.

They reached the farm; Daisy parked the car close to an open field arena. They leaned on the wooden fence watching an empty arena.

"What this arena for?" He asked

"This arena is for saddle bronc riding. Saddle bronc riding is considered rodeo's classic event. It goes back to the Old West when cowboys would throw saddles on wild horses to break and train them for their cattle ranches. "

A rider on the back of a wild horse entered the arena. The horse was bucking and kicking. The animal lowered its head and raised its hindquarters into the air while kicking out with its hind legs. The rider lost control of his mount and was sent flying into the roof of Daisy's car. The horse was kicking and rearing just inches away from Mostafa and Daisy. Some workers ran to the rider to check his injuries and see what can be done. The horse was left lose in the arena bucking and kicking.

"I want to subdue this beautiful beast." Mostafa said after contemplating the horse for a long moment.

"Are you crazy? You will not last a second on his back. I will not allow you to ride one of these beasts."

"I can manage with the help of the stirrup and the bridle."

Seeing his stubbornness, she warned him further: "You are not trained for such dangerous sport, so forget about riding one of these horses."

The horse was still bucking near the fence. Mostafa jumped from the fence onto its back not paying attention to Daisy's warning shouts.

The horse ran bucking and kicking determined to throw Mostafa off its back. The horse brought its head up, shifted his weight back and stroke out with its front feet. He then dropped his head and kicked out behind. Mostafa spurred in rhythm with the horse's bucking action. Mostafa stayed firm in position through all the bucking, until all the activity of the horse was spent, and the horse was so tired he could not fight anymore. The horse realized that bucking, didn't work to relieve the heavy pressure he felt when Mostafa got on his back.

Mostafa rode the horse gently around the arena a few times, then dismounted and patted the horse glistening neck tenderly. He walked over to Daisy covered with sweat.

"You have done something miraculous. You subdued this beast though you have never been on a horse before! You used your strength to overpower the horse without any training!"

"I didn't like it when the horse bucked off his rider. I saw him wild and vicious. I wanted to give him a lesson."

"A lesson! This is a sport and not vengeance."

"Now the horse understands that he cannot escape a tough rider."

"You like challenges, don't you? Don't let the challenges get the best of you."

"I don't like challenges for challenges, but I pitied the rider when he fell to the ground and lost consciousness."

"How were you able to subdue the horse without training?"

"A horse with his head up cannot buck; so, I sat deep in the saddle, kept my heels down and my shoulders back. I gave strong pulls on the reins to discourage the horse from putting his head down. I pressed the horse's sides with the calves of my legs and made sure to keep my leg on."

Sweat poured down his face. She stared at him fascinated. He was a beautiful man – taller than most men she knew before. His face was proud and strong. Something fluttered in her belly and she felt a burst of wetness between her thighs.

"I am soaking wet." He said as if apologizing.

"You have to take a bath and relax. You must change into dry clothes. We have a nice house here with a swimming pool. We will spend the night in it."

"I didn't bring a change of clothes."

"I would lend you some of my father's clothes.

"No thank you. Take me to town to buy some clothes."

She drove him to a mall where he bought cotton underwear, a bath suit, a pair of jeans and a pair of pyjamas. He then invited her to a cup of coffee and ice cream. They sat in the coffee shop enjoying the strong taste of the Italian coffee and the sweet taste of the ice cream. His beauty was so intimidating that women sitting around with men or without could not help themselves but to stare passionately at him. They eyed Daisy enviously and stared lustfully at Mostafa with glittering eyes. Some girls sitting close to their table, went to the extent of snapping pictures of him on their cell phones. Daisy was immensely irritated. She gave them a hard-jealous stare.

"Why wherever you go to a place women stare at you?" She shot at him.

"Some women stare because they don't know what else to do." He said naively.
"Women stare at you because you are attractive enough that they want to have sex with you. Finish your coffee and let's get out of here." She snapped at him.

Chapter 6

Daisy and Mostafa went back to the farm. Daisy showed Mostafa to the guest room.

"You can spend the night in this room. It has a private bath. You can put your things in the closet. After you have finished showering, the maid will wash your clothes and send it to dry cleaning."

Daisy headed to her room and Mostafa ran to the shower. He took off his clothes and soaked in a hot bath for half an hour. He rubbed himself dry with a towel, changed into pyjamas and jumped into bed seeking a long nap. The day was hot; he took off the pyjama jacket and slept with the upper part of his body naked.

With Mostafa close and living next door, Daisy ached with heat and need. A profound passion and lust had taken possession of her. She needed to have sex with Mostafa.

As Daisy took a shower, she tried to get herself under control. She dried herself with a towel, put on a bathrobe and walked across the hall to Mostafa's room. She silently opened the door and padded across the bedroom until she stood before his bed. She stood for a moment contemplating him. His broad shoulders, lean stomach combined with a muscular upper torso, and his square-jawed, masculine face attracted her immensely. She could smell his strong aroma - the scent of sex. Lust clawed at her and she felt burning out from the inside.

She stripped off her bathrobe and let it fall to the ground. She whispered: "Mostafa?"

Whispering his name was enough to startle him awake. His eyes opened wide with surprise as he saw her standing beside his bed completely naked. He felt stricken. He had not seen a woman naked before. He couldn't help himself from glancing at her, admiring every inch of her enticing body, from her cascading blonde hair, her beautiful face, her sensual body. Her nipples were so hard from arousal that set his body ablaze. His heart pounded in his ears. He continued staring at her, bewildered and frightened. Big beads of sweat covered his forehead.

 "Daisy is something wrong?" He said swallowing his saliva. "I am melting hungry for you. I want to have sex with you." "Daisy how dare you say something like that? This is not right. Go back to your room and.."

She did not give him a chance to continue. She quickly sat beside him and surrounded his neck with her arms kissing him heatedly. Her blood took heat from his body. Her hand moved along his body, moaning, into a lustful frenzy.

"My God, you are so beautiful." She said fuming with desire. He disengaged himself tenderly from her arms and stared into her lustful eyes. His wide eyes drove her into frenzy. She gave him a long kiss on the lips ripe with passion and infused with need. His heart raced from her kiss. He felt his need growing, coming to life inside him. He loved it when she touched him. It was so thrilling when he felt her hands on his body. An explosion went off in his body. His entire body was on fire. He thought he might combust at any moment. He wanted her with a hunger he had never imagined possible.

She hissed in his arms: "You brought me to a boil, take me now."

Breathing heavily, he pulled away tenderly from her arms.

"Daisy please - get back to your senses." He said with a big effort trying to fight back the lust that washed over him.

"you got me burning up inside. Make love to me now."

"Daisy please, you drive me to the edge. You drive me out of my mind." He muttered.

She threw her arms around his neck and kissed him hard on the lips again. He pulled back and looked at her. "Listen to me." He cleared his throat. "In our religion, there is no sex outside marriage. Please try to understand." He said embarrassed trying hard not to hurt her feelings.

She hit his chest with both hands. You mean I should marry you to have sex with you?" She said angrily.

"I am afraid so."

"Do you want to marry me."
"No."

"Why not?

"I do not marry women of questionable character."

"You think I will not make a good wife because I am a loose girl."

"I was just telling you the command of our religion in this matter."

"Silly explanation and awkward religion. If I want to marry someone, it is not going to be you for sure. I look for men on my level. You will never be on my level. Get this through your head, you silly rude backward peasant."

"This is an unlawful love and a betrayal to your father. I promised your father to protect you and now you want me to commit a terrible sin with you! Cast off evil. Cease to be a slave of passion."

"I have never been rejected with any of the men I knew before.You rebuffed me, you humiliated me. I hate you."

"You had affairs with other men!" He said annoyed.

"Of course, I had. What are you going to do about that Mr. Hercules?" She said in derision.

She got out of bed, picked up her bathrobe from the ground

and left the room burning with anger.

He sat in bed trying to visualize her beautiful body. The smell of her perfume was still lingering in the room. He has not seen a naked woman before. Heat shot through him at the memory of the softness and fullness of her lips; at those perfect curves outlining her spectacular body. The sensation of her curves against his body was exquisite torture. He ached for her. A sudden burst of savage possessiveness overtook him; she is his responsibility, she is his woman. He wanted her with so much intensity.

A fierce surge of possession went through him. There is something about her, something about the way he felt when she touched him that he could not deny. She turned him inside out. What is happening to him? He couldn't ever remember having these kinds of intense feelings for a woman before. Was that love? He wondered.

Daisy tossed in her bed unable to sleep that night until the sun penetrated her room. She went to the window and opened it to breathe fresh air that might suppress her mounting desire. She saw Mostafa swimming in the pool. She had not finished with him yet. She will humiliate him as he did to her. She changed into her bikini, put on a bathrobe and went down to the swimming pool. She took off the bathrobe and settled on a lounge chair and watched him swim.

Mostafa came out of the water to see her stretched on the lounge chair comfortably. He moved his eyes towards the beautiful curves of her breasts, hips and long lean legs and felt suddenly hot as adrenaline surged through his veins charging him with an orgasmic rush.

Daisy let her gaze travel the length of him, from broad, muscled shoulders to sculpted abdominal muscles to slim hips, and muscular thighs. She swallowed hard when she let her eyes rest on his sex for a moment and felt renewed outrage at his rejection of her last night. Had he not turned her away she would have known what it was like to enjoy sex with this rigorous man.

He sat on the edge of the pool near her. A slight irritated look crossed his face.

"You were not fair last night when you accused me of being silly, rude and backward peasant. You have mocked me. I was really hurt."

"I meant what I have said, because that is what you are."

"You said I am not in your level and that you look for men on your level. You also said that you had affairs with other men. Is that what you are after, sex and money? Is that life to you?"

"Yes, what else you think worth living?"

"Many things."

"Such as."

"I will try to explain to you but you will not understand."

"Try me."

"Don't mock a small bird because it can reach far places you cannot reach. Do not belittle a small butterfly because it has colours and emotions you cannot comprehend. The silent tree might speak several languages you do not understand because you live in the illusion that the universe is subdued to serve only you. Maybe you do not know that by cutting that tree down, you are killing an embryo it carries in its bowels or opening wounds it carries in its depths. Do not humiliate a modest man because he might be better than you are but you cannot see."

"I am afraid I do not understand."

"I knew you won't."

"It is really absurd to see a religion preventing lovers from making love and live freely without fetters. Freedom in our society is a crucial component of our civilization. Do you understand Mr. wise man?" She said mockingly.

"Societies whose developmental dynamics become alienated from religion face inevitable doom. "

"Our societies are rich and successful; yours are poor and suffering backwardness and enormous failure. Is that the civilization you are talking about?"

"You are incorrigible, you will not understand."

"Try me." She said again.

"Wondrous is the affair of the believer for there is good for him in every matter. If he is granted goodness, he praises God and is grateful. If he is afflicted with a calamity, he surrenders to God and is patient. The believer is rewarded for every matter, even lifting a morsel of food to his wife's mouth. God does not decree anything for the believer except what is good for him."

"Is this your civilization? I do not understand."

"I knew you wouldn't."

"Explain further."

"Ethics and values are the moral and spiritual aspects of every religion. If these aspects disappear, man will lose his moral warmth, which is the spirit of life and existence; mercy will quit his heart; his conscience will not be able to play its role; he will no longer know the truth of his existence and himself; and he will be bound with material restrictions, from which he cannot escape."

"Well, what else Mr. pious?" She said sardonically.

"Morality is one of the fundamental sources of a nation's strength, just as immorality is one of the main causes of a nation's decline. Religion support morality and matters that lead to it, and stand in the way of corruption and matters that lead to it. The guiding principle for the behaviour of the believer is virtuous deeds. The most fundamental characteristics of a believer are piety and humility. A Believer must be humble with God and with other people.

He must be in control of his passions and desires."

"I do not want to live like that. What you are saying is fanatics and backwardness."

"You should not be attached to the ephemeral pleasures of this world. You should keep God in your heart and the material world in your hand. Do not allow the material world to fill your heart."

"And you consider these fairy tales civilizations? Bullshit." She retorted.

"Yes. In my perspective, civilization is the civilization of ethics."

"Nonsense. I do not believe in all this. I am not a believer."

"You should believe in God Daisy. You will not get rid of your sins unless you believe in God and ask His forgiveness. Fearing God, obeying Him, following His commands and avoiding His prohibitions bring goodness, remove evil, sickness, calamities and keep God's bounties."

He rose to his feet and said: "You better cover yourself. You are nearly naked. Prepare to leave. You have lectures to catch."

She hated his domineering way in telling her what to do and what not to do. She hated his crushing masculine beauty that totally subdued her to his charm. This man is not easy. He is deep like an ocean and wise like a prophet. He is also astoundingly strong. He frightens her, but she is strongly attracted to him. He is more desirable, more thrilling than any other man she had ever met. She could not remember being so strongly attracted to anyone before. Is that love? She wondered.

Chapter 7

Mostafa called his father and asked him to send him ten thousand dollars of the money he had in his possession. With this money and some of the money he had saved during the past months, Mostafa bought a Harley Davis motorcycle. He took a rider course in the Harley-Davidson Riding Academy and became acquainted with the wonderful machine. Mostafa enjoyed riding and cleaning motorcycle. Riding the Harley became his passion. He drove across New York into Nevada and then came back the next day. That's 4,480 in two days.

When Daisy first saw Mostafa on the Harley, she thought she was looking at a knight coming to take her to a world of wonders. "I just can't seem to get it together. I have no idea how I am supposed to act around you now?" She said laughing. "Come to a ride." He said happy to see her laughing.

She walked toward him and got on the back of the Harley. The engine roared to life, and Mostafa drove leisurely down the street. He was happy to feel her behind him. As she put her arms around his waist, he felt that he had her for himself. As the Harley picked up speed, the wind stung her cheeks and made her hair mingle with his. She inhaled sharply and could smell his masculine scent mixed with the fragrance of summer air.

They stopped at an ice cream shop. Daisy went inside to get her favourite flavour. Mostafa waited for her outside. She came back with two Italian-style Gelatos. She stopped smiling before him and kissed him lightly on the cheek. He blushed, and a chill drew up his spine. "Well, it's a beautiful day. I'm just getting in the spirit you know." She said laughing while giving him the ice cream.

Daisy stopped going to the college by car and preferred riding on the back of the Harley holding Mostafa's back. To her, the ride with him was pure exhilaration.

Tom Wilson came from a long trip abroad. He was having breakfast when Daisy entered the dining room. The way Daisy was dressed infuriated him. Daisy was dressed in a short blouse, mid-section exposed, and a very short mini skirt revealing her thighs and long legs.

"For heaven's sake Daisy, put on something decent please." He shot at her.

Please, Daddy, please don't start again," pleaded Daisy.

"I personally feel like ashamed that where is our society going. This is really embarrassing."

"Just because it makes you uncomfortable doesn't mean you get to tell other people what to wear."

"You should cover up more Daisy. If a woman wears little clothing on her body she is most definitely insecure. If you're walking down the street dressed like this some people may think you were asking for sex."

"I, being a votary of personal freedom, believe each person has the right to decide how he or she wants to live and that includes as to how he or she wants to dress."

"Are you suggesting that the freedom is absolute? Any Freedom that is not tempered with responsibility is a sure recipe for disaster. Women should avoid dressing like sluts in order not to be victimized".

"I mean that every woman should have the right to decide what she should wear."

"You're not a child Daisy. You're an adult and you know what is good for you. Care for appropriate dressing, it is very easy to decide."

Mostafa entered the dining room to say Hello to Tom. He was embarrassed to see Daisy in such revealing clothing.

"Hello Mr. Tom. I hope you had a pleasant trip." He said lowering his gaze.

"Yes, I had a nice trip thank you." Tom said while getting on with his breakfast.

Daisy shot at her father: "I don't think I am in so much danger that you need to get me a bodyguard." She said pointing at Mostafa.

"Unfortunately, I could see no other way to protect you. You come late drunk. You wear revealing clothes. I fear you might get sexually abused by bad guys."

"Don't tell me what to wear, it's my choice not yours. I wear what I see fit."

"Just shut up and listen. You wear miniskirts and over exposed tops. Men draw bad conclusions about you from how your dress." Tom yelled at her.

"I don't fucking care what men think about me. I want to feel sexy and desired. I want to feel the centre of attention."

"You still have to wear decent clothes. Women wear can give a powerful insight into who they are. You are what you wear Daisy." Mostafa intervened.

"Keep out of this. You came from an underdeveloped world where women wear headscarf, burka, and hijab. You want me dress like that?"

"I haven't said that, but our women clothes are a sign of modesty, and a symbol of religious faith. A symbol of woman's intellectual ability over her physical beauty and sexuality."

"Don't step into your mother shoes Daisy. She should have helped you find your way through the years, but she deserted you and ran away with her lover. I don't want you to follow on her footsteps." Tom said angrily.

"Leave my mother alone daddy. She left you because you paid no attention to her. You were too busy with your work."

"I am worried about you Daisy. I am so engrossed in my work that I can't give you the attention you need. It is such a relief that Mostafa is here to care of you."

"Thank you for the privilege for being a part of your family Mr. Tom." Mostafa said.

"Being a part of our family doesn't mean you put restriction on my private life. I have my life to live and stay out of it. You hear me?" She said raising a threatening hand to Mostafa's face.

"You are a very headstrong, foolish girl who does not know her own interest. Mostafa is here to protect you from the temptations of life and the evil of your soul." Tom said concerned.

"You appointed a guard to suffocate me and limits my freedom. Do not force me to get your own way. Accept me as I am. I am responsible for myself. I make my choices and live with them."

"I am doing this for your own sake. I fear you might take the wrong road. If you take the wrong road you shall be dashed to pieces."

"I am free to go where I like, sleep where I like and do what I love without being monitored."

"Many young people who were given freedom walked the wrong path, not because they wanted to but because the guidance isn't there anymore. You do bad things because you have freedom to them. You must limit your freedom. As your father, I am here to correct you and discipline you." Tom said disappointed.

"Your father wants to protect you from the burden of sin and failure. He wants to guide you from sin to righteousness." Mostafa said supporting Tom's view.

Anger shot through Daisy. She gave Mostafa a sour look and shot at him while leaving the room: "If you could shut the fuck up, that would be just lovely."

Though Mostafa was still prepared to protect her, he was no longer prepared to let her humiliate him.

Daisy stopped going to college riding the Harley behind Mostafa. She went by her car and Mostafa had to follow her with his bike. It was funny to see Daisy driving her car followed by a Harley drove by a handsome strong man. It looked like a young woman followed by a bodyguard. Her colleagues made fun of her saying that she was a naughty girl guarded by a bodyguard lest she might succumb to sexual temptations. Their sarcasm outraged her and made her more determined to escape Mostafa's surveillance and live the life she has chosen for herself.

She must free herself from Mostafa's hold and she knew how. She can see his admiration from the way he looks at her. He can't take his eyes off her when they were together.

She will take advantage of that and persuade him one way or another to leave her alone without disturbance.

It was midnight when Mostafa heard a knock on the door. He opened it to see daisy in her nightgown with a broad smile on her face.

"Daisy! It is not proper that a woman visit a man in his room at midnight. What would your father say if he sees us like this?" He said annoyed.

"Can we talk inside? Can I come in?" She said to embarrass him.

"Come in, but you have only two munites, you hear me?"

"I hear you."

"What do you want from me at this hour of the night?" He said irritated.

She sat on the edge of his bed and he stood looking at her swamped by feelings of guilt and anxiety.

"Well, say what you have to say." He said impatiently.

"How long I should wait to have sex with a person?" She said bluntly.

"You really are perverted, aren't you?"

"You haven't answered my question?"

"You can hold out until I disappear from your life, and I do not intend to."

"Why don't you try to understand? I am a modern-day feminist. I believe in equality. I don't think there is any need to label ourselves just for sake of society. I am just a woman with free thoughts free mind set and I love the way I am."

"You just want to get laid like an animal and then kick men out."

"Sex is the utmost admiration of love."

"You can have sex after marriage. All religions said there is no sex outside marriage. Do not sin against God."

She suddenly stood and walked towards him. Her move was too fast for him to see, and the next moment he was in her arms, feeling her lips on his. She moved her mouth over his with seductive power.

"Stop this. What in hell got into you?" He managed to say.

"Not until I see sense."

"What sense?"

"Stop following me like a watching dog."

"How many times have I told you that it is wrong for a man to treat a woman as if he has free reign with her body before marriage."

"I don't know how to act when I am around you. You make me lose control. I know that you love me. I can see this in your eyes. Make love to me." The feel of him in her arms sent her wild.

"Don't you feel guilty about what you are doing?"

"I don't feel guilty about it. It makes me feel so powerful and fucking beautiful."

"I don't want to get into this." He said pulling himself away from her, and this broke her heart.

"Damn you. I hate you." She shouted at him.

He took her by the arm and grabbed her to the door. She jerked her arm, but his grip was strong and hurting. He opened the door and pushed her out and closed the door.

Chapter 8

Daisy went to college with her car. Mostafa followed her with his bike. She parked her car and he parked the Harley few yards from her car. After the end of the lectures she didn't appear at the front door as she used to do. He entered the college building and asked one of the students about her. The student said: "I saw her with Arnold heading to the back door," and he pointed to the other side of the building.

Mostafa rushed to the Harley, but it took him long to reach the other side of the building. When he got there, he saw a car leaving the park and heading to downtown. He followed the car from a distance so not to be noticed.

The car stopped at a cheap motel. Arnold and Daisy stepped out of the car and disappeared in one of the rooms. Seeing her disappearing with Arnold in the room was like a sharp knife stabbing his heart. Seeing them together in a private room aroused furious jealousy in him.

Daisy and Arnold took their clothes off. Naked, they jumped into the bed hugging and kissing. A terrible blow came from behind to send Arnold crashing to the ground. Arnold fell on the ground like a log. Mostafa grabbed him up by his hair and dealt him blows like thunderbolts that made him fall senseless to the ground.

Daisy shouted in horror: "Stop it, you are going to kill him, you barbaric brute."

He turned to look at her. Her throat tightened when she saw tears in his eyes. She however yelled in anger: "How dare you invade my privacy like this, you monster?"

He slapped her face hard. She felt the blood oozing down her lips into her mouth. He shouted in her face: "Cover the flesh of your nakedness; get dressed, you despicable whore."

Arnold began to regain consciousness and opened his eyes. Mostafa kicked him hard in his chest and broke one of his ribs.

When she finished dressing he pulled her by the arm to the Harley and drove her home. Although he was harsh on her and slapped her face she wrapped her arms around him, rested her head against his back and gave him a big squeeze. She knew if he sleeps with her only once, he would be the only man who could subdue her strong sex drive and bind her to him forever. Yes, she must admit to herself that she loves this beautiful beast, but sex In her opinion is the highest form of love, and in his opinion, sex comes after marriage not before. Marriage however, is far behind her horizon. She wants to live freely like a bird and not to confine herself to a man who wants to restrain and rule over her.

They stepped inside the house and he grabbed her by the wrist to her bedroom. He flung the door open and stormed into the room. He pushed her down on the bed in contempt and sat in a chair beside the bed.

She sat in the middle of the bed looking at him as if he were the scum of the earth. Her delicate face was contorted with anger. Tears gathered in her eyes.

"What's the matter with you? You suffocate me. You are not normal, you are a psychopath." She said weeping."

"You are much trouble. Your existence is an act of rebellion. I can't understand how your brain works. Talk to me. What do you think life is all about?"

"All I want is to live a life where I could be me, and be okay with that."

"You do not know where you stand. You are a slave to your passion. You are engulfed in flames Daisy."

"I live in my own flames and it feels good. I am the slave and ruler of my own body, and I wish to do with it exactly as I please. I look my best when I am totally free."

"No woman is free who cannot control herself. No one is free, even the birds are chained to the sky."

"I don't have to be what you want me to be. I am free to be what I want."

"Tell me again Daisy. What is your purpose in life?"

"I seek wealth, indulging in sex, eating and dancing." Pity and deep sorrow were shown on his face.

He said after a brief silence: "The sun is set to disappear; the flowers wither, bend their heads in awful sorrow and lose their fragrance; the spring turns to autumn, yellow leaves spread as far as the eyes could see; health declines with age; life ends with death; empires rise, flourish and then perish; continents swollen by oceans, the stars explode in the space and disappear; the world of appearances is deceitful, covered by lies and move toward extinction; nothing holds together, everything falls apart. All that dwells upon the earth is perishing, yet still abides the face of God, majestic splendid."

"Sad words but I don't understand what you mean." She said perplexed.

"All these lusts for money, food and sex are transient and passing ones. You need for a permanent purpose Daisy. You should understand that the only way for your salvation in this life and in the hereafter is to know God by believing in Him and abiding by His rules. This is the wisdom of creation Daisy."

"I am not a believer. I told you that before. Religion can never reform mankind because religion is slavery. It is far better to be free."

"You continue with your aggression and sins because you are deceived by the delay of God's punishment. Beware of the anger of God. Those who transgress the limits set by God expose themselves to punishment in this life and the next. You have to repent to God and return to Him and avoid all that brings His wrath and anger."

"I don't give a shit about religion. I want a man to attract me with his masculinity and then move forward to kissing, and sex. Having sex only after marriage is obscurant and retrogressive. Today, most women like to have sex to start off the relationship and then see where it goes from there."

He knew it was useless to talk further with her, so he remained silent for long moments. Her voice was enough to alert him when she suddenly said: "What I saw from you today was strong jealousy. You love me, don't you?"

"Have I ever said that?" He said trying to hide his true feelings.

"You don't have to say it. Whenever you set eyes on me, love is clearly shown in your eyes."

"If you want sex so badly, then marry me. I will give you sex until it comes out of your ears."

"So you don't mind marrying me. This is an admittance that you love me though I scratch your pride. Forget about marriage. I don't want to get married. I want to live my life away from any restrictions."

As if she got the opportunity she was waiting for to humiliate him, so she shot at him: "You think your piety will win me over? I am going to be honest with you. I derive from a wealthy family. I am beautiful, have style and good taste. If I am going to marry, I wish to marry a rich man of my social status, and not of your lower and poor status. I want to marry a man who is independent and who would be more of an asset than liability. If I marry a poor man like you, you will become a liability to me."

"Rich men want women that are smart and chaste not an immature materialistic idiot that only talks about sex. When you say you want to marry a rich man, you are basically saying that you are too weak to fulfil the responsibilities of being human and would rather become a lifeless object instead. A woman should look for discipline, responsibility and good character first. I can earn millions if I want to."

"We live in a money-oriented society. The love of money is the root of all virtue. Wealth is well known to be a great comforter. It pays to get rich. Smart women marry rich men. No romance without finance. You are however poor. You work for my father. You are my bodyguard."

"Your tongue is strong enough to break a heart. So be careful with your words." He said feeling sorry for her and for himself.

Her heart slammed through her ribs when she saw him hurting. She said comforting him: "You are an awesome guy. I am strongly attracted to you. But that is not enough. It's humiliating to beg for your love, I wouldn't have to deal with the pain of being rejected repeatedly by the person I truly loved."

"Do you really love me?"

"Yes, I do."

"Then why having sex with other men?"

"Because I wanted it. I enjoyed it."

She saw an incredible sadness on his face.

"Hey, don't look so sad. My affairs with them are just one-night stand."

"Your ugly words are like a knife tearing my heart apart."

"Do not forget that I showed my interest in you in different ways, but you turned me down. You wait too long to make a move. You make me feel ugly, unwanted, unloved. Instead of wasting more time on you, I opened myself up to opportunities to be with other guys."

"What do you expect me to do, build up sexual tension and then release that tension with kissing and sex?"

"Now that you got it, how about kissing and having sex?"

She left the bed and sat on his lap. She wrapped her arms around his neck, gazing into his eyes. She kissed him on the forehead, the eyes, the cheeks, and the lips.

"Sex between two lovers leads to feelings of happiness, connectedness, closeness, and commitment. Having sex often and passionately is an extremely positive thing for our love to continue." She said while raining his face with her kisses.

A strong passion seized him. He must take drastic measures to keep himself from surrendering to her deadly charm, but he was amazed to see the weakness of his will. He was swayed by the love he felt for her, as though he were a leaf in the wind. He felt paralysed and had no self-control. She kissed his lips long, and he responded without hesitation, her body melting against his. Her lips were silky and soft, and it felt like his entire soul stilled the moment he tasted her.

His black long hair mingled with her hair, and they held each other for a long moment. The scent of her skin and hair filled his senses. She looked intently into his eyes. She smiled as she had found what she was looking for.

"Do you love me that much?" She said sure of herself.

"Yes, I do, but hear this well. Until I convince you to marry me, if you flirt with another man I'll peel your skin from your body and watch you scream. Do you understand?"

"Yes, darling I understand." She held him tight, kissed his lips long and cried in his arms from joy.

Chapter 9

It was nearly 8 pm when Daisy surprised Mostafa by telling him that she was going to a party.

"My friends and I are celebrating the birthday of Audrey. You remember her, don't you?"

"Yes I do. The vulgar girl who wanted to have sex with me."

"Don't you want to go?'

"I'm not much for parties."

"I am a wild party goer."

"Where is the party?"

"We have rented out the back bar of Analogue bar."

"I know the place."

He regarded her with a frown on his face. "I don't like your kind of parties. You drink a lot and dance intimately in vulgar ways simulating sexual activity. What is there to be happy about if all you do is that?"

"There is nothing boring about wanting to explore and be

free, there's lots of people who feel the same. Come with me and enjoy life being you."

"I can't understand the crowd that just drinks, and parties. It's just not your thing. You need different friends Daisy. Find people more like yourself. There are many people like you who prefer other activities and don't drink. For example, you can join rock climbing, hiking, biking, traveling and other stuff."

"If you are so worried about me then join me and be my companion to the party."

"I am afraid I can't. I have joined the Harley Davidson family. We will make a New York sightseeing tour by night on the back of the Harley. Why don't you come with me? It's enjoyable. You will like it I am sure."

"Oh dear, it's going to be quite boring."

"You will love every minute of it. We will be stopping at various locations throughout the city. Every stop is a party you don't want to miss. You will enjoy friends, food, soft drinks, live bands and so much more! "

"Don't worry I can take care of myself. I am not going to get drunk."

"It's obvious my opinion doesn't matter. You are being unreasonable. So, you will go to the party regardless of what I think?"

"I want to have fun and act my age."

"If anything happens to you just give me a call okay?

"Okay."

Daisy went to the party in a nude slip dress exhibiting every inch of her sexy body. The strappy silver shoes were impossibly high and added definition to her already slender legs.

Daisy met her friends at the bar. They chatted, laughed and had a lot of whisky. There were four men next to Daisy talking. One of them was a devilishly huge beast touching every woman's butt as he walks by them. The man went to Daisy and attempted to isolate her by grabbing her arm and leading her to a more secluded area to talk.

"Leave me alone you pervert." She yelled at him.

The huge man spent the remainder of the night staring longingly at Daisy and watching every move she made.

Daisy drank profusely that night and was in no position to drive home. As Daisy exited the bar, the four men quickly followed behind and stood beside their parked van. Daisy walked unsteadily on her feet and was unable to move forward to her car. As she walked past them, the huge man grabbed her from behind and tried to drag her into the front passenger seat of the van. Daisy fought back and was able to break free. The three other men came to the man's aid.

Daisy ran few steps away and opened her purse, took out

the cell phone and called Mostafa with a frightened voice: "Mostafa please come quickly. Four men are attacking me."

At that time Mostafa was touring New York with the group of the Harley family. He separated himself from the group and drove at a high speed to Analogue club.

The huge man attacked Daisy again and raised his hand and slapped her on the side of her head. Daisy felt the blood running down her neck as she landed on the floor. The man bent down, picked her up with one hand, and was about to toss her into the van, when he heard a lethal voice saying:

"Get your damn hand off her. Put her down."

The huge man looked back to see Mostafa looking at him with eyes like blazing fire. The huge man looked at Mostafa and knew that he was not looking at an ally. The man stared at Mostafa in contempt, Mostafa seemed to him fragile and far weaker to perform physically against him. The man did not care about Mostafa's request and continued heading to the van to put Daisy on the passenger seat. He stopped however when he received a hard slap to the nape. He turned around to receive another slap on the cheek. He had to put Daisy down to confront the stubborn intruder. The moment Daisy's feet touched the ground she ran away from the man and hid behind Mostafa.

The man charged forward, but Mostafa evaded the attack and gave him another slap to the nape. The man turned back outraged to receive a hard slap to the face. He rushed forward to attack again, but Mostafa kicked him viciously in the stomach. The man bent over in agony, and here Mostafa kept slapping his exposed nape repeatedly. The man stood erect in defiance to Mostafa. Almost faster than the eye can follow, Mostafa back handed the man across the face. The man's face quickly turned to rage, but Mostafa slapped the man again and again.

"You son of a bitch." The man said and reached around behind his back and drew a knife from a leather holster. Mostafa kicked out the knife from the man's hand and began to land solid blows on the man's face and body. The man fell face down on the ground. Mostafa grabbed cruelly at his hair and pulled him up to his feet.

Mostafa said angrily: "So you wanted to kidnap the girl and rape her eh? Then take this." Mostafa gave the man a painful blow to the groin causing him to double over in pain.

"Of course, you were going to strip her off eh?" Mostafa continued reprimanding him while stripping him down to his boxer shorts. Mostafa pulled the man from his hair and toured him nearly naked through the place. Mostafa kept humiliating him by slapping his ass while taking him around.

"People, this is the hulk who frightened you. The hulk who thought he has the right to rape innocent girls to satisfy his animal desire. See how he is so weak, and so humiliated. He thought he was the stronger, the mightier, but in fact he is the dirtiest, the meanest and the most despicable of all mankind." Mostafa said to the watchers.

Mostafa kicked the man again in the groin. The man fell

unconscious to the ground accompanied by Mostafa's words:

"I think you will never get in bed with women again."

Mostafa looked around searching for the three men, but they were not there. They disappeared with the van from sight.

Mostafa mounted the Harley. "Get to the back." He ordered Daisy roughly.

Mostafa drove to Daisy's house. He brought the Harley to a halt in front of the house. She unwrapped her hands from around his waist and got off. Mostafa shut the Harley down and got off. Together they mounted the stairs to her room. When they got into the room, he closed the door behind him and started reprimanding her.

"Aren't you ashamed of yourself? We had an agreement, but you breached it. You promised not to drink but I found you totally intoxicated and barely able to stand on your feet. You are to blame because you act flirtatiously. Your nude dress provoked men to assault you. Women are responsible for being raped if they wear revealing clothing or are drunk. Men respect women who covered up."

"Mostafa please calm down and try to understand. I realize that you came from a world sunk in piety and religious beliefs. But the fact is that you are not familiar with women progressive ways of thinking. I view my body as beautiful, strong, and considers highlighting those physical attributes an intrinsic part of my identity. Women don't cause rape by what they wear. The clothing that I wear is, in many ways, a projection of what I am going through emotionally and mentally."

"Daisy stop this nonsense. A woman's clothing is an incitement to rape."

She encircled his neck with her arms and kissed his lips light feathery kisses. She said through her kisses: "The number of assaults will not go down if women make sure to cover up. Plenty of assaulted women are not dressed sexily, including women draped in head-to-toe burqas. Interestingly, veiled women are blamed, too. The abuser must have seen a bit of her ankle, wrist, hair, neck... who could resist!?" She laughed lightly.

"Daisy you were dressed like a slut. You have shamed me. You have humiliated me."

"So I am your slut. Your bitch wants you to love her, drain her, and squeeze her. Come on and treat me like a whore." She pressed her body tight to his and kissed him longingly.

With a deep thigh, he succumbed to the intense delight that washed over him. He closed his eyes and inhaled deeply, wanting to fill his lungs with her. They stood that way for several long moments before he pulled away.

 "You think I give a damn about a bitch?" He said frowning down at her.

"You love the bitch. You must be crazy." She laughed with a heart filled with his love.

Chapter 10

Mostafa celebrated Daisy's birthday by taking her on the back of his Harley to a tour around New York City. The Harley was really comfortable and there were headsets in the helmets, so she could easily communicate with Mostafa and chat all the way round.

She sat behind him, wrapped her arms around him and gave him a big squeeze. He showed her areas of the city that she never would have explored otherwise, or even knew existed. They stopped along the tour to take pictures and grab snacks. They stopped around Bryant Park where they had good coffee, pastries and cakes. They rode through Times Square at night and cruised down the West Side Highway along the Hudson River at sunset. The tour was superb.

Every morning Mostafa took Daisy on his Harley to college. When she finished her lectures, he took her back home. He was like her shadow guarding and protecting her. More than that, he was deeply in love with her, a love that was always threatened by the possibility that she might slid into a temporary affair behind his back.

In New York strong winds, rain and flooding wreak havoc as coastal storm moved through New York area. The strong wind huffed and puffed and blew roofs off buildings landing on some cars in the parking lots. In this stormy night, Daisy rushed into Mostafa's room wearing a short nightgown revealing her sexy thighs and long legs. She stood before him barefoot, dishevelled, immodest, with her hand holding a burning cigarette.

"You're worse than the storm outside." Mostafa said perplexed.

"We must talk." She said trembling all over.

"Okay let's talk." He said pointing to a chair beside his bed. She sat in the chair cross legged. She inhaled the smoke deeply to the bottom of her lungs, held it long, and then exhaled slow. She looked as if she loved the feeling of drawing smoke into her lungs.

"Well, what do you want to talk about?" he said while sitting on the edge of the bed.

"I do not like this kind of platonic love. I want to get my emotional needs met, and you do not give me sex."

"I am willing to give you all the sex you need, but this must be after marriage. Marry me Daisy please, I love you."

"I don't want to get married. I want to live my life freely without shackles, without commitments. And this is what I am offering you. We live together without pledge and have sex and enjoy life. I love you. I don't want to lose you, but your hard-conservative views prohibit you from freeing yourself from the fetters of your religion."

"Get to your senses Daisy. You push me to commit a terrible sin. Just marry me and I will satisfy your sexual desires. So as you see darling, I am offering you lawful sex through a legitimate bond – marriage."

"I don't believe that having sex outside marriage is a sin. Premarital virginity had been going out of fashion for decades now. American women took their sexuality into their own hands since the 1960s."

"It is wrong for a woman to engage in premarital sex, even with a man she is going to marry. Your society paid the price for free love. Now you have homosexuals, gays, lesbians and sex outside marriage. This is destroying the traditional American family. This brings God's wrath on the evil doers."

"It's hard for you to understand because you came from undeveloped immature world."

"I am trying to reason with you Daisy. Having sex with different partners besides being a major sin, is joyless, uncomfortable and humiliating. A good sex life is a grain of affection between only husband and wife.

"You are fucking annoying sometimes. Give me space and room to breathe, will you?"

"No Daisy, I must tell you this: do not regard what you are doing is good for you shall be held to account for the sins you have committed. You should always be on your guard against the traps of evil. If you persist in doing such evil things God will punish you in this life and Hereafter. Remain chaste. That is purer for you. God is aware of what you do."

"Put off the conversation about God and let's talk about our life together. I offered you my love, but I was the one being brushed off. There are many who die to be in my shoes. Yet I preferred you to all others, but you were not interested in loving me."

"You seem to forget that I proposed to you but you refused claiming that I am naïve, crude, poor and unworthy peasant. I must tell you that men in our part of the world do not marry women indulging in sin and neglect obligatory duties prescribed by God. You have a disgraceful past Daisy, a thing that cast a slur upon my name and my honour, yet I want to marry you because I love you. If you marry me I will protect you from evil and satisfy your sexual needs."

"Marriage shackles women in fetters and chains and you are over-strict and stubborn. I don't want to get married. I want to live my life to the fullest so not a minute is wasted. I intend to live life, not just exist."

"Marriage and family provide the sense of belonging, the sense of loving and being loved. Marriage is believing that one has a purpose in life and a reason for continued existence."

"O Mostafa please stop that nonsense."

"Do you want to live life, or do you want to escape life? God has made woman and man to abide with each other in the closest companionship, and to be even as a single soul. They are two helpmates, two intimate friends, who should be concerned about the welfare of each other. Marriage will keep you chaste and protect you against temptation. Marriage will protect you from unlawful sexual intercourse or taking secret lovers."

"Mostafa, do not distract me from what I want to tell you, let's talk sense. "

"Sense! Was I talking nonsense to you?"

"Please listen. Just listen."

"I am listening."

"In order for our relationship to continue let's have a sex agreement."

"And what is that?"

"Consent that you and I can have sex." Mostafa's cheeks burned dark red.

"Sorry I don't accept such rubbish."

"Then I offer you another alternative. I would like to open our relationship. This would mean allowing each other to sleep with other people. It would be just sex, temporary love affair. This affair would be harmless when it couldn't last. We would make the rules in advance, no feelings involved. You see, it is so simple."

"And you can handle me having intimate relations with another woman?" He said aghast.

"Of course, I can. It's healthy for our relationship to survive."

"Daisy are you out of your mind?"

"The idea would be to just spice things up and keep things fresh."

"I am outraged by the suggestion as I feel it is a major threat to our relationship. I love and value you way too much to allow you to have sex with other men. I would be extremely jealous and could not handle it."

"Your negative attitude towards me get me bored really fast. I get excited when you take me in your arms, but your strict manners make you too negative, and negativity is a drain on energy for both of us. So, stop being such a douche and be more positive. Your cold behaviour makes me feel undervalued. I need your attention to see that you care, but you don't give any; that is why I look for it elsewhere."

Mostafa regarded her in disbelief.

"You know something! We might be able to save our love if I can just have time to myself. Time apart is the only hope of improving our current situation" She continued.

"You want to free yourself of the restrictions of love and spend more time with your lover. You look for passion and sex with a new lover?

What kind of life is that Daisy? The life of deceit and cheating. Keep predators out of your life. You made yourself accessible to anyone you thought will cherish and respect you, but believe me they despise you instead." He said with tears in his eyes."

She said weeping: "Stop messing with my life okay.
Stay out of my life. You appointed yourself guardian over me. You didn't give me the freedom to come to my own decisions."

"What decisions you are talking about Daisy."

"You took control of my life. I wanted to take back control of my life by making my own decisions and my own choices, I wanted to live my life and go about my choices and owning my mistakes. I wanted to choose the man I like but you hit the shit out of them."

"Then quit making the wrong ones. I was protecting you from you. I thought I was your man Daisy. You frighten me. You dishearten and depress me down."

"It's time to let me take care of myself. Don't ruin my one chance at happiness."

"Happiness? You will never be happy if you go along this evil road. Happiness is a quality of thought, a state of mind. Tell me what happiness in your opinion is?"

"Happiness is to feel the sexiness, to satisfy my insatiable hunger, and to enjoy a powerful, fulfilling sex life."

"Your thoughts are low, and your mind is dirty."

"Why need to be this hostile? If you don't like me I don't give a fuck at all." Depression took hold of her. She rose to her feet and left the room feeling down.

Chapter 11

Daisy had a strong sex drive which shapes her interactions with men. She gets as horny as not to say no to sexual advances. As a result, she could be in love with someone and have sex with another. She wants to have sex with Mostafa, but Mostafa believes that sex must only be after marriage, and marriage is not in her horizon. She wants to live a free sexual life without control or commitment. Her relationship with Mostafa is therefore incomplete, platonic love is not enough!

By refusing having sex with her, Daisy felt like she was undervalued, ignored and dismissed. She wanted sex with other men, but she also didn't want to lose Mostafa. She will cheat on him and he will never know – she thought. She loves Mostafa sincerely, but a little chocolate now and then doesn't hurt.

Daisy's behaviour with Mostafa began to change. Mostafa was surprised when she said to him one day: "I want time for myself."

"What do you mean?"

"I am bored I need time apart."

"We are so good together why needing time apart?"

"Time is the key for a successful relationship. It is a way to avoid the death of passion in our love."

"Why don't you be honest and say that you see me as an obstacle to what you desperately want and aren't getting."

"What do I desperately want and not getting?

"Sex of course."

"You are absolutely wrong. You know something – I lost interest in sex."

"Do not play games with me. Do not deceive yourself with false reasoning. My ethics are at odds with the immoral and humiliating life you are living. I came from a Sa'idi family living in Upper Egypt. In its culture family honour is highly valued and is linked to female modesty, and chastity. Preserving family honour is deeply rooted in our society. Our women are expected to be modest and sexually pure to preserve the honour of the family. If a family's honour is breached, it brings shame to the entire family. In such cases, the family would decide the fate of the female that brought shame. This might involve killing the woman who is involved in the dishonourable act."

"This is backwardness. You came from undeveloped people. You have been here for a year now and you must have seen the difference."

"What difference? You brought dishonour to your father

and to me. Even blood, will not be able to wash out the disgrace you brought to your father's name. Listen carefully young girl. I will chase you until you have nowhere to run. I make you this promise."

His warning was as if a heavy iron collar with a big chain was put around her neck.

"Please give me a space to breathe." She begged.

"My love for you made me sacrifice my ethical goods. I will put you under surveillance, I'll watch your steps. I love you. Your life is mine."

"You will never be able to conquer me. I defy you." She said challenging him.

In the following days, he was growing suspicious because she started acting strangely around him. She began to disappear from the house in times of his afternoon naps. He thought that probably she had met a stranger that had a large influence on her. He was right; from his room's window, he saw a man collecting her outside the house in a van and then dropped her home, at 2 am. She was wearing revealing clothes and too much makeup. He decided to track her down to know what she was doing.

He followed her one day as she walked down the street, then turned left for two blocks. She stopped and stood there. Ten minutes later a black van stopped where she stood. The door opened, and Daisy climbed in. Mostafa ran two blocks back to his Harley and was barely able to find the van before it disappeared completely from sight. He patiently followed the van from a distance. The car stopped before a building and Daisy and the man got out and entered the building. Mostafa parked the Harley and followed on their heel. He climbed the stairs to the man's apartment and knocked on the door. A man bare from the waist up opened the door.

"Where is Daisy." He asked the man.

"Who are you?" The man inquired.

"Where is she?" He said slapping the man hard on his face.

The man pointed at the bedroom frightened. Mostafa slid the door open and saw Daisy completely naked in bed.

"Get dressed you whore." He shouted at her.

"It is not serious it is just a…"

"Shut up you slut and get dressed now I said."

When she finished dressing he grabbed her by the hair out of the apartment, to the Harley. She climbed behind him, and he drove back and pulled to a quick stop in front of the house.

In her room, he waved his large hand in front of her face and then pointed one of his large fingers at her.

"I can't do it anymore. I will quit this job. You are incorrigible. It's easy to protect you from men taking advantage of you but it is impossible to protect you from your evil self."

"I know that I have done nothing but lie and cheat and betray you. But in reality, all I want is to be near you for as long as I am able."

"Don't say that you love me, because if you do you wouldn't have done what you did. You frighten me Daisy. What scares me most is the thought that I won't be able to protect you. How can I protect a corrupted heart against the temptation to rebel? Your father appointed me to walk in front of you at night with a lit lantern, showing you the right way, but you loved darkness and decided to tread the wrong path."

"The affair was accidental, just a one-night stand."

"Liar! You saw him more often behind my back. Why did you do that?"

"Because you do not give me sex. I had to relieve myself from the intense horniness." She said helplessly.

"What a despicable answer from a slut like you. You know nothing about the honour of the body. You don't know the value of loyalty and friendship. These are virtues to be cherished, for without them we are no more than beasts roaming the land. You have less honour than a piece of shit."

He said leaving the room: "You are a disgrace. I don't love you anymore. You are the woman who broke my heart. For the rest of my life you will always be the one who hurt me the most. Don't forget that."

Chapter 12

A thought stirred in Daisy's mind for the first time – there was no place for her here. She felt terribly alone, a loneliness that drew her further away from Mostafa. A loneliness that sounded the death knell for her relationship with him. Here in this house she was observed in all matters, she was constantly under threat of correction, judgment and criticism from Mostafa. She became a child fettered under watchful eyes.

Mostafa constantly opposed her behaviour with all the men she knew. He came from an underdeveloped world treating women as goods, as furniture and not as human beings having the right to love and breath. Mostafa deprived her from every love feeling she wished to enjoy with a man. He snatched from above her every man she wanted to have intimate relationship with. He deprived her from sex as other women usually had. "No sex outside marriage," that's what he always said to her, but she didn't want to get married, she wanted to live her own private life without fetters, and without confining herself to one man.

Mostafa detested the way she looked at sex. He hated her attempts to hunt men and bring them to her room. He hated to see her naked in the arms of strangers. He broke bones and slapped faces because of her. She knew that she hurt him so much, but what she could do, and he had even rejected her love when she proposed to be his woman and live with him a free sexual life. She wanted to wound him and bruise his pride because he rejected her.

Her heart constricted. She wanted to run. She wanted out of this prison. In response, she will channel her defiance and anger into a new affair.

She needed air. She needed space. She needed drink. She drove her car not knowing where to go. She stopped by a pub to have some drink. The public bar was crowded.

"What would you like to drink?" The bartender asked her.

"I want a stiff drink to calm myself down. A bottle of whisky please."

"Have a seat while I get your order ready."

She sat at an empty table crossed-legged. Her mini skirt revealed her thighs and long sexy legs. The bottle of whisky came with an empty glass.

She began to drink thirstily. She drained her glass and poured another, then another. A man half drunk was sitting at a small table in the corner, watching her and sipping his drink slowly. The man got up and went to her table. "May I join you?"

"No I don't think so. You are drunk."

"So are you."

Daisy looked intently at the man. She saw him handsome with a ruddy complexion. He pulled out the chair opposite and sat. He settled his bottle and glass on the table.

"Tell me your story. Tell me why you are drunk?"

"It's none of your business."

She took her glass and drained it. She poured herself another glass and drank it in a gulp.

The man leaned forward and smiled.

"My name is Alfred. I have an apartment few blocks away. Where do you live?"

"Nowhere."

"Then come to my place and spend the night in my arms."

"It is not a bad idea. I am hungry, I must eat something first."

"How about eating sexy food to get you in the mood?"

"What do you mean by sexy food?"

"Special food to get you in the mood for love. They serve here sexy food. Let me order for you."

He raised his hand for a waiter and ordered oysters, asparagus and chilies, liqueur-laced coconut macaroons and chocolate-covered strawberries.

Although they were drunk they ate with great appetite. It was a kind of possessive hunger that appears with great ferocity in states of intoxication.

He paid his bill and hers. "Now let's go back to my place and spend a good time together." He said stretching his hand to her.

She stared at him. She took a big swallow and said: "What do you mean by good time."

"Fuck you, suck you, and eat you."

"Any time handsome boy." She said laughing.

He took her in his car to his apartment. When they entered the apartment, he held her and kissed her hard.

"Come to bed. I want to melt in your flesh." He said pushing her to the bedroom.

In the bedroom, she took off her clothes and stood naked before him. He examined her naked body and could not help but think how beautiful she was. She lay down in the bed waiting for him.

He finished taking his clothes off. He was hot and she was ready for him. He slipped in to her with a groan. He went deeper and deeper, with a shout he said: "You are a woman well fuckable." His body moving over hers as she lay stretched out on the bed, his length embedded deep in her heat. He was in her until they both finally went limp.

In the morning, she felt a euphoric sense of satisfaction – the handsome man with her sees her desirable, sexy and attractive.

They woke up late at noon.

"Let's see your watch. What time is it?" He said.

"It's noon."

"Oh! Hungry you must be. How about having lunch at the New York Marriott Marquis Hotel?"

"That would be splendid. I love fancy clubs and restaurants." She said cheerfully.

At the Marriot restaurant, he ordered Mongolian shrimp and broccoli. The meal was superb and very tasty.

"Thank you for the most delicious launch I ever had."

"You are most welcome." He said with a broad smile on his face.

"Can I confess something?"

"Sure!"

"You have the prettiest smile I've ever seen."

"Can I confess something as well?"

"Yeah."

"This smile only exists because Of you!"

"My heart beats for you, only for you and will continue to beat till you love me most.

Her heart leaped. She could live with that man - a man who could be everything she had ever wanted. She liked herself when she was with him. He made her feel more loved, cherished and admired than anyone she knew before. He knew how to please her. He made her explode in a fiery explosion when he brought her to orgasm several times in one night. He gave her the big finish she deserved. With him her soul settled. With him she felt free. No fetters put upon her by Mostafa or her father. Now she can do with her body what she wants. Now she can surrender to Alfred, trusting him with her body, without fearing the sudden appearance of Mostafa to humiliate her and shackle her with his sermons.

On their way back to his apartment, Daisy stopped and said: "I am dying for a drink"

Alfred nodded his head agreeing. "As if you were reading my mind. Let's go to the nearest pub and get one."

They headed off to the nearest pub and sat at the bar.

"What do you like to drink?" He said looking at the glass shelves holding liqueur bottles before him.

"Anything you wish."

"How about scotch Whisky?"

"I am not a liquor-taker you know, but whisky is okay I suppose."

Alfred ordered a bottle of scotch. He poured two glasses, one for him and one for her. They sipped their whisky slowly, both of them enjoying the flavour.

"Scotch Whisky is one of those drinks that can be an experience. Only whisky born in Scotland can be called Scotch whisky. Whisky is aged in wooden barrels and the aging process enhances the flavour experience."

"Oh! You seem knowledgeable about booze."

"You are drinking now the best type of Scotch – single malt Scotch. It is widely considered the gold standard of Scotch and must be distilled at a single distillery, from only water and malted barley, without any other cereal grains added. Most single malt whiskies are bottled at ages from 10 to 21 years. Some rare whiskies are aged 50 plus years."

Daisy looked at him fascinated. He has extensive knowledge about life. He is a man who can take control. He is a confident leader. She can give him the reins and let him lead.

"I drink because I like the way it feels. I associate the feeling of being tipsy or drunk with the feeling of joy." A strange feeling of excitement filled her as she stared at him.

He had already poured her three glasses of Scotch, which she had swallowed and looked dizzy. He whispered into her ears, making her tingle all over.

"I can't stop thinking about you. Cheers and bottoms up." He said pouring her a fourth glass.

"No thanks. I have had my limit."

"Drink darling. Too much of anything is bad, but too much good whiskey is barely enough. Whisky is the water of life. Whisky is the liquid sunshine." He said patting her cheek with his fingers and tucking her hair behind her ear.

She gulped it down, even though she had to force it. As soon as she finished it he poured her another.

She raised her hand in a gesture of rejection and with a look of loathing on her face.

"Drink it now." A hard look filled his face.

"I don't want another please, my head is spinning." She begged.

"It is not spinning enough, go ahead and finish your glass." She lifted her glass to her lips with a trembling hand, and a little whisky spilt on the bar. She drank the remaining whisky and became totally intoxicated.

"Alcohol is like love: the first kiss is magic, the second is intimate, the third is routine. After that you just take the girl's clothes off." He said laughing at the helpless girl laying her head down on the bar.

Chapter 13

Daisy was clearly very drunk. Head spinning, she held Alfred's arm for support as they walked out of the bar. He helped her to get into his car and drove off to his apartment. He escorted her inside the apartment and up to the bedroom. She fell flat on her face on the bed before falling asleep almost instantly. She slept through until sunset. She woke up to see herself completely naked and covered with the bed sheet. Alfred must have undressed her. She lifted her head to meet Alfred's gaze. He was standing before her in the room with just his boxers.

"I am really sorry. I really don't drink much. You must feel I am a drunken idiot." She said feeling like her head was going to explode.

"No, I am very familiar with drunken idiots, and you are not one of them."

She wondered if they had sex while she was asleep! She was too dazed to absorb the details. She remembered however, the feeling of him filling her, consuming her.

Alfred opened the wardrobe and brought out a robe of pure silk. "Put that on and come to the kitchen. I will cook you seared salmon with avocado salsa Verde." He said heading to the kitchen.

She sat down on a tall chair and watched him prepare the meal.

"I need to see what kind of cook you are." She said enthusiastically.

He started mentioning the ingredients of the meal and how it is prepared: "4 salmon pieces, chopped red onion, avocado diced, chopped onion…"

After he finished preparing the meal, he yanked open the kitchen cabinet to pull out a couple of dishes, set them down on the kitchen table, and folded white napkins at each place setting. He filled the plates with the salmon he prepared and served them with large spoonful of avocado salsa Verde and squeeze of lime. The food was so delicious. Daisy kept saying wow every time she tasted another bite.

"Everything is so delicious I am completely full."

"I am a good cook. I love food, wine drink and beautiful women."

"You see me beautiful?"

"Yes. That's why you are here."

He loaded the dishes and eating utensils into the dish washer.

"Can I get you a drink?"

"No thank you I have had enough to drink."

"I tell you what. I will bring you a sweet cocktail, it's light and tasty."

"I never heard of sweet cocktail before."

"Sweet cocktails are popular after dinner and include cordials made with a variety of liqueurs. Popular cordials include Amaretto - almond-flavoured, Kahlúa - coffee-flavoured, Grappa - grape-flavoured and Chambord - raspberry-flavoured. How about Amaretto?"

"It sounds tasty. I don't mind trying it."

He poured her a glass of Amaretto. She liked it, so he poured her another, then another. Since whisky was the main component of Amaretto she began to feel dizzy as the liquor worked its way through her body.

"Is it safe to drink alcohol after having dinner?" She asked.

"Yes, it is safe. It reduces the effect of alcohol on your liver." Alfred poured himself a scotch. She loved the way he drank his scotch. He held the glass, rolling it gently so that the ice knocked musically against the side of the glass. She loved the warmth that came out of him when they were alone together. She sat quietly enjoying his company. Loving feeling flooded through her.

"Drinking good wine with good food in good company is

one of life's most civilized pleasures. As I sat in your cosy kitchen eating your delightful meal, I longed to share all meals with you as a wife."

Suddenly he realized that the perfect opportunity was glaring him in the face.

"Will you marry me?"

Her heart thumped against her ribs. "I don't know, Alfred. It's a slip of a tongue I think. As they say, those who marry in haste do repent at leisure." She hesitantly said.

"We've been together for almost two days. That's not long in the grand scheme of things, but it's long enough for me to know how much I love you. We can marry in haste in Reno."

"Why Reno in particular?"

"In Reno we can marry in as much secrecy and with as much haste as possible. We can get our marriage license at Washoe County Complex; bring the license to the Antique Angel Wedding Chapel, and make reservation; if we do not have a witness, the wedding chapel will provide us with one. You see how simple it is to get married in Reno?"

She contemplated his words. The way he is living his life would certainly make her free from the shackles her father and Mostafa fettered her with. In two days she experienced grand sex, fancy food and superb drink. She was free in her wildness. She was a free bird, the queen of the world.

Sexual frenzy is her compensation for the moments of deprivation she spent at her father's house. The world lays itself out beautiful before her with this stranger. With him there is a rich tapestry to explore with love in abundance.

"Just forget it," Alfred said. "Don't trouble your little head about what I said. You have been with me for two days now. Your parents must have been worried about you by now."

"The thought of going back gets my skin crawling. I don't want to go home to my father. He limits my freedom, and places increasingly severe restrictions on my life. I want to forget anything that reminds me with my previous life."

"Forget your troubles and just get happy. Ignore anything else around. I will make you forget all your troubles today."

"How?" She said with eyes brimmed with tears.

"The food and drink we have consumed will help us last longer in bed. Tonight, I will take you like you have never been taken. You will lose yourself in my arms and reach heights like never before."

"You have no idea of the amount of happiness you brought into my life." He continued.

Suddenly, all her troubles melt away. All her worries were gone.

"I think I'll have a few more drinks to prepare myself. Go to bed. I will be with you in a minute."

Alfred took a tablet of Viagra, drank a double vodka and then joined Daisy in bed. He wrapped his arms around her and pulled her tightly against his torso. His mouth came down on hers. She surrendered willingly to his embrace. Their bodies met, chest to chest, hip to hip. Her body and his locked, inseparable, consuming each other in feverish bliss.

A searing fire spread through her. Shudders wracked her frame when he filled the aching void inside her. She fell into an abyss of splendid tormenting sensation. Sensation followed sensation. Shimmering waves of ecstasy drowning her in delight.

 She opened her eyes in the morning. There was a delicious languor in her blood, a delicious ache in her bones in her heart. She sighed deeply and whispered: "I love that man. I feel home in his arms."

He opened his eyes and saw her glancing at him smiling. He gathered her to him.

"I love you. Do you marry me?" He said.

"Yes." she said.

His passion for her stirred again into flame and it began anew. They quickly melted into the heat waves again. Wonderful this time, even better, prolonged measure that mounted and filled her with the same shimmering bliss.

Now he possessed both her body and soul.

On the same day, they took a flight to Reno and got married.

Chapter 14

After the wedding Daisy and Alfred flew back to New York; Daisy to pack her things and Alfred to wait for her in his apartment before they both travel back again to Nevada where he lives and works. She went to her room and packed her things in two big travel Duffel bags. She knew that she had to tell her father about how she met Alfred and the sudden wedding. She rode down to the lobby pulling the bags behind her.

Her father Tom Wilson and Mostafa were in the library talking about her disappearance for two days now. Daisy had never confronted her father before, but now she will. Daisy entered the library to see her father sitting in a large fauteuil, and Mostafa standing leaning against the wall with his hands crossed over his chest.

The moment Tom laid eyes on her, he yelled at her: "You could have made a little phone call to tell me where you have gone."

"I have been busy getting married." She said willing to defy her father.

Tom looked at Mostafa. "You see what she had done to herself? She married a stranger without even telling me."

The fact that she got married hurt Mostafa to the core. Anger fumed out of his eyes. His greatest defence is to ignore her until she no longer exists. He glared at her with a blank expression on his face.

Tom: "And who is the man you married?"

Daisy: "His name is Alfred."

Tom: "Has he any family name?"

Daisy: "I didn't ask him."

Tom: "What does he do for a living?"

Daisy: "He says he is a businessman working in industry, but he never explained exactly what he did. He seems rich but didn't seem to have regular business hours."

Tom: "How long have you known each other?"
Daisy: "Two days ago. But I feel like we have known each other forever because we are so much alike."
Tom: "You married a stranger, a man you knew nothing about. You didn't even care to invite me or any person from the family to the wedding!"

Tom: "What made you marry in such a haste? What is so special about him Daisy?"

Daisy: "He could wrap his arms around me and take away my rejection and hurt."

Tom: "What hurt Daisy? Nothing is missing you."
Daisy: "I want to break the chains that tie my hands."

Tom: "You mean Mostafa?"

Daisy: "Who else."

Tom: "What are your plans for the future?"

Daisy: "I will live with him in Nevada. He works there."

Tom: "This man doesn't really care about you. You didn't even care to introduce me to him until now. You've chosen the wrong person Daisy."

Daisy: "Why is it so hard for you to believe that he is a good guy? This wrong person is right for me. Is it wrong to fall in love?" She burst out.

Tom: "Do you really love him?"

Daisy: "He seems sweet, charming, and thoughtful. I see him a true gentleman that is charismatic, handsome, chivalrous, and funny. We both shared quite a lot of interests."

Tom: "You will grieve forever. You will not get over regret. You will beat yourself up because you have made a bad choice."

Daisy: "I am matured enough to look after my own affairs."

Tom: "He will drag you down to his level."

Daisy: "No. He will make me happy. He loves me."

Tom: "You can't stay for long in any relationship, you cheated with many men before him."

Daisy: "The men I cheated with meant nothing, purely physical. But this time it is true love."

Tom: "Corrupt women are for corrupt men, and corrupt men are for corrupt women."

Daisy: "Stop blaming me. I am the result of your toxic relationship with my mother."

Tom looked at his daughter sadly, watching the guilt play out on her face. He yelled at her: "Whatever you sow is what you shall reap. You sowed evil, and you shall reap evil. You are an indecent girl. You hurt me. You tortured me."

Silence reigned over the room for a long while. Daisy then looked Mostafa directly in the eyes. And said: "You should have opened your eyes. I was crazy for you."

Mostafa: "What did you want from me? More romantic passion involving sex?"

Daisy: "I am sorry Mostafa. You wanted to make me into something I am not. I think what happened between us was not true love. When love is real it doesn't make you feel unwanted."

Mostafa: "I stayed by your side and protected you. I broke my heart loving you. I proposed to you, but you rejected me. I cared for you more than you deserve."

Daisy: "You have no idea how chattering it is to be rejected. It wasn't enough to know that deep down, you loved me. It was the actual execution that mattered, and you just didn't. Not enough."

Mostafa: "Why did you have to hurt me so much? I was a fool for loving you. I was a fool once again for trusting you with my heart. You wanted love without marriage, but you have married a stranger! Maybe because he is richer, a man of high social status not a poor guy like me."

Daisy: "You still don't understand. There is always something nice about being wanted. I need love that casts me into the wind and sets me ablaze. I want love that burns."

Mostafa: "You lied to me. You cheated on me. You hurt me. I thought you would change but you didn't. Your love was like a cut, it will heal, but there will always be a scar."

Daisy: "Sometimes love means letting go when you want to hold on tighter. Believe me Mostafa, there will always be a place in my heart that belongs only to you." Mostafa could hear the guilt in her voice.

Mostafa: "Everything I did, I did it for you. I just wouldn't want you to get hurt Daisy." Mostafa said sadly.

Daisy: "This I know perfectly well. You do care for me, but

you are simply not for me. I am not an angel I am me. I know I am weird. I am sorry I am not what you wanted. I love you in my own way. You fixed me when I was broken. You comforted me when I was hurting, you gave me strength when I was weak. Sorry if I broke your heart."

Mostafa: "It hurts when you realize you aren't as important to someone as you thought you were. You were my dream, but you turned my dream into shame. I will get over you." Tears rolled down his face.

Daisy: "Time heals even the deepest wounds. You will always have a special place in my heart no matter how much I have hurt you. Please try to understand Mostafa." She said with a bleeding heart.

Tears coursing down her cheeks, and with a heavy sigh, she bent down, grabbed the handles of her bags and headed to the door. She stopped and turned back to face Mostafa. "I am not afraid to walk my new life alone because I carry your love in my heart. One day you will again think about me and come to rescue me." Bitterness simmered beneath the surface of her words.

Mostafa sighed and turned his head away refusing to acknowledge her leaving. Out of the corner of his eye he watched as she heavily pushed herself toward the door. She seemed like a defeated woman.

A single tear slid down from his warm, black eyes, followed by another one, and another one, until soon, a steady stream of tears flowed its way down his cheek, releasing the sadness and sorrow that has been held inside of him for all this time. His hands open and closed, rhythmically clenching as if there could be some violent solution to his pain if only he could find it.

Chapter 15

When Daisy and Alfred first met, she asked him about his profession, he said that he worked in industry, hiding the fact that he worked in sex industry i.e. pornography, stripping, nude modelling, and erotic dancing.

Prostitution is legal in Nevada. Alfred owns a brothel in the State of Nevada where people come to engage in sexual activity with prostitutes. The brothel offers a Vegas-style lounge atmosphere with spacious VIP rooms, a Jacuzzi tub, and a well-stocked bar. The brothel has a strip club where clients can enjoy a couple of drinks before taking things further with women of their choice. The women are a mix of white and black girls in their 20s and 30s.

After she packed her things, Daisy met Alfred in his apartment. He pushed her to drink glasses of whisky with packets of tranquilizers into it until she became completely intoxicated. They then took a cheap flight to Nevada. All through the trip Daisy laid her head against Alfred's shoulder nearly unconscious. Now he had her where he wanted.

When they reached the brothel, Alfred carried her upstairs to a spacious room. He undressed her, put her in bed, and got under the cover beside her. They both slept for hours. Daisy awoke to see him still asleep. She ran her fingers through his hair, gave it a gentle tug to wake him up. He opened his lazy eyes glancing at her half asleep.

"I am having an orgasm. Make me feel better. Fuck me, wear me out." She said throwing her arms around his neck. Alfred mounted her. Her body was heating, straining to meet his. Daisy was little away from her extreme point when Alfred stepped up his speed and, in few seconds, explode inside her. She grabbed him more tightly, wrapping her legs around him, suggesting continuing the pace somehow. But much to her surprise, Alfred pushed her away and got up from the bed. Without uttering a single word, he dressed himself up. Daisy got shocked: "What the hell happened" she asked him holding his wrist. "How dare you leave me like that? Don't you see I am not fulfilled?" Daisy looked like a packed bomb of excitement and anger.

"Okay I will meet your needs. I will be back in a moment."

Tom left the room and shut the door behind him. After a few moments, the door was opened and a huge black man with a bare torso entered the room.

"What are you doing here? Get the fuck out of my room," she shouted at the black man.

"Don't shout bitch. Mr. Alfred told me that you need to get fucked."

Daisy screamed calling Alfred, but she got no answer. The black man slammed the door shut and came to bed. She tried to fight him off but to no avail. He raped her repeatedly all night until morning.

In the morning, she woke up to the black man in bed with her. She sat up on the bed and pulled the sheet over her trying to cover her naked body. Her body went numb when she remembered the hours of brutal penetration that happened to her last night, and then more when she saw the black man lying awake beside her in bed.

The black man left the bed and said: "You will be locked up in this room. You are not allowed to go out. You can live comfortably here. The room has all what you need. Do not attempt to escape. The door is locked. There is a private bathroom over there, and in the closet, you will find revealing clothes for the customers."

"Where is my husband, where is Alfred?" She began to cry. "Husband? Alfred didn't tell me that he got married! I thought you were one of the new whores he usually brings to the brothel."

"Brothel! What brothel? This place is supposed to be a family home!"

"Family home! Call it home if you like, but here men pay to have sex with prostitutes." He said laughing.

"You seem new here. Try to make yourself feel good about being a whore. You have a beautiful body. I enjoyed having sex with you. I will be happy to share you with other men. You are going to be a desirable whore I am sure." He said shutting the door behind him and locking it.

The door opened, and her heart jumped in her neck when

she saw Alfred entering the room with a woman close behind carrying the breakfast tray. The woman placed the tray on the bed before Daisy and left the room.

"Good morning darling. How are you today?" Alfred said as he walked past the end of the bed to open the tapestries and shutters, letting the early morning light flood into the room. He then sat on the bed before her smiling a smile of pure vengeance. Daisy shook with fear, she felt that there was something terribly wrong.

Alfred rolled himself a cigarette, sprinkling it with hashish. When it was ready, he drew a lighter from his pocket and lit it, inhaled deeply, then blew the smoke in Daisy's face.

How dare you offer my body to a stranger?" She shouted in his face.

"You mean hibou the Niger? He is my right hand here. He is the professional - an expert in bed. His job is to explore our women bodies, especially the newcomers, and discover how truly libidinous they are. He said that you showed strong arousal and intense sex drive. Here we arrange our women according to their strong sexual feelings, and darling you came on top of the list. I will offer you to my best customers. Alfred said coolly as he puffed the smoke of his cigarette in her face.

Daisy saw the expression of pure vengeance on his face. She shook with fear, every primal instinct telling her to flee. "So how did you like the fucking last night?" He said laughing. Adrenaline shot through her veins like rockets. Her body stiffened, and her head sprung around like someone had smacked it hard.

"How dare you offer my body to a stranger you pimp?"

"Pimp is the wrong word darling. I work in commercial sex. It's a regulated profession. The annual revenue generated by prostitution worldwide is over $100 billion."

"A person who works in this field is called a prostitute. Prostitution is illegal in the United States. It is considered a vagrancy crime. You know that?

"It is legal in Nevada darling. It is also present in most parts of the country in various forms. 15-20 percent of men in the United States are engaged in commercial sex. This is a good business dear, a good business."

"So you are trafficker - a pimp. You married me to push me into prostitution. Why are you doing this to me." She said crying.

"Ah, here come the big question: why did I marry you? My father Thomas Richardson owned a plastic company by the name of Aton. The company earned around $26 million per year on sales. My father owned 51% of the shares.

"After several years of selling plastic products and domestic expansion involving complicated deals and contracts, Aton was millions of dollars into debt. All this debt was concealed from shareholders through partnerships with other companies, fraudulent accounting, and illegal loans.

The huge debt wiped out the shares of the shareholders. Having their expected profits completely evaporated, the shareholders assigned Tom Wilson your father to defend their interests when they conflicted with those of the company.

"After studying the case, your father was able to prove that the company falsified earnings reports to show continued profits. Your father's investigations revealed that Aton entered secretly in fraud deals with entities funded by Aton to purchase plastic products from Aton, then later sold them back with high profits going to my father, the main shareholder and key Aton officials and their families. Your father charged my father with conspiracy and fraud. My father was found guilty on 19 counts of conspiracy, fraud, false statements and insider trading. The company had to admit to overstating income from 2014-2016 by $30 million.

"My father was indicted and sentenced to 10 years and six months in prison. After two years in prison, my father died from a heart attack brought on by severe coronary artery disease. I therefore decided to take revenge against your father. You are the victim of such revenge darling. Now you know why I married you. Now you know why I brought you here."

Daisy sat in bed feeling terrified. Her whole body was shaking. She married a criminal, a fraud, a pimp. His story turned her stomach.

"So you are working in prostitution. Is that the business you were talking about?" Tears rolled down from her eyes.

"You deserve this, bitch."

"I will go to the police." She said trying to threaten him.

"You have nothing against me. First, we are legally married, and you are living where I live. Second, prostitution is legal in Nevada and I have a certified licence. This makes it difficult for prostitutes to seek help of law enforcement when they are victims in crimes. Third, you will be imprisoned here without phones, you will be dead to the world."

 "It's unfair." She said desperately through tearful sobs.

"Calm down honey. You will enjoy your job I am sure. You will satisfy my customers a lot because your sex drive is animalistic and ravenous." He said in a cool dry tone.

He stared at her with an icy calmness and said before leaving the room: "To me you are nothing more but a whore wanting to be fucked hard. I have a lot of regular clients. I care for the pleasure you will give them. I am confident you will make them see how talented you are. You will make me a nice profit I am sure."

Mostafa's voice echoed in her head: "You were my dream, but you turned my dream into shame."

Chapter 16

Alfred covered Daisy with heroin, cocaine, and alcohol. She became a drug addict and couldn't stay away from heroine. Overtime her perception of things as they should be became warped and twisted.

On her first night, she was given only three clients, which grew to nine on busy shift. Alfred gave her enough heroin during the day and alcohol during the night to keep her going.

Daisy became a sex slave for a whole year and Alfred made thousands of dollars in cash off her.

Trapped in a world she never expected, Daisy was forced to make the ultimate decision: surrender her life to this miserable life or risk escape. One night she tried to escape but Alfred and pimbou beat her and broke her ribs. They tied her up for twelve days, tortured her with burns, sexually abused her and forced her to take drugs. They took her to Nevada desert, threw her in a hole and started shovelling dirt over her before pulling her out. They beat her with a leather belt every day and kept her locked inside the room, with no food or water, for days. The door was then opened only twice a day, a little food was slid through, and then darkness returned. They threatened to kill her if she doesn't allow the throngs of filthy men to have their way with her all hours of the day and night.

Many horrible thoughts came to Daisy's mind. She imagined being arrested for prostitution, her picture in the paper, what would her family and friends say? She imagined being choked to death, unable to scream.

A customer entered Daisy's room to have sex with her. He put his cell phone and car keys on a small table beside the bed. He took off his clothes and had sex with her. After he finished he entered the bathroom for a shower. Daisy took the opportunity and rushed to the phone and called Mostafa.

She whispered into the telephone in a trembling voice: "Mostafa?"

"Yes." His heart raced in his chest when he recognized her voice. His voice warmed her heart for a second.

"Come quickly and get me out from a brothel in Nevada owned by my husband Alfred Richardson. Pretend you are a customer that is safer for you and me. Do not mention my real name. Ask for Selina. That is my name in the brothel." She ended the call and breathed a sigh of relief.

Mostafa knew that Daisy was in deep trouble. He preferred not to tell Tom about the phone call. Mostafa rode his Harley 2,240 miles to Nevada during which he spent two nights in roadway motels.

In the reception, he asked for Selina. They made him pay

500 dollars and then to wait for his turn. The receptionist pointed at a corridor where the customers were sitting in rows waiting for their turn. Mostafa sat on a chair for a few seconds, but he couldn't stand to wait longer. He broke into the room. He saw a man sitting on his knees between her thighs about to penetrate her. He grabbed the man from his hair and pulled him away. The man yelled: "What is the matter with you idiot? I paid lots of cash for that slut."

The man received a slap on the face that took him down to the ground. The door opened and Alfred and pimbou entered the room to see what was going on. Mostafa delivered them blows that broke their teeth and fractured their skulls.

Mostafa opened the closet door, went through the hanging clothing and found a robe and a pair of boots. He threw the robe over her exposed body. "Put that on." He said turning his face the other way not willing to look at her body trodden under foot. She put the robe on and sat on the edge of the bed and put her feet on the ground. He shoved the pair of boots her way. "Put that on too." He said in haste. Her hands were too weak to put the boots on, so he helped her put them on.

"Come let's get out of here." He said pulling her from her arms. Unable to walk, she fell nearly unconscious to the ground. He carried her to the Harley and helped her sit on its back. "Hold fast." He said, and off they flew to the land of freedom.

Daisy was so exhausted that she couldn't stand the long trip back to New York. Mostafa had to stop at the nearest motel. Unable to walk Mostafa carried her to the room he rented. "Try to get some sleep"

"I can't sleep."

You should get some sleep. You are tired, and we still have a long way to go."

"No degree of fatigue would allow me to sleep."

"They intoxicated my body with alcohol and drugs to keep me awake. I had to satisfy a long line of men waiting for their turns." She burst into tears.

A knife pierced his heart

"Let's give your inhibitions a bath. Nothing like a hot bath to ease the tension and help you calm down." He said with a torn heart.

He prepared a hot bath for her to cleanse her body and help her relax. He filled the bath with hot water and added in oils and salts. Daisy slid in the tub and felt herself shivering. She stayed in the tub for half an hour feverishly washing her private parts from the dirt she was brutally forced to accept.

When she left the tub, she felt like all her muscles were on strike. She put on the robe and headed out to the room. She was barely able to walk. Mostafa carried her to bed. He thought she would sleep after the hot shower, but she was trembling all over and couldn't sleep. She was addicted to alcohol and cocaine and needed gulps of alcohol or a shot of cocaine to sleep.

"I am addicted to alcohol and cocaine. Can you get me some whisky from the bar please?" She said trembling all over.

Mostafa went to the bar and brought a bottle of whisky and a glass. He poured her a glass of whisky, she finished it in one gulp and asked for more. She got another four glasses of whisky down her throat before she surrendered to sleep. This addiction disorder was repeated in two other motels along the road to New York. Mostafa parked the Harley before the house and carried Daisy to her bed. Tom saw them and came to see his daughter a total wreck.

Tom: "What happened to her?" He asked Mostafa.

Mostafa: "She phoned me three days ago asking for help. She gave me the address of a brothel owned by her Husband Alfred Richardson in Nevada. It seems that she married a pimp trading in women flesh. He forced her into flesh trade." "How would you know that?" Tom yelled at him.

Mostafa: "I saw her imprisoned in a room, and several customers were waiting for their turns. I entered her room and saw a man sleeping with her. A white man and a black one came to stop me, but I knocked them down."

Tom: "She disgraced me. She wallowed my face in mud. I wish she were dead."

Mostafa: "She is barely alive. She needs medical care."

Tom shouted angrily at the unconscious body: "You are some irresponsible slut. I think you need this. Reap what you sow."

Mostafa: "She is physically and emotionally wounded. She is addicted to alcohol and cocaine."

Tom: "I don't want to see her face again. I will put her in a drug Rehab centre. Take care of her. She is still your responsibility."

Chapter 17

Daisy was put in a Drug Rehab Centre. The doctors treated her with Methadone - a slow acting opioid agonist, in concert with behavioural treatment. Mostafa visited her in the centre for hours every day. Daisy left the hospital after two months. Her face was drawn and pale. She felt like someone had shaken her brain and erased it.

 A car with a chauffeur was waiting at the entrance of the Rehab Centre. Mostafa stood beside the car to take Daisy home. When their eyes met, her skin flashed red with shame.

Mostafa opened the car door for her. She got into the car and he sat beside her. Face filled with remorse, she dropped it in her hands to hide it from Mostafa. She was shaking uncontrollably, so he took off his jacket and wrapped it around her. She felt his sympathy. She cried for herself, for Mostafa and for the cruel fate that drove her to the lowest point.

She was so weak to get out of the car. The moment her feet touched the ground the world spun around her. Mostafa lent her his arm to lean on. She felt good to lean on his strength in her hour of need. He was always her rock, her mountain, her true love, but unfortunately, a love that was never complete. Something told her that she was going to

love him forever. She whispered in her tormented soul: "I loved you then, I love you still, always have."
They made their way to her bedroom. A maid was waiting for her to undress her and put her to bed. The maid covered her with the bed sheet. In just few minutes Daisy went into a deep sleep.

A month had passed, and Daisy became better. She regained her health and her pale beauty was associated with a light skin tone. She toured the house several times searching for Mostafa, but he was absent most of the time. She knew that he was outraged and angry with her. She was dying to make amends with him and ask his forgiveness, but would he allow her? Would he accept her love and let her come back to his life? She had done everything he hated and stood against. She humiliated him and wounded his pride. She had lost his respect forever when he saw her trodden by men's feet and despised by all. Her heart jumped in her chest when she spotted him one day leaning against a tree in the garden. Her heart felt like it was going to beat its way right out of her chest while walking toward him hoping he would understand and forgive. She was so embarrassed, Mostafa had seen her at her lowest moment.

She stood before him shaking, unable to stand firmly enough to confront him. He saw her unsteadiness. "There is a stone bench just there." He said pointing to the bench. When they reached there, he helped her sit and sat beside her.

She took his hand in hers and started talking: "What I did was truly horrible, selfish, and disrespectful. I do truly feel guilty, and I am truly sorry for what I have done."

He didn't reply. She glanced at his face and saw it contorted with anger.

She continued: "I made the biggest mistake of my life. I am so torn with guilt."

He did not reply and snatched his hand free.

"I don't want to cause you pain, but you are the only one whom I can talk to."

He looked before him not willing to talk. Signs of sorrow and grief were drawn on his face.

"I know that I am unworthy of your love. You are the only person who has ever really been here for me and I ripped out your heart with my lies and unfaithfulness. I will regret all that for the rest of my life."

He said while suddenly standing up: "It's over daisy, it's no use to talk. I am leaving here. I need to get over you even though you were never mine. I will never get close enough for you to hurt me again. You will never be bored again. You will not see my face again. I promise."

She got to her feet and tightened her arms around his neck. "Please stay. I need you. Please stay long enough to love me again. Give me just one more chance. I love you and I need you. I promise that I will never hurt you again." She said crying.

"You killed me. I watched the woman I love, love many others. Only a fool would take back someone who was covered with shame and trampled underfoot like mire in the streets. I don't marry whores. You are a disgrace. You are abomination." He said pulling his body away from her.

"I loved you despite all your flaws. I even proposed to you, but you wouldn't marry a naïve, crude and unworthy peasant." Tears welled in his eyes.

He continued sobbing: "You hurt me. You tortured me. You wounded my pride. I tried to keep you pure and clean for me, but you insisted of being contaminated, stained and defiled. I tried hard to protect you from your evil self, but you continued your rioting and impertinent dissipation. But it was my fault. It was my fault that I loved you. I tried hard to stop my heart from loving you, but I just couldn't. I shackled my heart so not to love you, but it bowed down to you and praised your name. It rebelled against me and became enchanted when you were not even around. What did I see in you? I saw nothing but deception and perfidy. You betrayed the trust I gave you, and you thought I was not aware. You excelled in finding ways to run away from me just to hurt yourself.

"I cared for you, but you considered my care fetters tying your freedom. Is that what you call here sexual freedom? To open your legs to everyone you have relationship with? Tell me, what was the pleasure you got from having sexual relationships with strangers? Tell me, just how many people have you slept with?"

He looked away to stop himself from crying, but he couldn't hold back his tears. He said still sobbing: "You slaughtered my heart. It bleeds in my chest. It hurts every time I breathe."

She rose to her feet and turned him around to see his face. His tears pierced her heart. She held him and cried aloud in his chest. He didn't hold her back. He kept his hands spread wide at his sides.

He said through abundant tears: "You do not respect your body. You leave it to the predators to snap at it. I loved you. I did anything I can to keep you safe. I was afraid you are getting hurt. Nothing hurts more than being disappointed by the person you thought would never hurt you. You have no idea how worthless you made me feel. I wanted to protect you from all danger and keep you safe. I just wanted to love you and be loved in return. Was that hard for you to do? Was that too much for you?"

He staggered away from her body. "You did not see my longing heart because you were busy making connections with bad people." He said wiping away his tears.

"I don't love them. I love only you. I wanted to make you jealous because you rejected me."

"You wanted to make me jealous by sacrificing your body to strangers! You do not love me. You only wanted to have sex with me. I came from a people who do sex through a marriage contract. It's more decent Daisy. I wanted you as a wife. I wanted you pure, but you preferred to be cloudy and defiled."

"It all happened against my will. They kept me locked in a dark room for months. They imprisoned me in the brothel for over a year. They forced me into prostitution. Despite my resistance, Alfred and pimbou tortured me until I succumbed to the rules of the brothel. They concealed the outside world from me. They threatened to kill me if I left the brothel. My whole world shattered into pieces. I've been tortured and abused, and survived serious injuries inflicted by Alfred and pimbou. I have been through so much, suffered so much. I literally couldn't believe that it had happened. It seemed completely unreal to me."

"This is the result of your deeds that you sent forth with your own hands. Alfred Richardson was one of your bad choices. You got nothing but humiliation and bad reputation. I thought you were my costliest flower, and no one was going to breathe your odour but me, but you preferred being corrupted and tainted. What type of bitch are you? You are a woman of questionable character. Stay away from me. I hate you. I don't want to see your face ever again."

He strode towards the iron gate of the garden, leaving her alone to struggle with her pain.

"How would I live without you when you are gone?" She shouted after him with a tearful voice.

A week later, Tom received an envelope with a letter from Alfred and pictures of Daisy having sex with customers. Tom called Mostafa and told him to come to see him immediately.

They met in the study where Tom was sitting boiling with anger, and Daisy was sitting opposite him resting her head on her hands and crying.

"Sir, what's up?" Mostafa said ignoring Daisy's existence. "What do you think?" Tom said handing the pictures to him. Mostafa stared at the pictures dumbfounded. A boiling anger seized him. He felt like hot metal rod penetrated his skull and seared away parts of his brain. He couldn't but say: "Why Daisy?"

The tremor in his voice broke her heart and her crying increased.

"Do you feel comfortable with that? It is about respect Daisy. How could you expect to have a future and there is a man taking advantage of you and has a cart Blanche over your nudes?"

Tom: "He would certainly post these pics everywhere and tarnish my reputation. Why you did that to me Daisy? You ruined your life and my career as a respectable lawyer."

Tom rested his hands on his knees and shook his head sharply rejecting what had happened. He said after a moment of sad silence: "I collected all the relevant information about him. He is taking revenge on me. I am the lawyer who charged his father with conspiracy and fraud. His father was indicted and sentenced to 10 years in prison. He died after two years' imprisonment."

Mostafa's expression grew more sorrowful when Tom

said: "He sent pictures threatening to publish them on the internet if I contact the police. It is not just that, he sent a letter with the pictures asking for three million dollars in ransom so not to release the pictures on the internet. I don't know what to do. I feel so powerless!"

Mostafa: "Giving him money is very unlikely to end the matter."

Tom: "You think we should report this to the police?"

Mostafa: "No. Keep the police out. Her husband has good cards in his hands. Prostitution is allowed in Nevada, the brothel is licensed, she is his legal wife, the brothel is the marriage house, and he can prove that she knew his profession in advance and chose prostitution of her own free will."

Tom: "Yes, quite likely. Let alone the horrific scandal we are going to face."

Mostafa: "He is pushing us to do what he wants, but we will not give in to the threats. He thinks he has the upper hand. But the moron doesn't know that he is already insecure enough."

Tom: "What's in your mind Mostafa?"

Mostafa: "Revenge is commonplace in southern Egypt, the region I came from."

Tom: "You mean vendetta?"

Mostafa: "Yes. In our village, we do not see the issue of vendetta as a problem. We think it is something natural. You may think as if it were something strange and uncivilized, but to us, it is not considered something negative, but rather positive. We see it as a tradition that needs to be respected. Vendetta is justified based on protecting honour, pride, or land. We apply God's law "an eye for an eye". Only by killing a member of the murderer's family can a clan regain its honour and mourn its deceased."

Tom: "Stay away from revenge. Vengeance may lead to furthering cycle of violence. Besides, you may face charges of retaliation."

Mostafa: "Still, it's a risk that must be met; and the greater offense is to allow the guilty go unpunished."

When Daisy realized that Mostafa was putting himself in so much danger; she broke her silence:

"Mostafa please, keep out of this. They are dangerous people."

"Shut up. Don't tell me what to do. I will ignore and forget you till you wonder if you still exist." He said leaving the room.

Chapter 18

A stranger arrived in Nevada and spent two weeks observing life inside Alfred's brothel. The brothel was outside town and out of the way corners of the lonely expanse of rural Nevada. The stranger paid special attention to the women working inside the brothel. All the women get a day off on Sunday.

The same stranger wearing a black mask that seemed more like a scarf fastened tight around his face entered Alfred's brothel at dawn. He broke into the brothel through an opened first floor window. He carried a gasoline can in his hand. On his way to Alfred's room, he spilled gasoline all over the floor and the furniture. He opened the door of Alfred's room to see him and the black man sitting at a desk counting the cash the brothel made during the day.

In a glimpse of a second, an iron fist descended on the black man's jaw to throw him unconscious on the ground. Alfred tried to open the drawer to get his gun out, but he received a punch on his throat that knocked the air from his lungs. He fell grasping his throat and eventually passed out.

The masked man poured gasoline on the two bodies and all over the room. He lit a match and threw it on the gasoline. The furniture and the bodies caught fire and began to burn. On his way out, he threw another match. The gasoline he spilled on his way to Alfred's room exploded, and the fire on the floor moved rapidly to burn everything in its way. The whole brothel was on fire. The flames engulfed the brothel and reduced it to ashes.

The masked man ran for two miles to a Harley Davidson hidden among the trees. He mounted it and took off the mask. The man had a beautiful face with jet-black hair spilling over his shoulders. The Harley roared forward disturbing the silence of the night.

The news of the burning brothel spread in the newspapers. The police stated that no criminal intent was suspected or observed.

Mostafa met Tom at his office. Tom welcomed him heartily and ushered him to sit.

Mostafa: "I am here to thank you sir for the hospitality you gave me during my stay in your house. You have been like my father."

Tom: "I have no son, and to me you were more than a son. I don't find the words to thank you for all that you have done to me and Daisy."

Mostafa: "I am requesting permission to leave."

Tom frustrated: "Where to? To Egypt I suppose!"

Mostafa: "No. I will stay here. I will earn my living somewhere else."

Tom: "What are you going to do?"

Mostafa: "I will find a job that is right for me. WWE could be just for me."

Tom: "I know you are a strong young man, but wrestlers there are twice your size, they are giant monsters that can smash your bones and break your skull."

Mostafa: "God has gifted me with a divine power that others don't have. I can rob these monsters of their strength anytime I wish."

Tom: "Your father told me that you can easily lift a rock weighing 200 kg and pull out of the river the boat you were sailing without toil or pain."

Mostafa: Yes, and I can do more than that if I wish."

Tom: "I know that you are running away from Daisy. You loved her, but she hurt you. She hurt me too, but she is my daughter, and I have to accept my ill fate."

Mostafa: "I have sworn to myself never again show my face to her, never again let my love for her show."

Tom: "Do you have enough money to start your new life, your new project?"

Mostafa: "Yes sir. I lived in your house, I ate your food and I saved every dollar you gave me. I have sufficient savings to start a new life."

Mostafa rose from his seat and extended his hand to Tom. Tom reached out to shake his hand. "Let me hear from you. If anything, you need please call me."

Mostafa: "Of course sir. Thank you for your kindness and hospitality."

Mostafa strode to the door, but Tom stopped him saying: "The burning of the brothel was a clever job. You made it look like an accident. The police found no evidence for attempted murder. The fire was attributed to faulty electrical outlets and old, outdated appliances. No more threatening, no more humiliation. I don't know how to repay you."

Mostafa: "I don't know what you are talking about sir." Mostafa smiled lightly, muttered a goodbye and then left.

Daisy was sad because Mostafa left the house. His departure agonized her and made her feel like a worthless scum. She was now naked, uncovered; her rock had disappeared from her life and left her to misery and disappointment. She realized that life away from him was meaningless. She felt worthless, loser, nobody, and no point to live.

She hated to call her friends and have fun with them. Enjoying life with men was not a joy anymore. She lost her sex drive and resorted to seclusion.

Mostafa left New York and lived in a rented apartment in Stanford Connecticut where WWE headquarters was located. Due to his formidable inborn strength, He found that professional wrestling would be a convenient career for him. But how could WWE scouts discover him, and they mostly recruit new wrestlers from independent wrestling promotions, college football programs, and college wrestling teams? He must start out as a skilled amateur wrestler before signing deals with WWE. He decided to get training at a private wrestling school, then join a wrestling promotion to become good enough to get WWE's attention. In the private wrestling school, Mostafa focused on building strength in his upper body, his core and his legs. He worked each body part once a week but changed exercises and worked body part combinations every week. He did 4 exercises per body part, and 12 reps each exercise.

Mostafa found his body morphing into something quite spectacular. Although he was six-feet-tall and slender, weighing 150lbs, his muscles responded surprisingly quickly with weight-training. Seeing these results Mostafa continued to train with a vengeance. In a very short time he was able to form well defined bodybuilder muscles. He also focused on high intensity cardio by running long distances every day. To get coordinated, the trainer gave him intense long exercises and dance classes.

Mostafa took dancing classes, composed of cardio, strength, endurance, balance and flexibility exercises to increase all over flexibility and improve dance technique. As time passed, his passion for dance grew. He learned movements and steps that matched the speed and rhythm of pieces of music. He has been passionately involved in jazz dance, salsa, merengue, samba and many more. He became extremely fond of dancing, since it was a sort of cardio training and helped him get his incredible physical fitness.

In the gym, he created a fun relaxed atmosphere. He listened to his favourite music while he trained. Music with a strong beat helped his movements stay consistent during exercise. The music fuelled his workout and became the motivator to get him in the right mood and set the tone for a great workout.

Mostafa then joined a wrestling school ran by a former wrestler. He learned how to take bumps, how to fall properly and protect his head and neck from more serious injury. He learned how to fall on his back safely, as well other skills involving locking up, striking, running the ropes, and taking specific moves.

The intensive bodybuilding workouts Mostafa exercised reshaped his body into a well-defined muscle mass. Mostafa wrestled for an independent promotion for three years during which he easily defeated all his opponents. Due to his outstanding skills in wrestling, and inundate power, the independent promotion advised him to try out for WWE reality program "Tough Enough". The show follows wrestlers who compete for a contract with WWE. In these try-outs shows Mostafa exhibited formidable wrestling skills.

Now he knew how to increase his energy, enhance the way he looks, make himself more vibrant, stronger and more confident. These things in fact, decorated a divine gift granted to him by the Lord — a divine inborn strength distinguishing him from all others.

Now he is confident of his strength. Now he is unbreakable.

There is nothing he can't accomplish. The world needs his gifts, it is now time to bring himself to the world.

At last the recruiters noticed his wrestling skills and got him a WWE contract. He gradually climbed the ladder of success by contending one opponent after another and defeated them all. He had proven to be a fighting champion. He earned the right to challenge for the title after he defeated his opponent in the semi-final.

His formidable physics and overwhelming beauty made women call him 'the handsomest built man', and his fans called him 'the unbreakable'; a ring name that spread over the American states like wildfire.

Mostafa contended in the WWE heavyweight championship and won. He then contended in the WWE Universal Championship and won. People were fascinated to see this amazing stamina and extraordinary power. But Mostafa knew the source of his power. In addition to his physical power, he had this God-given strength, which made him practically unbreakable.

Mostafa wanted to know the limit of his power, so he fought for TNA World Heavyweight Championship and also won. He climbed the top of the rope and flaunted the title belt for all to see.

Among the audience there was always a pretty woman with brown hair watching Mostafa's grand matches. The TV cameras caught her jumping and clapping with tears of joy in her eyes. The TV cameras frequently zoomed in on her face to show her hilarious reaction after Mostafa winning his grand matches.

Chapter 19

Mostafa goes running around his neighbourhood every day. As he set off, a pretty woman came running up beside him. She went for two miles with him then stopped gasping for breath. He was about to continue but she stopped him saying: "I am Janet Berry. I work as a fashion designer. I want to discuss an important matter with you. Do you have time for me?"

"I am a very busy sort of person and I have no time for…"

"Please it is an important matter." She said interrupting.

"You know where I live?"

"Yes."

"How about six in the evening?"

"That would be perfect."

The woman arrived at six sharp. He met her at the front door and led her to the terrace overlooking the spacious garden. They sat there talking.

Janet: "I want to thank you for allowing me to have some words with the champion of WWE. People love you and consider you their hero."

He smiled modestly without saying a word.

"Let me put it to you bluntly. You are a very good-looking man. Men and women are fond of you, and so am I. As a fashion designer, I see that you meet all the requirements needed for a successful fashion model. Your male beauty, handsomeness and strength can make you one of the most notable men fashion models in the United States."

"What I have to do to be a fashion model?" He said not interested.

"You will be a runaway model. You will wear the fashion and accessories of designers for runway shows."

"I know nothing about this profession and..."

"I will teach you everything about fashion modelling. I am sure you will be a brand of your own. I want you to give modelling a shot."

"So, you think I have what it takes to be a model. "

"Absolutely."

"I know nothing about you. Tell me about your work."

"I am an American fashion designer based in Connecticut. I have my own clothing line for men and women wear. I own a factory responsible for design, sourcing, development, retail buying, sales, marketing, and of course, manufacturing. I own a grand fashion salon and a fashion magazine. My fashion is presented bi-annually at New York Fashion Week. Signature Janet Berry stores are in New York City, Charleston, Chicago, Boston, Montauk, Japan, South Korea, Taiwan, as well as at the company's web store. The collection is also represented in departments and specialty stores both domestically and internationally. I am seeking a broad range of licensing agreements to make my business a lifestyle brand instead of just a fashion brand."

"It is very brave of you. I mean to do all this work alone."

"I was married to Steve Jackson. We were equal partners. He helped me in the business and put equal money into it. Steve and I were joyfully anticipating the celebration of our ten-year wedding anniversary, when he unexpectedly passed away. He wrote a bill and gave me his share after his death. Now I own the whole business."

"Tell me about your parents – I mean father, mother, brothers and sisters."

"I was raised and born in Kansas City. My father was a math teacher. My mother was a music teacher. They both worked at the same school. I am their only child."

"Do you visit them quite often? I miss my parents. I haven't seen them for long.

"I used to visit them yes, but not anymore. They died in a car crash four years ago."

Oh! I am sorry to hear that."

"Do you manage your business successfully?" He said after a moment of silence.

"It's tough especially after my husband died. But yes, I am doing okay so far."

 "What I have to do to be a fashion model?

"You will wear the fashion and accessories of my designs for runway shows."

"I am sorry, I just can't…"

Janet interrupted: "Your physique is lean, yet strong, and that is the body the designers want to display their clothing."

Janet finished talking and looked at him afraid that he might reject her offer.

He contemplated her. She speaks in a low penetrating voice. Her thick brown shining hair was cut to an above the shoulder length. She had strawberry sweet lips. Her body appeared voluptuous, showing youth and fertility. He saw her a pretty woman, sexy, and attractive. He admired her struggle to achieve her goals. And above all, he knew that she was one of his ardent fans. When he watched his matches on TV, she was always there among the audience with a beaming smile on her face, celebrating his winnings by clapping her hands, and jumping, and screaming for joy.

His long silence worried her. Fearing of rejection, she broke the silence: "You are a celebrity. Joining us would certainly increase sales. Men will come from everywhere to watch their hero presenting their favourite fashion. Women will also come to see the man they are enamoured with." She added.

He looked into her smiling pleading eyes. Her smile threw light into his soul and he appreciated the beauty of it.

He amazed her when he said: "How do I get started?"

"Any time you want." She said hilariously not believing her ears.

In Janet's salon, Mostafa sat listening to Janet's lessons about how to walk like a model:

"Envision a taut string threaded from your spine through the top of your head. The key is to imagine that you are on a puppet string, being prodded to stand up straight, with shoulders slightly back.

"Take long strides, placing one foot in front of the other. Let your arms fall next to your body, with hands relaxed. They shouldn't swing too much, and keep your eyes focused straight ahead. Try to look at an imaginary point straight in the distance. Project an attitude of utmost confidence. Walk with a purpose. Wherever you're going is where everyone should want to follow. Listen to the music and walk to the beat. Feel like you're dancing, almost."

"Is that all?" He said laughing.
"I think so. Do you have any comments?"

"Yes, I'll walk my own way."

The first fashion show was held in Janet's salon. It featured male and female models. Mostafa walked his own way. The rhythm of the music and the way he moved impressed the watchers, especially women. Janet was impressed by the way he moved. His muscles were taught. In his smile, she saw confidence. When he walked on the runway, women forgot the fancy footwork and the outfits he wore, they were excited about Mostafa as a famous wrestler performing and as a beautiful man sending them into a frenzy. Women released passionate sighs upon watching him presenting bathing suits and swimwear.

The show was a smashing success; one of the female attendants couldn't hide her joy and described Mostafa as the 'most attractive man ever'.

Mostafa presented Janet's men's wear in many fashion shows. He participated in Mercedes-Benz Fashion Week at The Stage at Lincoln Centre in New York City; Smashbox Fashion Week Los Angeles at Smashbox Studios in Culver City; LA Fashion Week (LAFW) Spring/Summer 2016. The fashion shows extended to include England, France and Germany.

In addition of becoming a super star wrestler, Mostafa became one of the most notable men fashion models in the Unites States. His pictures appeared in top fashion magazines.

In one of the fashion shows held in Janet's salon, Mostafa entered the dressing room to change his clothes for the next show, he was surprised to see Janet waiting for him in men's room.

"Janet! What are you doing here?" He said perplexed."

"Mostafa can I confess something to you?" She said shaking all over.

"Of course, Janet."

Tears swam in her eyes before slowly rolling down her cheeks. His heart clenched.

"I love you so much that I can't hide my love anymore. I want to share all my dreams and passions with you. I want you to love me. I want to marry you."

He stood looking at her tenderly. He knew that she loved him; that was clear in her passionate looks. She attended all his matches, and whenever she saw him her eyes sparkled like glitters.

"Every girl needs a man in whose arms she can find her peace, her world, her solace. You are my man, my only love. Would you marry me?" Now she was sobbing aloud.

"Yes, I would. I want you Janet." He said smiling.

He opened his arms and said quietly to her: "Disappear here."

She ran to him and threw herself into his arms crying. Her arms went around his neck, and her body pressed against his.

He kissed her hair and said: "I want to change for the next show aren't you coming to watch?

She disengaged herself from his embrace and stood before him, holding him in her gaze. "No. I will stay here to cry a little."

Chapter 20

Mostafa and Janet got married. The wedding was the talk of the nation. The bride was the queen of the American fashion designers, and the groom was the Champion of WWE, TNA world heavyweight, and the king of male fashion models.

The wedding was held in Saint Clements Castle & Marina. The place was situated on over 90 acres in the Connecticut River Valley. The staff did everything Janet had demanded for her wedding. The food was fantastic, scenery gorgeous and weather perfect. Janet and Mostafa's photos together turned out incredible with the breath-taking river view in the background.

Janet looked so cool in her wedding. She wore a wedding dress chick and modern, open back, knee-length to reveal a pair of deliciously long legs and curves any woman would openly envy. Mostafa looked dashing utterly gorgeous in his tuxedo.

Guests on both sides came to the wedding; Janet's close relatives and acquaintances, and wrestlers from WWE. Mostafa's guests were also from prestigious dance studios and centres in which he had been trained. Tom Wilson received a special invitation and attended the wedding.

With a glass of juice in his hand, Mostafa stood talking

animatedly to his guests. Janet was talking to some of her close acquaintances, but she occasionally stole smiling glances at Mostafa out of the corner of her eye. In fact, she couldn't take her eyes off him. How could anyone think of that raw masculine delicious man as anything but beautiful? Mostafa returned her smiles, the look in his eyes showed that she was his entire world.

Suddenly, she caught her breath as her heart gave a sudden painful jolt. She couldn't seem to shake the worry that had clouded her senses and mind. Their night together would be just after a few hours. Mostafa must have been the spouse with the highest sex drive. What if she was unable to satisfy his own needs? What if he wanted to have sex all the time? She will feel embarrassed about not being able to keep up. It will be a huge blow to her self-esteem not to satisfy his raging needs. She adores him fiercely so much that she can't stay a moment without him. Having mismatched libidos however, can drive a wedge between them. She was afraid to lose a relationship over a raging libido.

The orchestra played a slow tango. Mostafa excused himself from his guests, handed his glass to a passing waiter and strolled toward Janet. Her heart pounded loudly in her ears when she saw him coming her way. He stood before her stealing her breath. He looked so marvellous she had almost forgotten to breathe. Her gaze lit up and she flashed the brightest smile she could muster without showing how worried she was.

"You look divine. Shall we dance?" He asked offering his hand.

She cleared her voice to speak. "No… no." she managed to say. "My coordination and sense of rhythm are horrendous. I'm quite awful really."

"It is our first dance as husband and wife. It will be a dance to remember." He insisted.

"You are a wonderful dancer. You will chew me out."

"Relax darling. It's simple. Just keep pace with the music and imitate what I am doing."

"You don't need to reduce your own dancing skills just to match my poor dancing."

"You will love dancing with me. I will hold you and you will hold me back. You will feel me, and I will feel you…and…" The slow burn of his gaze made her feel as if he was seeing right through her soul.

"Okay, okay. I am not much of a dancer but for you I will try." She said laughing, taking his hand and walking with him to the centre of the dance floor.

The orchestra played the music of the slow tango 'feelings' and Janet nestled against Mostafa. The song was slow and the steps simple. They danced in silence, cheek to cheek and hip to hip. They were like one body moving in vitality and grace.

"Enjoy the romance of tango. All you have to do is follow."

"I love how you dance the tango. It reflects how woman and man should relate."

"Yes darling. It brings you back to old-fashioned basics. Courtesy, chivalry, seduction and sensuality."

"I love that song, it's slow, smooth and fluid." She said breathing deeply, basking in his musky male scent.

"Good. It will keep you from scuffing my shoes if you are as bad as you say." He said laughing, happy to have her in his arms.

Mostafa held Janet very close. Her breasts pressed against his. She loved the feeling of being so close to him. They danced in each other's arms lost in their own private world. The music then changed into a fast tango. It was the song of Tina Turner 'You are simply the best'.

"Terrific! The fast tango. May I have this dance too?" He said pleading.

"But I have barely learned the tango," gasped Janet and stopped dancing.

"Don't worry, just follow my lead."

"Fast tango is unfamiliar to me." She looked unsure of herself.

"People are watching us. The press and media are here. If I

make a fool of myself I shall blame you.”

“Relax, just feel the rhythm and let me dance this fast tango with you.”

“Do you know the lyrics to this song?” She said looking up smiling with her eyes.

“I remember few words – I get washed away, I get lost.”

“It also says, something I feel towards you.”

“I am eager to know your feelings about me.”

 “The words also say, ‘you are simply the best, better than anyone I ever met.”’

“O God Janet. You don’t know how much I love you. You filled my life with joy, with happiness, with dreams. You brought meaning into my life. I love you so much and that will never change.”

She put her arms around his neck, bent him down to her, and kissed him long on the lips. He tore his lips from hers and said laughing: “The press and the media are watching.”

“Hell, who cares. Let’s threw all caution to the wind and dance like we have never danced before.”

His hand on her back, hers are on his shoulder, his arm at the small of her back, he led her in the fast tango. He used his dancing skills to make Janet look good. This helped her overcome anxiety, loosen up and dance better. They danced intimately to the fast music. She beautifully communicated with his body language and matched his significant movement above the waist with up and down shoulder movements and shifting of the ribcage. They danced quickly, then slowly, then quickly again as the beat of the drums became more and more rhythmic and increasingly intense. Her steps keeping up with the sudden turns and long strides of the tango. They rhythmically rocked from side to side, their bodies reproducing the motion of a flowing wave.

The music reached its crescendo, Mostafa spun Janet round one last time and with a flourish of saxophones, and guitars the dance ended.

They stood sweating. She smelled his musk, his sweat. He smelled hot. She inhaled deeply finding his masculine scent hot and seductive. She clung tightly to him basking in his glorious scent. A quiver ran through her entire body.

"I am surprised about your talent in a dance that required the play of passion and sensuality, hardly to be expected from a wrestler." She said disengaging herself from his embrace.

"You are a hell of a dancer Janet, and sexy as well. I could get lost in your cleavage while dancing with you, I swear."

Hot desire spilled from her belly at his words. She looked straight up into his eyes with love flowing. She wanted to show him how deeply she cared. She wished at this moment to make exquisite love to him and as intimate a way as she could. She wanted to show him how deeply she cared.

Daisy stayed at home watching the wedding on TV with sorrowful tearful eyes. She wanted sex at any cost. She didn't think of consequences or the disgrace and shame she brought to herself, to her father, and most of all to the man who loved her sincerely and protected her against her frequent digressions from the right path. In that very moment she realized, just how evil she had been. Now she was all alone decrying the miserable fate she brought on herself by her own hands – she had lost her man to another woman.

Chapter 21

Mostafa moved from his apartment to Janet's spacious house. It was their first night together. Mostafa went crazy when he saw Janet naked in bed for the first time. He had never made love to a woman before. He tried to keep a cool demeanour, but he got nervous to the point where his hands started sweating. He was too nervous to react, he just stared awkwardly at Janet's lush body.

Janet knew that he was virgin and inexperienced in dealing with women in bed. This robust masculine man that oozes charisma from every pore of his body, certainly doesn't know the value of sexual foreplay in lovemaking. Her fear increased that he might hurt her, but she saw him hesitant to touch her. She calmed down when she realized that the fear was his not hers.

"Well, you know, it's the first time that I…" He said utterly embarrassed.

"I understand darling. You need more time to adjust to intimacy. Do not be afraid of my warmth and closeness. I love you."

"I am sorry darling. My body, mind and soul yearn for you, but I am lost within myself."

"Let me show you how much I love you." She said stretching her hands to him. She gathered him to her, weaving her fingers in his hair. She caressed him with feathery kisses on his lips until he grew a bit bolder and calmed down to find his voice: "I don't want you to feel pressured. I will go as far as you want."

When he said these words, her passion escalated and her love for him exploded.

 "I am okay darling. I just want to please you." She said kissing him deeply.

He kissed her back. His masculine body pressed against her, and electricity sparkled through her. His powerful body continued to move frantically against hers. His hands moved down her sides, wrapping her slender legs around his waist as their passion rose higher and higher. When the moment of culmination came, she cried out into his mouth and he into hers.

When he tasted her for the first time, he became like a wild river sweeping away all obstacles put in its way. The raging waters never receded. His deep caress of every inch of her intimate parts excited her and made her want him more. She loved his touch, all she could feel that moment was his masculine sexiness, his gorgeous features and strong, tall athletic body. He smelled of salt air and man. The heat of him surrounding her, the feel of his body pressed to hers, he turned her into a liquid heat.

A surge of power coursed through her veins and they

ignited one another like a raging fire. He was driving her completely insane and she loved every minute of it. He took her to a realm of passion such as she had never experienced before. She gasped at the wild sensation he evoked. When they finally came, she collapsed against him feeling limp and replete.

She moaned huskily: "Oh my God! Mostafa, you are incredible. You shattered me into a million pieces."

Her late husband never had that kind of effect on her. Passion was there yes, but there was never this spark that made her enjoy Mostafa's lovemaking as she never had before.

They lay breast to breast on their sides. "Did I hurt you?" He said pressing a gentle kiss on her forehead and wet brown hair.

"No. You made me feel wonderful, vibrant and alive. I have found in your arms rapture beyond belief." She said drowning in the beauty of his wide black captivating eyes.

"You are going to be a wonderful mother Janet." He said holding her close to his masculine body. His words washed through her like a warm wave of calm. She closed her eyes enjoying his thorough position of her, and revelling in the secure sensation of being held in his arms.

They passed each night in acts of passion. Each act was more sensual and arousing than the one before it. He made love to her so sweetly and so tenderly that when they awoke the next morning she could not help but awake with a smile on her face.

It was a pleasure to her to see him each morning naked lying next to her. She loved to watch the terrible beauty of his face, his long black hair spread on the pillow and his wonderful masculine body.

Snuggling close, she pressed her lips to the hard bulge of his shoulder and smiled contentedly. He opened his eyes and glanced at her smiling.

"I knew nothing about love until I met you. I knew true love when you welcomed my body and took me in your arms. You nourished my thirsty soul and caressed my lonely heart. I love you deeper than my love can comprehend. I love you with every fibre of my soul."

Her heart sped mercilessly against her chest. She said as tears flowed down her face: "These are the sweetest words I have ever heard. You are a blessing from God to illuminate my life and keep me strong. You came to my life to make my life more meaningful. I love you beyond reason. May God shower his blessings on you and makes you happy. May the Lord shine His face on you and be gracious to you. May the Lord lift up His countenance on you, and give you peace."

He wrapped his arms around her and held her against him. She burrowed her face into his chest and began sobbing aloud.

"Hey! What's up?" He said alarmed.

"Tears came to my eyes when you loved me so ardently, so beautifully and so tenderly. Your love sneaks out of my eyes and roll down my cheeks."

"I understand. Tears are the words to express true love. Sometimes love is spoken mainly in our tears." He said gathering her in his arms.

"I want to collide with your heart. I want to stay curled and cosied in your arms forever."

"You are my beautiful world. We have the rest of our lives to spend together. I love you Janet and I will always love you deep in my heart."

"I do know you are that person to me. You are the one. The only one. And you always will be. You are here in my life and that's all that matters."

When Mostafa came home from wrestling, the urge for sex was so intense that he demanded it all the time, but Janet was always ready to contain his strong sex drive and calm him down. She disciplined him to have sex with her two to three times a week and he obeyed willingly fearing to hurt her feelings. She contained him body and soul. He was her robust husband, her great lover. She was for him and he was for her.

Chapter 22

Fashion shows debut every season, particularly the Spring/ Summer and Fall/Winter seasons. The two most influential fashion weeks are Paris Fashion Week and New York Fashion Week, which are both semi-annual events. Janet wished to expand more by exhibiting her new collections in several other European and Asian countries.

In traditional fashion shows models walk the catwalk dressed in the clothing created by the designer. The clothing is illuminated on the runway by the lighting. The order in which each model walked out wearing a specific outfit was usually planned in accordance to the statement that the designer wanted to make about their collections. Janet however, wished to present her new collections in a theatrical way accompanied with music and a variety of technological components like holograms. This new approach overburdened her thin shoulders. Janet was possessed by the idea of making women feel strong and powerful. She wanted her creations to instil self-confidence in women; to empower women through design and to give them the clothing they need to go out and fulfil their goals and dreams in their life.

Janet was also launching a menswear line. She wanted to create an exciting and captivating presentation, showing the many moods and attitudes of the men's clothing brand.

Mostafa shared with her the toil of preparation for the shows. He grouped men and women models into teams of 8 and started to teach men models how to present the collections designed for them. Janet showed women models how to present women collections accompanied with music and holograms.

Mostafa asked her: "Why are female models appearing in menswear shows?"

"She replied: "Presenting men's and women's together can result in a stronger and more cohesive brand message. I use this opportunity to enhance my brand identity."

Mostafa: "You may have a point, but the reason could be that most fashion designers, find menswear a bit dull. So, they add womenswear in to mix it up."

She laughed: "Pretty women are always in your mind eh? They find you attractive because you are a strong handsome man."

Mostafa: "It's only you whom I love."

"Yes, I know." She said laughing.

He gave her a big hug and kissed her.

"Your hug makes everything better." She said feeling blessed to have him in her life."

To keep up with the dense work, Janet began to suffer. She suffered from insomnia and couldn't sleep. Mostafa noticed that she had taken an overdose of sleeping pills when she feared failure and pressures got too much for her. She had lost weight, and excessive stress interfered with her productivity and affected her physical and emotional health.

"I like to win and achieve high standards. I am terrified of failure. Any failure is unacceptable. O God. I am tired and awfully stressed." Janet confided one day to Mostafa.

"It's normal darling. Successful people like to win and achieve high standards. This can make them so terrified of failure."

"I feel powerless Mostafa." She said exhausted.

 Mostafa: "Stress isn't always bad. A little bit of stress can help you stay focused, energetic, and able to meet new challenges."

Janet: "Yes darling, but long hours, tight deadlines, and ever-increasing demands can leave you feeling worried, drained, and overwhelmed. And when stress exceeds your ability to cope, it stops being helpful and starts causing damage to your mind and body."

Mostafa: "If stress on the job is interfering with your health and work, it's time to take action. There are steps you can take to protect yourself from the damaging effects of stress and regain a sense of control at work."

Janet: "Such as?"
Mostafa: "A short vacation."

Janet: "Yes my love. We can fly to my summer place in North Carolina where we could spend few days on the beach away from the hectic preparations I have been doing for the upcoming shows.

Mostafa: "Wonderful idea. We have been together for long weeks and we haven't been able to get time alone for us."

The beach is known for its soft, sugar-fine sand and tranquil atmosphere. They walked the beach early in the morning to spot whole seashells, and starfish. They had lunch in restaurants serving good seafood, and back home, they relaxed together on the sofa listening to Andy Williams lyrics, 'Summer place'.

In bed, his body ached for her like he hadn't ached for anyone in a long time. Janet savoured his heat and his strength. Her body heated with need as her body quivered against him. They soon found each other's mouths, hungry, desperate. Desire for him grew within her, and she melted into his arms. He made love to her vigorously as if he were stamping his ownership upon her. He poured his adoration into her so strongly, that she cried for joy. He was starving for more of her and gave her multiple orgasms.

He was great in knowing all the right pressure points and how to give her the pleasure she needed. He brought her to long and strong orgasm several times until she buried her face into his neck and begged: "Honey, darling, you worn me out, it will be just better if you relax."

He rolled over and stared into her eyes. "I love you Janet."
"I know, I love you too."

"You have taught me what true love is. You made my empty life become whole. You have given me a reason to live."

"To me love was just a word until you came along and gave it meaning. You took away my loneliness. You made me complete. I am blessed to be your wife."

"If I did anything right in my life it was when I gave my heart to you. I love you so much." He said gathering her in his arms and pressing his lips to her own.

She nestled in his chest like a baby bird settling in its nest. He whispered in her ear: "We together will overcome our fears and keep moving towards our goals."

She wanted reassurance and he gave it to her. She admired the power and strength he possessed. His power dispelled doubt. She communicated her reassurance by kissing him long on the lips.

They lay together quietly, their limbs entwined, neither wanting to move, lest something might disturb their moment of complete contentment.

Chapter 23

The first show started in New York. Hours before the show started, Janet checked the models' outfits, haircuts and makeup, and the order in which the clothes will be shown. Female models presented womenswear collections. Mostafa presented Janet's menswear line. He was a big hit during the shows. He walked with men models presenting Janet's new collection, then walked the runway in bathing suits. He sizzled on the runway. Women feasted their eyes. Photographers took hot shots of him.

One of the fashion magazines wrote: "Mostafa, the formidable wrestler, the hottest male model, the breakout star has had a substantial presence on the modelling scene. This rising star has racked up coveted campaigns and impressive editorial work in a short period of time and is set to leave a lasting mark on the industry."

Another fashion magazine wrote under the title: The body and face that launched a billion likes. "Mostafa has an expressive personality that shines in front of the camera. we look forward to seeing a lot more of him. He proved his worth as a top male model of 2016."

After the shows, Mostafa was chosen model of the year awards 2016.

The impact of the show was overwhelming. At the end, Janet walked with her horde of models along the runway amid thunderous applause.

Janet and Mostafa had to travel to all other cities in which the shows were to be held to be sure that everything is done properly and in order. They travelled to Paris, Jardins des Tuileries; Milan, Prada Foundation; Hong Kong, National Exhibition and Convention Centre; Germany, Berliner Mode Salon; China, CHIC; Dubai. The success of the shows was also striking in all these cities.

The success of Janet's fashion shows was so smashing that in London's Regent Street, scuffles broke out among people who had been lined up for hours. In Paris, customers flooded the store, knocking over displays and scrambling to grab anything they could. Shoppers in Dubai pushed past security guards and climbing under a security gate to get inside as stores open. In other cities, shoppers had lined up days before the collection.

Fashion magazines strived to take Janet's statements about her shows: "Our ability to perceive the world around us, our unique ways of thinking and understanding- these are the ingredients that I pull from."

The fashion magazine praised her work: "Janet is a true inspiration to women in fashion, and more, around the world. She set the world on fire with unexpected mixes of colours and patterns. She uses the most ingenious fabrics and rigorous tailoring techniques to painstakingly construct and envelope the womanly form with flourish of couture."

Janet now operates 48 freestanding stores in several important locations. Her collections are now distributed in 60 countries through 700 doors including specialty shops, and department stores, as well as shipping to 105 countries online.

Now it's time to thank God for this smashing success. Janet must do something to the poor and the needy.

Research on cancer shows that health and wellness is an important aspect of battling and surviving cancer, which includes emotional support and finding hope and inspiration.Fitness Formula Clubs (FFC), in collaboration with the fashion community, is an important partner in providing that much-needed emotional support and provides ways to regain hope and inspiration. FFC's therapeutic workshops and seminars are offered free to cancer patients and survivors. These workshops and seminars use fashion- and design-related disciplines in a variety of activities that act as soothing therapy.

Janet participated in combatting cancer. She contacted FFC, which helps cancer patients to express themselves through fashion and design creations and, in the process, allows them to turn their experiences into expressions, fears into fashion, and renewed hope into healing. She devoted part of her precious time and studio space to teach cancer patients the principles of fashion design. In her view, fashion can fight cancer when it comes to helping cancer patients and survivors enrich their mind and body. The compassionate and therapeutic program brings strength and hope and faith into their minds. The patients get the strength that they need for their bodies to fight cancer when interacting together while engaging in a creative process.

Janet further established "The Berry Foundation" - a non-profit charitable organization that supports humanitarian and charitable projects in Africa, Asia, and the Middle East.

The Berry Foundation fights hunger, prevent malnutrition and improve the lives of boys and girls in Africa.

Conflicts across the Middle East have forced millions of people to flee to neighbouring countries or to refuge within their own countries. Refugees and displaced families from Syria, Iraq and Gaza need shelter, food, water and medical care. With lifesaving and life-changing programs, the Berry Foundation is helping them meet their urgent needs.

Chapter 24

To celebrate their outstanding success, Mostafa invited Janet to dinner in Casona Restaurant. The dinner was fish collar, fried Brussel sprouts, cup of fish chowder and French fries. Janet marvelled over every bite she ate, and they both cleaned their plates.

The song "save the last dance for me" played, and Janet started tapping her fingers to the lively music. Mostafa dragged her to the dance floor. They danced beautifully together as though they had danced together all their lives.

Janet was so thrilled by music that she sang the first words of the song: "You can dance – every dance with the guy who gives you the eye, let him hold you tight."

Mostafa continued in earnest: "But don't forget who's taking you home and in whose arms, you are gonna be. So darling save the last dance for me."

She held him close: "It's always been you. For the rest of my life it will be only you."

"There isn't one person in this world that I want more than I want you." He said kissing her lips.

"I am always afraid of losing you. I want to wrap my arms

tightly around you and never let you go. Being in your arms is the best feeling ever." She said pressing her soft warm lips deeper into his.

"No amount of time and space can separate you from me. I want you for always." He said holding her closer, as if afraid he might lose her.

They melted into each other, and she enjoyed of being the centre of his world.

That night in bed, she smelled of woman, a husky, sweet, faint scent.

He reached for her, his deep voice was husky with desire:

"I want to love you endlessly." he spoke in a husky voice as his arms surrounded her. His husky voice sent shivers through her body. He kissed her from head to toe. He loved her, slowly and sensuously. He loved her in so many delicious ways. His love making was intense, fiery and beyond anything she'd experienced before in her life. He put her in a frenzy, and she lost all control. She cried out of delight.

"That was the hottest thing I have ever seen." She said lying spent beside him.

"Every day we are together is the greatest day of my life." She said smiling contently.

"You are my love, you are my life, you are my everything."

He said raining her face with tender kisses.

"Call me yours is all I want." She whispered with so much sleep in her eyes.

In the morning, she opened her eyes to see him looking at her smiling.

"Good morning love." He said kissing her sleepy eyes."

She embraced him with her naked arms, then looked deeply into his eyes and said: "I am so blessed to have you in my life. I thank God for giving me a husband as loving and wonderful as you are."

"I love you more than words can show. There is no one I would ever love the way I love you." He said kissing the corner of her mouth.

"Give me half an hour to freshen up and cook up a good breakfast for you."

They sat at a small table in the kitchen enjoying the rich breakfast. Mostafa took a large bite and found it utterly delicious. "It is really tasty. Is that a pie?" He said wonderingly.

"No, it's not a pie. It's baked crème brulee oatmeal." Janet said laughing.

Mostafa: "What it is made from?"

Janet: "From rolled oat, apples, cherries, and raisins backed in crème brulee custard then topped with caramelized sugar."

They ate with good appetite. When they were through eating, Janet went to the cabinet and brought two mugs, one for her and one for Mostafa. She placed one before Mostafa and poured him coffee. She poured some coffee into her mug and sat sipping the coffee and staring intently into Mostafa's eyes.

"It is not my regular cup, you gave me a new one I suppose." He said amazed after he noticed the difference.

"Yes darling, it's a new cup. I bought it especially for you."

"Oh! It's printed on it, 'you + me = baby'. What does that mean?'"

"You scored, stud. You are going to be a daddy." She said with delight.

He rose and came to stand before her. Abundant tears rolled down his face. He knelt before her and held her crying incessantly. She threaded her fingers through his thick hair and held him close weeping with him.

She said through her tears: "Oh God, you sent him to me knowing that I would love him beyond reason."

He said sobbing: "Thank you for making me happy. I thank God for giving me a wife as loving and wonderful as you are."

She said still crying: "I love that you are mine. Every second I spend with you is a gift from Lord. All that is within me bless His Holy Name."

He lifted his tearful eyes to her and said smiling: "Thank you for the beautiful mug. It will be my favourite mug."

"But that is not all. Come with me."

She took him to the bedroom. She opened the closet and brought out a stylish box covered in see-through paper and sealed with a sticker. She gave him the box and he opened it. It was a T shirt imprinted on it: 'Best dad ever.'

His arms went around her. He held her tight as if he were holding his own heart.

Chapter 25

After Mostafa left the house, Daisy felt like she will never survive the sadness that overtook her. The whole world became cold and unfeeling. Her sadness was so overwhelming that she fell victim to depression. Her physical health was also affected. She was constantly fatigued, lost weight, suffered night sweats and unexplained fevers. Bleeding without apparent reason was also common. She travelled with her father to the University of Texas MD Anderson Cancer Centre in Houston, TX for physical examination. She was diagnosed as having acute lymphoid leukaemia. The doctors advised that she begins chemotherapy immediately. Her father reserved a room for her in the hospital. Daisy travelled back home to get her clothes and personal possessions.

Mostafa flew to New York city to be interviewed by Fox Sports National Networks about WWE professional Wrestling. After finishing the interview, he went to the airport to take a flight back to Connecticut.

Daisy walked in New York airport holding her handbag when she saw Mostafa by accident pushing a cart carrying his luggage. Her heart sank. Her eyes were wide open and her mouth the same. She stood still for a moment. Everything seemed to stop. She held her hand to her heart fearing it might stop beating. She walked over to him and reached behind him. She called his name with a trembling voice:" Mostafa!" He heard his name called. He instantly recognized her voice. He froze in his place not willing to turn back to see her. She stepped forward and stopped before him, looking up into his face. She saw pain and sadness in his eyes.

"How are you Mostafa? I haven't seen you for a long time."

His eyes blazed at her wild and wide but without any expression on his face. He did not speak.

She sighed, swallowing the heaviness. She had hurt him deeply to make amends, and she had to accept that.

"Are you still mad at me?" A faint smile played on her lips.

She received no answer. His eyes were open wounds beneath his heavy brows.

"I see pain in your eyes. Sorry for all the pain I caused you."

He saw her pale and small, trapped within her pain. He could see the signs of strain in the dark circles underneath her eyes. He remained silent.

"Your sad eyes tell me all - no need for words. But I must tell you this: 'You are the best thing that has ever happened to me. You were my sun. My safe harbour. Your heart was pure, and kind, and I should not have acted blind.'"

Silent tears rolled down his face. She couldn't help but take him in her arms and kiss his wet cheek. She then ran away to meet her black doom.

Janet was now five months pregnant. She and Mostafa had to find out the sex of the baby. They had their 20-week ultrasound and found out they were having a boy. The clinic had a big screen Plasma TV so they were both able to see the baby very clearly. They couldn't be more excited!

Janet experienced pregnancy symptoms in the 5th month: heart burn fatigue and loss of sleep. Mostafa was always there for her urging her to relax, but she continued to carry the torch, designing new products that are always exceptional, gorgeous and imminently wearable.

One day, Janet walked up to Mostafa and surprised him by saying: "I will travel to some counties in Africa to see how far the lifesaving programs of my foundation are helping the starving children meet their needs."

Mostafa shouted amazed" Janet! What's got into you? What's so urgent that makes you travel to dangerous remote locations, and you are five months pregnant?"

Janet: "I will not be away for long darling, it's only five days or so."

Mostafa angry: "Janet listen to me. I don't agree that you…"

"I am having a child and I want to see all the children of the world happy." She said interrupting and holding her swollen belly.

"What are you trying to do, kill me? We have never been separated before. I can't live without you even for a second. Why do you have to go Janet?" He blubbered. The tears now became uncontrollable.

"I love you darling, I always have, and I always will". She said trying her best to calm his increasingly agitated mood.

"I have committed myself to this mission because the matter is serious. Conflict and the worst drought in 70 years has left nearly 20 million people in Africa in urgent need of food and water. Somalia is on the brink of famine. In Nigeria, up to 90,000 children could die this year from severe malnutrition. Millions more in Kenya and Ethiopia need help urgently. The situation is growing worse by the day. children are struggling to survive. The littlest children, weakened by malnutrition, are more susceptible to life-threatening diseases. If we don't act now the unthinkable will happen."

He saw the determination in her eyes and realized he couldn't dissuade her from travelling to the dangerous spots. He stood frustrated, disappointed. She saw the frown of sadness covering his face. She looked into his eyes and said comforting him: "God has given us all what we wished for, it's time to give others."

A wave of sorrow overwhelmed him. He said through abundant tears: "You have a great big heart Janet."

"That won't be long you will see." She said kissing away his tears."

On July 17, 2016 a Boeing 747 carrying 212 passengers and 18 crew, exploded and crashed into the Atlantic Ocean near East Moriches, New York, shortly after departing from John F. Kennedy International Airport on a flight to England - Nigeria. Aboard that flight was Janet Berry.

Mostafa sat in shock when he heard the news. Janet died with their five-month-old son in the crash. When he was asked about his feelings he said: "One of the nice bright lights of the world has gone out. She has given me the greatest joy in life. It is hard to believe that she was gone. It's hard to take it. This is something that you don't get over."

The hurt was horrible. Her death devastated him. Mostafa was so stricken with sadness that he requested to be allowed to grieve in peace without intrusion at this difficult time.

A lengthy investigation concluded that the probable cause of the accident was a short circuit in a fuel tank that contained an explosive mixture of fuel and air vapour.

Chapter 26

It has been almost four years since Mostafa had broken up with Daisy. When Daisy knew the news of Janet's death she decided to visit Mostafa to console him. She wanted to share his grief.

 A guard stopped her at the door. "I am afraid I can't let you in. Mr. Mostafa is grieving the loss of his wife. He doesn't want to be interrupted." The guard said.

My name is Daisy. Please tell him I am standing at his door." She said persistently.

The guard disappeared into the building, then came back ushering Daisy to come in. She found Mostafa sitting on a sofa in the living room, holding his head in his hands. She sat quietly beside him. He looked sad and terribly devastated. Her heart went out to him.

He lifted his head and looked at her with eyes filled with tears.

"It was really nice of you to come. Forgive me for being this way.

"You are important to me. Together with you is my favourite place to be." He saw tears in her eyes. This brought more tears in his eyes.

"This can't be happening to me. Why is this happening? O God. Why her? Why not me?" He said crying.

"Cry my darling. Don't bottle up emotions of grief and sorrow. Have hope for tomorrow. Keeping a sense of hope through the feelings of grief can help you make it through each day." She said placing a consoling hand on his arm.

" No words can help me. I'm too sad to do anything."

"Time tends to heal wounds. Everything becomes more bearable with time. Be at peace with what has happened." "The death was sudden and unexpected. I miss her a lot. I just want to be with her. She was a true gift in my life. I am missing her every moment, waiting for us to be together again." He increased in weeping.

"Be kind to yourself. Joy comes in the morning."

"She was five months pregnant with a baby boy. Now that they have gone, I'll see them no more. They have all gone and I am sitting here alone. I am not sure what to do. I feel so awfully hollow, almost like it's me that died."

"Death has stolen her and the kid away. There's nothing left I can do." He said sobbing aloud.

"I know this is hard, but you can make it through. You can find peace in the good memories that you had with her."

He cried with intensity, with lament, with anger and with pain. He kept crying incessantly.

"She was my lover and friend. I thought we'd have so many more years, and so much more time to spend. I want to walk right up to Heaven and bring her and my son home again."

"I am longing for the moment we can be together again. She built a home in my heart. She has gone with no return, but I am still staring at her empty seat."

Daisy couldn't stand seeing him like this. She held him tight and both cried in each other's arms.

She said loving his weakness, loving his tears, loving to be in his arms: "The strongest have their moments of fatigue. Stay strong and have faith. May God impart strength to your fainting heart. Everything heals. Bad times don't last."

She released him from her arms and looked in his eyes. She kissed his tears away. Kissed his forehead, then held him again tightly to her bosom.

"I'm a great big ball of pain. I worry about how I will ever deal with this. Sorry to be a nuisance." He said feeling safe and comfortable in her arms.

"You need to toughen up and get over it. Always remember that I am your friend and I am here for you, so if there is anything you need, please don't hesitate to ask. She said extricating herself from his arms."

"Promise me you will be okay." She said rising from the sofa.

"I promise." He said downhearted.

Janet died leaving behind a huge fortune in the form of cash - 50 million dollars and Janet Berry stores. Opening Janet's will, she left all her fortune to Mostafa. This affected him to the core and decided to preserve her fortune from any loss by working even harder and make it prosper abundantly.

After Janet death Mostafa buried himself in work. He hired more highly skilled fashion designers to work in-house as employees. Their job was to follow instructions and further the vision of the fashion house.

the power of the teenage and young adult market was too great to ignore. Mostafa directed his innovative fashion styles to the youth market and featured a wide number of diversified trends. The designers incorporated more colour and pattern into their clothing, using inspiration from vintage clothing of the 1960s, 1970s, and 1980s, 1990s and 2000s.

The fashion house also designed for the mature and elite members of society. Oftentimes, celebrities will commission gowns for awards shows. The celebrities will wear Mostafa's garments for the Oscars, or BAFTA, the Emmys, or other highly photographed or filmed events. The celebrity does not buy the garment, and it is returned after the event. The payoff for the designer is that they will have high profile exposure that runs at least one year.

In addition to Janet Berry stores, Mostafa expanded further by opening boutiques in several states housing his fashion lines. Mostafa kept himself busy by supervising steps of the process, from on-site construction visits to the actual layout and design of his boutiques.

Mostafa's brands were so successful that customers had lined up days before the collection. They patiently spent up to 20 hours in the rain just for the chance to shop the collection. In other cities, customers flooded the stores, knocking over displays and scrambling to grab anything they could.

Mostafa hadn't a minute to spare, He spent his morning in fashion business which expanded to cover the whole country and occupied his nights in winning WWE grand matches and harvesting the big money prizes.

Mostafa launched his line for spring 2017 at New York Fashion week. Tom Wilson always received an invitation to Mostafa's shows. Tom was seated in the first row with the honourees, movie stars and celebrities. After the show, Mostafa offered Tom a swag bag Packed with high-end makeup products to upscale travel accessories.

"Here is a little present for Daisy. I hope she like it." Mostafa said while handing Tom the bag.

Tom: "How long haven't you seen each other?"

Mostafa: "The last time I saw her was when she came to

console me for my wife's death. That was two years ago."

Tom: "So you haven't talked to her since your wife died?"

"Yes, I think so."

Tom: "Most hospitals have times at which you can visit your friend." Tom said sardonically.

"Is Daisy in hospital? What was she sick with?" Mostafa said alarmed.

"Tom: "The last two years she started feeling extremely fatigued and having severe dizziness. She was diagnosed with acute leukaemia. She has been hospitalized several times. The doctors tried all treatments but to no avail."

Mostafa: "O God, not leukaemia, not that." Tears welled in his eyes.

Mostafa: "I didn't know. You didn't tell me, and neither did she."

Tom: "I knew that you hated her for what she did. I didn't want to burden you with her problems. I just didn't want to disturb you."

Mostafa: "But you have, you have indeed." His heart contracted. The news of her illness with this malicious disease was like a giant fist smashing his ribs.

Chapter 27

When Daisy was diagnosed with Leukaemia, she was about to call Mostafa and tell him about her illness but she withheld. She will not show him that she was weak and needed him. She would rather die and not tell him she was dying. He left and burned all their memories together. He slapped her face and swore that she was not going to see his face again. He thought that this was what she wanted. But he had killed her the moment he left. Whatever he did to her was because he loved her and wanted to save her from her evil self. Whatever she did to him was because she loved him and wanted him to be jealous. But she lost him, and now she lives a life of sorrow and regret.

Daisy stayed in the hospital enduring months of dense treatment with chemotherapy and radiotherapy but to no avail. She was then further submitted to marrow transportation.

Radiotherapy and chemotherapy damaged her hair and made it fall out in clumps, so she had to shave it. In the bathroom, she looked in the mirror. Cancer had changed her appearance; she saw pale skin, bald head, and lifeless eyes. She thanked God that Mostafa was not with her to see her ugly appearance.

She sat on her bed terribly emaciated and utterly exhausted.

She didn't notice that Mostafa was watching her from behind the glass separating her room from the corridor outside. She wanted to go to the bathroom. With great difficulty, she got out of bed. She was so weak she could hardly stand. She crawled on her hands and knees to the bathroom. After a while she came back crawling to a solid chair situated beside the bed and used it as a support in getting up. With huge pain, she forced herself into bed.

She sat on her bed looking at the window. It was a sunny day. The sun penetrated her bed and illuminated her tired face. She felt as if she was being watched. She looked at the glass separating her room from the corridor and saw Mostafa watching her with eyes brimmed with tears. He was crying in silence. Her whole body quaked, and her heart throbbed in her chest. He must not see her like that. At that moment, she wished the ground would swallow her up. She turned her face toward the window so not to see his tearful eyes. Breathless weeping seized her. Her whole body shook with violent sobs.

He entered the room. She felt his weight on the edge of the bed.

"Go away I don't want to see you. I don't want you to see me like this." She said sobbing.

He looked at her baldhead and tried to be merry and pleasant. He wanted to sheer her up. He said in a merry voice: "Women shaving head bald is among top fashion trends nowadays. You remind me of Mia Farrow's pixie cut in her film Rosemary's Baby."

"When were you going to tell me? Am I so insignificant to you? Not one phone call to tell me that you were sick in the hospital?" He said as his eyes filled with tears.

"Why call? I am nothing to you. I am a dying woman." She said weeping and still tuning her face away from him.

"You are nothing to me? We once shared strong feelings remember?

"Feelings come and go like clouds in a windy sky." She seemed as if flying to another world.

"I know I was not in your heart all the time, but I am here now to remind you of me. Once you know me again, I'll be forever in your heart."

"O shut up. Get out of here. I don't want your sympathy."

She turned her face to him. The angular bones of her face threatening to cut through the pale flesh that barely covered them.

"You should have told me Daisy. You are still careless as ever?"

"What for? So, you would slap me and call me whore?" She burst into tears.

"You still remember? Sorry, I couldn't stand what happened. Forgive me. It was a slip of the tongue."

 "That's what you called me – whore."

He tried to wipe away her tears with his fingers, but her tears were abundant and dropping incessantly.

"Now let me hold you and ease your pain." He said trying to hold her tenderly in his arms. but she pushed him away.

"Why you came to my rescue? I am hanging by a thread."

"Let me hold you please. I will not break your ribs."

Ducking her head, she buried her face in the nape of his neck. She sobbed uncontrollably in his chest.

"My mind is still having trouble wrapping itself around the fact that you are gone. Hug me so tight that all of my broken pieces fit back together."

"I want you, just you. I love your weakness, I love your fragility. I want to pamper you in my arms." He held her tight close to his heart and cried like a child.

"I miss your love, I miss your hugs. I missed being happy." She nestled securely in his chest like a bird in a nest.

"I was trying to forget you, but I was also waiting for you to come back. A million times, I needed you, a million times I cried. In my heart, you hold a place that no one could ever fill. It broke my heart to lose you."

"I am here now darling. I will take care of you."

"You felt my agony and came to save me, but you came late."

"It's never too late. We together will change your life in a positive way."

"That is not possible. I am this fragment of a person too damaged by pain to become anything useful."

Uncontrollable weeping seized her. She nestled further into his embrace.

"I always thought of you. I just wished you were here, so I could tell you how hard every day has been without you."

She could see a small glint of hope easing her sick heart. She disengaged herself and looked at him with tearful eyes.

"Don't leave me at my worst, please." She said lifting his hand to her lips and kissing them.

"I will never leave you. I am here for you."

"How do you see me - an awful creature eh?"

"The most beautiful woman in the world." He said wiping the tears with his fingers from her eyes.

"I am a woman full of flaws. I am not fit for you."

"There is no flaw in you, just weakness. I will make you strong.

"I have never disobeyed God. He will answer my payers. He will make you whole again. I promise." Tears gushed from his eyes.

"Thank you for coming. I could just die in your arms."

"No beloved. You have just found arms assisting living."

"The doctors say I have only few days to live."

"They don't know the power of God. His command, when He desires a thing, is to say to it 'Be,' and it is." I will ask Him to cure you. He will answer my prayers."

"Oh God! You are so beautiful, so compassionate. I should thank God for bringing you to my life." She said with a sad smile.

"The sun will come out tomorrow to disperse the dark clouds." He said with tears rolling down his face.

She lifted her head and tried to wipe away his tears.

"Without you, it will never shine as bright again." She said with a tearful smile.

"I will get you out of here." He suddenly said.

"Where to?"

"I built a small house on a hill. It is here in New York. You will love it, I am sure."

"I dreamt that you and I were climbing a hill leading to a little house."

"It's yours now. You will brighten it with happiness and delight."

"I like to run away from you, but if you didn't come and find me I would die. O God I love you. I just love you." She whispered sliding her arms around his neck.

He kissed her bold head and said again:" Female Hairlessness became a beauty Norm, eh?"

"Now I must leave to prepare the house for you." He kissed her forehead then made his way to the door.

Chapter 28

Mostafa came the next day to take Daisy to the little house on the hill. She leaned on him while walking in the hospital corridor to the Harley motorcycle waiting in the park. She thought she would barely be able to walk, but she was surprised to see that she was walking with ease while leaning on him. It was because he came back to give her hope. She was walking with her beloved in a dark tunnel towards light. Her light went out and he rekindled it. Now she understands that for the light to shine, the darkness must be present. His encouraging words and encompassing love had rekindled the flame of hope within her. She will walk the road he chose for her until the end.

She loved the little house. It was her new home now. She will live here and die here. In either case, she will live with the man she truly loved. She will live with her only beloved.

He wanted her to breathe first and enjoys the beauty of nature. He walked her around the house. They walked in silence holding hands. The beauty of the trees, plants and wild roses increased manifold by the wonder of being together.

"I brought you here to combat cancer together. We will heal your body naturally. We wrestlers live on diets. I have read a lot about diets and among them were that healing leukaemia. We will tackle leukaemia with a simple change in diet. I will prepare for you a variety of healing diets and juices. I will add to them natural components known to destroy leukaemia. You will eat these diets without the slightest complaint."

"Of course, darling." She said happy to see him so interested in her health.

"The main things for you during your healing journey are your faith in God along with juicing and eating lots of fresh organic green vegetables, most of them raw. Also, you must believe in yourself and that you can heal, otherwise, no matter what you do, you will not get the results you want." He emphasized.

"Tomorrow we will start the healing process, okay?" He continued.

"Okay."

"Would I sleep in your arms tonight?" She said as if pleading.

"Yes love, every night."

"You mean the world to me. I would rather spend one lifetime with you, than face all the ages of this world alone. Being with you keeps me alive." She said joyfully while both continued walking toward their little house.

In the next morning, they sat in the kitchen drinking green tea.

"Are you ready to hear the procedure you will go through? I am not telling you it is going to be easy, I am telling you it is going to be worth it." He said tapping her shoulder tenderly.

"My body was drastically abused by the severe treatments they gave me. Your methods would certainly be less severe."

He continued: "The remedy must go through two paths, a spiritual path and a medical path. The spiritual path is to seek help with prayers by believing that God is the sole God of creation, and then bringing Him in the process by considering Him as the only healer. "

"Daisy, listen carefully to my words." He said pressing her hand tenderly. "You must understand that God is testing you, and that He did not send this calamity to destroy you or cause you pain or finish you off, rather He is testing your patience, acceptance and faith; it is so that He may hear your supplication.

"The first thing you will do every morning is to pray to the Lord asking Him to heal your body, but before doing that, it is necessary that you sincerely repent to Him. God loves those who repent, and those who cleanse themselves.

Daisy: "It is my iniquities that have separated me from God, it is my sins that have made him hide His face from me, so that He does not hear me. I have committed sins and I want to meet God pure and clean."

 "If you sincerely repent He will accept your repentance and

answer your prayers. Pray forgiveness of God, surely God is All-Forgiving, All-Compassionate."

"How to sincerely repent?"

"Regret deeply and truly for the sins you committed. Return to God for forgiveness and make a strong intention never to return to sins again.

"You must also believe that healing is from God, and physicians are just an instrument of the Healer. The physician dresses the wound and God heals it.

"No calamity befalls, but by the Leave of God. This means that whoever is afflicted with a calamity and believes that it is predestination of God and receives it with patience seeking His reward, God will guide his heart to certainty and belief. You also must realize that what befell you was not to miss you and what missed you was not to befall you. Be with God and pray to him ardently seeking his forgiveness, healing and good health. You must pray ardently, humbly and faithfully.

"How do I talk to God? Are there certain words I'm supposed to say?"

"Use whatever words feel comfortable to you. invoke whatever words bring you peace of mind. I wrote for you some verses about invocation. Use them in your prayers." He said giving her a small block note.

She said with eyes filled with tears: "I will read God's words; I will memorize them by heart."

"The second part of the healing process is the medical procedure we are going to use." Mostafa continued. "It includes healing with veggies and vitamins. You will stop eating all processed foods and abstain from eating animal products. I will eat the same diet you eat. I will prepare for you vegetarian meals specifically selected to treat cancer and boost up the immune system. The meals will include raw vegetables such as cabbage, green asparagus, broccoli, red beets, beet tops, cauliflower and related vegetables. Pepper will be added because it also has cancer-fighting substances. I will add to your vegetarian food garlic, carrot, olive leaf extract, Raspberry, curcumin, Ginseng, peals of citrus fruits, and black berries."

"You will drink green tea because it stops proliferation of cancer cells."

"Yes, darling whatever you say."

"For five weeks, you will eat nothing but these vegetarian meals and water. In addition to that, you will drink carrot juice twice a day. Carrot is the best cancer-fighting vegetable of all.

"As an alternative to carrot juice, you could also have a juice of raw fruits with known cancer-fighting abilities. It will be a mixture of purple grapes with skins and seeds, red raspberries, black raspberries, strawberries, pineapple and other non-citrus fruits, with their seeds, especially peaches and apricots."

Concern was shown on her face upon hearing the vegan medication.

"I ask for your patience. We have a long way to go." He said with an encouraging smile.

"You will find me obedient and patient. I promise."

"Cast all your anxiety on God because He cares for you."

Every morning Mostafa would see Daisy praying to God. She would use her own words or the words he wrote to her or both: "O God! Forgive me, have mercy on me, guide me, and grant me health; O Lord of mankind remove the harm; You are the one who heals and there is no healing expect Yours."

Chapter 29

Loss of appetite is a common side effect of cancer and its treatment. Daisy's delicate stomach couldn't tolerate any of the food Mostafa prepared for her.

I can't tolerate your cooking." She said nauseating.

"There is no cooking here, it's all sliced fresh fruits and vegetables. You need to stay well-nourished to help your body deal with cancer."

"Don't force me to eat please." She said looking like she was going to throw up.

"Appetite loss may lead to weight loss, not getting the nutrients from food that the body needs, and loss of strength. Please try to eat." He said pleading.

"I don't think I can eat this." Tears came to her eyes.

"I tell you what. I will feed you by my own hand."

From his own hand, he fed her bits of sliced vegetables and fruits. But her sensitive belly couldn't tolerate it.

Suddenly there was this nausea. "I want to vomit." She said and vomited all over him. She vomited for about five minutes and she was sweating profusely.

Mostafa looked down at himself. The vomit on his neck and chest. She pressed a hand over her mouth.

"I am sorry." She vomited on him again.

He sat by her side holding her while she vomited. She threw up everything that she ate. She collapsed into his arms crying.

"Just breathe darling and have faith that everything will work out for the best." He felt pity for her.

"Can you bath alone?" He said after vomiting subsided.

"I am too weak to run myself a bath. I can't get in and out of the tub alone."

He carried her into the bathroom and undressed her. She looked away embarrassed. He bathed her and hadn't tried to touch anything inappropriate. He grabbed a towel from the rack and wrapped it around her and carried her to bed. In a few minutes, she was sound asleep in his arms.

Black thoughts ran through his head. Daisy's health was failing and quickly. He watched her frail body with tearful eyes. What would happen if his program failed and she died. She was his first love and he still carry strong feelings for her. She needs him, and he needs her.

When Daisy woke up, Mostafa sat beside her on bed and

said firmly: "We must thank God for showing us what to do to get rid of this leukaemia which they say has no cure. I will add to the food you dislike Garlic and onions because they are two of the top 10 anti-cancer vegetables. And you will eat all the food I offer you, you hear me?"

She said disgusted: "Okay".

"You will drink with the food 10oz of carrot juice every morning, and 10oz again between 5-6pm every day for several months. You hear me?

"Yes, I hear you." She said pushed to the point of crying.

"You would eventually grow hungry enough to overcome your distaste for the food. You must eat on your own, I will not feed you every time. You understand?"

"Yes, I understand." Now she was crying.

"I am not going to pamper you. The food I offer you is your medicine to destroy the leukaemia cells and allow normal cells to form in your bone marrow. You will eat all the food and drink all the juice I prepare for you without objection."

Daisy was difficult at first, but gradually, she ended up eating everything in her dish. And drank every drop of carrot juice in the large tankards Mostafa offered her.

She insisted that each night they sleep in each other's arms.

There were however, incidents of recurrent episodes of

nausea, vomiting, and tiredness. The episodes lasted for days. Daisy vomited several times per hour, a matter that caused a dangerous dehydration, abdominal pain and diarrhoea.

Each time Daisy vomited, Mostafa takes her to the bathroom and bath her. And she weeps as he rinses the soap off her: "I had better die, Mostafa, for I am not fit to live! I know you are trying hard to keep me alive, but I am dying every day. My body is a wreck."

He says encouraging her:" Everything happens for a reason. Maybe this was something that had to happen to keep your immune system capable of combating leukaemia."

"I am devastated." She said still weeping.

"I acknowledge your pain. I'm here with you."

"I'm not really worth anything, I am becoming a burden upon you."

"Please stop talking like that."

"I don't even have the will to get better, I don't think I can. There is no use in living. Just let me die."

"You are not going to die."

"Please go back to your life and leave me alone.

"I will not leave you alone. We need each other."

"I will never get there."

"Only if you keep going."

Her skin was so pale that it was transparent. He could see the blue veins that ran down her arms.

He patted her dry skin, wrapped her in a towel and took her to bed. She nestled in his arms, her eyes still moist with tears.

Oh, what's the use? Leave me alone. Let me die. Don't be sad. I will breath my last sigh in your arms. How sweet in your bosom my slumber will be." She said wallowing her head in his chest.

"When will you stop with all this despair? When are you going to move on with your life?" He said reprimanding her.

What life? You may have a life, but I don't. My life is ruined. I have no future."

She looked plainly into his eyes: "Can't you see I am dying?"

"No, you are not. You are going to be okay, I promise. This pain you feel is going to pass. The hurt will fade. You may be wounded but you aren't broken. You will heal."

"It's time to come home. It is time to go to God."

"No darling, it's time to come to my arms, I will carry your heartbeat in mine."

In his arms, she heard the rhythm of hope. It was faint and thin as a thread, but it was there.

He said kissing her pale lips and emaciated cheeks: "Give your life a heartbeat, a pulse, open your eyes to the world."

She clung to him sobbing in his arms.

Chapter 30

After five months of drinking the carrot juice twice daily, combined with taking the garlic and onion daily, and eating the cancer diet, Daisy's health began to improve a little. When Daisy suffered from loss of appetite, spoonful by spoonful Mostafa fed her by his own hand.

Daisy slightly restored her weight, strength and fitness. She had to learn to walk again. Mostafa got her a German shepherd dog, so she would have to go for walks.

It was 6pm and Daisy was asleep after a long walk with the dog. She awoke to the sound of a stimulant music. The music amplified her spirits and elevated her energy. She knew that Mostafa was downstairs in the gym. She knew that music helps him exercise and eases the pain of working out.

The door of the gym was open. She sneaked inside and hid behind a paravane watching him.

He was wearing a black tight legging. His upper body was bare and sweat trickled down his muscular torso. Mostafa was doing pullups, which showed off all the muscles along his upper body. Then he worked out his shoulders and back; squats, and leg presses.

Daisy watched his muscles ripple in his back and arms and his legs. She watched with amazement the perfect abs rippled with strength. She loved the beauty of his masculine body and wished to hold it in her feeble yearning arms.

His back facing her, He turned on la salsa music and danced swaying his body to the music. He danced with ease and flexibility. His swaying torso mesmerized her. He was tall and strong, very experienced and knew what he was doing. The music was contagious and took a hold on her. She loved the music and embraced the rhythm.

She could not help but feel a little sway inside. She watched his steps, and she smiled because she remembered the moves so well. She knew the tune and she had an urge to dance as she did in the old days.

The music picked up, and she could not keep still. She walked towards him and held his back. He turned around to see her smiling and swaying with the music. She stretched her arms to him and he took her in his arms and together danced the hip-swaying salsa. She moved her hips, legs and feet.

Everything in her was shaking, everything was swaying. She was elated, almost giddy, and so happy she thought she might burst. She moved beautifully in his arms. They kept their feet tight, their legs firm, and their hips loose. In his arms, she felt hot, steamy and warm.

The music took them as they twirled around. The music swelled, and they ended as the song ended, holding on to each other. In that moment, Mostafa realized that Daisy had been cured of her illness.

"You have been cured. You're alive again!" He said, repeatedly as they laughed together.

"Daisy my love, I think it's time to take you in for check-up."

She trembled in his arms fearing the results of the check-up.

On the morrow, they went to the hospital to make a blood test. The cancer specialist knew Daisy; she was one of his regular customers. He welcomed her and offered her a seat. Mostafa sat opposite her. The doctor took Daisy to the examination room and took a blood sample and a couple bone marrow samples before Mostafa and Daisy left to a nearby café waiting for the results to appear. They returned to the clinic about forty minutes later and went back into the exam room.

The doctor came into the room scratching his head, and said, "Ms Daisy I was about to start you on chemo, but somehow your white cell count is back to normal, you don't have cancer. The leukaemia was gone. The disease has vanished."

Now Daisy achieved remission. No leukemic cells can be found in the blood or bone marrow and the bone marrow is working normally again. Daisy was happy and delighted and over the moon. She had achieved remission. She was now cancer free. Although Mostafa was exhilarated, he reacted more cautiously to the news, fearing that the leukaemia might recur, the longer Daisy stayed in remission the better it was. Treatment with vegies must therefore continue to destroy any remaining leukemic cells and give the best chance of a long-lasting remission or cure.

Daisy did not mind staying with Mostafa for longer periods eating vegies and drinking carrot juice. He is her beloved, her man, her rock. She loved him, and she knew that he loved her. She will take care of herself and make him love her more. She will look more feminine; she will change her hairstyle and change into more sexy outfits. She will set him crazy. He will be unable to set his eyes off her. She will cook him dinner, put him to bed and nestle in his arms enjoying the strong male sent of him.

Chapter 31

They went to bed and slept in each other's arms.

"I want that moment to last and not be taken away by sleep. I love sleeping with you. Not sex, just laying listening to your heartbeat and feeling like everything was at peace. Nothing matters except the two of us." She said nestling in his embrace.

He kissed her gently, his lips warm.

"I feel a renewed sense of hope. You taught me how to live. God redeemed my soul from going down to the pit, and I will live in your arms to enjoy the light."

"You were brave. It took you a lot of courage to do what you did. What makes you brave is your willingness to live through your terrible illness. You are a strong woman. You worked hard and won the battle."

"If I know what love is, it is because of you. I love you more than words can show. There is no one I would ever love the way I love you. Do you still love me? Do you still want me?"

"Never doubt that I want you, Daisy," he whispered raggedly. "Because I do – and nothing is ever going to change that."

"And now come closer to my arms. I cannot get enough of you." He said pulling her closer to him."

"I am terrified of even touching you. I find it very difficult to carry on a normal relationship with you. I am impotent in romancing you. I lost interest in sex."

"I understand. You have been through too much. You will regain your sex drive gradually."

"I am no match for you. I am too fragile and weak. You need a strong woman to put up with your massive body."

"Relax. I just want you here by my side. I want to feel you relax in my arms knowing that you are safe."

"I have gone through too much. I deserve to be happy for once."

"Let the past be in the past. Do not let the shadows of the past darken the future. Live for what today has to offer, not for what yesterday has taken away. Forgive and forget."

" I love you more than words can show. There is no one I would ever love the way I love you."

"I love you just the same."

"Hold me tight. I want to sleep and wake up by your side. I want to live."

He held her dearly and both slept in each other's arms in

love and peace until morning.

It was a gloomy day; days of clouds and rain were on the way. Mostafa and Daisy just had their breakfast, and were now resting in the living room, Daisy was drinking carrot juice and Mostafa sipping a cup of coffee. Mostafa started the talk.

"Haven't you thought about your future and what you want to do?"

"When I think about my future, I can't imagine you not being in it. If my future has you in it, I am not afraid of the rest. Every day we are together is the greatest day of my life."

"Of course, I will always be with you. It is just that I want you to learn, grow and become better than you have ever been before."

"I do not know what is important anymore. I am not sure that I could handle another change in my life at this point."

"Daisy let's be realistic. You must start making important choices. You must think very positive to create what you want in your future. Think about the outcome of the future and make the right choice."

"I don't worry about the future. Tomorrow is even out of sight for me. I am interested only in the present. Life is the moment we are living now, and I am living with you."

"You must start thinking about your future and what you want to do. Let today be the day you give up who you have been for who you can become. I am certain that you are capable to achieve your goals."

"And how do you think my future would be?"

"Before you left college, you were studying law. I think you should look into going back to college and continue your education. Be a great lawyer like your father."

"I lived with lawyers my whole life. They don't seem like happy people."

"Studying law opens so many doors. Lawyers are among the highest paid professionals in the legal industry and most attorneys earn salaries well above the national average. A career as a lawyer has been a hallmark of prestige."

"I don't like law school, and I don't know if this is for me."

"O Daisy dear. Please give it a chance. Wash away the past and start anew. Move on and go find yourself."

"I want to be with you. I want to be your wife, the mother of your children."

"Your future is more important now. You must work. Work will save you from the dullness and boredom of life. It will make your life meaningful and peaceful."

His words landed against her ears like heavy blows. She buried her face in her hands, sobbed, and shrank down in her seat. A thorn pierced her heart. Her life was just starting to look better but now all her dreams of being his wife were shattered. She wanted to hit him hard and make him feel the way she did. She was mad. His words messed up everything. She hated this. He was leaving her again. The thought of he is leaving her made her sick. She would die to marry him if he accepted her now. She loved him enough to marry him and he knew that. She wanted to be with him and have his kids.

"Daisy! What is the matter; did I say something that offended you?" He said confused.

She knew one thing for sure. She wanted to go home.

"I want to go home." She said feeling a clutch in her heart.

"Daisy darling, please try to understand."" He said with the sense of having been repeatedly punched in the stomach.

She stood and held up one hand stopping him. She headed to the door and walked out of it. Mostafa trailed behind her.

"Daisy! Have I said something wrong? It's all for your own good." He said extremely annoyed.

"Okay, at least let me get you a ride home." He said when he saw that she was determined to leave.

She sucked her breath in on a grasp of pain. "Stay where you are damn you, I will take a cap." Her eyes sparkled fury.

He stood by the door watching her leave. Bitterness engulfed him because he was the reason for her sadness.

Chapter 32

Daisy stormed into the house fuming. She found her father standing in the big hole. He smiled when he saw her. She marched straight past him and into the living room. He followed her to the living room amazed to see her so angry. Daisy sank onto the couch crying.

"I hate him, he broke my heart." She said sobbing, her rib cage shaking. "Why did you bring this primitive villager from Luxor? He came with decayed views about women. I thought his long stay in America had softened his manners and broadened his mind with the realities of life, but he is still wrapped up in his conservative views about women. In his view, love and sex must be through marriage and nothing else. I know. He will never marry me. He will never forget my ugly past." Her weeping increased.

Tom sat beside Daisy on the couch and took her in his arms. She burst into more tears.

"Daisy, what brought all this anger to the surface? You seem devastated."

"After I got cured I told him that I want to marry him and be the mother of his children, but he disappointed me by saying I must complete my law education and work with you in the firm."

"Sound advice Daisy, sound advice."
"No daddy. It was just an excuse to run away and escape my love. I hated when he acted like he didn't care about my feelings. I wanted him to show his emotions. I wanted him to love me the way I deserve to be loved."

"This man loves you Daisy. After all what he has done to you, and you think he doesn't love you?"

"He expresses his love by protecting me. His favours upon me are too numerous to count. He drew me out of deep waters. He protected me from my evil desires, from a pimp I married. He walked into my death room when the rest of the world walked out. He healed my body from a cancer that was about to destroy my life. I loved the days of my illness because I spent a whole year in in his arms. Spoonful by spoonful he fed me by his own hand. He bathed me, dried me off, and took me to bed every night to nestle in his compassionate arms. The days of my sickness were the best days I ever had. We were so close together I could still feel his body heat.

"I know he loves me with all his might, and I love him all the way down to my core. I want to be with him forever, but I know he will never accept me as a wife."

She lifted her tearful eyes to her father and said: "He thinks I am trouble, and too much for him to handle."

"No darling. You are just a challenge to handle. It takes a strong man to handle a broken woman, and he is a strong man. He is the only person who can change everything around when it is going bad."

He wiped her tears away with his fingers. "Do you love him that much?" He said kissing her forehead.

 "His love is all I seek. He is my everything. I can't imagine not having him in my life. It is driving me insane how I can't have him."

"I fear losing him. I know he will never take me as a wife, but I adore him anyway." She buried her face in her hands as long agonizing sobs wracked her body to the core."

"You never know. Can't you see he keeps coming back to you? True love has a habit of coming back. Maybe you were really meant for each other."

"O God. I feel awful. My heart is broken." She said feeling as if the whole world were crashing down on her.

"You have got to be strong Daisy. Sometimes you must go through the worst to get the best. It is just an emotional pain. Emotional pain cannot kill you. Have faith that things would get better. In time you will move through your pain. Time is a good healer."

"I am not sure this is true. There is not a day goes by that I don't cry for him. The hurt and pain are so big and so deep that I cannot forget him." She cried soundlessly, no sobs, just a steady course of tears down her cheeks.

"Believe in your potential not your past. Joining college to finish law study was the most valuable advice Mostafa gave you. This will change your life more than you can imagine. You will start thinking big and get new perspectives on the world."

"His reluctance to show his feelings towards me has ripped me into pieces so small I wasn't sure I still existed. Yes, I need help ending this tortured love. I will not let him break my soul. I will move on without him. I will start a new life. I will not stay any longer in the dark waiting for the pain to stop. I will join college and make my life worthwhile. I will show him what he could have had." She said angrily.

"That's my girl. You are still young, and your best days are still ahead. Turn your frustration into motivation so that you would never have to feel that way again. Join college, finish law study, and come work with me."

In her room, Daisy dropped to her knees and prayed through abundant tears:

"O Lord, heal my wounds.

O Lord, give me hope.

O Lord, strengthen my spirit.

O Lord, revive my soul."

Mostafa paid Tom a visit. Tom welcomed him and drew him into a big hug. They sat in the living room talking about

Daisy.

Tom: "I can never thank you enough for what you did to her. You did what I couldn't. I am thrilled that you are here."

Mostafa: "I am always happy to see you. I should have come earlier. Sorry I was late."

Tom: "Better late than never. Thank you so much for what you have done to Daisy. It was a miracle that she was cured from cancer. I was just there to calm her fears, but with your vegetable juices and greens, you were able to cure her from cancer. I don't know what I would do without you."

Mostafa: "I did nothing really. Daisy is a woman with heart. She deserves the world. She has taken a dreadful fall, but she will survive I am sure."

Tom: "Do you love her?"

"Yes." Mostafa said after a moment of hesitation.

"She came crying thinking that you don't care enough about her."

"Of course, I do care about her. I just wanted her to start a new life; to keep moving forward and opening new doors."

"And you think she will achieve all this by joining college?"

"I thought that would be in her own interest?

"You broke her heart by pushing her away from you."

"She may hate me for this, but I had to do it for her."
"I know what you think. You think you deserve someone better."

"I came from a deeply conservative culture where no physical contact with men was allowed. Adultery is rebuked and is considered amongst the gravest sins in our religion. There is not anything which God so abhors, as adultery."

"Do not be afraid to love Daisy because there is nothing more courageous than loving someone."

"I love Daisy, but I just can't stop thinking of her having sex with all these men. It kills me to think of her sordid past."

"What happened to her was against her will. You know that."

"Yes, but marrying that pimp was her own choice. She preferred him to me. I can't get over that."

"One of her bad choices I must say." Tom said annoyed.

"Someday she will find love with someone else. Someone will come along to offer her his heart." Mostafa said with a sad frown on his face.

"Don't lose someone who truly loves you. She loved you with honesty and you broke her. She wants a good man to depend on. She wants you."

Tom added with a frown: "Right now she is disappointed and angry. Every night she cries and dies a little more inside."
"I know she is angry with me now. Can I see her?"

Tom: "No. She is not ready to see you. She doesn't want to get close enough for you to hurt her again."

"Some people are meant to fall in love with each other but not meant to be together. Storms do not last forever. I am certain that Daisy can take care of herself just fine. She will shine amongst those who never believed she could." Tom said with signs of worry on his face.

Days turned into weeks, weeks turned into months, months turned into years. Three years had passed and Daisy graduated from law school and joined her father's law firm.

Chapter 33

Tom's law firm is a business entity owned by Tom and is run by associate lawyers. Hard work associates may become partners in the firm. An associate may have to wait as long as 11 years before the decision is made as to whether he makes partner. Associates who do not make partner are sometimes required to resign and join another firm. Making partner is very prestigious due to the competition that naturally results between associate lawyers. Partners known as non-equity partners, share directly in the profits of the firm, after paying salaried employees, the landlord, and the usual costs of furniture, office supplies, and books for the law library or a database subscription. Non-equity partners are generally paid a higher fixed salary than that of the associates, and they are often granted certain limited voting rights with respect to firm operations.

Steven Scott proved himself as a young lawyer in Tom's firm. He gained throughout the years, a genuine experience as a lawyer in various disciplines. He won cases in areas related to administrative law, appellate advocacy, civil rights, mediation service, and wills and trust.

Due to his hard work and devotion to the firm, Tom promoted him from associate to a non-equity partner in which the lawyer does not share in the profits or capital of the firm; a position is often an intermediate step toward full equity partner.

When Daisy first joined her father's firm, Tom assigned Steven to train her in major areas of law practice. Steven was clever in developing her future legal talent. He taught her that the law always changes, and the task of keeping abreast of those changes never diminishes whether by statute or case law. He taught her how to give better service to her clients and to grow her practice profitably whilst keeping fully up to date with all the relevant changes affecting the profession. He enriched her knowledge and skills to equip her with the tools needed to develop her talent and provide excellent client service. He taught her how to prepare for court. Adequate understanding of the facts allows her to present the case in an organized and efficient manner for a judge who is hearing the information for the first time. Courts today do not have the time or the patience for attorneys who are not prepared to present their cases in an efficient and organized way at trial. The more prepared she was, the more confident she will be, and confidence is a key to success in practicing law.

Steven and Daisy worked very close. He allowed her to help prepare his cases and discuss his trial strategies. She attended with him a variety of trials in civil, divorce and criminal courts with the intention to learn his techniques. She read books about manoeuvres by different attorneys, and the defence strategies of judges and clients, to better prepare herself for future cases.

Steven was a strong advocate for human rights. Among his interests was to bring the United States to change her relationship with Native Americans. The idea revived in his mind when the Indian tribes filed a lawsuit in the Supreme Court demanding sovereignty over their land and natural resources.

While collecting evidence for the lawsuit, Daisy entered with Steven into a deep conversation discussing the probability of winning or losing the case.

Daisy: "It's a losing case. Losing a court case sucks."

Steven: "I know, it's a losing game in the end."

Daisy: "Then why you accepted the case in the first place."

Steven: "I will struggle to persuade the Supreme Court to force the federal government to adopt a more productive manner towards American natives.

Daisy: "How can you do that?"

Steven: "This can begin by recognizing the cultural rights and human dignity of all people including American natives."

Daisy: "Yes, but the historical record of the Supreme Court with respect to its dealing with native Americans, does not leave room for a great deal of optimism. The Supreme Court continued to resist recognizing more expansive human rights for native Americans. The Supreme Court regularly upholds sweeping government powers over Indians that are completely outside the normal rules of constitutional interpretation."

Steven: "This is still the actual situation of the Supreme Court, but do not forget that the increasing global recognition of indigenous rights, may prove productive in bringing the United States to drastically change her relationship with native Americans. International pressure may force the United States to contend with her own human rights violations in a more effective way."

In the Supreme Court, Daisy sat watching Steven struggling to enforce international human rights law in a federal court was amazingly overwhelming.

Steve started his argument by stating that Indian termination was the policy of the United States from the mid-1940s to the mid-1960s. It was shaped by a series of laws and policies with the intent of assimilating Native Americans into mainstream American society. The belief that indigenous people should abandon their traditional lives and become civilized had been the basis of the government policy for centuries. With or without consent, tribes must be terminated and begin to live as Americans. To that end, Congress set about ending the special relationship between tribes and the federal government. In practical terms, the policy ended the U.S. government's recognition of sovereignty of tribes, trusteeship over Indian reservations, and exclusion of state law applicability to native persons.

Steven then struggled to persuade the court to give Native Americans their legal human rights. He reminded the court of the United Nations declaration on the Rights of persons belonging to ethnic, religious and linguistic minorities. He reaffirmed that one of the basic aims of the United Nations, as proclaimed in the Charter, is to promote and encourage respect for human rights and for fundamental freedoms for all, without distinction as to race, sex, language or religion. He demanded that the American states must protect the existence, the cultural, religious and linguistic identity of minorities within their respective territories and must encourage conditions for the promotion of that identity. States shall adopt appropriate legislative and other measures to achieve those ends.

The Supreme Court however, sided with the federal government against Native Americans. Daisy watched Steven fighting against the injustice of the Supreme Court, criticizing its decision as highly irregular, poorly reasoned, and even as schizophrenic approach to Indian rights.

The greatness of Steven in court inspired Daisy. She whispered to herself: "They sure don't teach you this in law school."

After overcoming her initial tongue-tied fear during her first trials, Daisy's manner and style became different, her zeal and the tone of her defence speeches placed her work well above the banalities usually committed by young lawyers in training. Tom watched Daisy's growing ability to construct a well-crafted argument that displayed a creative element in addition to well-organized facts. He entered her office to congratulate her. She and Steven were sitting at a long table discussing a case.

Tom: "You are no longer the child who dodges her defence

speech by imploring the indulgence of the court for your client. You have already evolved your creative flair for argumentation."

"Thank you, dad, all credit goes to him." She said pointing at Steven.

"I did nothing really. She learned fast. Almost anything I taught her." Steven said happy to hear her admiration for him.

Tom: "I love to see people happy and succeeding. I like this special connection between you two. Steven is a big asset to you. I want you to work very closely with him, shoulder to shoulder I mean. This would maximize your performance."

Daisy: "I am just a girl who decided to go for it. I have learned that is none else's job to take care of me but me. I am working hard towards everything I want."

Tom: "We cannot accomplish all that we need to do without working together."

Daisy: "I like to handle things my own way."

Tom: "Take a chance Daisy. You will never know how absolutely perfect something could turn out to be." He winked at her and left.

As time passed, Daisy became a famous lawyer. Her preparations for a trial, and her performance in the courtroom, were the equivalent of an artistic activity. In each of her cases, she struggled with different ways to present a persuasive and well- written defence for her clients.

Steven himself, did not understand her work mode, which was overexcited her brain, beating it up to the point which she worked her defence in a nervous burst. She impressed the spectators and judges alike with her dramatic capabilities by juggling drama with facts, creating an engaging presentation fascinating all audience present in court.

Daisy announced to Steven that from now on, she will prepare her cases on her own, following her own methods and style, and it became a habit for her to refuse his help, rarely even telling him which cases she had accepted, or discussing strategies for upcoming trials.

Chapter 34

Steven Scott – a lithe figure of medium height and slim build, with a prominent forehead, receding hairline and thoughtful eyes - possessed a magnetism evident to all who encountered him. He took no interest in sport or food, or personal comfort. He did not smoke or drink.

Steven was a lonely figure, distrustful of his close colleagues, rarely confiding in them. His work absorbed him, at work; he exuded vitality and had no time for women or love. He knew many women before, but feared intimacy. With Daisy however, the situation was different. She was intelligent, articulate and quite successful in her work. He loved her directness and confidence in herself. He saw her beautiful and lovely, and gorgeous and stunning. She was apparently physically attractive, and he wondered, whether she felt any attraction to him.

There was no question that Steven was smitten by beautiful Daisy. He could not remember the last time he was this happy; and it soon became apparent to him that he wanted Daisy to become a part of his everyday life.

But Daisy seemed always sad and lonely. There was always that shield that she had raised against the vicissitudes of a world that had misused her. If only he knew how to penetrate the shield she hid her true feelings behind. He will fill that void and make her live a life of passion and contentment.

"I am now an independent woman and I got my own life to live. I have been broken, but here I stand, still moving forward, growing stronger each day." Daisy whispered to herself.

After a long battle in court, Daisy was so worn out that she did not notice Steven standing at her desk. "You look worn out, how about having dinner with me tonight." He said softly with an engaging smile. She manged a tiny smile and accepted his invitation.

In a cosy restaurant, they ate dinner and shared a glass of wine. They talked while eating.

"I have a big opinion on you. You set the example of perseverance and hard work."

"I learned from the best. You showed me the way. You taught me how to practise law before the bar." She said appreciatively.

"Results don't come without commitment to the task, and you have been strongly committed to your job. I am at your service any time you need my help." He said pleased to hear her encouraging words.

"Sometimes I look at you and wonder how I got so damn lucky." He added with a broad smile on his face.

"It's me who is lucky to have you in my life. You helped me

close the door to my ugly past, and step through to a new life."
Ugly past? Did you suffer in the past?"

"I suffered a great deal in life. My suffering reached the limits of my ability to endure."

"Could you please be a bit clearer? I became anxious."

Not everything could be revealed. I will take my secrets to my grave."

"Was there a certain man in your life?" Steven suddenly asked.

She hesitated a moment then nodded her head: "Yes."

"Was he a perfect match for you?

"He is more than a perfect match. He is the only person I wanted to live the rest of my life with, but my love for him brought only pain." She tried to hide her suffering with a sad smile, but tears ran down her face.

"Please don't cry. I can't see you suffering." His heart went out to her.
"You don't know what it's like! You don't have a clue how much this hurts."

"Tell me about your life with him."

"Our life together was filled with desperation, of the bitter

knowledge that we could have had something perfect, but it just wasn't meant to be."
"I am sorry to hear that."

She said with watery eyes: "O God, what is wrong with me? Why does nothing ever work out? I was so desperate that I had the urge to lie down in the middle of the road and let the next car run over me."

"Do you love him that much?" Signs of jealousy crept into Steven's face.

"No woman could ever love him better. Not a day goes by without him on my mind. I will always have this piece of my heart that smiles whenever I think about him."

"How dare he let you suffer like that? I am anxious to know everything about him. How does he look like?" Steven inquired angrily.

"He is peaceful like a dove and ferocious like a lion. He saved me several times. He saved me from my evil self and from bad people trying to exploit me. He healed my sick body and put hope in my desperate heart. I ow my life to him."

"What is exactly your story Daisy?"

"My story is not to be told, it's a mystery."

"Why is he so important to you?"

"I made terrible mistakes. I let him down. I hurt him

tremendously. I was young and made thoughtless choices without thinking of repercussions. Despite being hurt, he protected me from my evil soul and from men taking advantage of me. He then erased all my mistakes, all the traces of my ugly past. I then got horribly sick, He healed me from the terrible disease and put hope into my dying heart."

"If you love him that much, why he left you."

"He couldn't forget the mistakes of the past, and thought I was not good enough for him." Sadness covered her face as she spoke.

"Did he tell you that?"

"No. But he told my father that someday I will find love with someone else."

"If you were mine, I would never let you go." He said feeling the wild throbbing of his heart."

"His love ravishes my heart; it is a power I cannot resist. Every time I see him I fall in love all over again." She said as if apologizing.

"I want to know everything about him. Is he handsome?"

 "He is a joy to look at. He is the kind of person you would follow to hell and back. Women cannot take their eyes off him. I forced myself to get over him, but it didn't work."

"You may love him, but there is no point holding onto someone who has already let you go. Don't follow someone to make you feel like you are not good enough for him. Respect yourself and leave what sounds like a destructive relationship."

"He left his mark upon my skin. I can't stop thinking about him. My heart is still with him."

"Do yourself a favour and delete him from your life. You are better off without him. You believed in him and he let you down. You think high of him. What is he exactly to you?"

"He was made to protect me, and I was made that I would always worth the effort." Her face smiled but her eyes did not.

""Take what happened in the past as a lesson and move on."

"It will take a while, but I will finally grow up."

"Are you sure?"

"Don't worry about me. I am the girl that picks herself every time she falls."

"You might not know this Daisy, but I really care for you. Your happiness matters more than mine."

"I can figure it out."

So why don't you love me? keep loving me. I will keep loving you. And the rest will fall in place."

She reached over and squeezed his hand. "You are such a nice guy Stevens. I love the way you understand my thoughts before I voice them. I am much more me when I am with you." She said with a pleasant smile.

Chapter 35

Audrey Miller was the head designer at the Janet-Berry fashion house. Audrey with her creative designs had taken the Janet-Berry name to new heights. She became renowned for creating designs to achieve a traditional style with modern influence.

Audrey Miller was ambitious and knew exactly what she wanted. She knew where she was headed and wouldn't settle for less.

Audrey was a beautiful brunette. She had sweet lips that were lilac soft. Her skin was smooth, the colour of cream. Her black hair was cut short - Audrey Hepburn style. Her short hair gave a strong focus to her beautiful face, and long sexy neck. Her body was slender, with a flat stomach, large breasts and a round, firm butt.

Audrey exercises regularly in the gym, switching between cardio and weights. She is an avid outdoor enthusiast. She jogs, climb mountains, and jump out of planes from time to time. She walks like an athlete with a cheerful smile on her face.

She had regular meetings with her team of designers to articulate what their brand really stands for and what they want it to accomplish in the future. In such meetings, she discussed with them how to collaborate and learn from one another.

Mostafa frequently participated in Audrey's meetings with her team and was impressed upon hearing her words to them: "There was a time when people looked to fashion designers to tell them what was beautiful or trendy, but this is no longer the case. Today, consumers dictate what they want, and the companies respond. The brands that will thrive are those that focus on understanding their customers and meeting them where they are."

Mostafa was also impressed to see her saying to her team with great enthusiasm: "We must all enjoy happy mind and healthy body. Sports improve one's mood, boost self-confidence, and reduce pressure and stress, and above all, sports teach teamwork and problem-solving skills."

Mostafa saw Audrey inspiring to her team. He admired her strong personality and talent and her determination to get her way. He heard one of her team saying: "she is a planet in her own inimitable orbit". Men admire women who know how to look and exude a high level of confidence.

Audrey had developed a strong relationship with Mostafa, her boss. She was keen to have regular meetings with him, admitting that she needs his guidance and support in her work. She appreciated his opinion about her fashion sketches, and approved them if were suitable, if not, she would gently express her rejection explaining the technical reasons behind her resentment.

It was at the beginning of the summer when Audrey took

Mostafa to the demonstration room to show him her fashion sketches. She started by explaining the fashion theory of the 'shifting erogenous zone': "The theory refers to a visual phenomenon associated with clothing and body adornment. According to the theory, erogenous zones are those areas of the female body, which men find sexually arousing and which women alter or adorn to attract the male eye. The whole of the female body is erotic to men, but the mind cannot grasp an eroticism extending over the whole body, so at different times, emphasis is placed on various parts, sometimes the bosom, sometimes the legs or buttocks, loins, and even ankles. I uncover them, accentuate them through cut and fabric, or subtly allude them."

She explained her work while moving from one sketch to another: "Fashion sketch is always a good method of recording or working out ideas for fashion design."

The sketches she demonstrated were trendy, colourful and mysterious at the same time. The unity of opposites grabbed Mostafa's attention. Like pure and delicate flower bud, the sketches showed how beautiful a woman could be if she was dressed, the way Audrey wanted her to be.

"Simple and delicate dress accentuates women beauty. Soft tones, gentle lines are features of my work. Through my work women can explore their own sensuality and femininity." She continued confidently.

After she finished her presentation, she said smiling: "Well, how did you find my work?"

He sat silent for a while contemplating her. He was fascinated by her fabulous look and skilful presentation and did not want to do anything to break the spell. He had seen Audrey quite often before, but he did not notice how beautiful she was. He had done injustice to her beauty in his remembrance of her. She was above even the beau ideal of fancy.

She woke him up from his reveries when she repeated her question: "Well what you think?"

He looked at her with a smile: "Your presentation was splendid. Every piece you presented is different and unique. Your illustrations are full of passion. You showed that women are more beautiful than they think. I liked your fashion sketches and illustrations. These remarkable pieces of art are going to be our fashion for the summer."

Her heart thrilled at his compliment. She broke out into a merry laugh and said: "You are a good boss, appreciative, communicative, you value your employees and help them do their jobs better."

"I see you like a racing horse jumping over all barriers." He said while rising out from his chair."

"Those who don't jump will never fly." She said laughing.

"Thank you for supporting me today. If it wasn't for your support I would be lost." She said with tears of appreciation rushing into her eyes. She said shyly without looking at his eyes and leaving the room in quick steps: "You are my shoulder to lean on, the one person I know I can count on. I could not have done it without your encouragement. You bring out the best of me."

Mostafa was troubled by Daisy's sexual past. She had slept with several men, and he wanted his wife pure, never touched by other men. Although he knew her sexual past, he was still in love with her. He had stood by her through painful and difficult times, but he can't marry her. His culture and tradition prevent him from living with her with that amount of shame. She will always be his beloved, his only love, but not his wife. She will always be somebody else's wife.

When he married Janet, he loved her the love of trust, loyalty and passion, but in every bit of emotion he had for Janet, Daisy was always there lingering in his mind.

He is young and robust, and he did not have sex with any woman since Janet died. He needs sex in his life, and according to his tradition, this could be only through legitimate marriage.

Audrey's competitive spirit was one of the things he found most attractive about her. She was a sexy flirtatious woman smiling with her eyes. She had that confidence that make her seem untouchable, yet so desirable all at once. He liked her good sense of humour. She was young and attractive, intelligent, tactful and made him feel needed.

Mostafa organized a fashion show in Artists Collective Inc. in Hartford. Photography, Graphics, printed textiles and fine art all had work on show while female models presented Audrey's collections on the catwalk in front of a big audience. The fashion show was a big success. The models wearing Audrey's stylish dresses rocked the foyer. Audrey was sitting beside Mostafa proudly watching the show. Mostafa glanced at her admiringly. She proved herself so very worthy every day.

Mostafa took Audrey out to dinner to celebrate the happy occasion. They dined at Max Downtown. They talked while eating.

"Tell me about you." Mostafa proceeded.

"I was raised by my mother and my mother's second husband who adopted me after my father disappeared when I was nine. My father was good to me. I simply adored him. Without him, I felt that I was alone, vulnerable, unprotected and obviously scared. I felt insecure and sometimes lost, even as I learned to navigate the world in my own way."

"I can understand. I am so lonely without Janet. I can't even begin to imagine living the rest of my life without her. We planned a future together. We had dreams and goals and now I am all alone. Even though time passes, to me the pain has not healed. I have learned to deal with that pain in my own way. The life I loved is over and I am trying to find a new life."

"I'm so sorry for your loss and the pain that goes along with it!"

"The first few months were so hard. They were all about surviving. Living without her stifled and strangled me. My spirit became so heavy with the weight of my isolation that I often felt like dying."

"I know. I've been there many times. But don't be sad. There is always hope. Loneliness is part of being human."

"The death of Janet was the most stressful and traumatic experience I went through."

"Don't allow yourself to sink into self-pity or feelings of helplessness. If you are feeling lonely, you must take charge and make changes. Nobody else can do this for you."

"That's what I am trying to do right now." He said looking deeply into her eyes.

For one moment, she thought she glimpsed a shadow of love in his eyes. Her heart pounded out of her chest. Is he infatuated with her? If he is, she must make the most of his infatuation with her while it lasts, to ensure a good deal out of it. The smart ones take advantage of a good opportunity.

"Is there a man in your life?" He said keeping his eyes fixed on her.

"No. I am still looking for the perfect guy."

"Who is the perfect guy in your opinion?"

"The perfect guy is not the richest or the most handsome,

he is the one who knows how to make me smile and will take care of me every day until the end of time."

"What is love in your opinion?"

"Love is when you look into someone's eyes and see everything you need."

"And what do you exactly need from love?"

"Love is overcoming obstacles, facing challenges, fighting to be together, holding on and never letting go."

"Have you fallen in love before?"

"Yes."

"But you have just said there was no man in your life."

"He only exist in my imagination but maybe someday I will find him in reality."

"What is it like to be in love with imaginary lover? "

"I feel the bliss and exhilaration of being in love. I envision the tender embrace of a lover, a supporter, a friend. A lover who would give me the strength and inspiration to continue to move forward."

"How does this imaginary lover look like?"

"He looks like you. Simple and honest. Strong and

courageous. So relaxed and so sure of himself. Open, considerate and caring."

"You see me with all these qualities!"

"You are the man I have always dreamt about. You are the love of my life."

 "Do you love me that much?"

"I loved you since a long time ago. Everyone says you only fall in love once, but that is not true, because every time I see you, I fall in love all over again."

"But I haven't seen you quite often in the company before."

"You were married to Janet, and busy building your career in wrestling and in the fashion industry, but you were with me even if you were far away. You were in my heart, in my thoughts, in my life always. You mean more to me than you will ever know."

He needed to touch her silken skin, stroke his hands over her lush body and sink into the fiery heat of her.

"I need a woman in my life. I have been single for far too long. I want a good woman to hold, and love. One who will flirt and play. Enjoy every aspect of life together."

The chemistry between them flared bright and hot. She knew he meant sex. She lowered her gaze; and said with a half-shy smile on her face: "We can beautifully connect with each other. We enjoy chemistry and compatibility, share common interests and share common life goal. Sex is a way to feel connected and would deepen our relationship." Something melted within him at her words. She'll bring a refreshing sense of heat and compassion to his life.

"Have you ever thought of getting married?" He said suddenly.

"Of course, I thought of getting married." She then opened her mouth and said amazed: |"Marriage! You mean you and me. Is that what you mean?"

"Yes that's exactly what I mean".

She reached up, encircled his neck with her arms, and kissed his head.

He said laughing: "We will have our wedding at Candlelight Farms Inn. It is perfect for our wedding day and it makes for an excellent honeymoon location as well. You will like the place I am sure."

"That sounds wonderful. I love my life when you are in it. I am so ready for our future together." She said hilariously.

"You must understand that marriage is not just a pair of rings, it is a vow to trust and always stand by your man. Marriage is a bond that last forever. A good loyal woman is one of the greatest things a man can have in his life."

"I know what you mean. Marriage is only a paper. It takes

trust, respect, love, understanding and faith to make it last. If you truly love someone, being faithful is easy. Without respect there is no love, without trust, there is no reason to continue."

She continued with tears of joy in her eyes: "I can't think of anything I want to do more than spend the rest of my life with you. You are the love of my life. I will become the best mother for my children."

Chapter 36

Audrey had a private life Mostafa knew nothing about. She had a lover called Alan Evans. He works as fashion sales representative. His job is to persuade buyers and retail purchasing agents to buy the products of clothing manufacturing companies. Audrey met him when they were students at the school of Fashion Institute of Design & Merchandising. Their relationship developed into a deep love. After graduation, Audrey moved into Alan's apartment and lived with him for years without marriage.

Alan proposed marriage to Audrey, but her answer was shocking: "I'm sorry. I care about you so much, but I do not think we want all the same things in life. I think it would be wise if we didn't marry, at least not right now."

"Why darling. I love you so much." He said with a bleeding heart.

"I'm flattered that you care for me enough to want to marry me. My career as a fashion designer is more important than marriage. I want to focus on my career first."

"Get married first then focus on career." He said pleading.

"Just now I am confused. I'll wait until I know myself better."
"Getting to know yourself is a lifelong process. Line up

the marriage first, then the career. I am more about the marriage than the relationship."

"I'm not ready to talk about marriage yet, maybe we can talk about marriage later."

"Why can't you just tell me what you feel, because how you act is confusing me?"

"I love you, but as I told you, my career comes first. I want to be financially stable, before being ready to settle down." Alan proposed to Audrey several times, but her answer was always no. Her frequent rejections affected him tremendously. One night he got so angry that he smashed with his fist the wooden windowsill of their bedroom.

Audrey was not on birth control when one night had sex with Alan. Alan's condom broke and she got pregnant. When she was two months pregnant, she told Alan that she wanted to get rid of the baby but Alan insisted that she keeps it. The baby was the only bond that would attach her to him. When she stubbornly rejected his attempts to persuade her to keep the baby, he smacked her across the mouth so hard he made her nose bleed; the blood ran like a tap down her face. She began yelling: "Susan, Susan for God's sake help me!" Susan, the landlord, who lived in an apartment so close to theirs, heard Audrey's appeal for help, she knocked heavily on Alan's door. Alan opened the door for her and Susan rushed in. She saw blood pouring down Audrey's face. She took Audrey to the bath and carefully washed her face.

Susan sat with them to smooth things out.

Alan said angrily: "She is two months pregnant and wants to get rid of the baby."

Audrey: "I know it is wrong to get abortion, but since it hadn't been my choice to get pregnant it is okay for me to get an abortion.

I am now much interested in pursuing a career. Pregnancy may cost me my job and career. I prefer to concentrate on my career rather than being a mother."

Susan: "God will bless the baby from your womb. The Bible calls children a "blessing". Don't ever worry about tomorrow. It is the highest privilege of any woman to be a mother. A child is a gift from God, and an occasion for celebration."

Nonetheless, Audrey went to the doctor behind Alan's back to get rid of the baby. The doctor however warned her: "Abortion not only kill an innocent human being in the womb; but it is also more dangerous to the mother than if she were to give birth to the child. Less than one in ten thousand pregnancies results in the mother's death."

 Audrey feared having an abortion and decided to keep her baby. She began to accept that she was pregnant, and that Alan was the father of her unborn child.

At work, no one noticed that Audrey was two months pregnant. She did not show any pregnancy bump, because of the type of loose fitting and comfortable clothing she wore, especially those that were loose around the stomach. That was the time when Mostafa proposed to her.

Audrey had to talk with Alan about her new relationship with Mostafa. She met him at their apartment.

"I want to have a very direct conversation with you to figure out our future together. I want to be true with myself and what I can truly be happy with." She started.

"Wat about." He said worried.

"Try to understand that I am going to marry another man."

 "What! Are you crazy or something?"

"Need not be disheartened. I know that sounds like a nasty idea, but it isn't that bad. Mostafa my boss proposed to me and I accepted his marriage proposal. Mostafa was more compatible with what I want in life. I always felt like I needed to find someone who could make my life stable. I wanted a partner who had money and ambition."

 Alan's anger got the better of him. "What meanings have you chosen to assess this marriage?" He yelled at her.

"I chose him for money, for security and for a better life than I had experienced growing up."

"There is no need to marry a rich man you are doing fine financially."

"I am keeping my head above water but never felt like I was secure. Money has always been a security blanket. I grew up without financial means. My decision to marry Mostafa is based on financial stability."

"Is he aware that financial stability played into your decision to marry him?"

"He understands that I am seeking security for myself. Being rich is not a crime but being poor is."

"You are greedy and ruthless. You are shallow and gold digging. You are traveling down a dark road Audrey."

"I will marry him for his money not love and he marries me for my looks. He is a multimillionaire and I am pretty."

"Aren't you ashamed of yourself?"

"I am not ashamed of it. Money can buy happiness depending on what you consider happiness. It is not wrong to marry a good man who can protect me and cares for my child."

"I will never give you up. You are mine now and forever until death do us apart."

"Calm down Alan and let's talk sense. Let's make a deal.

"What deal?"

"After marriage, I shall give you a high monthly allowance. I will deceive Mostafa into believing that our baby is his. This ensures our child's safety, gets all the benefits, and becomes protected and financially secured. You will not interfere in my life or tell my husband that the baby is yours. You and I will live our life without animosity."

"Sounds like a prostitution contract. I will play along with your games for now but on one condition."

"What condition?" She asked worriedly.

"After marriage our sex life will continue on at a similar pace."

"Not in your life Alan. Do not dwell in the past. Live for what today has to offer, not for what yesterday has taken away."
"I am the crazy guy that you should think twice about fucking with."

"I would generously give you thousands of dollars each month to keep your mouth shut. Keep your nose out of my life Alan. Do not mess with me. Do not let my demons out to play. Remember that."

Audrey assessed her future life with Mostafa like a business deal. She has settled things down with Alan. Now she will be filthy rich and live a luxurious life with Mostafa. Power excites her. She has met the man of her dreams. It is intoxicating to have a powerful man by her side. Now she has the whole world in the palm of her hands. The second step is to marry Mostafa right away before the early pregnancy signs appear.

Audrey thought of the life she would have had without Mostafa. She wanted to prove her gratitude to him by becoming an exceptional fascinating woman he would be unable to resist. She devoted so much energy to developing a far beautiful look and developing her flexibility with dance lessons.

They got married in Candlelight Farms Inn. They stayed seven days in the farm enjoying riding horses and the beautiful views of mountain ranges or cosy up next the fire.

Audrey realized that Mostafa as a formidable wrestler, needed passionate sex. Their nights were passionately hot and wild. He had sex with her all the time and would never be tired. He was super-hot, prolonged her pleasure, and gave her the best orgasm of her life. His erection was fierce, thick and painful. She couldn't think of anything else but having him buried inside her. His body was hard and hot spreading fire through her. His ardent kisses made her forget both past and future. The present moment's passion obliterated everything else. She has never experienced such a clawing need in her body, so much pleasure that it bordered on pain. He took her repeatedly, pushing her beyond anything she had ever imagined.

He drained her. She was exhausted beyond anything she had ever known, but she was ready for him. She was happy to see that level of complete satisfaction on his face after great sex. Sex was a mood enhancer for him. She loved to see that she was the reason he was smiling at work. She knew that he liked to see her sultry and sexy, so she worked hard to maintain her appearance. She trained herself to be flirty, affectionate, open and always ready for sex. She wanted Mostafa to always long for her and lust after her, and she succeeded in her attempts to please him better and meet all his needs.

During their frequent sexual encounter, his dark gaze held stark, raw hunger, ravenous lust and absolute command. She was trapped in his heat, in his lust, his needs and absolute command. His sensuality beyond her ability to resist. He played her body like a maestro; he dominated her completely and exhibited utter mastery over her. She accepted his dominance and welcomed his reign of power. She wanted this, a man who knew exactly what he wanted and took it, a man who push her further than she had ever been. She was now certain that she would never be able to pull herself back together and be the old Audrey she once knew. Something had happened to her and she never wanted it to end. She felt special tenderness toward him, and immense appreciation that he was her partner in life. She fell head over heels in love. He wooed her with his personality, with his charm, with his goodness. She fell into the warmth, passion and security he offered.

Chapter 37

When Mostafa married Audrey, a piercing pain tore through Daisy's heart. She had never felt so betrayed. Tears stung her eyes and blurred her vision. Tom entered her bed room to see her crying bitterly. The minute she saw him she left the bed and threw herself in his arms crying.

"Darling what's wrong?" Tom said concerned.

"How could he marry another woman without telling me? I was not even invited to the wedding." She said with tears coursing down her cheeks.

"Take it easy darling. He has his own way of seeing life. He cannot forget your past. He is different from us. He is no good for you."

"I cannot breathe without him. I cannot get him out of my mind. Being ignored, worst feeling ever." She said sobbing.

"Please don't cry. Wipe the tears from your eyes baby."

"I can wipe away the tears from my eyes, but I can't wipe the pain from my heart. It hurts when you want someone but can't have him. It hurts more when you have had that someone and you lost him."

"It was an experience of coercion dad. A bad experience I was forced to go through. He could have forgotten it if he truly loved me. She said still crying hard.

"What you have been through has prepared you for just what you are doing now. You are a big success now. Forget him. Look forward to the future, for the best things are yet to come."

"How could I forget him so easily dad? It hurts like hell to lose him. There are certain wounds that never heal, certain hurts that never leave you alone, like a broken bone that heals wrong and always twinges when it's about to rain."

She raised her wet eyes to her father and said: "Some people come into your life and you just know you will never be able to replace them if they left."

"He has never forgiven me for my past. A past that has been forced upon me against my will. Any past does not matter if he truly loves me, but he doesn't. He looks at me with his eyes not with his heart. I will stop crying over him. I will use my strength to get over him." She said wiping her tears with the back of her hand.

The river of life glided along smoothly between Mostafa and Audrey. Alan was receiving high monthly payments from Audrey to keep his mouth shut, and Audrey and Mostafa were busy displaying their genuine collections in the fashion capitals of the world – New York, Paris, England, and Milan. Audrey genuine collections had a powerful and impressive effect on the audience and the media. Her work was heart felt, genuine and appreciated. Her collections influenced trends for the current and upcoming seasons. In that year, Audrey won the "Best Fashion Designer of the year".

The painful split with Audrey, had left Alan deeply wounded. His job seemed to get him down and he felt worthless. He found the only way out of his inadequacy was going to the bookies and playing poker. As Audrey sent him high monthly payments, it gave him the confidence to continue with his obsession. He sank deep into overwhelming debt and was unable to pay up. His addiction to gambling made him imagine that things were not too bad and that he could pay the debt back, but his sick imagination led him further into the mire.

Alan called Audrey and begged her for more money.

Alan: "I have an insane amount of debt and I don't know how to deal with it."

Audrey: "I send you large monthly payments already, I can't give you more."

Alan: "I have obligations and commitments to fulfil."

Audrey: "What exactly, women and gambling?"

Alan: "If I don't pay the creditors they will take me to court."
Audrey: "You're a loser. Why don't you jump in front of a train and kill yourself?"

"Pay the money I need, and I'll be out of your hair for good."

Audrey: "You don't seriously believe that I am going to give you that money, do you?"
"If you don't give me the money I asked for, I will reveal our secret to a tabloid."

"Don't you threaten me, do you think you can just bully me around?" She snapped.

Alan: "I am not satisfied with the monthly payments you give me. You are in very serious trouble Audrey. If you don't give me the money I will sell our secret to a tabloid, I mean it. You don't have another option. You will do what you are threatened to do."

"Your insatiable greed for money is going to ruin both of us." She said feeling drowned by a black wave.

 She wanted to end it all. "Talking on the phone was not enough. "I will meet you tomorrow at your place at six pm." She said feeling a suffocating anger.

When Audrey met Alan at his apartment, she adopted this time a more lenient approach. He opened the door for her swaying as if on a rocking ship.

"Have you been drinking?" She said reluctantly.

"I drink a bottle of whisky every day, ha ha." He laughed hysterically.

"Understandable you're hurt, angry, emotionally in pain but you need to step back a bit and see it for what it is." She said trying to get him back to reason.

"We were together for a certain time span. We both enjoyed time together and both got benefits, desires, needs, want fulfilled." She continued.

"You want to hurt me and my husband. For what benefit? What gain? Is it for revenge because you didn't get me? I needed to be loved and I got that from you. I gave love and you gave me that too. These are good memories and though it didn't end well in that I am married to another man now. Can't you cherish the moments you had with me.? Embrace that you found love, sex, and great time for a while. Let me remember the good about you. Please Alan, don't destroy it all for revenge.

"Don't let me regret meeting you and falling for you. Don't think that if you destroy my marriage I will run into your arms. I won't. Let me walk away with good memories of you."

"What are you saying Audrey. Stop this nonsense. You killed me when you left me to another man."

"I am saying cherish what you had, move on and learn to appreciate our memories together. Leave me in the best way possible. Enjoy the memories, smile, and move."

"Bottom line. Double the monthly payments or I will tell your husband the baby you carry is not his. I want something else from you. Give me some of your genuine fashion designs to sell to retail purchasing agents."

"Are you out of your mind? This is a clear theft. I am loyal to my company."

"You talk about loyalty! What a cruel joke. You should have been loyal to me in the first place, but you deserted me for money. You don't understand Audrey. I miss the old you that cared about me and would treat me so well. I missed the old us, but you just left, like it was nothing. Fuck you for leaving me when I needed you the most, and now get lost there is a woman coming."

She knew that there was no way to shut him up but to surrender to his blackmailing by doubling the monthly payments and giving him copies of her brand new genuine fashion sketches.

Audrey endured Alan blackmailing for three years, yet Alan kept threatening her that if she delayed the payments as she sometimes did he would reveal their secret to her husband and to the media. He painfully pressured her, ruined her mind and put her under constant fear. She feared that Mostafa's image of her would be chattered if he knew about her secret.

A question kept lingering at the back of her mind and she couldn't brush it off: 'For how long she would have to go on sharing her secret with this being?'

After seven months, Audrey gave birth to a boy Mostafa called Ali. Mostafa thought the baby was born after only seven months instead of nine. This kind of irregular childbirth usually happens with pregnant mothers.

Chapter 38

Shortly before Christmas, Mostafa received an email from a customer with the subject line, "Your designs had been copied". The customer alerted him that a big-dress store had exact copies of his best-selling designs. The customer attached photos of the designs exhibited in the store. Mostafa scanned the store's website and, sure enough, it had multiple replicas. Mostafa had to take legal consultation, so he called Tom Wilson, his second father, and the owner of the reputable law firm worldwide. Tom asked him to come to his office in New York to give him legal advice.

Mostafa entered through the door of Tom's office to see him sitting at his desk reading some papers. When Tom saw him, he got off his desk and hugged him.

Tom: "How are you kid? I missed you. Have a seat." Tom said pointing to a seat opposite his desk.

Mostafa sat smiling while Tom resumed his place at his desk. Tom said laughing: "I know everything about your story. The media hasn't left a chance but to talk about the theft. But don't worry boy. We are ready for you.

Tom lifted the phone handset and dialed: "Daisy dear, please come to my office."

"Daisy!" Mostafa said bewildered. "Is she the attorney you are going to appoint for my case?"
Tom: "Yes. She is a real lawyer who does very good work for her clients. Daisy is a lawyer with a proven record of accomplishments."

After a few moments, Daisy came in through the door. Mostafa was thrilled to see her. She has put on healthy weight and looked beautiful as always. His face brightened up when he saw her.

Mostafa stood up and shook hands – "How are you Daisy? It's been long since I last saw you."

She shook hands with him and without smiling as if she were not interested in seeing him after such a long time.

"you look terrific." He said smiling.

She gazed at him in silence and ignored his compliment. She glanced at her father: "Yes father. What do you want to see me for?"

Tom: "Of course you might have heard that Mostafa's designs had been copied and..."

Daisy interrupted: "Daddy will you excuse us? I will take Mostafa to my office."

Tom: "Of course, darling. Take care of Mostafa as he took care of you.

Daisy: "Sure father, I will do my best to help him through it." Daisy sat at her desk and Mostafa sat opposite her. Mostafa took a good look at her in admiration. She was simply beautiful. His old love revived in his heart.

"I've been following your career over the past few years and I'm so proud of you."

"Thank you." She said with no expression at all.

"Well, how can I help you?" She said looking straight into his eyes.

Mostafa: "I want to file a lawsuit against Tom and Decker group holding Ltd for $10 million over trademark infringement. They copied 50 sketches of my designs."

Daisy nodded approval: "In the past, Tom and Decker has been criticized for its designs' similarities to high fashion brands."

"But how Tom and Decker knew about your fashion designs! Who is responsible for fashion designing in your firm?" Daisy inquired.

"Audrey my wife."

"Oh! Your wife's name is Audrey?"

"Don't tell me you don't know!" He said surprised.

"Have you ever introduced me to her? You didn't even invite

me to your wedding." She said smiling sarcastically.

He said shamefully: "Sorry Daisy, it was a rush wedding and..."

"Has she had any connection with Tom and Decker?" She said interrupting.

"Not to my knowledge." He said irritated.

"Maybe she was behind the leakage of the fashion designs to Tom and Decker."

"Daisy, how dare you accuse her of such terrible thing? She is my wife and I trust her. You accuse her without hard evidence." He said angrily.

"Easy gladiator. You are not here fighting in a wrestling arena; you are here to take my legal advice. Don't get emotional; it is just a systematic understanding of the situation. You got betrayed. Someone in your company betrayed you. The one who betrayed you is most likely involved in fashion designing and sold your designs to a big retailer."

Mostafa: "My business and personal relationships with my employees are based on trust."

Daisy: "And yet you got betrayed in your trust. If you had looked closely enough the signs were there but you chose to ignore and overlook it.'

Mostafa: "I had the feeling that things were not quite

stacking up, but I just didn't have the evidence to accuse someone in particular."

"Anyway, I don't see that filing a suit against Tom and Decker is a good idea."

"No. I want to retaliate by launching a lawsuit against Tom and Decker. Why this spirit of defeat Daisy? I want to fight until the end."

"I don't want to burden you with the financial strain that comes with lawsuits. The lawsuit could be settled out of court. This could potentially save the costs of a lengthy legal defence while also having to sustain your own business."

She rose up from her seat and stretched her hand for a handshaking and said: "The big store dealing with tens of thousands of products, may not have acted with intentional malice. Give me two days. I will make some digging and get back to you."

He got out of his chair and took her hand in his. A familiar warmth flashed through her, though he felt the absence of her warmth to the bone.

"Thank you for your time, I will see you in a couple of days." He said and walked up to the door.

After two days, Mostafa visited Daisy in her office. "Have you arrived at a decision?" He said sitting opposite her.

"I emailed them warning that before the law this was

considered a theft. They apologized saying that they relied on a manufacturer and wholesaler of dresses to stock their stands."

"So!"

"They removed the products from their store and site."

"It is shocking to see years of hard work given to another firm in an instant. They should have known the origins of everything that they sell. They should have known about their supplier's activities, before concluding the deal. I want to file a lawsuit against them."

"Stop being rushed. Going up in court against a retail giant is often financially unviable. Similar cases had been widely knocked off in court. To be spending such a big portion of your budget on legal fees when you should have been growing your brands is very difficult. You should drop this strategy."

"What is your opinion then? Have you arrived at a decision yet?

"It is my opinion that existing laws are failing the fashion industry and should be improved. In our country fashion doesn't enjoy the same protection afforded to creative media like art, literature or film, because clothes, shoes and bags are categorised as "functional items," which are exempt from copyright laws. Also, a lack of harmonisation between the laws in different countries makes it difficult for brands to protect their designs across markets. You may disagree with me, but copying is the engine driving the fashion industry."

"How come that copying benefit fashion?"

"Copying help create trends, and then help destroy them, paving the way for new ones to take their place. So, as you see, without copying, the fashion industry would be smaller, weaker and less powerful. When a new design first appears on the catwalk, its high price means that only elite customers can afford it. When the design is copied, it signals to the market that this is going to be a trend, and even more copies are produced."

"Yes, but copying my fashion really waters everything down. It makes our ideas less special, which ultimately hurts our business and our authenticity."

"Please try to understand. Buyers do want to engage with interesting suppliers. When a major retailer lists a start-up's products, it can be the turning point. Sudden exposure to a much larger audience often provides a catalyst for next-stage business growth."

"You mean my firm and Tom and Decker have to work together?"

"Today's changing landscape of business involves integrating with its immediate surroundings, looking for possibilities of transformation, and being one with the economic facet, while remaining true to the core of the business. Being a survivor in the business world means having the ability to cooperate directly or indirectly with other business models. By focusing on cooperation instead of competition, we keep the ecology of the business world diverse and healthy. There's no need for anyone to claim a generalized top position. We must work together to make the system function.

"Behind many successful companies lies a successful supply chain. Tom and Decker are a giant luxury conglomerate. They have built multi-billion-dollar businesses reproducing the latest catwalk creations for a fraction of their original price. This copycat economy keeps the wheels of the industry turning. Their market is huge, and they can buy directly from you and consume all your products. Severe competition in fashion industry is an incredible catalyst for you to come together. What you need is agreement in writing."

After a long thought he finally said: "That sound reasonable? I authorize you to deal with them on my behalf. Negotiate the right deal with them. If they accept, write a contract that meets all our requirements. I will check the details before signing up."

Daisy sealed a deal that offered specific advantages to Janet-Berry customers. Customers now have Tom and Decker as a single supplier who will provide the most-up-to-date fashion developed from Janet-Berry. Tom and Decker will offer the widest range of genuine fashion designs from Janet-Berry to meet the most diverse set of requirements. Janet-Berry will benefit from Tom and Decker's efficient retail distribution centres across America.

Chapter 39

Mostafa met Tom and Decker's lawyer at Daisy's office where he signed the deal. After the lawyer left, he sat chatting with Daisy.

Sitting across her, she contemplated his extraordinary physical beauty and elegance. He was even more beautiful than she has ever remembered. A little old perhaps, the lines of his jaw stronger and more angular.

He looked her straight in the eye. She looked mature, her figure slimmer, she is so beautiful yet so sad.

"Is something wrong?" He said concerned.

"No, I am just tired." She said trying to hide her sorrow.

"You are more beautiful than you have ever been." He said smiling.

Her heart pounded, and her mouth went dry when he said those words. She wanted to race forward without a second thought, flinging herself into his arms. But no. No more emotional distress, no more poignant pulls from the past.

She didn't say a word, she fell into a deep silence. Her eyes were hard and cold. Her lips were rigid and compressed.

Her eyebrows gave a stern expression to her countenance.

"We are still friends eh?" He said breaking the silence.

"No, we are not friends. You are not the friend who would always love the imperfect me, the wrong me. Can you mend where my heart is broken, can you erase the fears of my past and forgive?" A look of regret covered her face.

"I hate your flaws and imperfections Daisy. They ruined our life together."

"Life is not always perfect; like a road, it has many bends, ups and down. We are all damaged in our own way. Nobody is perfect."

"I hate your past Daisy. I can't get over the hurt and betrayal I felt from what you did in the past. I just can't imagine how an amazing, beautiful talented woman like you could have done anything that ugly."

She fell silent and eyed him with bitterness.

"I have known defeat, known suffering, known struggle, known loss. It is a fight to let go of a past that refuses to withdraw its sticky tentacles from my present. The world has messed me so bad I don't even know what I am anymore." She said bitterly.

"Sorry for the times I was not there for you. Sorry for the times I hurt you and for every other reason you are so angry with me. I promise to try to be better in the future."

"You ignored me. When you left me and gone, I stood in great darkness, frozen, broken and shattered into pieces.

You taught me to live without you. I honestly completely forgot about you."

"Never forget who was there for you when no one else was."

"I am moving on with my life without you. I am trying to make it better piece by piece." Tears came to her eyes.

"Do you still have feelings for me? Have I ever crossed your mind?"

"You don't cross my mind, you live in it. You do not know how special you are to me. I loved you because you have brought me back to life."

"I still care about you. I may not get to see you as often as I like, but deep inside my heart I truly know, you are the one that I love."

"Why did you marry her? What did you see in her? A woman with no past? A woman pure and untouched? Do you truly love her?" She said with a bleeding heart.

"She is attractive, beautiful, confident and loyal. She cares for me, loves me unconditionally. I need sex in my life- just being honest."

She said sobbing: "Why did you marry her, because I am

a whore and she is pure and untouched? You called me a whore remember?

"Please Daisy let us not get into that. Forgive me if you were offended by my stupid anger. I never intended for things to go that far."

"You should have accepted me for who I am, not who you wanted me to be. All that happened was against my will. I was being forced to do that and you knew it. How was it so easy for you to just walk away? Did I mean that little to you? Do you even realize how bad you hurt me?

"Please try to understand. There was the pit that I would feel in my gut at the thought of you being that intimate with some strangers. The past matters when it comes to deciding the future. I wanted my spouse to be pure of heart, mind, and body."

"I am not afraid of my past anymore. I will not omit pieces of me to make you love me. What did I ever do to deserve this pain? Why wasn't I worth enough to be your wife? You left me and married twice without even inviting me to your weddings. You treated me like shit. I would rather die in misery and pain than love you again. One day you will look back and realize how much I loved you. I might have been worthless to you, but you will miss me, when I become priceless to another."

"One day you will find someone better than me. Someone who doesn't care about your past because he wants to be your future."

"Remember, I didn't walk away, you let me go. I am going to erase you and leave you behind just as you did to me. I will find a man better than you could ever be."

"You seem to forget that you have broken every promise we made, and I have loved you just the same. I am protective over the woman I love, and I get jealous when she flirts with other guys."

"I wish I had never met you then there would be no need for pain or tears. No need for everything you have done to make me feel like absolutely nothing. I will move on with my life. I will look forward to a future you have no place in it."

"Now please leave and don't come back. Forget what we had. I no longer have the energy for meaningless relationship or unnecessary conversations." She said pointing to the door.

Chapter 40

Audrey's head had been pounding before she had gotten out of bed that morning, but even after a hefty dose of aspirin, it continued to thump.

 Late in the afternoon, Audrey got a call from Alan.

"The monthly payments are not enough to cover my debts. I need two million dollars now." Alan said with an unsteady voice.

Audrey shouted at him: "I don't take well to being blackmailed you miserable drunkard."

"Then I will make your life miserable. You got that? I don't seriously believe that you got any choice in the matter. Comply with my demand or I am going to make sure that you don't have no peace, no happiness, not a moment's rest or respite."

"You are simply threatening to ruin my life, my reputation unless I pay you $2 million!"

 "I don't have time to listen to your screams. Two million dollars to be exact and I want them now. Do not forget." He hung up.

Audrey felt she was walking through a den of lions with raw meat wrapped around her. The asking price was just beyond the range she could afford. She will lose all her savings, her respect. All her friends and employees will turn on her like a pack of dogs. She will lose her luxurious peaceful life and above all Mostafa's respect. Mostafa's life will be thrown into turmoil. He will become the focus of world press attention.

Audrey completely fell apart. She must meet Alan in person to convince him not to reveal their secret. She went to his apartment to make peace with him. He opened the door for her nearly naked with a bottle of whisky in his hand. "Did you bring the money I asked for?" He said swaying dramatically.

"I came to talk some sense into your head. Can I come in?" "Of course you can." He said watching her shapely, curvy hips as she walked in. He walked behind her swaying from side to side. He appeared to be on the verge of collapsing.

"You take alcohol like a fish to water. Are you okay?" She demanded".

He took a large gulp of whisky and said: "Alcohol makes me feel relaxed and mellow. I start with speed and liquor, then take a tranquilizer to calm myself down, then more speed to give me energy, then more liquor to relax in to reach the summit of clarity. So, as you see, I am ready for you. Have you brought the money?"

"Alan, please try to understand. I can't afford the money

you asked for. Be reasonable, let's talk."

"And how would I survive when I can't pay my debts? You don't give a fuck about me." He said with anger rising.

"Don't ask me to give you my hard-earned money to sit around and do drugs all day! I cannot afford those damn things. Stop borrowing money from me and borrow instead some sense of responsibility."

"You made me feel like a worthless piece of shit again. You ow me money bitch."

I don't owe you shit! I been buying your silence all this time and now you trying to talk shit? I ow you a bullet, that's what I ow you."

"I feel so fucked up. You betrayed me, and I am going to torture you, you slimy ass bitch." He screamed at her.

He punched her in the face sending her head slamming into the wall behind her. His face started to spin before her, and she realized with horrible clarity that she was going to pass out. She closed her eyes to drive her pain away.

"Look at me when I am talking to you." He said as he reared his hand back and slapped her across the face. He hit her again, except this time with his close fist, connecting squarely with her cheek bone.

He yelled at her while repeatedly punching her face: "It was your entire fault. You made me feel that you really love me and then you just left as if it was nothing. You gave our love away just for money. You are such a fucking bitch. Fuck you and all the shit you put me through."

"Come, let's have a good fuck as we did in the old days." He said grabbing her shoulders and kissing her on her mouth. She tried to push him away, but he held her tight.

"Get your dirty hands off me you make me sick. I bleed to death before I would let you touch me." She cried.

"You are a pig." She said scratching his face and punching him as hard as she could in the ribs.

In a fit of rage, he punched her so hard that she fell against the door and hit her head. He then picked her up, threw her across the room, and started kicking her. "You are no different from any other bitch." He said.

He reached down grabbing her by her hair with his left hand, picking her up to her feet. He smacked her across the mouth with his right and kept punching her face until they reached the bedroom. He threw her on the bed and started unzipping his trousers and pushing them down. She tried to get off the bed, but he knelt over her and began kissing her lips hungrily.

 "Let's fuck like the world is ending tomorrow." He said unbuttoning her dress, pushing the fabric open. Terror flooded through her, her entire body turning stiff as she struggled to free herself. Rage pierced her to the core. She struggled violently under his hands. With a wrench, Audrey wriggled free at last. She fled into the kitchen, Alan ran at her heels. She grabbed a steel knife from the drawer and turned around to see Alan standing in the doorway.

She yelled at him: "I will kill you before you ruin my life."

She sprung at him and both crashed to the ground. As he fell, she guided the blade between his ribs and into his heart. She repeatedly plunged the blade into his chest. As if that were not enough, she rose up, reached into her purse, pulled out a nickel-plated gun, and put the gun to his head. She pulled the trigger and the gun fired, sending a fatal bullet into his head. She dropped the gun and ran out of the apartment and out of the house. She rushed along the bustling street, blood streaming from her face, shouting hysterically: "I have killed him I have killed him." People came by and gathered around her. Seeing her covered in blood, they called the police. A patrol car came to take her to the police station for interrogation.

Audrey was arrested, handcuffed, and read her Miranda rights: "You have the right to remain silent. Anything you say can and will be used against you in a court of law."

Chapter 41

The incident spread like wildfire on social media – Alan Evans, a fashion sales representative was found killed at his home. His ex-lover Audrey Miller, fashion designer and wife of Mostafa the famous wrestler and owner of Janet-Berry Fashion House admitted to committing the crime, according to the police. She could face the death penalty if convicted...

Tom Wilson picked up the phone and called Daisy at her office. "Daisy please come to my office right away."

After a few minutes, Daisy entered her father's office to see Mostafa sitting on a chair opposite Tom's desk, leaning forward in his chair, his hands clasped between his knees, his head down with a dejected expression. Daisy sat in the chair opposite Mostafa's.

Tom: "You know about Mostafa's wife case of course."

Daisy: "Who doesn't? The scandal reached far and wide within our firm."

Mostafa was unable to hide his bitterness and humiliation. He couldn't look deeply into Daisy's eyes.

"Mostafa are you okay?" She said trying to look so cool.

"I thought that you could be helping me."

"How did that happen? Do you have any information about the crime?"

"Not much to say. I knew from the media just like everyone else."

Mostafa shook his head, as if the world disgusted him. He struggled to find the words for his feelings. "I am sad, angry, and hurt, and can't understand. Who was the person she killed and why did she kill him? She made a fool out of me, but she is my wife after all and I must stand by her. I am concerned about my son Ali; he will be raised without a mother. I am living a calamity."

Daisy: "Of course you must stand by her. In fact, that is the way it should be. Your wife is in real trouble."

"I don't know how to deal with the situation." A look of extreme worry crossed his face.

"God is testing me. If God wants to do good to somebody, He afflicts him with trials. He is testing my patience and perseverance. Whatever has reached me would never have missed me. Daisy, would you care to help me? Would you accept the case?" He said unable to hide his bitterness.

"Of course. You came to the right place. Whatever it is, we can handle it together."

"I don't know how to thank you." He said with tearful eyes.

"I don't ever forget who was there for me when no one else was." She said in a sarcastic tone
"Are you still mad at me?"

She looked hard and long at him and said: "Let's not get into that please. What we are into right now is not personal, but strictly business."

Her words disheartened him. "We are still friends, aren't we?" He said feeling an ache in his throat.

"Yes we are friends."

"I depend on you. I put my trust in you."

"You can lean on me. That is what I am here for." She said encouraging him.

 "What are you going to do next, what details are important to you now?"

"I will get a copy of the police report about the case and try to find out the root cause of the incident. You look like you haven't slept in a week. Go home now and try to get some rest."

"When will I see you again?"

" I'll see you on Tuesday, in the morning, at about 10 o'clock.

"Sure. See you then." He said as he walked out of the room.

Daisy got a permission from the judge to see Audrey who was held in a remand prison until trial. Audrey arrived to the visiting room with a female guard. She looked gaunt and disheveled. She sat at the table with clenched hands, and an angry countenance. She looked at Daisy with a severe gaze.

"Who are you? Wat do you want from me?" She said challenging Daisy with a stern look.

"I am your lawyer." Said Daisy.

"I didn't ask for a lawyer dumb bitch." She yelled at Daisy.

Daisy sat statue-like for a moment.

"I don't need no help from no goddamn lawyer." She screamed in Daisy's face.

Daisy raised her hands in a gesture of surrender and compliance.

"Excuse me," Daisy said as gently as she could. "I am here to help you. As your attorney, I expect you to listen to me. You must communicate with me. That is why I am here."

"Who appointed you as my lawyer?"

"Your husband hired me to handle the case. You are in serious trouble. You face a murder charge."

"There isn't no man-can save me. I don't need your help, I can defend myself. I am innocent. I have the proof. I killed him in self-defense."

"You lack both the skill and knowledge to prepare your defense. You require guiding hand of counsel at every step in the proceedings against you. Without it, you would certainly face the danger of conviction because you do not know how to establish innocence. You must talk to me. I can only work with what you tell me. I am not a mind reader. I cannot make it rain when the sun is out if you know what I mean."

"Are you fucking kidding me? I have already admitted to the killing. I have nothing to lose. I had lost everything. There was not anything wrong until this bastard destroyed my life, my plans, everything that I dreamed of. He made me live in fear. He turned my world upside down. I couldn't live with that asshole around. I wanted him dead and I killed him."

"Listen carefully to me please. Many strings are going to have to be pulled to get your case resolved. I must get your full cooperation. Please tell me exactly what happened."

The anger in Audrey's eyes was shocking. She screamed in Daisy's face: "I don't want to see you no more bitch. I'm perfectly fine sitting in my cell."

She stood and shouted hysterically: "Guard, take me back to my cell. Take me back right now."

At the appointed date, Mostafa met Daisy at her office to

know the results of her visit to Audrey.

Mostafa: "How was she?"

Daisy: "The situation is complicated. She was hysteric, unwilling to cooperate. She has already admitted to the police and to the district attorney (DA) that she has committed murder and she refused to tell me what her motive for the murder was. How could I handle her case if she refuses to talk to her attorney? With anything that important, the work is anything but easy. Obstacles, barriers, and road blocks are on the path."

"How are you going to help her?"

"My role is to ensure that she gets a fair trial, but how that can be, and she hides the true motive for the murder? I want to know the facts behind the murder to use them in her favor. This would help me prepare the best defense possible."

Chapter 42

In court, Mostafa sat with the audience while Daisy sat at one of the two front tables. Audrey sat in a locked iron cage, guarded by security officers. Bailiff announces: "All rise, this court is now in session. The honorable judge Thomas Clark is now presiding...

Judge: "Good morning, ladies and gentlemen. Calling the case of the People of the State of Connecticut versus Audrey Miller."

The judge addressed Audrey saying: "Audrey Miller, you stand accused today of manslaughter in the first degree of Alan Evans. How do you plead?"

Audrey responded: "Guilty."

Judge: Are both DA and defense ready?

DA: "Ready for the murder, your honor."

Daisy: "Ready for the defense, your honor."

The Judge asked Audrey: "How do you plead Mrs Audrey?"

Audrey: "I plead guilty sir, but I killed for self-defense."

Judge: "Is that all you have to say?"

Daisy: "Yes your honor."

The DA spoke his opening statement: "Your Honor and ladies and gentlemen of the jury. The defendant has been charged with the crime of murder against Alan Evans. The evidence I present will prove to you that the defendant is guilty as charged."

Daisy spoke her defense statement: "Your Honor and ladies and gentlemen of the jury; under the law my client is presumed innocent until proven guilty. During this trial, you will come to know the truth. The evidence will prove that my client meant no harm. She is not guilty of first degree murder."

Judge: "The DA may call his witnesses for cross examination." All the witnesses of the DA testified that they saw the defendant rushing along the street covered in blood and shouting hysterically: 'I have killed him, I have killed him.' They called the police and a patrol car came to take the defendant to the police station.

The police testified that during search of Alan's flat the victim was found dead with stabs in the chest and a gun shot in the head.

Judge: "The defense may call her witnesses for cross examination."

Daisy: I don't need any witnesses your honor. The defendant has already pleaded guilty and the DA witnesses confirmed her statement. I will concentrate on clarifying to the court the actual motives behind the murder because the evidence is still ambiguous about how the victim died."

Judge: "Yes, this point remains unclear and needs further elucidation."

Daisy addressed the judge and the jury saying: "No matter what the defendant has done, she is not legally guilty until the prosecutor offers enough evidence to persuade a judge or jury to convict. I am not going to lie to the judge or jury by specifically stating that the defendant did not do something I knew the defendant did do. Rather I will focus on the DA's failure to prove all the elements of the crime. Perhaps most challenging of all is the need to remind the court to protect the rights of the defendant rather than treat her as a docket number to be quickly processed and sent to jail."

Daisy addressed the judge: "Your honor may I ask that the defendant takes the witness stand?"

Judge: "The defendant takes the witness stand to explain her reasons for killing."

 The Bailiff took the witness to the witness stand.

Clerk: Raise your right hand. Do you promise that the testimony you shall give in the case before this court shall be the truth?"

Audrey: "I do."

Clerk: Please state your first and last name."

Audrey: "Audrey Miller."

Clerk: "You may be seated."

Daisy: "Audrey Miller, remember that you are under oath. Now answer my question. Did you kill Alan Evans?"

Audrey: "Yes," Audrey said softly, turning to look at the jury.

Daisy: "Why?"

"The simple answer is that he attacked me, and I defended myself."

Audrey turned to the jury and said: "No jury would ever convict me of murdering Alan. It was self-defence."

Daisy: "You are on trial because you stabbed Alan several times and shooting him in the head. Tell the court exactly why you killed Alan Evans."

Audrey: I had been taken advantage of. He blackmailed me over a period of several years. I gave him 6000 dollars every month, but he was not satisfied and asked for more. I raised the money to 10,000 dollars but again he was not satisfied and blackmailed me further for two million dollars to keep our secret safe."

Daisy: "So you killed him for blackmailing you. Was that the only reason for the killing?"

Audrey: "I went to him trying to smooth things over; instead we got into an argument, which ended up killing him."

Daisy" How the killing occurred?"

Audrey: "He was drunk and tried to rape me. He Kicked me and punched me. He threatened to tell my husband about our previous affairs if I do not have sex with him. Since I broke up with him just before marriage, he said that now he had nothing to lose and was going to ruin my life and my family, he wanted me to hurt as bad as him."

Daisy: "What good reason did you have for killing him? Is it just for blackmailing?"

Audrey: "My husband is conservative in his views about sex. He is Muslim and sex before marriage is not allowed in Islam. It kills me to think that he will never forgive me for what I have done. I love him deeply and I was so scared of losing him. Nothing in my life has ever meant as much to me as he did."

Daisy: "That could never be a sufficient reason for the killing. I mean nowadays, it is common that women sleep with men before settling down. Please tell the court the true story behind the killing. You must confess the truth, it is for your own benefit."

Judge: "Audrey Miller, you have been charged with the murder of Alan Evans. You have made commitment to tell the truth. If it is later found that you have lied whilst bound by the commitment, I would charge you with the crime of perjury."

Audrey spats. "Oh yeah, go fuck yourself."

Daisy amazed of Audrey's impudence: "You must be crazy to talk to the judge like that."

"Oh yeah? Fuck you too. I don't like to be accused of something I did not do."

Daisy: "Your honor, may I approach the bench?"

Judge: "You may."

Daisy approached the judge's bench and spoke out of earshot of the jury: "your honour I apologize for the inconvenience. She is hysteric and needs medical treatment. But before I resort to that, I need to make more adequate examination of the homicide scene and to make further investigations to find out more about the cause of death."

Judge: "All right, go back to counsel table and proceed."

Daisy went back to the counsel table and addressed the judge: "I ask for an adjournment to obtain further evidence your honour."

Judge: "The case is adjourned until next week to allow additional information to be prepared."

Chapter 43

At Daisy's office, Mostafa and Daisy sat to talk.

Mostafa: "What further investigations you are going to make. Everything is clear. She pleaded guilty and…"

Daisy interrupted: "The true causes of the murder are not yet clear until now. Audrey is hiding something from us. There was something fishy about her confession. The reason she offered for killing her boyfriend was not strong enough to justify the killing."

Daisy continued: "It seems that I am going to be your defence attorney not hers."

Mostafa: "You puzzle me. What do you exactly mean?"

Daisy: "I have a hunch you are part of the secret she is hiding."

Mostafa: "You have gone too far in your imagination."

Daisy: "Trust me I am talking from experience."

Daisy shook her head wearily and said: "I wonder what she might be hiding from the court." She then looked at Mostafa and said: "Now leave me alone I am going to be busy for the next few days."

A week had passed, and the court was in session again. Mostafa sat with the audience watching the trial. Audrey took the witness stand and Daisy interrogated her again.

Daisy: ""Tell me about your early childhood."

Audrey: "I was subjected to frequent, violent beatings by my mother and father, who used belts, a wooden spoon, and their hands to discipline me. The beating happened at times as often as four times a week. As I became a teenager, my dad would get rougher and rougher. He would sometimes throw me against walls and doorframes when he was angry. He knocked me out once."

Daisy: "How would you describe your father?"

Audrey: "Sarcastic, negative, critical, and gossipy."

Daisy: "Did you finish high school?

Audrey: "I dropped out of school after my junior year after getting "mostly D's and F's" because I had moved out of my parents' house and in with my boyfriend. I had to get a full-time job at a restaurant to pay bills and support my boyfriend and myself. I worked full time buying groceries and clothes for my boyfriend and helping to pay the bills while he struggled to find work."

Daisy: "Was he the boyfriend you killed?"

Audrey: "No, I met Alan in college after that. The man I lived with was three years older and did not have a job."

Daisy: "Was he nice to you?"

Audrey: "He cheated on me and abused me several times, but I continued to live with him because I didn't have a place to escape to."

Daisy: "How he abused you?"

Audrey: "Hitting, slapping, punching, kicking and sometimes burning."

Daisy: "He did that while having sex with you or without?"

Audrey: "While having sex. Finally, he moved away to Oregon and got a job."

Daisy: "Tell the court about your relationship with Alan Evans."

Audrey: "I met him when we were students at the school of Fashion Institute of Design. After graduation, I moved to his apartment and lived with him."

Daisy: "For how many years did you live with him?"

Audrey: "Six or seven years."

Daisy: "Did you have sex with him?"

Audrey highly irritated "Yes."

Daisy: "What kind of sex? Was it normal or abusive?"

Judge: "Is that a necessary question?"

Daisy: "Yes your honour. It is an assumption question necessary for the argument."

Judge: "The defendant can answer to the question."

Audrey stared at Daisy furiously and retorted: "You are a bit of a cunt you know."

Daisy: "Being offensive to me does not help. Answer the question please."

Audrey shouted at the judge and pointing her finger at Daisy: "This woman is crazy, and you agree with her? Go fuck yourself."

Judge: "You have acted in a manner, which disrupts the administration of justice. Behave or I will hold you in contempt of court."

 Daisy: "Please answer the question. What kind of sex you had with Alan Evans was it normal or abusive?"

Audrey furious: "We had wild crazy sex all the time. We had sex in the car, sex on the tennis court, sex when we got home, sex up and down the stairs, sex everywhere, all the time. Are you satisfied now bitch?"

Daisy: "Your honour, I have made further investigations and I came to crucial facts that would reveal the secrets the defendant was hiding from the court. My questions to the defendant are to clarify any confusing testimony for the jury.

Judge: "Please proceed."

Daisy: "Audrey Miller, please remember that you are under oath and I will expect you to answer my questions honestly and accurately to the best of your knowledge. The police found in Alan Evan's apartment fashion sketches signed with your name. How these sketches reached your boy friend's apartment?"

Audrey: "Alan threatened that if I don't give him the sketches he would reveal our relationship to my husband, so I gave the sketches to him."

Daisy: "So you bribed him with money and the sketches to shut him up?"

Audrey: "Yes, I had to."

Daisy: "Normal childbirth lasts about 40 weeks. A baby born three or more weeks early is premature and is at risk for problems. Doctors and nurses often call premature babies "preemies." When a baby is born too early, his or her major organs are not fully formed. This can cause health problems. Babies, who are born closer to 32 weeks just over 7 months, may not be able to eat, breathe, or stay warm on their own.

The doctors watch them closely for infections and changes in breathing and heart rate. Until they can maintain their body heat, and as they haven't had the full amount of time to develop vital organs, the premature babies are kept warm in special neonatal intensive care units. None of these happened to the defendant's son because he was born healthy and after nine months pregnancy."

Audrey shouted defiantly at Daisy: "Liar. I gave birth to my son after 7 months pregnancy not nine. Where did you get that information, from Alan? He is already dead. Did someone give you information that I gave birth after 9 months pregnancy? Do you have a witness?

Daisy: "Yes, there is a witness. One who can prove that you were lying to your husband, to the court and to the jury."

Judge: The defence got a witness?"

Daisy: "Yes your honour. I have a witness who will take stand and testify."

Judge: "Call your witness."

Daisy called Susan, the landlord to the witness stand.

Daisy: "The defendant claims that she delivered her baby after 7 months pregnancy. What would you say to the court about that?"

Susan: "I knew the defendant and Alan, her boyfriend for several years. Alan rented an apartment in my building and

Audrey lived with him. They quarrelled a lot and I was like a mother to them trying to help them tame their tempers. One of their quarrels was about Audrey's pregnancy. She was two months pregnant and wanted to terminate her pregnancy, but Alan wanted the baby. I advised her to keep the baby."

Daisy: "Why she wanted to get rid of the baby?"

Susan: "As a professional, high-earning, independent woman, she thought pregnancy would jeopardize her career."

Daisy: "does that mean she was two months pregnant when she married her husband?"

Susan: "Yes. I heard about her marriage three weeks later."

Audrey screamed: "Your honour, the witness is lying."

Judge: "Calm down you are hysterical?

Audrey spat. "Oh yeah?" She shouted. "Well, so is your grandma."

Judge: If you don't calm down and behave, I will sentence you to two years in prison for contempt of court."

Daisy: "I went to the hospital where the defendant delivered her baby. I contacted the medical records department and went over defendant's birth notes. The records revealed that she was nine months pregnant and gave birth to a healthy baby boy. She faked being pregnant for 7 months to mislead her husband that the boy was his. And who the boy's father really was, none other than the boyfriend she killed. I present to court this official document as a proof that the defendant gave birth to a healthy child after nine months pregnancy." Daisy said while placing the document before the judge.

Real fear began to paralyze Audrey's mind. Her heart pounded hard almost bursting through her chest. Her eyes bulged from their sockets. She screamed at Daisy: "You crazy maniac how could you say this shit?"

Mostafa looked miserable and very disappointed. He was taken aback to realize how far he was cheated on. A healthy relationship cannot exist without trust. He was living with Audrey an unhealthy, dysfunctional relationship. He wiped his hand over his face, his hand came back damp.

Daisy: "Your honour. I ask for a Court-Ordered DNA Paternity Test."

Judge: "the defence explains to the court how relevant this test to the case is."

Daisy: "A DNA paternity test would be required to prove that Alan Evans, the deceased, is the biological father and not the defendant's husband. This would involve testing the child, the mother, the real father and the husband to see how closely related their DNA is."

Judge: "The court order the biological mother, the man who may be the father, the child and the husband to have paternity tests. The court is adjourned until the next week."

Chapter 44

The DNA samples from Audrey, Mostafa and the baby were collected from buccal swabs. The destruction of soft tissues takes place shortly after death and is due to the action of micro-organisms on the body, which will rapidly cause a breakdown of the cells and the cell nucleus. To avoid any degradation of DNA, the DNA samples from Alan whose corpse was lain frozen in the morgue, were taken from hair and bone.

The results showed that Alan's DNA matched Audrey's son and not Mostafa's and so Alan was identified as the biological father. The court accused Audrey of lying to the court and of deceit and murder of the second degree.

Court was in session again and Daisy gave the results of the DNA tests to the judge as a crucial evidence that Audrey had deceived her husband by falsely claiming that her child was his.

The judge pointed at the DA and said: "Please proceed with your closing argument."

DA: "The defendant pleaded guilty before even the trial started. All the evidences confirmed that she deliberately killed the victim Alan Evans in cold blood. The victim was found stabbed in the heart and shot in the head. This is murder. The defendant deliberately killed Alan Evans to take away his life when she walked into his apartment and stabbed him several times with a knife and shoved that gun into his head and she pulled that trigger. She deluded her husband by keeping her pregnancy secret and robbed his money by spending it lavishly on her lover to shut him up. The defendants showed no consideration for the life of a young man who had a full life ahead of him. The defendant is guilty of first-degree murder. I call for death penalty for Audrey Miller.

The judge glanced at Audrey and said: "Do you wish to address the court with a statement?"

Audrey: "Yes I do, your honour."

judge: "Very well, proceed then."

Audrey: "It is with great regret that I stand here. My actions were not intended to cause physical harm, I was defending myself against rape and deliberate intension to ruin my life."

Audrey struggled to hold her composure and tears flowed down her cheeks as she spoke. "This day I stand before you and take full responsibility for those actions and accept any punishment that this court deems suitable and just. Regardless of that punishment, for the rest of my days I will carry the burden of knowing I have taken a life through maddening behaviour."

Audrey glanced at Mostafa and said: "Mostafa my beloved husband, the only man I truly loved, I hope with time you will be able to forgive me for what I have done to you. A last request Mostafa, please take care of my son." She wiped her eyes and took her seat.

The judge turned to Daisy and asked, "Do you have anything to add, Counsellor?"

Daisy stood up and said her closing statement: "Audrey Miller had a wicked childhood and a miserable youth. Being miserable during childhood has a special ability to wound, especially when it includes emotional, physical or sexual abuse or neglect. A troubled childhood can also lead a person to alcohol and drug use as a way to numb the pain, but Audrey tried so hard to get rid of the bad impacts and managed to create her own successful life. She struggled to adjust, and her tragic past had made her the famous fashion designer she is today. It's no wonder that women want to marry a rich man when so many resources are still not equally available to them. Audrey wanted to be financially secure, so she married Mostafa, the king of fashion and the formidable heavyweight wrestler who had never been defeated. But she done him wrong by hiding from him that she was two months pregnant with her lover's child. She betrayed her husband by deluding him into believing that her son was his. The defendant had no intention to kill Alan Evans willingly and intentionally, but she was just defending herself against her brutal attack and vicious beating.

Because the defendant does not have a history of legal problems; given her young age and her genuine remorse, I ask the court for leniency in the sentencing."

After hearing the final statements, the jury retired to the jury room to begin deliberating. After reaching a decision, the jury notified the bailiff, who notified the judge. All the participants reconvened in the courtroom and the decision was announced. The announcement was made by the foreperson.

The jury rendered the following verdict: "We, the Jury, recommend that the defendant, Audrey Miller, be punished by life imprisonment without parole.

The Judge addressed Daisy saying: "In addition to the jury's verdict, the court decides that the defendant's child to be taken into care."

After the end of trial Mostafa and Daisy met at her office to discuss the fate of Ali, Audrey's child.

Mostafa: "You were aggressive in the courtroom."

Daisy: "Because I believe that jurors will respect an attorney who goes all out in a client's defence. I consider closing arguments to be important, and I believe that I do them well."

Mostafa: "No doubt you are good at your job. He continued after a moment silence: "I love the boy. I thought he was mine. He is an innocent soul needing care.

Daisy: "His right place is in an orphanage. I can apply for a guardianship court order if you wish."

Mostafa: "What do you exactly mean by guardianship?"

Daisy: "The probate court appoints a guardian to care for the child and a conservator to oversee the management of the financial details of the guardianship. Sometimes, a court may select one individual to serve in both capacities."

Mostafa: "I don't want to be part of her life anymore. Begin the process."

Mostafa said after a silent pause: "My life with her wasn't supposed to end like that. You have no idea how worthless she made me feel. She betrayed me and made me feel like a jerk." Deep sadness washed over him as he stared blankly before him.

"She was a bad choice." She said staring intently at him to see if he has gotten her message.

He turned his head and looked into her eyes. He realized what she meant. She had made a bad choice when she married a pimp, and he accused her at the time of being a bitch, a whore. He then walked away to marry other women. Now, he had made also a bad choice by marrying a deceitful pregnant woman who had sexual relationships with other men he knew nothing about. Daisy's words caused hot colour to surge into his face.

"It seems that you are fond of whores. You called me a whore once remember. Now you married another whore."

She continued sarcastically.

He raised his eyes and eyed her tightly. "There's no need to be downright impudent, Daisy."

Impudent! The word infuriated her. She wanted to humiliate him and wound his pride as he did to her. She wanted to show him that he does not mean anything to her anymore. She thought by attacking him, she had opened the door to a debate she was going to win.

 She took a deep breath and shot at him without reserve: "Well Mr Wise man. Mr know it all. You loved me before, and then walked away because you thought I was a whore, but you repeated the same mistake and married a slut from the swamps."

 "You're pissed and looking for a fight Daisy. Please do not get that up. Some old wounds never truly heal, and bleed again at the slightest word." He said enraged.

"You walked away and left me scarred. Have you ever thought that even if I am Satan and an adulterous bitch that I still might be the love of your life?"

"Don't blame me for your mistakes. This is all your own doing, Daisy. You had sex with men behind my back. You left me and married a pimp without even telling me. He forced you to prostitution. Your dirty conduct disgraced me and brought shame upon your family."

"No one is perfect. Everything happens for a reason."

"But sometimes the reason is that you are stupid, and you make bad decisions."

"I certainly have made my share of mistakes. We must accept whatever life throws at us. We live only once – one life, no regrets." She said defying him.

"Why you are doing this to me? I never meant to do you wrong. I never meant to do you harm. Why hurt someone whose only intension was to love you? I thought you loved me as much as I loved you. How wrong I was. I never expected you to betray me like this."

"Don't keep putting the blame at my door. I won't have you talking to me like this. What is done is done. You don't realize what you have done to me. You left me just when I needed you most. I never thought you could cause me so many tears. You are heartless. You do not feel my pain. The pain you left me with was much deeper than you will ever know; it hit me like a hammer to my head. You made me feel dirty. What was I to you? A worthless whore!"

Sorry if I have said something that offended you. It was out of anger."

"There are certain things that respectable, mature individuals never do, no matter how angry they are. Calling your woman, a whore is one of them. You probably had been thinking and believing this long before you even said that."

"I am sorry. I am such a disappointment to you. I know I hurt your feelings but…"

She interrupted saying: "My feelings? Don't worry about my feelings, no one else does."

"You seem to forget that I was always there for you when no one else was. I stood by your side and covered all your mistakes. I did not walk away, you pushed me away, don't you ever forget that."

"Don't define me by my past. I am not my mistakes."

"I don't know where I stand with you, nor do I know what I mean to you."

"We are just two people who talk sometimes. Nothing more, nothing less. You did me favours and I returned them." She said picking up the case file and waving it in his face.

His body contorted, and hot pain slid through him. He got to his feet, bent over her desk and stared into her eyes.

 "O no Attorney Daisy Wilson. You did me no favours. I paid for all your services." He pulled out a check from his jacket's pocket for one hundred thousand dollars and threw it in her face.

He continued fuming with rage: "You laugh at me because I married a stupid bitch like you. You should have shown some sympathy for me, but you are ugly inside and out. You are pathetic obsessed jealous crazy bitch. Do not play the victim to circumstances you created. I hate you."

"I hate you too. I sure as hell do not love you, nor do I want to have anything to do with you. How could you do this to me? I will never run back to what broke me. I will not allow you a second chance. Now please leave and don't come back around here again." She was on the verge of crying, not so much from sadness but from anger.

"I hate all the men you slept with. They were dirty, filthy, stinking pigs, and for that, I hold you entirely responsible.

I gave you my all, you left me in pieces, and now you laugh at me because I married a bitch like you. You did not love me. Because you do not destroy people, you love." He fired back.

"You are not worthy. You do not deserve me. How can you be so cruel? I loved you more than you deserve. Why am I so fool? If I could show you how awful you made me feel, you would never be able to look me in the eyes again." He continued reprimanding her with tears in his eyes.

"What's the matter with you are you nuts? You can't treat people like shit and then expect them to love you." She screamed in his face.

"Love is giving, and I gave a lot. I have done my best with you Daisy." He continued feeling suffocated.

"Still, it wasn't good enough."

"What do you mean?"

"It is sad when you realize you are not as important as you thought you were."
"You have changed a lot."

"Why not? My heart has been broken."

He turned around and left the room. She heard his feet disappearing down the corridor. A blade pierced her heart as she watched the man whom she really loved, the man who always took care of her, leaving so sad and so hurt.

She shrank down in her seat. The trickle of tears quickly became a torrent. She buried her face in her hand and wept as she had never wept before.

Chapter 45

It has been three years since Mostafa last saw Daisy. They went their separate ways. He knew that he loved her but the thought of getting back together was the furthest thing from his mind. In his opinion, marriage is regarded as the end goal of a relationship between a man and woman. There are two keys to an enduring marriage. Love may be important, but respect and trust are essential.

He still remembered Daisy's open sexual preoccupations that placed her under his surveillance all the time when she was not in school. And he can't forget when she preferred over him another man. What on earth did she see in him? He was a nationwide pimp!
He killed for her. He helped her recover from a terrible disease, but she had apparently thought of him as a little more than a hired peasant boy appointed for her protection.

He had been seeing a house and kids in their future, but she had damn near crippled him when she had walked away and married that man. Yes, he still wanted her just as badly as he always had. But he wasn't ready to risk his heart again.

Marriage could never work out between them. Marriage needs trust, and this is the hardest of all, because if you have ever been let down, reconstructing the trust is difficult. Marrying her will drag the weight of her past behind him, and this will drag him down in the end. It's better then to concentrate on his work and try to expand more.

As for Daisy, she was consumed with the goal of becoming successful. The goal of success became her primary driver. But she was unhappy even when her planned goals were realized. Somewhere along the way, she realized that something was terribly wrong with her life. She wasn't just unhappy; she was full of sorrow. She climbed the ladder of success and when she got to the top fell off that ladder and into a well of depression. She couldn't navigate the waters of difficult emotions. There was a basic truth lacking, she had thrown away the only true chance of happiness she ever had. She walked away from Mostafa convinced that somewhere out there, a better, more exciting, more fulfilling life awaited her. She was sure she would find Mr. perfect around the corner. Only there wasn't. Instead, she ended up in a brothel with a pimp selling her body to sex buyers. He treated her as a commodity for personal gain. Mostafa, as he always did, came to rescue her after one year in prostitution, pulled her into consciousness, and made her feel like a living being again.

She could never find another man who can protect, understand and love her as Mostafa did; someone who was her best friend as well as her lover.

Now she is a successful lawyer, but she doesn't have one thing she crave more than anything: a loving husband and family. She knew she can't have Mostafa back. Despair enthroned around amid the desolation which surrounded her. She was not happy with her life and she continually ventured the same road of unhappiness never willing to change. She was so wrapped in herself, that she didn't have a motivational force to jump up of bed every day.

Stevens however, failed not to comfort her in her distress. He convinced her to have a passion, without a passion, her life will never truly be fulfilled. He urged her to squash these pessimistic feelings before they ruin all chances of refining her life. He taught her that optimism is the key to success. He made her enjoy the small pleasures in life: the smell of rain; happy hours chatting and dancing with him in bars and restaurants; getting home so late that the sun is coming up...etc.

Stevens offered his affections to her, but he knew that her heart belonged to another man whom she worshipped.

They became close friends. They were seen frequently in a sit-down dinner in a private room or chatting for a happy hour that extends into dinner and dancing later in the night.

WWE enjoys a large, dedicated following in India, with the highest TV viewership after only cricket. To meet the requests of WWE fans in India and deliver the biggest main event in the country's history, WWE announced that it would hold a special edition of the show in India. The live event will be held on December 8 at the Indira Gandhi Indoor Stadium in New Delhi. The event will feature Mostafa the legend of WWE, and ten of WWE super stars. The wrestlers will compete among themselves, while Mostafa will wrestle against Kasi Bansal, the Indian wrestler who won one of the company's top championships and held it for nine months. Kasi was the 45th WWE Champion and the first wrestler of Indian descent to win the title. Kasi was the talk of India since winning the WWE championship title. Towering at 6 feet 9 inches and weighing 115 kilograms, Kasi was a brute force in the ring.

In recent decades, with increasing exposure to the West, the Indian fashion industry had become a growing industry with international events such as the Indian Fashion Week and annual shows by fashion designers being held across major cities of the country. Lakme Fashion Week is a bi-annual fashion event that takes place in Mumbai. Its Summer-Resort show takes place in April while the Winter-Festive show takes place in August. Lakme Fashion Week is considered a premier fashion event in India. International models and Indian film stars usually participate in it.

There is a growing movement towards Western and casual wear in India as more and more urbanised Indians are wearing Western clothes on a day-to-day basis, although Indian clothes remain the default for special occasions.

Mostafa took the opportunity of being in India and decided to kill two birds with one stone: fighting Kasi Bansal, and later, runs a professional fashion show in Lakme fashion week in Mumbai.

The Indian fans filled the Indira Gandhi Stadium to watch their favourite champion Kasi Bansal fighting the undefeatable Mostafa and to enjoy the fights between the other WWE superstars.

The fans enjoyed the experience of being able to go and sit within yards of their favourite superstars while they perform their wrestling skills, and most of all, the competitive spirit. They watched tag team matches, wrestlers leaping off the top rope; wrestlers performing submission holds against their opponents; pin falls; wrestlers taking down opponents with wrestling moves. After the tough fights, the wrestlers performed less-stressful, comical matches to allow the viewers to catch their breath and take in the dramatic moment they just previously witnessed.

Quick bursts of explosions marked Casi's arrival. The crowd chanted, "Best in the world". A waterfall of fireworks behind him, arms up in victory, Kasi looked so proud of himself. Grinning devilishly, Kasi tore toward the ring. He mounted the second rope and displayed his physique, under strobe light. Casi climbed the ropes of the ring and took great big swipes into the air at the crowd. The crowd cheered as if he was the mightiest warrior ever.

Mostafa's entrance was simple but memorable. Loud cheers greeted his entrance and chanted his name. He walked down the aisle wearing a blazing black satin robe looking ready to destroy anyone in his path. He climbed through the ring ropes and removed the black robe; he looked massive with bulging arms and chest muscles. He was aesthetically pleasing to the eye. Mostafa walked straight to his corner, hitting at imaginary targets with his fists.

Mostafa and Casi put out a thrilling bout with their high-flying, hard-hitting, and sometimes humorous antics. The crowd was yelling for Casi trying to urge him for victory. It was a long match and it had to be finished. Mostafa delivered Casi a variety of punches and kicks, then shoved him into the corner and finished him off with a bull hammer. The audience went quiet and turned angry at seeing their hero defeated. But Mostafa offered a hand to Casi helping him to his feet. Casi grabbed Mostafa's wrist and thrust his arm straight up. "It was a very enjoyable match, and a fair finish," Casi shouted at the audience. The audience erupted in cheer and roared its approval.

Two weeks after the WWE show, Mostafa set up a fashion runway show in Lakmy fashion week in Mumbai. Because Jane-Berry is one of the top American luxury fashion designers, and because a formidable wrestler known among WWE wrestlers as the most powerful and the most handsome owns it, the show attracted hundreds of Indian celebrities and entertainers.

Janet-Berry Fashion House presented a completely modern look; the East and the West came together by mixing Indian wear with western pieces. The mixing of indo western dresses created a beautiful traditional look.

Indian women who attended the show were able to see how they could reinvent themselves without having to change their inherent style. The female models presented kurta and shorts, kurta and palazzo pants, Indian vest with western clothing, and dupatta with a Western Top.

As a growing number of Indian women are choosing to wear Western clothing, or less formal Indian garments, the female models presented kurtis, salwar kameez and Indo-western sarees of vibrant colours and intricate designs, thus reviving the traditional sari in a modern avatar.

Mostafa as a leading model participated with the team of male models in presenting the best men's suits and blazers of the season. He also presented with his models Indo western collection: kurta pyjamas, mag men's kurta churidhar, red dhoti and men's linen kurta.

The women stared in awe when Mostafa walked down the runway presenting men's swimwear: board shorts, swim trunks and swim briefs. His physique was visually stunning, symmetrical and proportional where nothing looks out of place and everything seems to flow and taper into a harmonious whole. His body represented what a bodybuilding physique should look like - flawless and beautiful.

The famous Indian actress Genelia Kapoor is also one of the famous brand ambassadors of Bollywood. She has made India proud by not just making heads turn at the annual Cannes Film Festival but by also being a regular at the great fashion shows and a distinguished guest on talk shows revolving around the world of beauty and fashion events.

Genelia Kapoor attended Mostafa's show and admired his creative collections. "Congratulations on the wonderful success of your fashion show. I loved your show. It has an element of classic sensibility exhibited with a modern understanding. You did a splendid job as moderator and terrific performer." She said to Mostafa while shaking hands with him after the show.

"I am honoured that Genelia Kapoor, the famous Indian movie star and India's most celebrated fashion icon, attended my show. How about having dinner with me tonight?" He said with a smiling joyous face.

"Of course, I will be delighted." She said cheerfully.

At the restaurant of Oberoi Mumbai, Genelia looked gorgeous in a traditional lace sari and a long-embroidered jacket. Mostafa looked elegant in white tuxedo jacket and black tuxedo trousers. The dining table was graced with a large vase of red flowers in the centre.

They talked while having their delicious dinner - lamb vindaloo and pulao.

Genelia: "My favourite thing is to have a great dinner with friends and talk about life. I like to be bought flowers and taken out for dinner." She said admiring the red flowers.

Mostafa: "Every lesson I learned as a kid from my father was at the dinner table. It is where we laughed, cried and yelled, but most importantly, where we bonded and connected."

Genelia looked intently into Mostafa's eyes and said: "You are a man of substantial physique and a fashion celebrity. Besides your handsome looks you have a wonderful taste and knows how to dress. Even if you were not in the spotlight, you look very elegant in an effortless way. If people see me having dinner with you, they will think I am having a love affair with you."

Mostafa: "You are a beautiful woman with a beautiful taste. Your gracious manner makes everyone feel warm and welcome." He said laughing merrily.

He continued. "Apart from being one of the greatest Bollywood actress of all time, you are also one of the most stylish female celebrities who managed to capture attention with your stunning fashion choices. You look ravishing in that dress."

She laughed happily at his words. She straightened in her seat and firmed her lips and said: "I heard about your wife. I am sorry that it has come to this. I am very sorry for what happened."

"Do not worry about me. I love challenges, be intrigued by mistakes, enjoy effort, and keep on learning. The wounds of my body have healed." A sad smile crossed his face.

"Are you happy?" He suddenly asked.

"As long as I can hide the real tears with fake smiles."

"It seems there is a story of struggle behind your words."

"I have known defeat, known suffering, known struggle, known loss, and have found my way out of those depths."

"From the moment we started talking I knew that you are a strong woman."

"I am strong because of the pain I have faced and won. I made mistakes along the way, but I stayed focused and kept moving forward. I love the woman I am because I fought to become her."

"I understand. You mean failure is not the opposite of success, it's part of success."

"Exactly. I am not a product of my circumstances. The finest moments are most likely to occur when we are feeling deeply uncomfortable, unhappy, or unfulfilled. For it is only in such moments, propelled by our discomfort, that we are likely to step out of the ruts and start doing what is necessary, then what is possible, and suddenly we are doing the impossible."

"I know what you mean. Write your own book instead of reading someone else's book about success. Predicting rain does not count. Building arks does."

"I am happy to be me. I may not be perfect, but I am honest, loving, and happy. I do not try to be what I am not, and I don't try to impress anyone. I am me. I love people, places, and things, as they are not the way I want them to be."
"What about you? You certainly had your shortcomings and flaws?" She said wiping her mouth with a napkin.

"Of course I had my shortcomings, but sunlight is capable of entering a broken window and illuminating a dark room. Failure keeps me humble. Success keeps me glowing. Faith and determination keeps me going."

"A mind that is stretched by new experiences can never go back to its old dimensions, eh?"

"Right you are." He said admiring her logic and her struggling through the negative circumstances of life.

He said after a moment: "I was just wondering if you accept working for my brands in the United States."

"Be more specific please." She said with signs of interest on her face.

"You sign up for the Janet-Berry fashion house to become its global brand ambassador for next year."

She paused long on her answer. At last, she spoke in a hilarious voice: "I will be happy to promote your wonderful clothing line in America. Thank you for the privilege of joining your team. I am delighted to accept your offer." She said extending her hand across the table to shake Mostafa's hand.

Chapter 46

In the New York Fashion Week, models walked the catwalk dressed in the clothing created by Janet-Berry designers. They walked the runway accompanied by a female voice describing the design, the colours, the cut and describing what sort of accessories could be worn and adorn the outfit. The show was produced as theatrical production with elaborate sets as live music and hologram.

Genelia Kapoor walked like an ostrich down the runway. She rocked the runway presenting Janet-Berry new collection. She marched all the way to the end, looked out at everyone with a big smile, turned and then walked back like she was late for a very important meeting. She looked elegant in the golden one-shoulder attire draped around her curves. In other outfits, she wore a light peach off-shoulder, figure-hugging gown with an interesting floral cape. She strutted in like a princess in the metallic self-patterned frock. Genelia also presented women's formal wear like scarfs, shirts, blazer, and trousers, and struck a style statement with her hands in the pockets. No matter what she slips into, she makes every look special with her style appeal and confidence. Kapoor received loud applause from the audience appreciating her outstanding beauty and the refinement of the dress collections she presented.

Facing photographers, Kapoor posed knowing her good

angles and how to position herself in a way that's flattering for her body.

The night before leaving for Mumbai, Mostafa invited Genelia Kapoo to dinner at Swing 46 restaurant. The Indian star sizzled in a floral print Dolce and Gabbana dress. The attire not only made her look graceful and demure but also accentuated her curves. Mostafa was dressed in a tuxedo that made women smile, whisper and think 'wow'!

The waiter greeted them and showed them the way to their table. Quite adjacent to their table was an empty table with a plain white reserved sign on it.

"You are a real gentleman." Genelia said beaming with delight. "You dress with taste."

"I prefer informal style, but this is a happy occasion." Mostafa said laughing. "You are an amazing woman with good heart. May God pour His love and warmth on you." He said returning her compliment.

"May this happy occasion bring in your life countless joys, prosperity and fulfilling life." She said elated by their victory.

"Thank you for the contribution you made to make our brands exceptionally successful. It wouldn't have happened without you." He said gratefully.

I want to throw my hands in the air and let out a big fat wohoo!!!!!" She said elated.

"You made the show especially charming and elegant. Your genuine passion for the show and your willingness to make our brands successful was admirable."

He looked around and said: "This elegant dining room is the perfect place to celebrate our success. What you should have for dinner?" He said smiling.

"Order for both of us. I trust your taste."

He ordered escargot for their appetizer, and for their entrée, he chose the best stakes on the house, with asparagus and huge potatoes. For dessert he ordered a slice of cheesecake with chocolate syrup and two scoops of ice cream. They enjoyed their dinner.

Genelia watched the dancers swirling along the dance floor with a wistful expression. "Would you care to dance?" he asked.

"I would love to." She flashed him a smile. He reached for her hand and led her to the dance floor. They moved with perfect rhythm. Her laugh one of pure joy as they danced on slow dance songs. One song played, then another, then another. After the third song, they went back to their table to finish their dessert.

Suddenly he saw Daisy entering the restaurant escorted by Stevens, the senior lawyer in her father's law firm. Daisy had all eyes on her as she entered the restaurant. She sizzled the eyes in glittering one-shoulder black sequinned gown flashing her long sexy legs with a thigh-high split. Brown eyes sparkled like a brown quartz diamond in her round face, and a dimple danced at the corner of her generous mouth. Their appearance was greeted with a slight nod of recognition by several of their clients.

Daisy looked amazingly beautiful. Mostafa could not help staring at her. He sat transfixed with disbelief, his mouth open.

The waiter led them to their reserved table quite next to Mostafa's and Genelia's table. The sign was removed, and the table was occupied by Daisy and Stevens. The waiter took their order, scribbled something onto his pad and quickly disappeared into the kitchen.

From the corner of her eyes Daisy snatched a hasty look at Mostafa. A smile played at the corners of her mouth and danced in her eyes. He smiled at her nodding slowly. But she returned her head rudely as if she didn't even recognize him. A battle of thoughts began in Mostafa's mind: she was keen to make him jealous; to make him realize how attractive she was to other men. She was punishing him, taking revenge because he abandoned her. He got annoyed because he detected a rival. He felt a feeling of desperation overwhelming him when he saw her with Stevens. She has found someone else more appealing! He got angry. He wanted to pick Stevens up and punch him in the face.

The waiter brought the food to the table. "People will travel anywhere for good food. I could talk food all day. I love good food." Stevens shouted happily.

"I love live music and good food." Daisy said elated by the catchy, euphoric song penetrating her ears.

"I promised you an interesting life and good food." Stevens said laughing. They looked like the happiest couple in the entire restaurant.

Caught in the spell of her beauty, and seeing her with another man, made Mostafa feel jealous. He was surprised by how jealous he felt.

Stevens words to Daisy, 'I promised you an interesting life...' showed that their relationship was going seemingly well! Genelia noticed that his expression revealed a pang of jealousy as he struggled to finish his dessert.

Daisy and Stevens ate with great appetite. They chatted and laughed while eating. After dinner, they sat there enjoying more wine, and they talked forever, trying to catch up on the latest. Later, they made their way to the discotheque, where they danced to the most romantic songs; They danced very close. They looked completely at ease with each other. Stevens held her close. Very close. Her arms wrapped around his shoulders and his around her waist. She looked as if she were enjoying every second of it. They danced with comfort and intimacy. They were like a pair of teenagers in love.

She was tossing her head with abandon, moving her arms and swinging her hips in time to the music, showing off her ripe curves. She was smiling with pleasure as she moved sinuously to the beat.

Daisy danced around Stevens, running her hands over him, at times tickling his ear with a sexy whisper. Stevens kissed her unexpectedly, and this really caught Mostafa off guard. She was tormenting Mostafa, she was driving him crazy.

They dipped and whirled and danced around the dance floor until the music ended. They returned to the table out of breath. They sat laughing and chatting tête a tête. Mostafa kept staring at her with disbelieving eyes. Their eyes met, she looked at him as if she didn't recognize him.

Stevens kissed her hands repeatedly. She kissed his too.

Mostafa's world turned upside down. Time seemed to have stopped and sounds faded, as a black jealousy overtook him when he saw her so intimate with Stevens.

"Damn it, I'd kill her before she loves another man. I will kill that bastard." Mostafa's whispered angrily.

"You love her, you are jealous because she is with another man, right?" Genelia said cautiously afraid to offend him by her remark.

"What do you mean?"

"I've watched how you look angrily at her."

"Oh no, you got me wrong." He said surprised at her sagacity.

"But you look jealous. I can spot jealousy a mile off."

"I don't want to bring up what might be a painful subject for me." His voice was gruff, and his brows were drawn together in a frown.

"You don't have to talk about it if you don't want to."

"Let us go from here." He said rising from his seat.

She caught his hand and said firmly: "Sit down. let's talk."

"There is nothing to talk about." He said sitting reluctantly.

"Jealousy can rip apart a relationship and leaving you awful. It would be a relief if you confide what you are feeling to me. I might be able to give you a good advice.

"I grew up in a society where it's forbidden for females to have pre-marital sex with men. I protected her several times from her evil soul, but she kept messing around with bad guys. And in the end, she dumped me and married another man."

"What kind of husband was he?"

"A pimp. He intoxicated her, tortured her, and put her to work as a sex slave."

"Did she know about his profession before she married him?"

"No. It all happened against her will."

"And you love her still?"

"She genuinely loves me, I know I hurt her when I left her. I was a stupid person who fell for her when I never meant much to her. She is just not what I want in a partner."

"Maybe she is trying to make you feel jealous."

"Is she making me jealous or trying to blow me off?"

 I know it's hard. This must be eating at you from your insides."

"I rescued her from her sordid life, but I couldn't approach her again. How could I and all the beautiful things I loved in her had been stained with the lust of pleasure seekers."

He stopped talking for awhile then continued with a frown: "I wanted to be with her, to create a life together, but none of that happened because of her. I ended my relationship with her because of her past."

"I can feel her pain. I was sexually abused in my teens. Being sexually abused might cause lifelong negative repercussions if victims do not find the support they need to heal."

"The ugly past comes back and tortures me. It was the hurt of having been wronged, of having had something taken from me that was rightfully mine."

"No one is perfect and we all make mistakes. Instead of kicking yourself for her past mistakes, cut yourself some slack and focus on a beautiful life with her. Once you're not carrying that anger and resentment, you'll be able to move on."

"And how would I do that?"

"Do you really love her?"

He didn't answer and looked away.

"Look me in my eyes and tell me do you love her?"

"Yes." He said looking in her eyes.

"Forgiveness is the best form of love. It takes a strong person to forgive."

"I can't forgive her for the obscene things she had done."

"I feel her pain. When I was in a situation that was empirically awful, I was frustrated, exhausted, defeated, and terrified. The incident took my worth, my energy, my confidence."

"But I know that now you are happy with your marriage!"

"I thought that marrying a man who was gentle, and kind would lead to a healthy sex life together. My past would then be "my past." But I was wrong. It's not that my husband did everything right to help me deal with things properly.

He said and did things in his frustration that sometimes complicated matters even more. But that was not his intent to hurt me further.

"I pleaded with God to either help me stop the nightmares and flashbacks I was experiencing or help me to die. I couldn't take it any longer. God spoke to me in a way that made Himself real to me. He let me know that if I was serious, the road would be tough, and it would be long. But He also let me know I would get to the point of healing that I desperately needed, if I was willing to take the tough journey. I was and I'm so glad I said, "yes" to God in this.

"I won't lie and say that it was an easy journey. It was a very, very painful one. And it took several years to get through. Yet, even when I was reaching out for help, I never truly thought I would be able to get to the place where I would be completely healthy and whole in dealing with the sexual part of my life and the memories that haunted me for so many years. I was willing for any relief that I could get.

And yet, I can honestly give testimony that God has helped me to do an amazing work. My past is no longer being dragged around in my life. I am healed, and I am whole. And my husband and I have an amazing connection in every way in our lives together."

"But still Genelia, rape victims should take responsibility for what happened." Mostafa retorted.

Don't blame women for bringing rape on themselves. Blame the rapist not the victim. It can be easy to sit back and blame her for what happened to her. Don't use that as an excuse to condemn her. It's time to understand what forgiveness really is. Anything can be forgiven. Forgiveness is simply giving up the hope that the past could have been any different than it was. We can instead accept that the past could not have been any different than it was. The problem is, we cannot go back and change the past. We are powerless to change what has already happened. It's over and done."

"I find it difficult to forgive what she put me into."

"The power of forgiveness is an amazing thing. Forgiveness doesn't happen between two people. Forgiveness only happens within you. Unforgiveness stays within you causing pain and suffering for you, and you alone. Unforgiveness doesn't create justice... ever. Instead of reliving the past and getting consumed with negativity, keep yourself active and enjoy the current moment."

"I truly do love her more than I would have thought I could ever love another person. I cannot and would not want to imagine my life without her. And yet every now and again the pain would return. I found myself wishing that I was her only one. I fought with images of her with other men. It made my mind recoil and my heart sink. At times I would feel almost sick, disheartened with the thought of what had gone on in her past. She made my life miserable"

"You create your own little drama out of jealousy. This insane jealousy is going to tear you apart unless something changes. Do not dig up the past; digging up sins that God had long since cast away."

" I can't extend forgiveness with one hand while holding bitterness tightly behind my back with the other."

"it's time to let go. At this point, you can choose to let go and make way for a new chapter in your life. Or you can stay and suffer a great pain that slowly eats away at your heart and soul."

Mostafa let out a big sigh and said: "Dear God, teach me to be careless."

With a heavy sigh he continued: "We knew each other as much as we knew ourselves. I always believed she was the one I would end up with. I was convinced that no matter how many times she screwed things up I would eventually come back to her. I know that she is no good for me, but as it seems I feel for her immensely."

"Don't close the door on a love affair that broke you.

All you must do now is to figure out a way to make things work."

Genelia said rising from her seat: "It's becoming late. I have a plane to catch early in the morning. Take me to the hotel."

On their way out, he didn't look at Daisy and Stevens, but glanced away. At the hotel entrance he caught Genelia Kapoor in his arms and said smiling appreciatively: "Thanks for everything."

"Anytime handsome man." She said holding him close and kissing him goodbye.

In his hotel room he was really annoyed and hurt. He didn't know why Daisy had such control over his feelings. He is still in love with her. The dust has settled after their separation, but his emotions are still high.

The night was pleasantly cold, yet he couldn't sleep. It was almost like she was in his room. He could hear her, he could see her, smell her. He was overwhelmed with feelings of distress and worthlessness. He was afraid of his own anger, he was having difficulty controlling his anger.

Chapter 47

A she lay awake on her bed, too early for a Sunday morning, Daisy wondered how she would fill her day. She will spend the whole morning in bed enjoying the steady sunlight spreading over her rumpled sheets. It will be a long lazy morning in bed with a book followed by a lazy afternoon in the garden.

After reading for an hour she decided to get out of bed. She sat up and swung her legs round, sled her feet into her slippers and went to take a shower. After showering, she descended into the kitchen for a bite. As she rushed through the kitchen door the telephone rang.

It was Mostafa calling. "Daisy, it's a beautiful sunny morning. I do strive for a good cup of coffee Would you like to grab a cup of coffee at Lark cafe?"

Her heart pounded rapidly against her chest. "Mostafa!" She exclaimed. "Please don't call me again, okay." She hung up before Mostafa said anything. She sat at the kitchen table and all her body shook from anger and desolation. The telephone rang again. "Daisy, please listen to me. I have something important to say to you." He said pleading.

All the emotions kept inside her from the day of their separation caught in her throat. "I hate you. I don't want to see you. You always hurt me. I will never get close enough for you to hurt me again." Her voice broke and she couldn't go on. He heard her sobs.

"I am truly sorry. Just know I never meant to hurt you. I missed you a lot. I will be right here waiting for you. Please come."

She snapped the phone closed and cupped her face with her hands and tried to control herself, taking in deep angry breaths that made her whole-body jar.

She arrived at Lark café at 9 am and saw Mostafa sitting at a table waiting for her. He rose from his seat to welcome her. He took her hand in silence and raised it silently to his lips. She sat across from him smiling sadly.

The waiter came to their table to take the order. "How would you like your coffee?" He asked.

"Ethiopian Long berry." She demanded.

"And you sir?" the waiter inquired.

"Black coffee without sugar."

The waiter brought their order. They talked while sipping their coffee.

"Daisy, we need to talk." He began.

"What do you wish to talk about?"

"Our life together."

"Oh, for Christ's sake, can we please just try to have a good time?'

"please listen I have something important to tell you."

"There is nothing for me in your life."

"I just want you to know that I still love you with all my heart, and even though we don't talk anymore, I still think of you every single day."

She straightened herself up in her seat and looked straight into his eyes: "What am I to you?" Her eyes showing the hurt her heart felt.

"You are everything I think about, everything I want."

"O please don't say that. I tell you who I am to you Mr perfect. You think I am polluted, unworthy of being your wife." She flung out at him, and then, before he could answer: "You can find a woman much better than me. I don't want my past to spoil your life and dreams." She wrinkled her perfect brows in mock distress.

"Daisy, I love you. Please believe that I love you from the bottom of my heart."

"I don't want you in my life. I have learned more about myself in solitude. I have realized the power of just letting things be. There is no room left for you."

"Just because you are lonely doesn't mean you should invite a stranger to your life."

"What stranger?"

"I saw you with that guy at the restaurant. You pissed me off when you danced with him close and intimately."

"You got pissed because you saw me with another guy. You are such a jealous bastard." She screamed in his face.

"Daisy, please don't screw it up. Nothing better than enjoying life with the same person you struggled with. You belong to me. You are mine. Daisy I am losing you." He felt rejected.

"I was never yours and you were never mine. I wanted you to love me the way I deserved to be loved. I don't need you anymore, I no longer misses you, you never made me a priority. You took for granted that I would always be there." Tears rolled down her face.

She said sobbing: "You think I am a tramp. But you must understand that I am proud of my scars; I am proud that I am still standing. I want to fall back in love with life again. There are men out there that appreciate me. No matter what you think of me, someone loves me."

"No one will ever love you like I do."

"You knew I loved you, but you broke my heart anyway.

You made me feel like absolutely nothing. You made me feel unwanted."

He reached for her hand and pressed it tenderly to calm her down, but she pulled her hand away.

She continued through her tears: "What hurts like hell is when you make me feel special, and then make me feel so unwanted."

"I love you Daisy. There isn't one person in this world that I want more than I want you. Please try to understand that." He said begging.

"I need to learn how to love and take care of myself as well as be able to do things without relying on you. I am the only person that will heal and carry myself through life. I will not give you the power to make me feel like I can't survive on my own. I am walking my own path; your approval is not needed." She said sobbing.

"Your concern was always my priority Daisy. You know that perfectly well."

"You told my father that I can start my life with someone else. You told my father that one day someone will walk into my life and make me happy. You said to my father that someday someone will come along to offer me his heart. Well, I have found the one you were talking about. I have met the person I am going to end up marrying. I am lucky in having found the perfect partner to spend my life with."

"The man I saw you dancing with! What' so special about him?" He said with a frown of disapproval on his face.

"He loved me for who I am. He is decent, uncorrupted, and educated. He says there is no pressure and he will wait for me to be ready, that we can have children, and that my past doesn't matter to him."

"He is not a good match for you Daisy. He is taking advantage of you by marrying into a wealthy family. You have to set boundaries."

"I don't think it is any of your business. Get off my back. It's my life not yours."

"He wants to marry a woman whose daddy owns the business."

His words infuriated her more. She wanted to smack his face. She said hoping to hurt him as much he had been hurting her: "Stevens loves and respects me. I call him in the middle of the night and he always calms me down. He makes me feel safe. He always makes me laugh, dance, sings romantic songs, takes me to long drives, cooks tasty meat for me. I will arrange my life around loving him."

"I loved you despite the fact you failed me every day. I was the one who loved you even though you gave me a thousand reasons not to."

"You came from a conservative world looking at sex from a different perspective. After what I went through you think I am not pure, pure enough to start a new life with you. But I must admit; you are so special. I loved you when you first came to our house. I loved you when you saved me from all evil, when you burned the brothel to hide the darkest part of me that no one else has ever seen, you even cured me from cancer. You are different. Beautifully different. You left your mark on me. My moments with you are to be treasured forever."

"I stood by you because I loved you. You ow me Daisy, you ow me a lot."

"I owe you nothing. And you are nothing to me. You broke my heart. Thank you for curing me of my ridiculous obsession with loving you."

"Don't be ungrateful Daisy. I pushed you to success. You finished college and now you are a good lawyer."

"My set back was a blessing. I survived what was meant to destroy me. I walked away from anything that no longer makes me happy. I came back fabulous, wiser, and stronger than ever."

She continued with tears overflowing: "I am beautiful and gorgeous in my own way. You want me to feel ugly, but I am perfect just the way I am".

"yes. I see you now stronger, smarter and wiser."

There was a moment of silence, and then Mostafa spoke:

"I love you Daisy but in my own way. We are on the same page but on two different books. Please try to understand." His eyes brimmed with tears.

"I didn't lose you Mostafa, you lost me. While you took me for granted, I drifted a million miles away."

"I want you in my life Daisy. I love you, I really do."

"You know how to shape your life away from me. You married two women before."

"I love you. I want to start a new life with you. I forgot all your past, let's start anew."

Daisy rose from her chair and glanced down at Mostafa. "It's no use talking to you. I am talking to a wall. You don't understand, and you never will."

"Wait, Daisy, I haven't finished talking to you yet."

"For the rest of my life you will always be the one who hurt me the most. Don't forget that. You ignored me when I needed you. You suck. Get off my back. It's my life not yours."
"Just remember, I was there when no one else was."

"Don't act like you care because if you did, you wouldn't have done what you did."

"I don't want anyone else to have your heart, kiss your lips, or be in your arms because that's only my place."

"If you love me, then remember, I didn't walk away, you let me go. You broke my heart, but you forgot I have claws."

She proceeded to the café entrance. He stopped her saying: "When will I see you again?"

"I am getting married after four weeks. I would be happy if you grace me with your presence. I want to share my happiness with you. Happiness is only real when shared. Now fuck off and have a nice day." She said walking out of the café door.

He stopped her saying: "I am not coming to your wedding."

"Sure, you will. I will invite you myself." She said heading to the door in quick steps.

He kept watching her until she disappeared out of view.

Chapter 48

A sense of affection developed between Daisy and Stevens throughout the years. They enjoyed social and emotional intimacy but not sexual. Stevens was not sure that Daisy loved him because he did just about anything to have sex with her as a prove of love, but she rejected all his attempts. Stevens felt horrible when she always knocked him back.

Daisy never told Stevens about her sordid past because she knew that this might ruin their relationship. At the beginning of their relationship, whenever Stevens approached her she became alarmed. When Stevens puts a hand on her shoulder her whole body shook with terror. "Don't touch me," she cries, "don't let your hand touch me," she screams and runs like a wounded bird, and her breath comes in little gasps.

Daisy didn't love Stevens a bit. She couldn't have the idea of having Stevens or any other man in her bed. She had lost interest in sex after the terrible experience she went through. But still, after Mostafa broke her heart and deserted her, she must torture him by having a normal life, with a husband, home and kids. She didn't know how to do that when she hated being touched by men, but she will move one step at a time. First the wedding preparations, which will take weeks, as for her life with Stevens, it remains to be seen how her boring life with Stevens will last.

She set boundaries with Stevens that must not be crossed. She said no to Stevens whenever he violated her borders. She totally avoided his flirtation and put the rules: no flirting with her; no exploration of sexual compatibility before marriage.

Stevens was perplexed by Daisy's odd behaviour, however, to him, Daisy is a special gift of God, a gold mine that would push his future further ahead. Forbes magazine estimated her father's net worth at $800 million. He is now an important partner in her father's law firm; a promising future awaiting him. He must be patient with Daisy and accept her strange behaviour until he becomes a member of Tom Wilson's family.

Daisy and Stevens broke the news to Tom Wilson - Daisy's father, and to their families and close friends. Tom was happy to see that Daisy was going to have at last a marriage home, a husband, and if it is the Lord's will she may cradle infants she can call her own.

The wedding preparations were stressful. Stevens was organized from the beginning and created a wedding folder on his computer, which included everything about the wedding.

They set a date, got accurate costs from suppliers, and checked the availability of venues and facilities. They allocated together the wedding budget, they put together the guest list, they chose their attendants, picked a wedding date and organised a small engagement party to announce their engagement. After the engagement party, they looked for venues for ceremony and reception.

After weeks of planning, the wedding day has finally arrived. Now it's time to invite Mostafa personally to her wedding. The wedding ceremony was scheduled for 2pm.

 Three hours before the wedding ceremony began, and with the wedding invitation tucked in her jeans back pocket, Daisy drove her car to Mostafa's little house on the hill. She was dying to see the marks of distress on his face when she gives him the wedding invitation.

She rang the doorbell; a maid opened the door. "I want to see Mr. Mostafa please." She demanded. "He is exercising in the gym." The maid said.

She walked forward to the gym. She knew the place. She was here before. In this house she spent a whole year in Mostafa's arms trying to recover from a deadly disease. Her heart raced when a whiff of his body scent travelled through her nose and to her odour receptors. Although the trauma of being raped was chattering leaving her scared, ashamed, and hating to be touched by men, Mostafa is the only man who can excite her sexually, boost her arousal and get her tingly and wet in no time.

She whispered to her tortured soul:" We have built too many walls and not enough bridges. Enough hatred. Enough desire for revenge. I don't know how I would have managed without your help. You the cliff against which my waves of anger and sadness are crashing. I love you because you have been always there for me."

She entered the gym and stood in a corner with her back to the wall watching him training. workout music blared from a CD player in the corner. She looked at him in awe. The look at his rock-hard muscle pleased her eyes. She saw before her an ideal body composition; an expression of perfect and ideal human symmetry and form. He wore black tight jeans, his muscled torso bare except from a gold mashallah chain hanging from his neck.

She watched him doing squats, leg presses, and pullups. He then shifted to exercises with heavy dumbbells. His back and arms were massive and sexy. It was impressive to see him doing some CrossFit handstand push ups against the wall.

After he finished training he began the dancing fitness. He turned off the workout music and danced beautifully in a rhythmic way, simply taking delight in his own movements.

Daisy was thrilled watching him dancing. His coordinated movements were pleasing to her eyes. She found herself attuned to the movements of his body. A fond smile broke out over Daisy's face. Just looking at him makes her smile. She hated that she responded to him, but how could she not? She loves him.

A surge of joy swelled within him when he saw her. He walked up to her calmly. He stood close enough for her to smell his strong body odour and feel his heat. Emotion swirled through her eyes. Her mouth dropped open, the air whooshed out of her lungs and her throat went dry. She

liked his smell, his warmth, his strength. Her soul calling out for his every touch. He felt her face warm.
He could feel a blush heat her cheeks.

"What are you doing here?" He asked with a frown.

"I came to invite you to my wedding." She said taking out from her back pocket the wedding invitation and handed it to him.

"And when that would be?" He said carelessly.

" After a few hours."

"No man is going to be in your life but me. We grew together. I loved you. I cherished you. I protected you. You are mine. You are my property."

"Are you crazy? How many times do I have to tell you that I don't love you."

He threw the wedding invitation away without reading it.

"Why are you being so rude. It's impolite of you to…"

He interrupted: "There is no wedding. You are my woman. You belong to me."

"You jerk go to hell."

"End this preposterous nonsense! You love me like hell."

"You mean nothing to me. I don't ever want to see you again."

"I never hurt you."

"You made me cry." Her eyes suddenly brimmed with tears.

"Sorry for hurting you. I never meant to be so heartless. Please forgive me. Without your love, I am worthless. Let me hold you. Let me heal your broken heart."

"Don't even try."

His gaze brushed over the cream of her skin, the long sweep of her lashes before finally settling on the lush of her lips.

"Let me make all your broken pieces fit together. I want to kiss your lips. My lips will ravish your lips, my mouth will burn down your neck."

"You wouldn't dare."

She tensed, her eyes checking for a way to run. His hand lashed out, grabbed her and whipped her into his arms, where he held her tight. She was intoxicated by the feel of his arms around her.

His long warm fingers infusing her flesh with heat that seeped through the fabric of her blouse and straight into her bones. She loved how his touches made her feel all excited and jittery and breathless, but she hated how a simple brush of his fingers could weaken her knees and her will power and turn her putty in his hands.

"You like it when I touch you, his voice was hoarse and rough. The sound of it sent shivers dancing down her spine. Her whole body tensed up. Her skin burned where he touched her, and the places that were untouched longed for that heat.

She stiffened and tried to pull away, but he held her tight. He pushed her backward to the wall and pressed his belly into hers. He then kissed her forcefully. His kisses were strong and hard as he gripped the back of her head and ravished her lips. She stiffened and resisted him, but he was a creature of fierce passion and decisive action. She tried to push him away from her, but she was just too weak. She sighed and breathed in the scent of his warm skin.

She pulled back and looked at him hurt. She slapped his chest with both hands.

"Don't you dare touch me." She stared at him in disbelief.

"You are mine. You are my woman. You don't belong to any other. You belong to me." He said decisively.

She looked at him hurt. But with a groan and a fierceness, he captured her lips again in a bruising kiss. He deepened the kiss, his tongue plundering her mouth. His strong male scent penetrated her nostrils. She tried again to push him hard with both hands, but he was rock still.

"I don't want you. I don't need you in my life. I don't love you anymore." She said nervously.

He kissed her cheeks, her eyes, her chin, her lips. She moved her lips away. He then slowly went towards her neck.

"Please stop. I can't catch my breath." She pleaded.

"What do you want from me?" She said trying to squirm away.

"I just want you. All your flaws, mistakes, everything. I love you. I care about you." He said looking deeply into her eyes.

"If you cared about me, you never would have left me." She burst into tears.

"I have never left you. I have been always there for you."

She said through her sobs: "You destroyed me inside. You left me when I thought you were mine. You left me when I needed you most."

The tears burst forth like water from a dam, spilling down her face. The muscles of her chin trembled like a small child. The sobs punched through, ripping through her muscles, bones, and guts. She pressed her forehead against his chest and sobbed unceasingly. He held her tight until she softened and relaxed.

All her defences washed away in those salty tears. Her wall of rejection collapsed. Moment by moment they fell.

He glanced down at her. He saw fear in her eyes. She said broken: "You left me alone too long. Please don't leave me again. The world is a scary place. Take me with you."

A single tear slid down from his eyes, followed by another one, and another one, until soon, a steady stream of tears flowed its way down his cheek, releasing all the love that has been held inside of him for all this time.

"I will always be with you whatever happens." He said while tears coursed down his cheeks.

"Promise me you will never leave me again."

"I promise to walk this life with you forever."

She stroked his hair and kissed his forehead. He stared down at her smiling with tenderness. The smile he gave her filled her heart to overflowing. Dear God, she loved him. Had always loved him and would never love another man but him.

"You think the scars of the past are going to change how I see you? Feel about you?"

She swallowed and struggled to find her voice. "It's ugly."

"You're beautiful to me." She opened her mouth to say something, but he leaned down and kissed her passionately. His fingers closed around hers in a warm grip. Strong and reassuring. "Accept who you are. Be proud of your body. You are and always will be the love of my life."

He knelt to his knees before her. He put his arms around her waist and fixed her firmly in her position.

"Tell me that you love me, Daisy, he ordered gruffly."

"I love you. I love you more than you will ever know." She murmured grateful to have him back to face any obstacles to their happiness.

"You won't leave again," she demanded, "No matter how difficult things might get for us."

"Never again," he promised."

Suddenly, she remembered her wedding which was due after less than an hour. If she stayed with Mostafa how would she ever move on with her life with Stevens. Stevens and her father would be so disappointed for her waffling. A sense of entrapment made it difficult for her to breathe. She hesitated, wondering if she should voice her thoughts.

"What's up?" He said noticing a twinge of worry in her eyes.

"I remembered my wedding, it's only after one hour from now."

"Call Stevens and tell him that you have found your true love."

"I don't know what to tell Stevens, it's embarrassing."

"Use your imagination. Rack your brains." He said with a sneaky smile on his face.

She couldn't help but smiling at his words.

"You look the best when you wear your smile. There is no beauty like the one that comes from inside you." He said laughing.

"I swear Mostafa you are the devil himself." She said laughing too.

"It doesn't make you a bad person to want to live your own life, but you can live it with me. Be with someone who is proud to have you." He said encouraging her.

She took out her phone from her front pocket and dialled:

"Stevens dear I am sorry. I just couldn't go through with it. You know, there is this guy…he's stolen my heart, wrecked my world, and calmed my soul. He is all I could ever want. And he is mine."

Stevens: "What is that supposed to mean? Are you breaking up after the invitations have been sent, the space has been reserved and the honeymoon booked?"

Daisy: "Planning to get married doesn't always mean getting married. Sometimes, the wedding ends before 'I do' – and sometimes it ends immediately after. "

Stevens: "How am I supposed to tell the guests there will be no wedding?"

Daisy: "Tell them the bride ran away the morning of her wedding day." She hung up the phone.

She let out a laugh, and he burst into laughter.

Mostafa turned on the song 'sway with me' by Michael Bublé.

"Let's dance." He said stretching his hand out to her.

Daisy hesitated: "I am not good enough. I don't really have the moves."

"Come on. I will catch you if you stumble, trust me."

She took his hand and they started dancing. He adjusted his lead to put her where he wanted her. She beautifully followed his moves sketching them.

They danced spinning and twirling, round and round; a skip, a gallop, a leap and a bound. Happiness flowed from within her, exploding up and out. A bubbling transformation from stillness into life. They swayed together to the lyrics of the song in perfect harmony:

When marimba rhythms start to play

Dance with me, make me sway

Like a lazy ocean hugs the shore

Hold me close, sway me more

Like a flower bending in the breeze

Bend with me, sway with ease

When we dance you have a way with me

Stay with me, sway with me the music stopped. He looked down at her eyes and kissed her lips passionately. "How about watching sunrise on the beach? With the sun rising above the glistening water every morning the display of colours is breath-taking."

"Whatever you say." She said resting her head against his chest, trying to catch her breath

Chapter 49

Mostafa and Daisy flew from New York to North Carolina to enjoy a relaxing week in his summer place on the beach. They reached the chalet by night and spent the night in each other's arms. She rubbed herself against him. The feel of her, the scent of her, the warmth of her body ignited a strong reaction in Mostafa.

Exhilaration coursed through him. His senses ran high. His massive body pressed against hers as he leaned down and dipped his tongue into the hollow of her collarbone. His tongue slid against hers. His kiss ignited something in her. The sexual tension was unbelievable. A volcano of near euphoric erotic energy erupted inside her. Every vessel in her body was on fire. Her body ached with wanting and she became fully aroused. She wanted him with a fierceness she had never experienced. She wished she had the courage to ask him to finish her off.

He was a minute away from exploding, and wanted to make, slow, sweet love to her. "I want you. To taste you. To feel your heat." He said passionately.

He pulled away however, fearing of what would become of him if they continued. "I hate that I want to slide deep inside you. I don't believe in sex outside marriage." He said apologizing. Silently disappointed and still horny, she turned her back to him, and spent a restless night tossing and turning.

It was already dawn. Rising, on one elbow, Mostafa gazed down at Daisy. She was so incredibly lovely, and he wanted her desperately. Her eyelids were long and thick. And her lips – those full, luscious lips. Her hair looked like brown silk in the shadowy room. He lifted a strand and brought it to his lips, then dropped it, watching it fall back to her shoulder. He touched her cheek with his fingertip, tracing the lines of her face, slowly, lovingly.

Whatever tomorrow brought, Mostafa knew one thing for certain. He was not going to let anything, or anyone hurt Daisy again. Not ever. He leaned over and kissed her tenderly on the lips, then drew her into his arms. She woke up looking into his black wide eyes and smiling.

"I like that feeling I get when I see you smiling." He said as he placed a tender kiss on her lips.

"Being in love with you is the most beautiful thing that has happened to me. It gives me the reason to wake up every morning." She said loving the feeling of being curled up in his arms.

"You are that part of me I will always need. I have you. I found you, and I'm not letting you go." She said hugging him close and kissing his lips.

 The first fingers of dawn rendered the light of the room grainy and grey. "Are you ready to catch sunrise over the

Atlantic Ocean? Dawn would soon break across the horizon."

This is what we came for. Is it not?"

"Yes, but not quite. Come, let's get ready." He said helping her get out of bed. Daisy wore sleeveless tank top, pair of shorts and pair of flat sandals. Mostafa wore Swimming shorts, pair of deck shoes and tropical shirt. They looked pretty in their summer dresses. They walked out hand in hand to watch the sunrise on the beach.

They sat quietly on the beach glancing at the yellow stripe of dawn nudging back the night sky. The dark sky began to host light splashes of colour. Streaks of pink, orange and yellow painted the sky before the sun peeked over the water and began its ascent to signal a brand-new day.

The yellow shining sun filled the sky with mighty colours of red and splashed the clouds with endless rays of pink. Bit, by bit, it covered the pearl morning haze with a pale, pure white light. The sun and its brilliant rays began to warm the air. She loved the feeling of the fresh air on her face and the wind blowing through her hair. A thrilling feeling of happiness swept over her.

"Every sunrise gives you a new beginning and a new ending. Let this morning be a new beginning to a better relationship and a new ending to the bad memories. It's an opportunity to enjoy life, breathe freely, think and love." Mostafa said. A look of awe crept into his face.

"Sun must rise for the darkness to sink. It sets only to rise again." Daisy said while enjoying the beauty of the scene.

"At every sunrise I renounce the doubts of night and greet the new. I love you. I can't live without you. My body and soul are yours. He said kissing her forehead and caressing her cheek.

"You are my shoulder to lean on, the one person I know I can count on, you are the love of my life, you are my everything." She said kissing his cheek.

"I want to feel free like a bird. Happiness is walking on the beach. Let's walk on the beach." She said rising.

They walked along the beach hand in hand. Daisy's first thought was to pull off her sandals. Mostafa did the same. They walked barefoot on the warm sand. The sand was gentle beneath their bare feet. Clumps of seaweed got washed up on the beach. They continued walking and stopped to collect interesting shells.

They glanced at the ocean. The ocean stirred their hearts and brought joy to their souls. "Let's smell the sea and feel the sky." She said.

They ran together to the edge of the ocean. The sea was jewel-blue. The sky was like a curtain of silk white clouds drifted past. The waves were rippling gently. They cooled their feet in the ocean.

"My God. I never knew there could be such beauty. There is no colour quite like this. To some it's just water, to me it's where I regain my sanity." She said mystically.

She glanced at him happily. He detected the formation of tears in her eyes – tears of happiness and love filling her eyes. His heart overflowed with joy.

"Happiness is a moment with you. Can we please last forever?"

When she heard his words, she knew that their love would outlast time and will endure forever.

They laid on the beach and soaked up the sunshine.

"You are the best sight of the day." He said kissing her passionately on the lips.

"So are you." She said laughing against his mouth.

His kiss tapped into deep mines of memory, and the years that had separated them fell away as if they were nothing.

"Kiss me until I forget how terrified I am of everything wrong with my life." She murmured returning his kiss ardently.

He kissed her again. It was a kiss of a man who had waited years for the moment and feared that it would never come again. He kept kissing her as though he never wanted to let her go. She enjoyed his kisses. She held him tight. She loved him being so close - the feeling that she was really wanted. His kisses were like a tub of roses swimming in honey.

He buried his face in her neck, taking in the scent of her as his heart rate kicked up. She flashed a wicked grin and pressed her mouth to his. With each breath, Daisy sparked to life. She laughed against his mouth as water splashed over them both. The sea retreated, and His body on top of hers.

Seagulls and pelicans flew by in flocks. The sun continued to move across the sky. The sun warmed the sand making it increasingly difficult to keep up, and they could feel the burn of thirst beginning to demand water. Their stomachs aching and empty, they went to a nearby beach café.

Daisy ordered scrambled eggs, toast, orange juice and coffee. Mostafa ordered scrambled eggs, waffles, cranberry juice and coffee. They ate up their food, drank their juice and sipped their coffee.

A butterfly landed on her fingers for a while and rested cool.

"Every time I see a butterfly, it reminds me of how precious life can truly be. To be able to fly away so freely and gracefully wherever she may please, without no one in the world to tell her what to do. I wait for that special moment in time when I get to live freely, without no worries, pain or tears. One special day I'll get to live my life just like that beautiful butterfly. I will no longer feel blue inside." Daisy said watching the colours of the butterfly admiringly.

"Butterflies represent transformation. The caterpillars go into cocoons and then transform into magnificent butterflies. So, the message is transformation in your life.

God has a wonderful plan for you, plans to prosper you, not to harm you. Plans to give you hope and a future."

"You think so? You mean my life will change for the better? I will have a new course in life?"

"Yes darling. Soon your life changes. You are about to undergo a major shift in your life."

"Oh! How is that possible?"

"There are moments in life when we believe that everything is falling apart. What we don't know is that at time like these when we feel hopeless, and at a point of no return, the truth is that everything is falling in its place."

"How so?"

"You will never walk alone again. I will marry you. Make you the mother of my children."

She stared at him in disbelief. Emotion swirled through her eyes. So many thoughts whirled around her mind. Wasn't that what she wanted the most, marrying him? And now she was afraid to marry the man she loved! She had done things that she was not proud of. She had a terrible past and she can't change it. She wouldn't get Mostafa in such a pain when those hurtful images of her past haunt him on and off.

She buried her face in her hands as long agonizing sobs wracked her body to the core.

She lifted her tearful eyes to him and said: "Marry you! Mother of your children! I am not fit for you. I am a woman built upon the wreckage of herself. I am a barren desert; I am infertile land. You and I will always be unfinished business." Deep uncontrollable sobs squeezed the breath from her lungs.

"Find another woman with less misery and live happily ever after." She continued weeping.

"I want you, just you. I want to pamper you in my arms."

Her head began to ache, everything spun around her. She felt like she might pass out. She closed her eyes tightly.

"You chose to love someone who is damaged. Maybe you can stop the bleeding and help me scar over but I will always be a little broken. Can you accept the dents and the cracks of the past?"

He left his seat and sat beside her. "I love you more than you will ever know. For now, and always. I loved you, I always did. I tried my hardest to hold on, but you didn't want this as much as I did. And now that I have found you I won't let you go."

Her forehead was creased with tension, and she kept shaking her head, her mouth twisting in dissatisfaction. His arms encircled her waist. Her face remained troubled, and she shrank away from his arms.

"Let me hold you. Let me take your pain away. He wrapped

his arms around her. He kissed the top of her head, stroked her hair, and wiped her tears away with his thumb.

"I have a bad past and..." She said with a trembling voice.

"But it is pure now." He interrupted.

"You don't need to do this. My past will haunt you."

"I can get beyond this by coming to term with it. I will let go past hurts and move on."

She sobbed at his words. "Do you love me that much?"

"I live for you."

"You don't care enough to look past my flaws." He held her tight and kissed her tears away. He was awfully masculine, firm, and certain in the face of her disturbed emotions.

He gently touched her face and gently dragged his finger along her jawline. A smile grew upon her lips and she slowly blinked. "You were hot that night. We would be good together I am certain." He said humorously.

"You always make me happy whenever I am down. I don't think I can ever forget someone that once was the reason I smiled. Can you make me smile again?"

"I am going to make you the happiest woman in the world. I will love you through all the ups and downs."

"Now darling, let's get one thing straight. Will you marry me?"

"It seems like we are certainly walking into a doomed marriage. Why can't we be just lovers?"

I've already waited long enough. You either want me or not. I want you to be my wife. Let's make some babies and make it official.

"I am afraid of falling."

He smiles: "I will catch you."

"Yes, I want to live with you for the rest of my life. I could die from the thought of losing you again. You are all I need."

He kissed her lips tenderly. "Nothing you wear is more important than your smile. Smile please."

She turned her face away with a big sigh. He turned her face toward him. "You will find life is still worthwhile, if you just smile." A sad smile played on her lips. Tears were still seeping down her cheeks.

"Life is short. Smile when you still have teeth." He said teasing.

A lovely smile dawned on her face. He saw her smile like the dawn playing upon a small stream. She then burst into a big laughter. "I love you so damn much, it hurts. I am not afraid of tomorrow because I have you by my side. Even after the

torture and tears I would chose you every time." She said burying her head in his neck.
He held her tight as though she were all of life and it was being taken from him.

"Will you marry me?"

"Yes, I will." she nodded, tears sliding down her cheeks.

"I love you."

"I love you too." She sniffled through her tears.

"I can't wait to make you my bride." Tears of joy ran from his eyes.

Chapter 50

Acario Torres was of Mexican origin. He was 7 feet high with broad shoulders, huge and strong like a bull. He had a bull neck and eyes like a tiger.

Acario spent his teens engaging in hundreds of street fights in Mexico. Much of his body – arms, legs, torso, and even the palms of his hands have deep scars. A drug cartel coordinating the production and distribution of cocaine recruited him at age 16.

The cartel depended upon him in the disposing of its opponents. He would cut off their heads, and burry the heads in remote desert areas, leaving the bodies out in the streets so no one knows who was killed. He reveled in torturing them before killing them. Sometimes, he just beat them to death with wooden planks, or he would place them in a large drum filled with petrol and burn them alive. In short, Acario was a bully to his own people and a menace to the world.

When the Mexican police caught the cartel, Acario decided to migrate to the United States. He applied for a green card, and then tried hard to meet all naturalization requirements, and in 2013, he succeeded in being a US citizen.

Because he was a sex maniac, he spent his nights with prostitutes and became a regular customer in Nevada's brothels.

At first, he didn't know what type of career he should have. He found it convenient to join professional wrestling because it would best fit with his violent bestial nature.

Acario had to work his way up to being in the ring with WWE superstars. He began his pro wrestling training with the mid-Missouri Wrestling Association. He showed enough talent to earn a contract with the WWE. In five months, he defeated three WWE superstars and earned the name "The legend Killer". These matches resulted in Acario earning Hard Core Champion Crowns.

Acario became known as being a beast in the ring, and the ability to strike fast and hard at any time. He believed he could not be defeated. He humiliated his opponents, by calling them bad names and spatting on them not caring about audience disapproval.

Acario hunted down opponents one by one until he won the heavyweight championship.

Although the crowd and WWE officials supported him all the way until he got the title, Acario breached his contract with WWE by performing for another wrestling organization. WWE sue him, and both went to court. However, WWE made peace with him because he was talented in wrestling and the goose that lays the golden egg.

WWE believes strongly that its athletes must uphold certain standards both in and out of the WWE. But Acario breached his contract with WWE once again when he was accused of murdering his girlfriend, Eldora Perez. On the night Perez died, Acario called an ambulance and told the police that he had returned to his hotel room to find his mistress gasping for air and fighting for her life. An autopsy suggested that Perez had been beaten to death, and Acario became a prime suspect, but the evidences were not sufficient for conviction on charge of murder, and the court acquitted him.

Acario left court a free man and continued wrestling down his opponents, smashing their bones.

Acario never met Mostafa in the ring because he took his three years leave before Mostafa joined WWE. During this period, Mostafa fought his great battles, and won his great championships.

According to his new contract with WWE, Acario's coming matches were supposed to start after two months. During that period, his misconduct jeopardized his contract with WWE again.

Acario was pictured passed out on brothel bed where he had sex sessions with two prostitutes. The images showed him during a near-fatal overdose before he was found unconscious the following day and foaming from the mouth. It seemed that Acario consumed a toxic cocktail of drink and drugs. Reports soon surfaced stating that medics had found a needle mark on Acario's arm and every drug imaginable in his system.

WWE announced that it had reached the point of no return

with Acario, and that he will never be brought back into the company. WWE stripped him of the heavyweight title and suspended him permanently.

Things got really sour between Acario and the WWE when they sent him a fax notifying him about the release. Acario retaliated back by announcing in TV and newspapers that he had a contract with WWE, but he was released because of backstage political maneuvering by influential guys, who simply didn't like him and apparently wanted to bury him quickly. Acario went as far as to say that no matter how talented you are, at the end of the day the company will manipulate those they want to see succeed. The WWE would plant fake fans in the audience to put certain wrestlers over. He added that the WWE was a monopoly that treated their employees like shit.

Acario took things a step further by filing a defamation lawsuit against WWE and for being released from his contract without logical reason. Acario torn the company to shreds about various other topics as well, especially the issue of classifying the wrestlers as independent contractors, a matter that frees wrestling companies from paying health insurance, social security and medicare contributions and unemployment insurance.

The Court-ordered arbitration. WWE and Acario accepted the court's order because it was simpler, inexpensive and a quick way to resolve disputes. The court chose Tom Wilson's law firm to resolve the dispute between him and WWE. Daisy worked as an arbiter to discuss solution to the problem. WWE lawyer and Acario convened in Daisy's office to find a solution for the dispute.

Acario: "I don't want to sign for WWE again. They classify us as independent contractors to cut costs. They don't pay for medical treatment or health insurance. Even more alarming is that the contract ensures that the promoter cannot be sued or held liable if the wrestler is seriously injured or dies. WWE must stop taking advantage of us."

WWE lawyer: "The contract is a contract. It says that you are independent contractor. However, we can change your contract and get you a new one."

Acario: "professional wrestlers are being made to work while hurt. The vicious cycle is this: they are injured, they don't heal, because they wrestle for 275 days a year. They try to mask an injury, so they can continue to work. They work on injuries on top of injuries, and they don't take the time to rest, because this is the only way they know how to make a living."

Daisy addressing Acario: "A fair new contract would certainly close the door to any dispute between you and the organization."

Acario: "It is not just that. The wrestler must seek the WWE permission to appear in other works, such as films or product endorsements. The wrestler then needs to pay the company a 10 percent management fee, while all monies earned by wrestler from such permitted activities in a specific contract year shall be credited against the minimum annual compensation for that contract year."

Daisy: "Could you explain further please?"
Acario: "In other words, had I appeared in a permitted project outside WWE, whatever I would have earned would have been deducted from the $100,000 the company was paying me over 52 weeks."

Daisy: "We can write a contract expressly stating your terms."

Daisy: "I know that due to his wrestling talent Acario is indispensable to the organization. How about changing his contract and offering him a good new deal?" Daisy said addressing WWE lawyer.

Acario: "Yes, I want to change my contract and get a new one."

WWE lawyer: "I was delegated by the board of WWE to offer Acario a new unique deal."

The lawyer then opened his leather bag and handed Daisy a contract saying: "This is the contract you and I had been working on for the previous ten days."

Daisy read aloud to Acario the import of the contract:

"The contract allows you the option to go and work for the other wrestling organizations. You do not fall under the wellness policy. You have the advantage to re-negotiate the terms every six months to make sure that you are happy with everything and the WWE do not own the name Acario

Torres as an intellectual property."

Acario said hilariously: "Yes, this is what I was looking for. I cannot refuse a good deal."

"Will you excuse me; I have other work to do." The WWE lawyer said and left the room.

Acario however, stayed in his seat. He had questions to ask.

"I want to thank you, for the wonderful job you did."

"Thank you for your kindness." She said rising from her seat attempting to leave.

He stopped her by saying: ""I have seen you somewhere, I think, but cannot tell where." He smiled naughtily at her.

"I don't think so. We have never met before." She said with a lump forming in her throat.

"And now will you excuse me. I have an important meeting to attend." She said leaving her seat.

"Of course. Thank you very much for your time, I really appreciated." He said rising from his seat and extended his hand to her for a handshake. She shook hands with him. He squeezed her hand hard and kept it in his for long.

Are you sure, we haven't met before? I think we…"

"No, we haven't met. I haven't seen you before." She gave

him an annoyed suspicious look and snatched her hand away. Her heartbeats drummed in her ears.
Acario shot her a look of lust. "I am sure I have seen you somewhere, but where, I don't recall." He said heading towards the door.

Three days later, Daisy was at her office losing herself in work. "I thought of surprising you." She looked up to find Acario hoovering over her. Her breath caught. A ripple of nervousness went through her. She'd never expected to see him again. He sat on a chair by her desk without being invited.

"It wasn't very civil of you to sit down without being invited," She said extremely annoyed.

He shot her a lustful glance. "I have been waiting for you. I've searched so long for you, but you disappeared after the brothel was burned. And here you are, a fucking lawyer."

"Are you screwing with me?" She shouted at him.

"I fucked you before. I want to fuck you again. I would love to eat you. You taste so good. I know."

"How dare you talk to me like that?"

"If you only knew how much those moments with you mattered to me. Sex with you is unforgettable; You have an unforgettable body. You are so perfect. I know who you are. You are a whore I fucked before."

"Stop this nonsense you are freaking idiot." She screamed in his face.

"I will never forget the moments I spent with you. I need to get you alone. I want you all to myself. Why not? A fucking good time never hurt nobody." His eyes were harsh glaring with lust.

Tom Wilson entered Daisy's office to see His daughter's eyes filled with frightened tears. Acario not willing to confront Tom excused himself saying while walking away: "Maybe one day we will meet again and start all over."

The last thing Tom has ever wanted was to see Daisy hurting like this. Tom put his hand on her shoulder: "Is it a thing of the past?"

"I don't know. Maybe. What should I do? How do I trust and believe in myself again?" She said bursting into tears.

"What's been done has been done. Accept that we all make bad decisions in life. Accept that we are not perfect, and we are all humans and it is normal to make mistakes. Forgive yourself. Learn to forget about it, and don't keep blaming yourself."

She threw herself in her father's arms with a shriek that pierced his heart.

Don't worry the future will be much better than you think." He said patting her back gently trying to comfort her but there is little he can do.

Chapter 51

Acario parked his car not far from Daisy's house. For now, all he could do was wait. As he waited, he greedily gulped at the fiery liquid, only releasing it to another until the whole bottle was gone.

It was about midnight and Daisy was almost about to go to sleep when the front door knocked. John the butler opened the door to see a drunk staggering man. Acario rushed in without a word. As soon he has got into the house he shouted: "Where is the woman of the house?"

Daisy got out of her room to see who was coming. She was frightened to see Acario looking at her from downstairs, His body staggering left and right. He shot her a glance of lust then ran up the stairs to her. Daisy ran frightened to her room, but he caught up with her, pulled her inside the room and closed the door behind him.

"You are fuckin beautiful." He said seeing her quite sexy in her short nightgown. He grabbed her neck and pulled her toward him, kissing her lips ardently. "Get out of my room you monster, or I will call the police. She said yelling and struggling to free herself. He put his hand over her mouth to stop her screaming. She tried to move but was encased in his arms.

"Those sweet lips. My, oh my, I could kiss those lips all night long. Your breasts are too pretty to resist."

She kicked him. He spun her by her hair so her back was against his chest, his other arm clamped hard across her ribs.

"Someone helps me!"

She screamed as loud as she could.

He laughed. He thought her fear was funny.

She was driving him crazy with lust. "You are a common whore I fucked you before."

She turned and dug her nails into his wrists. Her resistance maddened him. He roared: "You are nothing but a hole, I'm going to ride you hard and good until you beg for mercy."

"Go away from me, you freak."

Lust dropped into his blood. "I want you naked, and in your bed, right now."

"Release me you bastards." She said suffocating.

John the butler called the police after he heard Daisy's screams. Within five minutes a state police car arrived, two police officers burst into Daisy's room, arrested Acario and took him into custody to investigate what exactly happened. The incident appeared in the morning papers. The ugly words the drunken Acario said about Daisy during the preliminary investigation were written in large letters.

Daisy filed a lawsuit alleged that she was sexually harassed by Acario. The news spread like wild fire in the newspapers and on TV. Mostafa was shocked upon hearing the news. He felt compassion towards her because her miserable past was striking her from all sides. She disgraced him again. He felt justifiable anger.

Tom found it wiser to settle the case without a trial. The WWE CEO also found it a good opportunity to protect Acario from severe attack by the public and the media. Acario is best for WWE business. He generates revenues in millions every year for the organization.

The settlement meeting was held in Tom's office. WWE CEO and Ocario attended the meeting. Daisy sat in a remote chair listening to the conversation.

"We would accept some form of compensation." Tom started the talk.

CEO: "How much?"

Tom: "One million dollars as a compensation."

CEO: "All right, but this must come with the agreement that Daisy won't speak about what happened to her."

Tom: "Of course. Daisy doesn't want to defame herself by disclosing this dirt to the public."

CEO addressing Acario: "You are a troublemaker. You violated the policy of WWE several times. I have repeatedly stood by you as you faced a series of allegations of sexual harassment and other inappropriate behaviour. You have failed a pre-fight drug test before, and you were suspended for one year as a result. You were accused of killing your girlfriend, and now you accused a decent woman of being a prostitute. I have had enough of this. I should dispense with your services and kick you out of the organization, but I don't like losing a wrestler who has reached the pinnacle of professional wrestling and became a top attraction for our shows. I will therefore pay the cash compensation Mr. Tom asked for. The money however, will be taken from your basic yearly salary."

"I don't like this. I am not supposed to pay anything. There was no illegal harassment. I didn't say something wrong. I am sure she worked as…"

WWE CEO interrupted: Shut your ugly mouth up. Don't make me behave in a way I never have before."

Tom stared at Acario and said: "If you claim there was no illegal harassment, why not just defend yourself in court? Fighting a lawsuit costs a lot of money. Estimates are usually between $50,000 and $250,000 just to fight. Those are just the direct financial costs. More than that, you end of fighting not only in court, but in the media as well."

Tom glanced at the CEO and said: "I insist to make the compensation figure public in a statement alongside its apology."

WWE CEO: "Okay."
The door swung open and Mostafa entered the room. The moment he walked into the room Daisy became breathless and speechless. Daisy was about to jump from her seat when she saw a deep frown on Mostafa's face. Mostafa sat in an empty seat after he nodded hello to Tom and the CEO. He didn't look at Daisy or Acario as if they didn't exist.

"Mostafa is like my son and Daisy is like his sister. He cares about her, he commits to her. He goes out of his way to make sure she is comfortable and happy." Tom said introducing Mostafa to the CEO.

WWE CEO: "Mostafa is one of our greatest wrestlers. He won several great matches until he won WWE heavy championship. I hope we can get Acario and Mostafa together in a grand match.

Acario: "You want me to compete against this shaky weak-kneed? Against this coward pussy; the fashion designer who walks the runway as a woman?"

CEO: "He isn't no pussy. He won WWE championship before and you are supposed to meet him in the upcoming championship after just a few weeks."

Acario: "I will eat him alive I am sure. He needs a fucking miracle to save his own life." He said with a sarcastic laugh.
CEO: "Stop being arrogant. Turn your life around and come down to earth."

The CEO glanced at Tom and said while rising from his seat: "Now will you excuse me I have some work to do."
The CEO shook hands with Tom, and nodded good-bye to Daisy.

"We will get all the papers ready for you to sign." Tom said.
"Of course." The CEO said while heading to the door.

The CEO left the room. Tom walked through a door into another room to prepare some papers. Acario and Mostafa stayed in their seats. Daisy became weary and annoyed wishing Acario to perish from her sight.

Mostafa turned to Acario and said: "You know nothing about me Acario. You don't know the culture of upper Egypt where I came from. Revenge killings is common. Killing for honor is a legitimate act and a part of our heritage. We believe that vendetta is better than disgrace. You disgraced me and the lady I care for."

Akario: "You call this bad ass bitch a lady?"

"Listen very closely Acario. I will make you pay dearly for what you did to her. Now get out of here and enjoy your days; for you never know whether it will be your last."

"The moron is so baffled by her beauty that he doesn't know that she works as a prostitute." Acario said aloud while heading to the door.

"I will teach you a lesson of what it is like to face hell. I am going to torture you and then I will kill you! "Mostafa shot after him.

Tom came back to sit at his desk, but Daisy interrupted him by running to him weeping. He took her in his arms trying to find the words that would make her feel better.

"God is testing you now, putting you through the fire to burn out the dross. Try to forget the past and move on."

"The past is haunting me? I should be over it, but I am not."

"Time heals all wounds. Pick up the pieces and move on."

"The wounds remain. Time covers them with scar tissue and the pain lessens. But it is never gone."

"I want God to forgive me for my weaknesses. I am not strong enough on my own." She said lifting her tearful eyes to her father.

"God knows what you need, and He will provide it."

"Pray for me father." She said shedding abundant tears.

"Create in her a clean heart, o God, and renew a right spirit within her." He said with a heart burst with grief.

"I need a scotch to lighten my mood." He extricated himself from her arms and left the room.

Daisy wished the ground might open and devour her. She feared Mostafa's anger after he had watched the events of the day.

"O God I have lost myself again and feel unsafe." She said with a lump forming in her throat.

Mostafa shot a look at her so sharp that she shrank back into her chair. He showed her no mercy.

"I get nothing from you but humiliation and disgrace." He yelled furiously at her.

Daisy: "I'm just done. Done with the hurt, done with your cruelty, done with your uncaring."

"If you really loved me you wouldn't have sex with other men. You hate me. Sure, you hate me. You have made it very clear."

 No, I don't hate you. I'm just done with you."

 "Do I not have the right to hate you, Daisy? I set you free from a sordid past, yet it comes back to haunt you!"

A glitter came into his eyes as they clashed with hers. Daisy closed her eyes tight, unable to look at the fury in his black wide eyes. She swallowed back her pain.

"I am sorry..." She whispered brokenly. "I am sorry."

"Did you open your legs for him as well like the filthy slut you are?"

"They intoxicated me, they forced me to do it, it was all against my will, and you knew it." She felt her shame scorch her from head to foot.

"I gave you all the trust, but you betrayed me. I gave you my heart but you killed me day by day."

"Can't you see your words are killing me? I can hardly breath."

"I was your cure, but you were my disease. I was saving you, but you were killing me."

"I made a terrible mistake, now I am living with the consequences. I regret it, I really do. And I am sorry." She said crying ardently.

"I loved you at your darkest, yet you disgraced me. How could you do this to me? How do I get out of this? How do I stop this misery?"

"I wish you would just understand how I feel. You are killing me with your words."

"I want to pull my aching heart and tear it piece by piece, so I no longer love you. I want to go so far so I no longer must see you. "

"Don't you dare walk away from me. You make me feel loved and that's what I want to be."

"You are a disaster woman. I see nothing from you but pain.

You burned everything I loved in you. You let the wolves snap at your body."

"Please do not remind me with terrible things I was forced to do. Try to leave the past behind you. Don't let the past steel our present. Don't let our happiness slid into a black hole."

"Your wounds will never heal. The wolves of the past keep opening them up. You are not worthy to hold my heart."

"Stop! You make me feel like if I were a piece of shit. How bitter your words taste? Please choose your words carefully. Find ones that would not make me cry." She yelled putting her hands over her ears.

"You broke my heart; the pain I am feeling is unbearable. You turned me into a killer. I killed because I loved you."

His words had the effect of a hammer smashing her attempts to repress her anger. No, she cannot tolerate anymore.

"I had been through hell but you don't feel me anymore. I loved you, I always have, I always will. But you don't feel my agony. You are pressing me too hard."

"You humiliated me. You disgraced me. You buried my pride in the sand. I broke my heart loving you. I saw your worst and I stayed. The worst feeling is when something is killing you inside, and you must act like you don't care. I hate you. I just hate you. I will never get close enough for you to hurt me again. I will walk out of your life. You will never see me again." He said with eyes filled with tears.

"You want to run away as you did before. Swallow your false pride and go away. I don't want you anymore. I wish I had never met you."

She walked over to the door and opened it for him.

"I am tired of fighting. I am so tired of you treating me like shit. You want to walk out of my life, there is the door. Hell, I will even hold it for you." She said opening the door for him.

He stood by the door glancing at her tearful eyes and felt sorry for her and for himself. He was too angry to find words to comfort her or ease her tension.

"I am sick of feeling like I am not good enough. I will never beg you to stay where you do not want to be. Have a nice life I am done trying to be in it. Get out of here, you don't even worth my time." She said screaming in his face.

Her words hurt him to the core. "Shut up Daisy. Calm down." He shouted nervously.

"I will not keep calm and you can fuck off." She yelled at him weeping.

Her weeping touched his heart deeply. He felt her despair, her doubt, her dismay. He gave her a sad smile and with a bleeding heart, he flounced angrily from the room. Tom Wilson met him at the door. They didn't exchange words. Tom noticed that Mostafa was extremely upset.

Tom entered the room to see Daisy shaking from anger.

"What happened?" He said worriedly.

"I wanted him to realize that he was wrong about me. I felt misunderstood and judged."

"You should have expressed your anger without pushing him away."

 Don't worry daddy. He is okay, he left smiling."

"It was a very sad smile Daisy. I looked into his eyes. He is breaking inside."

"It's my fault." She started crying. "It has been always my fault. I knew that he loved me since he first came to live with us. He told me then, how odd and unnatural I was for wanting to have sex with strangers. There must have been something wrong with me. I was young and wild, I hurt him more than anyone could ever have, and it kills me to think that I could have been so heartless, so dishonest. I look in the mirror every day and think to myself I don't deserve this man."

She continued weeping bitterly: "I feel like God is punishing me for my past mistakes. Will God punish me forever for my mistakes? Will I have to pay for the rest of my life?"

Never had Tom seen Daisy lose control like this; she looked quite demented. Tom held her in his arms to relieve her distress and calm her. "God's grace is bigger than your mistakes. He will show you favour despite your failings. That's the mercy of God." He said brushing her hair back and kissing her forehead.

"God is punishing me for my past wickedness by keeping me alive and in as much pain as He can."

"Just trust God to open the right doors at the right time."

"I am every mistake I've ever made. I am made of flaws. I am tired of my life. I think lower of myself. I don't know what to do. I want him, but I also want to get over him, and neither are happening. Every time we get close, something happens, and I eventually lose him."

"Do I still deserve God's grace?" She said sobbing in his arms.

"Unless you let go, unless you forgive yourself, you cannot move forward. God's mercy is bigger than any mistake that you have made. His mercy is new every morning."

Mostafa sat in his car behind the wheel, his eyes filled with tears of pity and compassion for Daisy. He muttered through his tears: "O God, give me the strength to forgive. Poor Daisy may God would touch you with his healing hand and give you the peace you need to go through."

The features of his face then turned into a grimace of anger. He snarled: "Acario, I will eat your fucking bones. You will end up in an ice-cold grave."

Chapter 52

In August 4th, 2016, an Intercontinental Championship matchup was lined up between two seasoned greats, the Egyptian Mostafa Abdel Fattah and the Mexican Acario Torres. Daisy arrived with her father to watch the big event. As he made his way to the ring, Mostafa could hear the crowds raise the noise levels to an almost deafening pitch. And as he stepped up and entered the ring the crowds went wild altogether. Acario accompanied by rock music, danced his way to the ring. As he entered the ring, the crowds went wild with the excitement of the moment. The crowd went crazy and began jumping up and down as Mostafa raised his hand greeting them.

Acario looked huge, and super fit. Mostafa's body was comparatively slim but solid, well formed, showing good muscular definition when moving around the ring. Mostafa wore Stretchy Jockstrap briefs Bodysuit. Acario wore one piece stretch body suit.

Seeing Acario, the beast, jumping up and down in the ring Daisy became extremely worried.

"No one can beat this incredible hulk. You think Mostafa can beat him?" She said to her father concerned.

"I believe in Mostafa. Above his physical strength, he

possesses a God-given strength. t's Time for him to start using the gift God has given him."

"Oh, I didn't know that."

"He doesn't realize that he has such a great gift. But it will spring up when he gets over excited. His father told me about this God-given strength when I first hired him for your protection."

The announcer took the microphone and addressed the audience: "Tonight WWE introduce to you the beast, the conqueror, the undisputed heavy weight champion Acario Fernandez. A 400-pound hard hitter. Standing at 7- foot tall with his gang appearance was intimidating enough. His size and aggression made him a danger in the ring. He is known to smash his opponents with callous disregard. Most of the WWE giant wrestlers have fallen to the monster at one time or another. He left behind a long line of victims. In one of his matches he eliminated seven opponents in just 18 minutes. The beast earned Heavyweight championship and Core Champion Crowns.

The opponent against the monster is the Egyptian Mostafa Abdel Fattah. The unbreakable, the handsomest built man. He won the WWE heavyweight championship, the WWE universal championship and the TNA World heavyweight championship. he knows submission manoeuvres, top rope attacks, and has been called the best pure striker in WWE. Standing at a towering 6-foot tall and weighing more than 200 pounds, the unbreakable is one of the most imposing men to ever enter a wrestling ring and, perhaps, the most athletically gifted."

The announcer ended his statement saying: "The following contest is scheduled for a pinfall."

Acario climbed the ropes and looked at the audience and shouted: "My job is to get into the ring and hurt people." He glanced at Mostafa and said: "Tonight I am going to teach this pussy a lesson. He will realize after a few moments that he is not fighting a man but a beast." He pointed at Mostafa and said: "They say this pussy is a great wrestler but is he great enough to fight Acario the magnificent? I am an incredible powerful being with no limits. There will be no mercy but brutal force. I will knock his motherfucking head off." A look of shark showed on his face.

While Acario still standing on the ropes facing the audience, Mostafa came from behind and slapped hard Acario's nape. Acario turned back to receive a strong slap in the face followed by a hard kick in the ass. Acario was extremely humiliated. He jumped down from the rope in fury.

"You coward. You are good at sucker punches eh? Poor pussy! Let's get you some milk Saucy boy."

Vivid scenes of Mostafa lifting heavy rocks, pulling out of the river a boat weighing tons, and ripping out a big tree of the ground from its roots floated before his eyes.

"Here I am standing before you. Show me what you got - worthless scoundrel". Mostafa stared at Acario with fiery eyes.

Acario immediately charged. He ran straight at Mostafa. At the last second Mostafa slid to the side and shoved Acario to the steel post that held up the ropes. Mostafa smashed Acario's head into the steel ring post several times. Mostafa delivered him violent blows in the back on the right side just below his ribs with both fists; the severe hits ruptured disks in his spine.

Mostafa pinned Acario to the ropes and delivered direct blows to his face. Acario freed himself from the ropes, and when he turned around, the audience gasped at the sight. Blood poured from a cut on his forehead just below to his hairline.

Dazed by his impact with the steel, and by the severe punches Mostafa delivered to his back and face, it took Acario a long while to steady himself. Mostafa took advantage of Acario's dizziness and grabbed him by the hair and ran him headlong to the other side of the ring, and smashed again his head into the steel post, and then threw him to the mat.

Mostafa climbed to the top of the ropes, steadied himself then leaped into Acario delivering right left elbows.

"Now Mr. beast, now Mr. magnificent, how do you like the power of the coward pussy; the fashion designer who walks the runway as a woman?" Mostafa said to Acario while yanking him up by the hair.

Fear gripped Acario as Mostafa lifted him up and threw him out of the ring and sending him crashing down on the time keeper's table and all the way to the floor, hitting the back of his head on the steel guardrail. Mostafa jumped out behind him and brought him back into the ring by pulling hair. Mostafa then hit Acario with both fists in his chest until he fell to the ground struggling to take a breath. Acario was not able to go for the cover. He looked as a wounded beast. Acario came back to life and struggled to his feet.

"Come on you coward, come on you sissy, stand and fight." Mostafa uttered through clinched teeth.

Acario charged forward but Mostafa turned him aside again, but this time followed through carting Acario and smashed his head into the post and threw him to the mat. Acario sprang up off his feet and punched Mostafa hard in the jaw, and a second blow caught him in the stomach. Mostafa went to a knee. He felt a flash of anger course through him. Mostafa stood to the side of Acario and applied a side headlock. Mostafa then spun around in a circle and dropped into a seated position, driving Acrio's face-first into the mat. Mostafa heard his head crack as it hit the ground.

Mostafa continued to dominate the match. He toyed with Acario and tortured him at the same time.

Tom looked at Daisy and said: Mostafa is wearing down the monster before finishing him off.

"There's nothing I love as much as a good fight. You not man enough to fuck with me. Give me your best shot. Show me what you got." Mostafa yelled at Acario.

Acario got to his feet and ran to Mostafa and threw his weight on him, but Mostafa grabbed his left arm, holding it across his chest and then fell backwards, dropping Acario's face first as well as damaging his arm and shoulder. Mostafa then climbed the ropes and landed heavily on Acario's arm thus damaging it. Mostafa pulled him up then grabbed his head and jumped forward so that Acario landed in a sitting position and drove Acario's face into the mat.

His expression darkened with rage, Acario got to his feet trying to attack again, Mostafa stood behind him facing the same direction. He then passed both of his arms under his arms and put one arm in a half nelson and the other hand around the neck in front of Acario. The hand in front of the neck was locked with the other hand at the wrist. Mostafa then lifted Acario up and fell backwards, dropping him on his head, and neck.

Acario stood there helpless with a dazed and foolish look, his big, bleeding mouth wide open. Blood spilling from his smashed mouth and nose.

"Your time has come. I have arrived to end your fucking life. You don't know how evil I can be. when I am done with you, you're going to wish you never met me." Mostafa said fiercely.

Mostafa delivered Acario three headlock suplex. "I am not finished with you yet. I will cut your liver out, I am stronger than I look. I fought men of all sizes." Screamed Mostafa with rage."

Mostafa applied a full nelson hold to Acario from behind. He then lifted him into the air and fell into a seated position, driving Acario's tailbone-first on to the mat.
Mostafa then lifted Acario for a powerbomb and dropped him with enough force on his back to dislocate the vertebrae in his spine. He lifted him again for another powerbomb and dropped him hard on his head, thus legitimately breaking his neck.

The referee signaled the need for immediate help by doing an "X" formation with his arms over Acario's head.

Acario was carried out of ring on stretcher. The blows Mostafa delivered Acario might appear as just a glancing blows, but the blown spots ruptured disks in his spine, broke his neck, dislocated his arm, fractured his skull and one of his teeth hanging from his nose.

Mostafa was announced as the winner. The audience erupted in applause. Daisy dried her weeping eyes with her thumbs. She was crying silently all through the match because she knew that the excruciating pain Mostafa endured during the match was because of her.

Chapter 53

Mostafa sat quietly in a corner of the dressing room reliving the events that occurred during the heat of the match. It was a brutal match; it was manslaughter. He delivered fatal blows just powerful enough to kill Acario. Acario might die within the coming days.

He would have killed the man a thousand times over if he got a second chance. He would have raised the whole WWE stadium and slammed it down on the son of a bitch. He killed the bastard and doesn't feel sorry for him.

The door of the dressing room opened silently, and Daisy stepped into the room. She headed straight to Mostafa who was sitting in the far corner. She put her arms around his neck and kissed him tenderly.

Hey! I am soaking wet. I haven't taken a shower yet. I haven't even changed." He said trying to push her away.

"I like your sweat. I like your body odor, don't push me away."

"I have got to cleanse myself of the dirt of the day. I wrestled with a pig. I got dirty." Anger flashed in his eyes.

She sobbed against his neck, eyes streaming and burning,

throat raw and sore, chest aching.

"You tortured him, you killed him for me. It was hard. It was tough. You didn't have to do that. I am not worth it."

"I would kill for you. I've killed for you before." His face drawn with exhaustion and melancholy

 "There are many things worth living for, and nothing worth killing for." He retorted angrily.

She burst out crying. "You rescued me several times. I just want you to stop saving me." She said through her tears.

"I have done things for you that I haven't done for anyone else in my life."

"I am a big stain in your life. I am sorry I always stain you with dirt. I wished my life was stain-free."

"I cleaned the stain, so you can get up and fly again." He clenched his teeth, but he couldn't stop the tears from coming.

"You are destroying everything good in my life. Get out of my life, I don't want to see you again." Tears started flowing from his eyes.

"Please don't cry I don't deserve your tears. O God. I love you so much it hurts." She said sobbing with abundant tears. "I am tired of hurting, tired of being let down. I deserve to be loved in every way. I am fed up of you making me feel so down all the time."

"Shut up okay. I never stopped loving you."
"I am tired of getting my hopes up and being disappointed."
"You carried me through every storm."

"You create your own storms and then get mad when it rains!"

"You brought peace to my soul."

"If peace can only come through killing someone, then I don't want it. It would be better if we don't meet again. Leave me alone. Go home."

"Go home to where? You are home. put your arms around me and I am home." She said crying ardently and holding him tight.

 "Don't cry because it's over. I am done. I have had enough. Please leave."

"I never stopped loving you. Even when I tried desperately to forget you, I just couldn't." Sobs erupted from her, so violent that her whole body shook.

"I don't want to see you again. You are an evil woman." He felt tightness in his throat. Tears sprang from his eyes.

"Sorry for all the pain I caused you."

"Always remember that if you fall I will no longer be there

to catch you."

"I am sorry to have caused you all this trouble. I wanted to be all the things you loved. Yet sadly I am plagued with flaws haunted by the thought that I never met up with your standards."

"You and I have gone dark. I know this is the end of the line for us. The damage has been done."

"I love you and I am so sorry of making your life harder. I wish I could be a better for you, but then again, you are not even mine."

His heart jerked hard in his chest when she said: "I have scars left by people who did me wrong. It all happened against my will and you knew it."

She continued crying as she stepped away from him.

"I am sorry for the pain I have caused you, and I know I can't take it back. Nothing in my life has ever meant as much to me as you do. I fear losing you. I love you. I don't know what else there is to say."

She stepped forward. She slid her arms around him. "Hold me, gather the remnant." She said wetting his face with her warm tears.

After a moment he pulled her close gripping her tightly. They sobbed in each other's arms for long moments.

"Go find yourself. The world is yours. Life goes on." He said refraining from saying more encouraging words.

"You mean we have the rest of our lives to go our separate ways. I know you. The mind gets angry, but the heart still cares." A sad smile crossed her face.

"you can go on without me." He swallowed to remove the lump in his throat.

"Pain changes people. It makes them shut people out. I hate when this happens to me. I will never bother you again. I wish you all the best in this world and I am sorry you had to go through any of the pain I brought into your world. I will stay out of your way. Now let me quietly go away." She turned and ran to the door, sobbing loudly. She opened the door and disappeared down the long corridor.

He felt as if someone were continuously pushing a knife, deep into his chest. His eyes shed tears as she strode weeping to the door. It was too late. She didn't hear him when he shot after her: "Always remember that if you fall, I will be there to catch you."

After the match, Acario never left the hospital. He suffered brain damage and died two weeks later.

Chapter 54

Daisy was invited by the International Research Conference on criminal law to give a lecture on "Victims and Compensation". The conference provides a premier interdisciplinary platform for lawyers and researchers around the world to present and discuss the most recent innovations, trends, and concerns as well as practical challenges encountered, and solutions adopted in the fields of Criminal Law, Victims and Compensation. The conference will be held in Amatrice, a town in the province of Rieti, in northern Lazio - central Italy. Daisy made a reservation for a room at the hotel Albergo Diffuso Villa Retrosi.

In Amatrice she visited the lake Lago di Scandarello, the church Santuario dell'Icona passatora, the history museum Museo Configno, and the art museum Museo Civico Cola Filotesio. She dined at the restaurant Agriturismo La Grotta. Being in Amatrice was a good opportunity for her to breathe fresh air, feel free and stay healthy.

The conference came to an end and she decided to stay for two other days to enjoy the superb Italian food. She sat at a table in the restaurant Agriturismo La Grotta and ordered Spaghetti alla Carbonara. She looked before her to see Mostafa sitting on a nearby table eating lunch. "What is he doing here?" She whispered amazed. He must have arrived to keep an eye on her.

Every time she thinks she had finally moved on from him, reality would slap her that she hadn't even moved one inch. She hated him. He made her feel incomplete and worthless. She wanted to stay away from him and begin the healing process.

She rushed to his table and shouted in his face: "What are you doing here? Stop chasing me."

"I came here to tell you…"

She interrupted saying: "Or maybe you think I am too helpless to take care of myself. Stop pressuring me."

"I have had these dreams that you were in danger. "

She shook her head in a mocking manner: "My tolerance for idiots is extremly low today. Now you became a dream interpreter. I am not in danger. Your dream will never come true. I am perfectly safe."

"I have never dreamt before. This dream was recurrent and so clear."

"Enough is enough. Go back to where you came from?"

"I came to tell you that I will always be there to catch you when you fall."

"Oh no please, not again. Stop this nonsense. I don't need your services. Stop being like a mother dog watching over her pre-mature pups." She shot at him.

"Unfortunately, I am the person you can screw over a million times and I would still be there for you if you needed me."

At this very moment, Italy was hit by four earthquakes in four hours. The four quakes, which came in quick succession, caused buildings to collapse. They affected already badly-damaged towns and villages in the regions of Abruzzo, Lazio and Marche, where around 300 people lost their lives.

The building where the restaurant was located began to collapse. Large parts of the ceiling fell to the ground. People screamed in terror after the floor cracked under their feet. Mostafa ran to horrified Daisy and held her tight protecting her with his body. The whole building collapsed, and both were buried under its rubbles. Mostafa used his body to shield her from the blast, clinging on to her as she was to him. He had grabbed hold of her with every muscle beneath his skin and refused to let go. They stayed under the rubble for three days trapped and entombed but had some sort of oxygen supply from the outside world.

The firemen crawled underneath the rubbles and could just make out a man holding a woman protecting her with his body amongst the rubble.

Daisy was pulled out of the rubble alive without a scratch after Mostafa saved her life by laying on top of her body.

Mostafa was found unconscious and seriously injured. It was hard to separate Mostafa from Daisy. His muscles were so tight and stiff that they gave him a shot to reduce his hold on her and make his stiffen muscles relax. They put them on a stretcher and hauled them to the hospital. The hospital was crowded with wounded people, so Mostafa and Daisy had their hospital beds moved side by side. Mostafa was unconscious. His whole body was covered with bruises and sores and open wounds. The doctors wrapped the wounded parts of his body with bandages.

Daisy buried her face in his bandaged hand and wept ardently. She was buried under the rubble for three days without water or food, but she survived because he shielded her with his body and took all the blows. He felt the danger that was about to hit her and travelled some hundred miles to save her. In this crazy world, full of change and chaos, there is one thing she was certain, one thing that does not change, her love for him.

"You are every reason, every hope, and every dream I have ever had. And no matter what happens to us in the future, everyday we are together is the greatest of my life. I will always be yours." She said kissing his bandaged hand wetting it with abundant tears.

After two days Mostafa regained consciousness. The nurse adjusted the back of the bed, so he can sit up straight. He looked at the void before him with a sad frown on his face. Daisy tried to talk to him, jest with him, but he didn't respond, as if a dreadful lethargy oozed into him, lulling his senses into oblivion.

His oblivion to what was going around him lasted for

days. He sat in bed looking ahead into the void, his eyes unseeing, his lips clamped together.

At first, he couldn't figure out what happened exactly, but as time passed, he remembered everything that happened. He was about to die for her. He was buried under the rubble to protect her again and again as he always did before. When would he stop sacrificing himself for her? He laid down his life for her. He sacrificed himself for her over and over.

Are his sacrifices worthwhile? She broke his heart several times. He wanted all his love back. He wanted all the time she had wasted back. He saw himself as a victim...prey that fell for a monster. This time he was buried under the rubbles. Every broken bones, wounds, and bruises in his body indicate the failure of his love. He felt flat and lifeless, removed and resentful.

The cost of protecting her was becoming unbearable. His love was his misery, his undertaker, his defeat. He no longer wanted her in his life. He once gave her everything, but she gave him nothing but misery. He made dangerous sacrifices for her, yet she failed to see. He helped too much, he gave too much, and he hurt the most. He would have liked to cry, to hack up this bitter sadness lodged in his throat. He felt pity for himself.

He wanted to hurt her. He wanted to break her; or at least, that's what he thought.

The air around him felt thick and heavy. He wanted to breathe. He wanted to get rid of the tension filling him. He was just tired; just wanted the world to be quiet for a bit.

He wanted to scream: "Get me out of here."

Daisy glanced at him and saw burning sadness in his eyes. She struggled to gain control of the emotions that suddenly welled up within her, threatening to overtake her.

Daisy wrapped her arms around him and whispered into his ear: "Why are you so sad? Lighten up, smile. A happy life is waiting for us, let's live it to the fullest and focus on the positive."

Because Daisy was recovered intact from the rubble, the hospital had to take her bed and give it to another seriously wounded boy. Daisy rented a room in a nearby hotel. She always found Mostafa as she left him sitting in bed looking sad and staring at the wall before him. For five days she sat by his bedside, holding his hand trying gently to make him talk to her but to no avail. He just sat in bed in complete oblivion and unaware of his surroundings.

"Mostafa love, what's the matter. Please talk to me. Why can't you look at me? What are you hiding?" But she got no answer as if she never existed.

It was a bad day for Daisy when she visited Mostafa at the hospital and found his bed empty. The nurse told her that she tried to convince him that he must stay for a medical advice discharge, but he left before the treating physician recommended discharge.

Mostafa disappeared in his house in Stamford Connecticut. He treated his wounds at home. He completed the work of the physicians by washing and disinfecting the wound and wrapping them with sterile bandages. After two weeks his wounds were perfectly healed.

He needed a long vacation to forget Daisy and to make it easier to move on. He joined a Harley-Davidson motorcycle tour in Europe. He drove his own Harley with the other fellow riders. The tour focused on riding mountain passes in the Alps, set in dramatic and beautiful scenery. The Harley group toured Switzerland, and Austria. They traveled through picturesque landscapes and typical Italian mountain villages.

 The tour also involved riding to the Alps and back again, on great roads in Luxembourg and Germany. They slept in comfortable hotels and enjoyed good meals in local restaurants. Mostafa's roommate was a big old man called Timothy. He took his guitar everywhere he went. In their room at night the old man chatted a lot with Mostafa about life, women and love.

Timothy: "You don't talk much."

Mostafa: "Sometimes I shut down and don't talk to anyone for days. It's nothing personal."

"You talk but you want to be quiet. You pretend like you are happy, but you aren't."

Mostafa: "My heart is so tired. I want to sleep until I feel better."

Timothy: "You better talk young man. You need to learn how to pick yourself up and pull yourself together. Is it love failure that made you close your door and shut the world out?"

Mostafa: "My heart had been stabbed, cheated and broken. I gave her my heart, I just didn't expect to get it back in pieces."

Timothy: "Where do you stand now?"

Mostafa: ""I am somewhere between giving up and seeing how much more I can take. I am slowly giving up. I fell in love with her, but she played me. She put herself in dangerous situations and I saved her several times. I never Would think that she would do this to me. If you can read my mind, you'd be in tears. You'll never understand until it happens to you."

Timothy: I once had a wife. She gave me the most beautiful days of my life. A part of me died the day she died and what I have left was slowly dying. I would never have expected to feel such grief, but I managed to lick my wounds and got over it."

Mostafa "Oh! Sorry to hear about your wife."

Timothy: "O God. She was wild. I loved her beyond all reason and didn't expect her to love me back. I was just waiting for her to wise up."

Mostafa: ""You loved her so much that you can't forget her."

Timothy: "If tears could build a stairway, and memories a

lane, I'd walk right up to heaven and bring her home again."

Mostafa: "I have had many beautiful days with my girl too. As I was fighting for her, I realized I was fighting to be taken for granted; fighting to be disappointed; and fighting to be hurt again. So I started fighting to let go."

Timothy: "That does not mean that you should give up and never be happy."

Mostafa: "I loved her for long that it is so hard to move on."

Timothy: "One day you will look back and think.. damn, that girl really did love me."

Mostafa: "I don't know what I feel anymore. Emotionally I am done."

Timothy: "Sometimes the only reason why you won't let go of what's making you sad is because it was the only thing that made you happy."

Mostafa: "My heart needs more time to accept what my mind already knows."

Timothy: "You will never see all the awesome things ahead of you, if you keep looking at all the bad things behind you. You just must turn around, throw the match and burn the bridge. Live, learn, and don't look back."

Mostafa: "I loved her, but she never loved me as I loved her."

Timothy: "Is it your choice to stay broken? Try to pull yourself together. Your efforts won't go to waste."

Mostafa: "She broke my heart. Yet I am still in love with her. And I don't know why." His eyes brimmed with tears.

Timothy: "Why do you cling to pain? There is nothing you can do about the wrongs of yesterday. It is not yours to judge. Why hold on to the very thing which keeps you from hope and love? You must take the good with the bad. Love what you got. "

Timothy took his guitar, adjusted its strings and played:

How do I start?

What do I say?

I love you more than words can say.

I thank God for you every day.

This love I have for you will never stray.

When I say goodbye.

promise me you won't cry.

Because the day I'll be saying that will be the day I die.

Mostafa smiled. He loved the song. Timothy put the guitar aside and said: "No one is perfect. If you avoid people for their mistakes, you will always be alone in this world. So judge less and love more."

Chapter 55

WWE magazine announced that Mostafa had returned from a Harley motorcycle tour in Europe. The magazine added that the famous wrestler is now preparing for his match with the next contender. Right now, he is spending few days in his summer place in North Carolina.

Daisy flew to North Carolina. Arriving at the chalet, she rang the bell but no one answered the door. She pressed the bell again, hearing it ring inside, but there was still no answer, when she got no response, she went to the beach searching for him. She saw him sitting on one of the many benches staring out at the wide beach. She sat down beside him and smiled. He gave her a pained look, then arose and walked away. She left the bench and walked over to him. She came by his right side and pleaded: "Oh please Mostafa can we talk?"

"Where were you? You left for weeks without telling me where you're going. It's okay. I am not angry with you. You may be gone from my sight, but you are never gone from my heart."

It was as if she didn't exist for him any more - as if she were a ghost. He continued walking slowly ahead without looking at her. She caught his left wrist stopping him from walking further.

"You are ignoring me. Say something please."
"What are you doing here? Don't follow me back." He said sharply glaring at her.

"I just wished you knew what I feel about you. That's it."

"I want you. I want us. I still have hope of being yours." She continued with a broken voice.

"Get off my back. I don't have time for that bullshit." He said and continued walking ahead.

She walked closely to his side and started talking without expecting from him any answers.

"It hurts so much to love you the way I do, then look at you and realize you don't care. I get it. I am not that important to you. You don't care about losing me.

"I try to forget you, but the moment I lay eye on you everything comes pushing back faster than I thought was possible.

"You hurt me but not as much as I am hurting myself by still loving you.

"I hate that I miss you. I hate that you forgot about me. I hate that I still care about you. I am just tired of waiting and watching you avoiding me."

She sang: "The beat of my heart - the pulse in my veins - the life of my soul. You are my destiny and I am your fate."

"I won't beg for your time and attention anymore. One day I'll learn to live without you and move on."

He stopped walking and shouted at her: ""You are bad luck. There is no chance for me being your man. Don't spoil my life. I am moving with my life now."

"Maybe I am a bad luck. But you taught me that I mustn't sit at the side of the road showing my wounds and shouting."

"Just leave me alone I am tired. Get out of my sight. I am sick of your nonsense."

"You are a crude man. You offend me by your crude manners. You enjoy breaking my heart. I cried a lot because of you. Please don't make me cry." The tears welling in her eyes sent his heart in a flurry of wild beats.

She continued through her tears: "I don't think I could ever tell you how much you mean to me. I can't imagine what things would be like if I hadn't met you. You have been always there for me. You watch out for me. You check up on me often to see if I am okay. You want the very best for me. People like you are hard to find. I just want you, that's all."

"Just because I have been always there for you does not mean you can take me for granted. Don't get it twisted." He said pointing his finger in her face.

"I don't care how hard being together is, nothing is worse

than being apart. I still love you, I am just tired of trying." She broke down weeping.

"Just shut up okay? Don't poison my day with your silly tears."

"I was a desperate woman lost in the land of evil. You came like a super hero to take me in your arms and out of danger. I had never imagined love could be like that. I had never dared to hope a man like you could ever love me. Yet, here we are. God didn't bring you this far to abandon me. Why can't it be the two of us? Why can't we be lovers again?"

 "You will find the love meant for you with another man I am sure."

"You have no idea how worthless you make me feel.

Do you realize what you mean to me?"

"You are stupid and worthless. You threw away your innocence and tore apart your reputation. I see nothing from you but pain." He shouted at her, fury on his face.

She swallowed hard and faked a smile to hide her hurt.

"You always hurt me but it's okay, I am used to it. Do you still love me?"

"No. I don't. Not anymore."

"You are a terrible liar. If you don't love me then why you

keep saving me?"

I don't really know. There is just something about you I can't let go. Let's be friends. It's much safer."

"I may not be a perfect woman, but you will never find a woman who loved you the way I do." She said pulling him and kissing him on the left cheek. Her tearful eyes glancing at him smiling.

"Why are you smiling like that? I didn't say I love you."

"You treat me like shit, but I adore you anyway."

"I don't love you Daisy. I stopped loving you a long time ago. Please try to understand."

"Liar! You said I love you a thousand times before."

"How is that so?"

"It's hard to pretend that you don't love someone when you really do. If you don't love me why you keep saving Me?"

"Oh God what I got myself into. If I hadn't saved you, you would have been dead by now or still wallowing in the mud." Stop wasting your time on me. Get off my back and leave me alone."

Bullshit. You simply adore me. She put her arms around his back and rested her head upon his shoulder and sighed: "I am just happy, because you are here, you are real, and you are mine. When I was sick, I enjoyed living in your arms for one year. When we were under the rubble, I was happy being in your arms. My body had all of you. It softened against yours. I was not afraid of dying because I felt safe in your protective arms."

"I am not yours. I am done with you Daisy. I am suffering on your account. You are a constant headache."

He disengaged himself from her arms and continued walking at a quick pace. She scrambled after him, jogging to keep pace with his long legs.

"You can't get rid of me that easily. I just wished you knew I still love you, I wish you would grab me, and hold me tight in your arms, and whisper in my ear how much you loved me more like you did before."

"Shut up Daisy. You make me feel sick to my stomach right now. You won't get any sympathy."

"I love you and you love me and that is it, and you have to deal with it."

"Daisy I had enough of your bullshit. Stop talking please."

"I know you may be hurt but please don't push me away. You never told me how I was supposed to live without you for the rest of my life. O God. Why your love hurts so much?"

"Love is giving, and I gave a lot. I stood by your side. You pushed me away."

"I need you. I need you to give me strength again. Love is the only thing that we can carry with us when we go, and it makes the end so easy."

He stopped walking and looked at her, his face creased with worry.

"Go! Go where? And what end are you talking about?"

"I am exhausted from trying to be stronger than I feel. I am tired of trying to hold things together that cannot be held. Trying to control what cannot be controlled. I wonder how long I can keep this up." She said sobbing painfully.

"What's the matter Daisy, are you hiding something from me?" He said with concern.

"I want to strive with you again towards a better and healthy life."

What does that mean?

"Mostafa I am scared."

"What are you scared of?"

"I am afraid because I can't fight forever. This time I am not going to fight back. I can't do this anymore."

"Fight back what exactly?"

"Fight cancer. My routine blood test showed remission of leukemia."

He didn't expect to cry, but tears rushed into his eyes like violent waves. He turned his face away so that she could not see his tears, but he could not hide the heaving of his chest and shoulders. She stood staring at him utterly surprised.

He collapsed down on his knees weeping ardently like a child. She knelt in front of him, stood on her knees, and took his face in her hands. She kissed his mouth tenderly, then, cradled his head against her bosom. He sobbed against her breast, he searched for his voice, and when he found it, he said between sobs: "I don't know how to take this. O Daisy not again. I can't take it anymore."

Together they cried while she hugged him fiercely to her breast. He clung to her like a fluttering dry leaf in high winds that had suddenly found a shelter. He felt his whole world was falling apart. He felt lost and lonely.

"Daisy! You frighten me. I fear the moment I might lose you. I can't live without you. He said sobbing and choking convulsively.

'We're all dying, Mostafa. It's just that some of us are dying faster than others. But I am not afraid.

We fought cancer before together and won. The healing power of God is working in me right now." She said kissing his forehead.

"It's God this time Daisy. I can't fight God. I am tired. I just want to go someplace where no one know my name."

"God is not far from us. God is with us. God's presence overcomes our fear, and worry."

"You give me hope, although you suffer alone?" He said weeping aloud.

"I am the happiest woman on earth because now I knew you still love me."

"I never stopped loving you. I just stopped showing it. You always have a special place in my heart no matter how much you have hurt me. You are the world to me. I have seen the best of you and the worst of you and I chose both. No matter what the future brings, I will walk with you along the path you tread."

He held her tight and continued to sob as he pleaded with God: "O God. Why did you choose her instead of me? O God why you are taking her through troubled water? She has been through hell. She is too weak to stand that ache. She is a good person. She uses silence to express pain. She says I am tired when she is sad. She feels unwanted, yet she gives the love she thinks the world needs. God mend where her heart is broken. Erase the fears of her past. I can't manage a world without her in it."

Hearing his words made her cry even harder.

"Dear Lord, I need you now. I am feeling so broken and all

alone. God fill me with your spirit and warm my heart. Dear God, I am not strong enough on my own. Protect me from all this pain. Comfort me." He continued saying as he held her tight in his arms.

"Dear Lord, somewhere beneath that pain and bitterness is a good woman. A woman who had been abused all her life, a woman in desperate need of someone to care."

All he could do was cry. Tears spilled over, streaming down his cheeks.

He pulled back slightly and looked into Daisy's watery eyes. He cupped her face in his hands and said weeping: "The regret of my life is that I have not said I love you often enough. There is not anything in the world I would not do for you. We will step into the light and use every bit of power we have inside. We will start each day with a grateful heart. I will turn you to the beauty you have always been. I will heal your heart and soothe your soul." He said wiping her tears away with his fingers.

He continued sobbing: "Everything heals. Wounds heal. Happiness is always going to come. Bad times don't last."

"How do I tell you I am sorry? How I didn't realize that I hurt you so much? Can you forgive and forget?" He said pleading.

"There is nothing to forgive. I love you." She said smiling through her tears.

"I saddened your heart. Would you accept me again? Would you forgive me and give me the happiness I long for?"

"I will forgive you for avoiding me. I will forgive you for breaking my heart. I will forgive you for all the time you made me cry." She said crying in earnest.

"We have been hurt enough. I promise you the tears will dry. The hurt will fade. The heart will heal. Put on a smile, dry your eyes, hide your scars, I am here for you."

"You are the greatest thing that ever happened to me. Being with you keeps me alive. Hold me tight. A tight hug can do so much for someone that is hurting."

"I will wash away the dust that hurt your eyes. I will never let you go. I will never stop loving you. I will hold you till the end." He said gathering her tightly to him.

"Every day we are together is the greatest day of my life. I will always be yours." She said trembling in his arms.

"I want to hold you. I want to make food for you. I want to call you baby. If you just give me a chance, I swear I will make you the happiest woman on earth. I am not perfect, but you will never find someone who loves you as much as I do." He said weeping hot tears.

He suddenly went down on one knee and popped the question: "Will you marry me? You're the only one I want to share the rest of my life with."

"You're the love of my life, and my answer is yes, yes, yes!"

He got to his feet and held her closer cradling her dearly to him.

"We will have a big family with lots of kids, and we will all live in delightful bliss, happily ever after."

They married in a small gathering in his house on the hill. They danced a romantic dance and then spent a hot night together. She hated men and lost her sex drive, but he was the only man who can touch her and make her aroused and sure of herself.

 In their wedding bed adorned with rose petals, He took her passionately in his arms. She whispered in his ear: "I bruise easily so be gentle when you handle me."

He touched her with a gentleness that she had never known. His kisses melted into her soul, causing her juices to flow freely, and spasms of desire shot through her core. He made love to her tenderly and passionately. And she indeed matched him in his ardor as he took her to the pinnacle of pleasure and beyond, until she felt herself shattering into a million shards of starlight.

Wrapped in his strong arms she recalled the ups and downs, the fear, the crying, the doubt and the darkness. Tears raced down her cheeks.

"No tears, sweetheart?" He whispered.

"No. Oh, no. No tears of sadness. I love you, Mostafa, so very much. I just hope I will be worthy of you."

"You have proved that and more a thousand times. I could face anything – anything Daisy except the loss of your love."

She nestled tighter into his arms. "You have my love forever," she breathed.

"Forever and always," he echoed.

She twined her arms around his neck and her heart flowed with pure happiness. Forever with Mostafa, the only man she truly loved was all that she could want,
or need.

Their eyes locked, and she shot him a playful seductive eye. "How you love like crazy. You are strange, terrifying, strong and beautiful, something not everyone knows how to love." A radiant smile brightened her face.

They fell fast asleep in each other's arms, their naked bodies pressed together.

At dawn he woke up and touched her side of the bed, but she was not there. He searched every part of the house, but she was missing. He found her at last sitting with her transparent nightgown in the garden silently crying. He knelt before her perplexed.

"Darling what happened? Why crying?

She said wiping away her tears with her delicate fingers:

"I was thirsty – a dry land. My body was like a dead tree. I feared my limbs had turned to stone. Last night you soothed my dry bones and sent your rain to revive my parched soul. You watered my barren soul and turned it into fertile land."

She began to sob again. He held her close and kissed her hair. She buried her face in his shoulder. She could feel his warmth. She felt cared for. She felt safe. It was just what she needed.

She leaned her head back and looked at him, wiping the tears from her cheeks. "I need you to tell me that I am exactly the right one for you. I just want to know that you won't wake up one morning and feel differently."

"I know my life will never be complete without you beside me to share it. I promise you, no one will work harder to make you happy or cherish you more than me."

The sincerity in his voice brought more tears into her eyes. She said with tears coursing down her cheeks: "You make me complete. You give me a reason to live. I never dreamed that I would love somebody like you. I didn't know what love meant until I met you."

She continued through her tears: "I am desperate for your love. Refill my thirst, send your rain, let it pour. Turn my body into a lush meadow. I loved the way you touched me. I need your touch again. Touch me please. I need to feel your touch. I need to be touched and kissed. Make my soul blossoms. Turn my dry body into a lush meadow."

He held her tenderly in his arms for long moments, kissed her, and carried her to their room.

He truly loved her. He made her feel beautiful, loved, protected and taken care of. He made her feel special. For the first time ever in their relationship, she found herself blooming.

Chapter 56

Three years later

When Mostafa and Daisy got married, Daisy desperately wanted a baby. The presence of a child would certainly strengthen her relationship with Mostafa. Daisy carefully planned her pregnancy. She knew that a leukemia woman who is pregnant need not undergo an abortion if she does not desire, and that standard antileukemic chemotherapy can be administered safely during pregnancy without affecting the viability of the fetus. She also knew that the offspring of leukemic mothers appear to mature normally. Daisy let herself get pregnant. She gave birth to a baby girl after one year from marriage.

Daisy was the happiest mother on earth when she first carried her daughter in her arms. When Mostafa saw the baby for the first time, it was likely a moment of relief, amazement, and a little shock, too. The little girl was so tiny that he was afraid to carry her lest he might hurt her.

"She took my brown eyes and your black hair." Daisy said enthralled.

"she's as beautiful as can be just the way she is." Mostafa said unable to comprehend the situation.They called her Grace.

Two years after giving birth, Daisy's health rapidly deteriorated. When cancer came back to invade Daisy's blood, Mostafa put her on anti-cancer diet for weeks but to no avail. She had to receive chemotherapy drug whose side effects were ravishing like severe nausea, vomiting, and mouth sores. She also underwent five weeks of radiation.

Unlike many other cancers, acute leukemia is treated initially with several courses of daily chemotherapy. Daisy had to stay in hospital for long periods with occasional breaks at home. This was sometimes followed by a period of out-patient treatment involving regular visits to hospital. Once again Mostafa and Daisy heard the words no one wants to hear. "There is nothing more we can do." The chemo caused too much damage to the bone marrow and it was no longer functioning. The doctors gave Daisy three weeks to live.

Daisy fought cancer as much as she could. She had to do everything she could to ensure that she would be here to raise Grace. She wanted to see her grow up. She wanted to play with her. She wanted to see her start school. She wanted to see her birthdays. To listen to her problems. She needed to live.

Cancer changed Daisy on the inside. There were times during her illness when she wanted to give up. But she surrendered to her fate and learned to be thankful for all the good things that happen in life.

Daisy didn't let treatment sessions and doctor appointments

become her whole world. She started spending more time in nature. To her, nature was walking on the beach with Mostafa and carrying her little adorable Grace.

It was spring. One hour before sunset, we see Mostafa walking on the beach, with Daisy carrying her two-year-old daughter. Daisy wore a lace-up floral print maxi dress and wrapped her bald head in a silk scarf after hair loss from cancer treatment. It was clear that the illness had whittled down her.

Mostafa tosses Grace in the air laughing, and then sat her down upon the yellow sand to play with buckets and shovels, cups and spoons. Daisy engaged with imaginative play with Grace. They cooked, and baked sand pies.

She looked at Grace smiling. "Everything looks cute when it is small." She leaned forward and hugged her daughter kissing her cheek.

After they have finished playing, they walked on the beach enjoying the whiteness of the sand and the clarity of the water.

"At the beach life is different. We live by the currents, plan by the tides, and follow the sun." She said fascinated by the green blue water of the ocean.

"For others, it's the ruggedness of the coast and the power of the waves." Mostafa said laughing and placing one arm around Daisy's back and the other arm carrying Grace.

"All I want to do is sit down by the sea and not worry about a single damn thing. Nothing soothes the soul like a walk on the beach." She said breathing deeply in the ocean air.

It was near sunset when they left the beach. The sun started settling down and left a red, orange blue ray of light in the sky.

Promenading along the beach became an established feature of their relationship. Daisy couldn't express herself freely unless she was walking on the beach where the sky touched the sea. The sound of the waves relaxed her, as if all her troubles were washed away in the water. She used to laugh and say: "I need vitamin sea. I need some beach therapy."

The beach became their favorite place to walk or sit.

All Daisy's uncovered thoughts were released to Mostafa only at the beach. Daisy walked with difficulty leaning heavily upon Mostafa's shoulder with his left arm wrapped around her back.

"This is my happy place. The beach takes my heart to a place of serenity and peace. The ocean calms my restless soul." She said with a big smile on her face."

"I understand what you mean. The ocean stirs the heart, inspires the imagination, and brings eternal joy to the soul." He said happy to see her smiling.

They walked a few paces, but Daisy got tired easily and

gasped for air.

"Let's rest on that seat." He said pointing to an empty bench.

She said continuing to walk: "Don't wait, life goes faster than you think." Her words tore his heart apart.

"The smell of the ocean never gets old. Salt water cures all wounds". She smiled and took a deep breath, inhaling the salty air.

"I thought I'd have six months of treatment and that would be it. Never in my worst nightmares would I have ever imagined I would be taken so soon. I was given weeks to live. I wanted to live a full wonderful life with you."

"Please stop it Daisy. There is no pain greater than to be helpless in the face of a loved one's suffering. I can't endure to see you suffering." His voice cracked and caught in his throat.

"Well, one has to die from something, I suppose. I wished to see Grace grow up and possibly have kids of her own. I don't want to watch her see me go through a long, painful death."

"Don't talk about death. You are my life. I can't live without you." Repressed tears flooded out of his eyes.

She stopped walking and looked into his tearful eyes.

"You filled my heart with glowing joy. I know that someday

we will be together again, and that God will protect you while we are apart." She said wiping away his tears with her delicate fingers.

"I would do anything to help you feel better. I'll Get You through this. I promise." He said crying his eyes out.

She said sobbing: "Cry as much as you can. You cry not because you are weak, but because you have been strong for too long."

"This time it's God will, remember. You can't fight God." She said hugging him dearly. Her grief poured out in a flood of uncontrollable tears.

"Keep faith, hang onto it."

He said with tears pouring down like a river.

"Because I have loved you I shall have no sorrow to die. The only regret was leaving you behind."

He fell to his knees and held her waist crying out with a loud voice. Tears continued to pour down his face like a river escaping a dam. She knelt before him and indulged for a long time in weeping.

"I can't help the way I am acting. Can't be different though I try. The best of me is gone. Love me till my life is done."

Panic and despair overtook him, and he couldn't stop himself from crying ardently.

He rose to his feet and helped her to her feet, supporting her once she was standing. "Let's walk a bit further. The ocean brings eternal joy to the soul." She Said breathing deeply in the fresh sea air.

"Walking in sand requires a greater effort than walking on a hard surface. Your muscles will work harder as your foot moves around." He said fearing that she might get tired.

She said as if she didn't hear him: "The waves of the sea help me get back to me. To walk quietly on the beach — that's my idea of paradise."

The smell of the salty water, the wind in their faces, the gentle roar of the waves all combined to create a sense of peace and calm. They walked further down the beach. She got tired and leaned heavily on his arm. Her weak whisper came to penetrate his ears: "Seeing death as the end of life is like seeing the horizon as the end of the ocean."

"Please stop it Daisy. Your words about dying make me feel dead inside."

"God always speak to my heart when I am alone on the beach. I could walk no further. Let's go back home." She said trying hard to catch her breath.

Chapter 57

Now, Daisy was weak, and exhausted from the disease and chemotherapy and pain medication. She became dry like withered petal, Mostafa could count her ribs one by one. Her weight has gone down in a matter of days. In half opened eyes she watched Mostafa sitting by her bed. In aching voice, she said: "I looked in the mirror and what did I see? A bald person staring at me!

"Daisy my love, you haven't eaten for days. You must eat something. How about warm soup and a piece of toast?" Mostafa pleaded.

"Don't feel like eating." She smiled at him and held his hand. He squeezed back gently.

"I`m fed up laying in my bed, feeling sickly.

"You'll be fine I am sure." A tear rolled down his cheek and more came down until tears rolled down like a stream.

She saw his tears, her arms opened wide and closed him inside. He pressed his head against the side of her neck trying to hide his tears.

"Let me look in your eyes." She said tenderly.

He released her gently. "Be strong and have faith." She whispered wiping away his tears with her thumb.
Panic kept growing exploding in his chest. Tears kept falling on his cheeks. He said sobbing: "There are flowers growing outside your window. The coffee is warm, the air is pure. And I am here to take care of you, and it's spring again. It will always be spring again. And there will always be a new day. Don't lose hope."

She flattened her lips, fighting the urge to cry further.

"Go stronger from the pain. Don't let it destroy you."

"I am exhausted from trying to be stronger than I feel."

"I wish I could do more than give you encouragement. I wish I could really help you."

"Thanks for never giving up on me. Thanks for loving me. Thanks for giving me hope."

The long pain was taking its toll on her feeble body. Her bone marrow has become overcrowded with cancer cells and caused severe bone and joint pain. The terrible pain was accompanied by nausea and vomiting.

She screamed in pain. "Please help me Mostafa. Don' t make me go there."

Mostafa shouted hysterically: "Nurse!"

The nurse came quickly and gave Daisy a strong opioid shot

to relief cancer pain. Because of the severity of the pain, the drug was given at short intervals. Daisy would float in and out of states of awareness.

Daisy did not regain full consciousness till late in the day. She blinked to try to clear her vision. She whispered: "There is no pain so great as the pain I'm going through. If God knows I am hurting, why doesn't he help me?"

Mostafa felt a sudden tightness in his chest as his heart hammered and started feeling a lump in his throat.

"God loves and cares deeply about you Daisy." He said devastated and hurt.

"I am so tired. I am done with everything. My soul deserves peace."

 "I'm sorry you must endure such pain and discomfort. I wish I could take all this pain and sorrow from you." Tears stung his eyes.

"Tell me everything will be alright." She sighed faintly.

"Don't worry you will be fine. I am here for you. I will always care for you, I will always keep you safe."

"I have endured. I have been broken. The pain I feel is the only thing that reminds me I'm still alive."

"God loves you and has a purpose for you. Leave all your worries up to God. Don't give up."

"The world is no more mine. I want to give up. I am done with myself."

Anxiety ate him up and he cried silently.

"I feel much weaker now. I feel sorry for myself. My life didn't go as planned. Lord I need you to help me. Strengthen my heart. Your grace has brought me safe thus far. O You who changes not, abide with me. In life, in death, O Lord, abide with me." She started to cry quietly. Mostafa sitting by her bed sobbing with her. Everything darkened into nothingness as she passed into the oblivion of unconsciousness.

One day, late in the afternoon, Daisy opened heavy eyes after a restless sleep. She searched for Mostafa with tired eyes.

"I am here darling just beside you." He said jumping out of his seat and hurried to her bed.

"Oh, there you are. I have been searching for you. But it was darkness within darkness. There was nothing to seek and nothing to find. I missed you. Anywhere with you is better than anywhere without you. I want to touch you. Hold my body close to yours."

He held her close to his heart. "I drag myself out of nightmares each morning and find there's no relief in waking. I just wish I could die so I can have some sort of peace. I can't take the pain. I just want to die. I just want it all over. Take me to the ocean." She said as if pleading.

He knew what the ocean and the beach meant to her. He carried her tenderly to a wheelchair. He wrapped her bold head with a scarf and tucked a soft blanket around her. He wheeled her out to the shore. When they reached the first bench she ushered him to stop. "Carry me to the bench." She said in a faint voice.

He lifted her off the wheelchair and carried her to the bench. He sat down on it with Daisy cradled in his arms. He saw a pair of tears raced down her cheeks.

"Why those tears Daisy. Don't fear anything. I am here with you. We are together love."

"I don't fear anything anymore. I have reached my end."

"Easy my love. Please, don't talk about sorrow, grief or pain."

"Grief is like the ocean, it comes on waves, then it hits you so much harder than you ever thought it would. I have no regrets whatsoever save the pain I'll leave behind."

"your words are killing me Daisy. You mean more to me than you will ever know. I just can't live without you." She felt his tears wetting her face, falling on her cheeks.

"Grieve not, nor speak of me with tears, but laugh and talk of me as if I were beside you. I loved you so much. It was heaven here with you."

"I'd like the memory of me to be a happy one. I'd like to leave an afterglow of smiles when life is done." She continued in a low voice.

"I wanted to know you for longer, my love, but it wasn't to be. Marrying you was the best thing that ever happened to me. Even if death separates us apart, I would choose you in a hundred lifetimes, in a hundred worlds, I would find you, I would choose you."

"Daisy, enough please. You are torturing my heart. You talk as if you were leaving me. There is no life after you." His eyes dripped with tears. His walls that held him up and made him strong collapsed. The hot tears ran over and dripped from his chin to wet her face. He began to cry aloud unable to stop.

"Cry my love. Don't hide your tears. Tears are prayers. They travel to God when we can't speak."

She lifted her pale face and looked into his tearful eyes and said: "Thank you for our time together. You were my rock, my Fortress and my delight. You have made known to me the paths of life. You have given me the greatest possible happiness. I owe all the happiness of my life to you. You have been entirely patient with me and incredibly good. Everything has gone from me but the certainty of your goodness. I don't think two people could have been happier than we have been." She paused as if about to faint.

"You took my empty life and filled it with every good thing. When my life was without purpose, you gave me a reason to live. You gave me joy down deep in my soul." He held her closer to his heart.

"The road is getting rough. God knew that I would never get well on earth again."

"God knew that you were suffering. He knew that you were in pain. The deeper the grief, the closer is God."

"I can't fight any longer. If I should go now, it would never be goodbye, For I have left my heart with you, so don't you ever cry. The love that's deep within me, shall reach you from the sky, you'll feel it from the heavens, and it will heal your scars."

He kept holding her in his arms and she nestled peacefully against his chest. Daisy ceased speaking and closed her eyes exhausted.

"I will live this earth carrying you in my heart. I will be right there waiting for you." She suddenly spoke.

"I won't say goodbye my love, for you and I will meet again. Until we meet again, may God hold you in the hollow of his hand." She continued faintly.

She whispered: "The taste of death is upon my lips. I feel something that is not of this earth. Now is my final agony. No more. Now I can be at peace forever. My soul thirsts for God. God called me home. I shall have with God a life of joy and peace."

Her eyes widened, then her mouth opened slightly, her teeth chattered, her eyes froze, lost all glimmer and clouded; they were empty of all life. Her heart stopped, and her body twisted in a last spasm.

He looked at her terrified. His heart thudded against his chest. His face contorted with grief. He collapsed sobbing uncontrollably.

The tears burst forth spilling down his face. He felt the muscles of his chin tremble like a small child. The sobs punched through, ripping through his muscles, bones, and guts. He sobbed unceasingly, hands holding her dearly as his tears soaked the blanket. A tiny lapse let him pull away, blinking lashes heavy with tears, before he collapsed again, his howls of misery worsening. The pain came in waves, minutes of sobbing broken apart by short pauses for recovering breaths, before hurling him back into the outstretched arms of his grief.

He prayed for her weeping through rivers of tears: "Rest in peace my love. The Lord will lead you to a joyful end. God will bestow on you a great reward. He will admit you to Gardens under which rivers flow to abide therein forever. God will bring you into his mercy and will accept the best of your deeds and overlook the bad deeds.

"O God, I need Your mercy. I cannot believe she is gone forever. I can't bear losing her. She fought so hard for 14 months, but the cancer was so aggressive, and she lost her battle.

"O God, forgive and have mercy upon her, pardon her, and make honorable her reception. Expand her entry and purify her of sin. Exchange her home for a better home. O God, You are forgiving, and love forgiveness so forgive her, have mercy on her and admit her to the Gardens of Bliss."

Chapter 58

With a bleeding heart, Mostafa carried daisy to her bed. Tom was in the chalet waiting for their return. When he saw Mostafa carrying Daisy's dead body he collapsed crying. He knelt on his knees and cried out: "She wanted to live but not die. Grace will never have the chance to know her and experience how loving and gracious she was. She is not dead, she is just away. She is resting from the sorrows and the tears in a place of warmth and comfort."

Tom hugged him, and they cried together. They cried their grief, their loss. "She will always be a part of me. She has never left me even after she is gone. She lives on in the kindness and the love she brought into my life." Mostafa said crying his heart out.

Tom went to Daisy's bedside and hugged her crying: "You were my only daughter. You were my pet. You died at the height of your youth and beauty, died with your life ahead of you, you died and left me alone grieving. I prayed and prayed for a miracle, but it didn't happen. It is hard for an old afflicted father, to lose his only beloved child, his only comfort, the crown and joy of his old age." He sobbed out in a broken and faltering voice.

Daisy's mother was on her way to see Daisy when she knew that Daisy was going through a delicate situation. When she entered the room and saw her daughter lying dead in bed she rushed over to Daisy and held her in her arms and shed abundant tears. "I had not been able to protect my baby. You were unsafe enough to die. I am sorry baby. I was not a good mother. Had I come too late to save you? Oh Daisy! The only pang will be parting with you." She said wailing.

The funeral was simple. Daisy's corps was placed in a pine coffin and was buried in New York on a private property own by her father.

Losing Daisy was totally devastating to Mostafa, he wasn't the same after her death. He saw life through a black lens. He felt more alone and helpless than he ever had felt before. Grief usually eases as time passes but with Mostafa it never subsided. One year after she was gone, and Mostafa was still devastated by Daisy's death. He lost interest to move on with his life. He resorted to loneliness refusing to go out and mingle with people.

Tom Wilson noticed that Mostafa withdrew from public life, he paid him a visit to persuade him to embrace life again.

Tom: "Mostafa, how are you son, I haven't seen you for a while where you have been hiding?"

Mostafa: "I am tired. My heart prays for respite."

Tom: "it's been one year, about time you get over it, move on.

Mostafa: I am so frustrated and disappointed. I am a lost

man deserted and depleted."

Tom: "How do you view the future?"

Mostafa: "My whole view of life had changed. Things that once seemed important no longer seemed important."

Tom: "Loneliness is a sign of dryness. A feeling of departure from people forever. you've got to keep positive."

Mostafa: "I gave my heart away a long time ago and I never got it back. She was the oasis of hope in my dry life. I wonder if I'll ever feel joy again."

Tom: "Focus on something other than your loss, or you will be pulled into the downward spiral of depression. Go to work, resume your activities and make her spirit inspire you each day."

My life with her creeps up on me. It whispers in my ear her name, the name I loved so dearly. I feel like crying and screaming out her name. Her name is too precious, it will never grow old in my heart." His throat constricted, and unshed tears stung his eyes.

Tom: "Death is an invitation to open our hearts, to experience the feelings of pain and grief, and then to honor our loved ones by going back into the world with an open heart to do our work with an increased awareness and compassion for our needs and the needs of others."

Mostafa: "I grieve for the person I was before she died - a

young man who was happy and in love. I feel like screaming my problems, but something is choking me in throat. I feel like burst in tears but hold on to patience. I want to let go but I still hold on."

Tom: "Dealing with death is devastatingly hard, but our loved ones never really leave us. You were not born to drown. Cope with grief and change your life completely. Do look forward to the future."

Mostafa: "The pain doesn't go away." Tears coursed down his cheeks.

Tom: "Love life to the fullest and embrace it with no regrets. Focus on the positive."

Mostafa: "Nothing will be as before. I'm sorry that I was a disappointment to you." He said wiping the tears from his cheeks.

Tom: "A thousand disappointments in the past cannot equal the power of one positive action right now, Go ahead and go for it."

Mostafa gradually returned to normal life. He drowned himself in work to forget the pain of his heart, the loss of the woman he truly loved. He returned vigorously to wrestling and fashion designing. It was like a form of therapy that helped him come to terms with the fact that Daisy had gone. In the wrestling ring he smashed the faces of his opponents and broke their bones. In the fashion industry he presented fashion shows wherever he could get free space, and they were so outrageous. He blazed the trail in fashion design. His innovative techniques were widely studied and used by many of the great designers. His designs have graced the covers of numerous magazines and the red carpet at movie premieres and awards shows. The critics said he will remain an iconic designer for decades to come.

He also worked as a model for his own designs. He walked down the runway wearing men's wear. At the end of each show he combines men and women's models into a single presentation and walks with them down the runway greeting the audience and thanking them for appreciating his collections.

Women adored him because of his beauty, elegance, wealth and strength. But all they ever got was a broad smile on his face. His heart was closed, it belonged to a woman that cannot be seen or touched because she was living in his heart.

Mostafa lived near the beach in his summer chalet. He wanted to be near the ocean and the beach which Daisy loved. Here on the beach she loved him, and he loved her. Here on the beach she died in his arms.

After a long day at work, his favorite way to unwind was by going out with the setting sun on the empty beach to embrace his solitude and talks to Daisy.

The sound and visuals of the beach and ocean were soothing and peaceful. The beach felt like home to him. The sun was setting on the purple-pink-orange horizon and the waves crashed onto shore. Droplets of salt water hit him as he walked through the sand, birds flying everywhere, and the wind whooshing all around. The pebbles crackled as they walked over the beach. The seafront was empty apart from few seagulls, picking up the shellfish and dropping them down onto the rocks to crack their shells. The tide recedes but leaves behind bright seashells on the sand. The sun goes down, but gentle warmth still lingers on the land.

Mostafa walked along the beach. The memories kept flooding back. He remembered her words: "Grieve not, nor speak of me with tears, but laugh and talk of me as if I were beside you. I loved you so much. It was heaven here with you."

He looked around as if he heard soft footfalls moving over the sand beside him. With an aching heart he whispered to her: "Not a day goes by that you don't cross my mind. And I still miss you so. I miss you more than ever. I know you hear me talk to you. I know you are still watching silently from above. You didn't go away. You walk beside me every day. Unseen, unheard, but always near. Still loved, still missed and very dear.

"You have gone from my arms, but you will always be in my heart. I still remember the sound of your last breath. I can still feel your hands entangled warmly in mine. You are not just ashes. You're deep within my soul. You creep and crawl inside my body. Not a day has gone by that I haven't thought about you.

"God has you in His keeping I have you in my heart. No

words can really help to ease the loss I bear. You are very close in every thought and prayer.

"Surely you now dwell amid gardens of Paradise by the flowing streams in a sure abode in the presence of a King Omnipotent. Until we meet again, May God hold you in the palm of His hand."

Mohsen El-Guindy

www.ingramcontent.com/pod-product-compliance
Lightning Source LLC
Chambersburg PA
CBHW060755210726
48292CB00013B/149